BOUNDLESS

a novel

Brad Cotton

Prinia Press

Publisher's note: This book is a work of fiction. Names, characters, places, and incidents either are products of the author's imagination or are used fictitiously. Any resemblance to actual persons, living or dead, is entirely coincidental.

First Prinia Press Printing, August 2013.
10 9 8 7 6 5 4 3 2 1

Library and Archives Canada Cataloguing in Publication

Cotton, Brad, 1977-, author
Boundless / Brad Cotton.

ISBN 978-0-9919724-0-1 (pbk.)

I. Title.

PS8605.O8847B68 2013   C813'.6   C2013-903514-

Author Website: www.BradCotton.com
Twitter: @bradcott0n
Facebook: facebook.com/bradcotton

For Stephanie

PART I

CHAPTER 1

"YOU'RE TELLING ME he's in charge?"

"Yes."

"So he knows what's going on right now?"

"Yes."

Ray paused to absorb Duncan's response. "You say that as if I should have known," he said.

"Well, consider the alternative."

"I don't have access to him, Dun. I'm just taking your word for it."

Duncan removed the black bag from his lap and placed it beside him on the couch. It sank heavily into the soft leather. Duncan leaned forward and lifted a large book from the coffee table in front of him. Ray sat across from Duncan on a black chaise, his feet propped up.

"New Zealand," Duncan said. He showed the book's cover to Ray.

Duncan scuttled back into the couch. He opened the cover of the book and began turning its thick, glossy pages. The vivid greens and browns of the picturesque hills charmed him right away.

"It doesn't make you uncomfortable to think he knows what you're up to?" Ray asked.

"Not at all," said Duncan.

"I don't buy it."

Duncan continued to flip the pages of the book with an easy grin. Restless, Ray rose from his chair and scanned the picture frames atop the nearby marble fireplace. He lifted a wooden plaque that sat amongst the photographs. "Eagle's Glen flight two golf tournament champion, 1998," he read aloud.

The front door opened. The house was abnormally large, but the sound of someone entering and walking down the hallway towards them was easy to distinguish. The echo of shoes on a tiled floor began to draw close. It was an ominous sound, but Duncan's eyes never wavered from the shimmering turquoise lakes reflecting majestically off the snow-capped mountaintops.

"Hi Marty," Ray said from his vantage in front of the unlit fireplace.

Martin Bridge startled and turned quickly. He was standing before three wide steps that led to the massive sunken living room. He nearly tumbled down the steps when Ray called his name.

"What the fuck?" Martin yelped. The aging man grasped at a white pillar beside the steps.

"Don't freak out, Marty," Ray said, holding his palms out in a gesture of peace.

"Who the hell are you?" Martin asked.

"I'm Ray, that's Duncan."

Duncan closed the book and placed it back calmly on the coffee table, sure to tilt it back into the original position he found it.

"Oh shit, Ray," Martin said. "You scared the hell out of me."

"Sorry about that."

Martin unclenched the pillar – among other things – and walked down the steps and into the living room to meet Ray and Duncan. "What are you guys doing here?"

"We need to talk to you about something," Ray said.

"What's wrong with the phone? In four years you guys have never come by once." Martin walked over to Ray and shook his hand. "You're a lot younger than I imagined," he said. "How the hell did you get in here?"

"We need to cash you out, Marty," Ray said, still holding Martin's hand.

"I need a drink, can I get you a drink?" Martin said.

"Sure."

"Duncan?"

"None for me," said Duncan.

Martin unclasped Ray's hand and walked to the far end of the sunken room. He tapped his finger on a small white pad by the window. A discreet portion of the wall-long bookshelf began to rotate slowly and unveiled an impressive alcohol display.

"Scotch okay?" Martin asked, twisting open a twenty-five-year-old single malt. He then poured into his glass what could be considered the daily hydration quotient of a small farm animal. He did the same for Ray.

Ray took a seat beside Duncan on the couch. He lifted the book Duncan had been looking at and flipped it open to the middle.

Martin joined the pair in the center of the room. He placed a coaster down in front of Ray and then the glass of scotch upon it.

"Do you still golf, Marty?" Duncan asked.

"Yes, well, no," Martin said, "I don't get out that much anymore."

Martin was in his early sixties. His impeccably tailored suit made him look a bit younger, as did his fashionably narrow eyeglasses, but the lines on his face spoke the truth. Martin's hair could be described as salt and pepper, but only if the lid of the salt had been unscrewed as a prank before it was shaken onto his head. He stood six-two and weighed well over two hundred pounds. He was larger in stature than both Ray and Duncan. Martin walked with confidence, as if he knew where he was going and what he was going to do when he got there. In a boardroom, Martin could be an intimidating figure. In his living room, he made no such impression on Duncan.

"You still belong to Eagle's Glen?" Duncan asked.

"I use the facilities," Martin said, taking a seat on the black chair across from his guests. "How did you guys get in here? How did you know my wife wouldn't be home?"

"Your wife moved out years ago, Marty," Ray said.

"My daughter–"

"Lives with your wife, but is currently attending Stanford Law, so she wouldn't be at either house. And you leave a key under the fake rock in the front garden. Why don't you golf anymore?"

"My body is falling apart," Martin said pitifully. "Look at this."

He held up his left hand and clenched his fist a few times slowly as if he were milking an invisible goat.

"What are we looking at?" Ray asked.

"You don't see this?" Martin said. He opened and closed his hand a few more times.

Ray looked over at Duncan who had no answer either.

"Arthritis!" Martin said. "I can barely grip my clubs anymore. I have to wear padded batting gloves just to hold my driver. I just bought a $1,200 custom-fit TaylorMade and the thing keeps flying out of my hands. I nearly tossed it into someone's pool."

"Sounds frustrating," Ray said.

"So why the hell do you need to cash me out?" Martin asked, "Is something wrong? Are you guys in trouble?"

"Nothing like that. We're cashing everybody out."

"You need the money?"

"We're shutting down," Ray said.

"We're leaving Phoenix," Duncan added.

"You're leaving Phoenix? What for? Where're you going?" Martin asked.

"Don't know yet. Maybe L.A.," Ray offered.

"I've spent time in L.A., Ray, you'll hate it." Martin leaned back in the chair and took a gulp of his drink. "Coffee shops, plastic surgeons…actors. A million fucking actors."

"New York, maybe, I don't know," Ray said as he put down the book. Duncan reached across the couch and unzipped the front pouch of the bag.

"New York!" Martin said.

Duncan withdrew a black hardcover notebook from the bag and handed it to Ray. Ray flipped the book open and shuffled through the pages.

"I had a girl in New York once," Martin said. "1968. Maryanne McCurry. Red hair, blue eyes…great ass. She moved to Michigan and married a Protestant."

"Sixty-six," Ray said.

"Shame really."

"Marty…Sixty-six."

"No, I'm pretty sure it was sixty eight. It was the summer we saw Gary Puckett and The Union Gap…it was a leap year too, I think."

"Sixty-six thousand, Marty. You're at sixty-six thousand," Duncan said.

"Sixty-six thousand? That can't be right. Are you sure?"

Duncan took the book from Ray and walked it over to Martin. He turned it around and placed two fingers down the ledger.

Martin lifted his glasses and looked at the book. He shook his head. "Fucking Wake Forrest," he said. "Never bet on a team named after trees." Duncan turned and handed the book back to Ray.

"We need it in cash," Duncan said. "Today."

"Sixty-six thousand in cash?" Martin exclaimed. "You must be joking."

"You're the last person on our list, Marty. We need the money," Ray said.

"What, you guys gonna rough me up or something?" Martin asked, leaning forward.

"No, not really." Ray said.

"Oh. Okay."

Martin sat back pensively. "Well if you need it right now, I can get you ten, maybe fifteen," he said. "But there's no way I can get sixty-six. I don't have that kind of cash lying around."

"Few do," Ray said. "But we still need it. So you better come up with something."

"Okay, let me think for a minute."

Martin got up from the chair and returned to the bar. He topped up his glass, standing before volumes of un-creased book spines.

"Okay," Martin said after a healthy swig. "Give me thirty minutes." He gulped down the entirety of the brown liquid.

"Stay here, make something to eat, have another drink. I'll be right back."

Martin placed his glass on the table and hopped back up the three steps.

"I'm coming with you," Ray said.

"I'm just going to my brother's house."

Ray looked over to Duncan.

"He has a bigger safe than me," Martin added.

Ray and Duncan exchanged another glance.

"Guys," Martin said, walking back towards them and standing atop the steps. "I've been a lawyer in this city for thirty years. I sit on the board of a hospital charity. For fuck sake, I have a monthly dinner with the mayor. I'll be back in thirty minutes. Trust me."

Ray and Duncan continued their silence.

"Go," Ray said finally.

When it was clear that he had indeed vacated the premises, Ray walked back across the room and pressed the small white pad on the wall. The bar began to disappear and the bookshelf reemerged. When he clicked it again, the bar returned.

"How did you know about his wife?" Duncan asked.

Ray was still playing with the switch.

"Remember Hayley," he said, clicking the button. "Dated her about three years ago?"

"Vaguely."

"Hayley Bridge."

"His daughter?"

"It only lasted about a month, but we're still Facebook friends. Spoke to her last week actually."

"Good thing."

"I have another question for you," Ray said, finally bored with the switch on the wall. "If he knows what's going on right now – with everything, I mean – why doesn't he do something about it?"

"Who says he hasn't?"

7

"Well, I don't see him doing anything."

"If you say so," Duncan said. "But how can you be sure?"

Ray sat back down on the chaise.

Martin Bridge returned to the house in less than the allotted thirty minutes. He walked down into the living room carrying a black gym bag. He sat on the couch beside Duncan and placed the bag on the coffee table.

"Twelve," he said, with a lift of his chin.

"Not enough," Ray said.

"I know that."

"So what are we supposed to do?"

"Well what am *I* supposed to do? I have games this weekend."

"That's not our problem," Duncan said. "Find someone else to take your bets. We need the money."

Martin crossed one leg over the other.

"Is that your car on the street?" he asked.

Duncan nodded.

"What is it? 1978? 79?"

"76 Riviera."

"Nice car. They don't make them like that anymore, do they?"

"They do not."

Martin gave Duncan's knee a friendly tap. "Follow me," he said.

Martin rose from the couch. He grabbed the gym bag and led the boys through the kitchen, down a long hallway, and up to a dark metal door. The door had more than one lock on it. Martin flipped one deadbolt and used a key to open the other. He opened the door and turned on the lights. They stood in a large car garage. The room had a freshly painted grey concrete floor and an impressive twenty-foot ceiling.

The three men stood in the doorway.

"These all yours?" Ray asked.

"Something like that," Martin said. He began to walk, leading the duo across the impressive line-up. "Aston Martin V8 Phantom. Ferrari F430. Mercedes SL500. Bentley Continental. Maserati GranTurismo Sport. And, if you'll follow me this way…"

The trio reached the last car in the garage.

"The 2010 Metallic Silver BMW E92 M3."

All three gazed at the impressive machine. "Is this one special?" Ray asked.

"They're all special, Ray. But this one is yours."

"I already have a car," Duncan said.

"Consider it a trade-up, Duncan."

"This is our sixty-six K?" Ray asked.

Martin threw the gym bag filled with cash to Ray. "It's your fifty-four. And believe me, it's worth double that."

"So then why you giving it up?"

Martin pointed back to the first car in the line and made his way down the display. "Mine, mine, mine, mine, mine…hers," he said.

"I see."

"Won't she ask what happened to it?" Duncan asked.

"She will," Martin said. "That's why you'll have to do something for me."

"And what's that?"

Martin walked over to the wall and typed a code into a keypad. A silver box on the wall clanked and opened. Martin pulled a key ring off one of the hooks inside.

"Before you take this car," he said, dangling the keys on his finger, "one of you is going to have to punch me in the face as hard as you can."

"You can't be serious," Ray said.

"Oh, I'm serious."

"Why, exactly, does one of us have to punch you in the face?"

"Well, Ray, there are a few reasons," Martin said. "Including that it will make explaining the disappearance of a six figure car a little easier to believe. If I tell the she-beast that I had to give it up to settle a debt, it might look a little better if she thinks I was at least coerced a bit first. And, we do want to be sure that the police don't get involved, don't we? I imagine that's important to you. But also, Ray," Martin paused. "The truth is, I've never been punched in the face before, and this seems like a good opportunity. I want to know what it feels like."

Ray looked at Duncan. Duncan simply shrugged.

"You're serious?" Ray asked.

"Never been in a fight. I want to know what it's like."

"So you want one of us to just pop you?"

"That's what I want."

"Duncan?"

"I'm not gonna do it," Duncan said.

"Okay," Ray said, walking up to Martin.

"Ray…" Duncan said.

Martin tightened all his muscles, including the ones in his face. "Count to three first," he said.

"This is really stupid, Marty, you know that, right?" said Ray.

"I'm ready."

Martin braced himself again.

Ray made a fist and Duncan held back any further objection.

"This is weird, Marty. I don't know if I can do it."

"I believe in you, Ray. You can do it."

"All right then. One…I'm going to hit you in the mouth."

"Okay, go. No wait. Mouth or nose?"

"Mouth I think."

"Not nose?"

"Well I don't want to break your nose. Let's try and avoid a visit to the hospital."

"Okay, mouth. I'm ready."

"One…"

"Don't knock out any teeth, no dentist."

"Duncan should be the one doing this."

"Just do it, Ray…"

"I'm gonna do it. You ready?"

"Just do it!"

"Onetwothree."

Ray's fist landed on Martin's face. Martin's hands flew up to his mouth. He bounced up and down in pain and exhilaration. Ray swiped the car keys from the ground almost as quickly as Martin dropped them.

"Fuck me!" Martin yelled. He stomped his foot on the sleek concrete floor and the sound echoed through the immaculate garage.

"Open the door, Marty" Ray said, patting him on the back. "You'll be okay."

Ray threw the keys to Duncan and walked over to the passenger side of the car.

Martin scurried over to the same wall where he had retrieved the keys. He pressed a button and the garage door in front of the BMW began to rise.

"Put some ice on it," Duncan said as he threw the keys to the Riviera to Martin and got into the driver's side of the new car.

Martin nodded and waved him off. The car purred upon ignition.

Duncan pulled the BMW out of the garage with a delicate squeal. As Duncan and Ray drove down the bricked drive, neither of them looked back to see if Martin was watching.

CHAPTER 2

RAYMOND PERRY AND Duncan Miller met in college. Duncan was two years older than Ray, but the two shared a common interest and quickly became friends when Ray nearly doubled Duncan's sports book earnings in his first month alone. The two eventually came to share an apartment in downtown Phoenix while they both completed their undergraduate degrees at ASU. When Duncan finished his B.A. in political science he enrolled in just enough post-graduate classes so not to inspire suspicion with his steady audience on campus. Ray finished his studies in philosophy a year later and the pair slowly moved their bookie business from college nickels and dimes to a higher class of golden parachutes. Ray was twenty-eight, Duncan was thirty, and neither had ever had what could be considered a real job.

Both men grew weary of the life that had built up around them. Like untended ivy on a building wall, the business soon took over everything in sight, without consideration. Taking bets had started out as a convenience born from a youthful urge for extra money, but it eventually carried them well into adulthood, which was never the plan. Year after year the burden grew increasingly wearisome, especially for Duncan.

They had spoken about it many times; the lure of adventure and of the unknown and of what existed for them outside of Phoenix and the bookie business. Upon learning of the partially debt-induced suicide of one of their most fervent and friendly clients, it became a simple decision for the pair to finally leave it all behind. They had their whole lives ahead of them, and the first step was leaving Phoenix to find out what else might lay in store.

About a hundred miles up Highway 93, Duncan pulled into a gas station to fill up. He returned to the car with two bottles of water and a large bag of Rold Gold pretzels and saw that Ray had taken the driver's seat. Without a word he got in the passenger side and put on his seatbelt.

Ray smiled and turned on the car.

He pulled out of the gas station slowly with both hands on the wheel. Once on the highway on-ramp, he instantly stomped on the gas pedal as if he were crushing a bug underneath his foot. Duncan closed his window so as not to get smacked in the face by the warm night wind. As they reached speeds comparable to that of a small aircraft, Ray finally let up on the gas. The car roared like a satiated lion and gradually decreased in speed.

Ray put on the left blinker and merged with the sparse highway traffic, going no faster than the dictated limit on the roadside sign.

Hours passed.

The night was black and the road was quiet.

Then Ray finally spoke. "Have you ever heard of the Hadean?" he asked.

"The band?"

"No. There's a band called the Hadean?"

"There could be."

"It is a good band name. No, the geological era."

"Are you asking me if I've heard of a geological era called the Hadean?"

"That's what I'm asking."

"No, I have not."

"Over 4 billion years ago, during the Hadean, the earth was essentially just a fiery ball of goo."

"You don't say."

"The planet was still forming. Nothing existed yet. It was like a giant sphere of chemicals getting pounded by meteors over and over again. Just oceans of lava; the surface temperature was something like 250 degrees."

"Of course," said Duncan.

"There was no oxygen, no ozone, no protection from solar radiation…"

"What's your point?"

"My point is that the Hadean lasted about a billion years. A *billion*. Or at least what we would consider a billion years."

"And?"

"*And*…that seems like an awful lot of wasted time, doesn't it?"

Duncan thought for a moment. "For who?" he asked.

Ray looked over at his friend.

Then slowly, Duncan's face began to light up as if a mask were being pulled up over it. Ray turned his head and looked back out the windshield. That's when he saw the lights. Duncan and Ray both smiled. In a rush of excitement Ray pressed down on the gas pedal. The car jerked forward and shot down the road.

Ray and Duncan had been to Las Vegas more times than they could count, but the thrill of the approach on Interstate 15 never diminished. It was as if the lights of the desert paradise illuminated a new and different possibility each time they arrived.

They entered the city.

The BMW eventually pulled up to the curb outside a sprawling gate at the end of a long driveway. The gate was open, which was unusual.

"Should we pull in?" Ray asked.

He let off the brake and the powerful car glided across the cobbled drive.

For the first time, a car in which they drove fit in nicely with the array of vehicles that decorated the sizable housefront. Ray and Duncan pulled up beside a red Porsche and got out of the car. Ray threw the now hefty black bag over his shoulder as they approached the front door.

Duncan rang the bell.

There was no response.

He rang it again.

Ray peered through the ornamental glass beside the large metal door. He saw no movement.

After a pause, Duncan rang once more and added a few heavy knocks.

"Who is it?" blared a voice from nowhere.

Ray approached the voice box in the right corner of the arched entranceway. "Ray and Duncan," he said.

No response.

After a few moments of prolonged silence, they heard the click of the front door unlocking.

Ray shrugged. "I guess we go in…?"

Richard "Rico" Diero always had someone answer his door. In the dozen or more times Duncan and Ray paid visit, they had never been invited to let themselves in. But this time, let themselves in they did.

No one was around.

The large house was desert warm. Rico didn't believe in air conditioning.

Duncan and Ray scuttled about the main floor looking for someone, for anyone. They entered the massive kitchen in the dark.

Something moved.

Their attention turned to a feeble light emanating behind the long granite island.

"Hello?" Ray said into the darkness.

A shadow popped up. With a sandwich in his mouth and a bag of ice in his hand, Kentucky Joe's eyes met theirs. He reached up and took the sloppy sandwich from between his lips and with his knee he nudged closed the freezer door. "What're you guys doing here?"

"We need to see Rico," Duncan answered. "He's expecting us."

"Today?"

"In general," Ray said.

"Howdja get in?"

"Someone unlocked the door."

True to his nickname, Kentucky Joe spoke with a southern twang. His real name was Phil, but to everyone affiliated with Rico, he was Kentucky Joe. When he had first arrived in Vegas, the locals were quick to comment on Phil's accent, to which he'd respond, "I talk just like any other Kentucky Joe." No one was sure who first afforded him the moniker, but nevertheless it stuck.

Kentucky Joe had become a principal figure at Rico's house. His unwavering fidelity, unquestioning service, and intimidating size made him a valued commodity.

"Ya'll stay here a second," the big man said.

Kentucky Joe disappeared into the other room. He could be heard clomping down the steps to the lower floor. It's almost unheard of to have a basement in Las Vegas, mostly due to the difficulty and excessive cost of digging through the hard caliche rock layer upon which the city stands, but Rico insisted on it and didn't care the cost. Having grown up on the east coast, Rico was partial to conducting all his business below ground.

Joe appeared from the darkness, a white bag of ice still in his hand. "This way," he said. Ray and Duncan followed him down the stairs.

Arriving in a large, open room at the end of the hallway, Ray and Duncan joined a small party already in progress. Among the handful of guests were some unfamiliar faces. Rico stood at the center of the room, looking down on a bloody-faced man. Rico moved over to the bar at the side of the room and perched himself up on a stool. Kentucky Joe placed the bag of ice in front of Rico who promptly sunk his right hand into it with a sigh and a sneer.

"Hey guys," Rico said, acknowledging Duncan and Ray.

"What's up Rico?" Ray said, sincerely.

"This fucking guy…" Rico said.

The bookie business could be dangerous. The one thing you could always count on when dealing in large quantities of money is that people's emotions got involved, as much as they would claim they did not. Every once in a while a collector would run into someone less than willing to part with that which they had grown fond of keeping for themselves.

In the decade or so that Duncan and Ray had dealt with Rico, they'd never known him to be an intrinsically violent man. He dabbled in intimidation and occasionally had Kentucky Joe or another gorilla put a fright into someone, but rarely had he shed blood or been put in a position where he had to make good on threats widely considered to be nothing more than occupational necessities. Rico considered himself a classic numbers man, not a gangster or bully or thug. And, while he did own a gun or two or ten, he did so mostly for appearance. It was, after all, Las Vegas, where one is seemingly issued a cocktail and a firearm upon breach of the city limits.

"We have your bag," Duncan said.

"That was fast," Rico said. He raised his limp, reddened hand from the bag of ice as if it were a dead fish, and gave it a good look-over.

"We need to talk to you about it," Ray added, "but not here, if that's okay."

"That's fine," Rico said.

"What did he do?" Ray finally asked, referring to the bleeding man now kneeling on the floor.

"He was reaching for something," Rico said. "It looked like a knife."

"Why would I pull a knife, Rico?" the red-faced man whimpered.

"You know what you did, Quinn. And you knew that I knew."

Quinn Mckegg was one of Rico's newer associates. He was young, good-looking, and much more well-kempt than the usual type that Rico employed. Quinn was a Las Vegas local. He knew the ins-and-outs of the city and all the dealings that went on below the line.

"What did he do?" Ray asked.

"My sister!" Rico admitted, getting up from his perch and walking up to the new arrivals.

"Jenny?"

"Yeah, thanks Ray. No one here would've figured I was talking about my only sister."

"I love her," Quinn mumbled.

"What the fuck did you make a move for?" Rico yelled.

"I was reaching for a letter!"

"Who keeps a letter in their back pocket? It looked like a knife."

"It was a letter," Quinn repeated sheepishly. "I wrote you a letter."

"What the fuck? What is this, the 1800's? Who does that?" Rico turned to Ray. "Who writes a letter?"

It was obvious that Rico felt badly for hitting Quinn, and by the looks of Quinn's face, it seemed as though he felt worse.

"Do you wanna go upstairs?" Ray offered. "We can talk there."

"Yeah, okay," Rico said, "Quinn…fuck, sorry I hit you."

"It's okay, Rico," Quinn said, getting up off the floor. Quinn reached into his back pocket and pulled out a white envelope. He held it in his out-stretched arm. Rico didn't take it.

Rico led Ray and Duncan back up the stairs and into a small private office. He shut the door behind them. "How's everything with you guys?" he asked, settling up against the large wooden desk.

"Pretty good," Ray said. "We have something for you."

Duncan had taken the bag from Ray and was fishing his hand around within it. He pulled out a stack of cash.

"So you actually did it," Rico said. "You cashed 'em all out. I never thought you would. Not a lot of people can walk away from a life like that."

"It's time for something new," said Ray.

"Something new? What else do you know how to do?"

Duncan handed Rico a wad of bills. "That's yours," he said.

Rico took the money. "Now I gotta find someone down in Phoenix to take over for you guys. That's not gonna be easy, you know."

"Sorry, Rico," Duncan said.

"You're just lucky I like you guys."

"How nice," Ray joked.

"So what now? What's next?"

"Still don't know," Duncan said.

Rico thought for a moment. He stood up and walked closer to Ray and Duncan. "Well," he said, "I got a small job you can have if you're up for it."

Ray and Duncan exchanged a glance.

"What is it?" Duncan asked.

"It's a small collection, nothing major. You can even keep the pick-up."

"Keep it?" Ray asked.

"It's 12K, including juice and it's yours if you want it."

"What's the catch?"

"No catch. It's so long overdue I don't even care about the money anymore. But I can't let a debt slide. I do care about that. The guy has to know that he can't hold out."

"Why haven't you sent Kentucky Joe or Mikey?"

"I would have, but the pick-up is in Boston."

"Boston?" Ray blurted.

"Don't you have someone out there?" Duncan asked.

"Yeah, Willy." Rico said. "But he had a coronary three months ago and dropped dead. This fucking 12K is the last holdout."

"Boston," Ray said again.

"Yeah, Boston. So? Whadaya think?"

Ray just shook his head.

"We were actually thinking of heading east." Duncan said.

"Who couldn't use another 12K? It's an in-and-out job. Just promise me if you do it, you do it. Once you have the cake just let me know so I can close Willy's book."

"And why don't you want the 12K?"

"That's my business. Don't worry about that. So you gonna do it or what?"

Ray and Duncan weren't following any particular timeline or planned route. Part of the appeal of cashing out and moving on from Phoenix was the prospect of freedom to do whatever came next. Putting the plan to have no plan on hold for one more job and a few extra dollars didn't sound so terrible.

After nearly a decade of bookmaking, both Duncan and Ray embraced the idea of picking up and essentially starting life over from scratch. People rarely, if ever, get the opportunity to do it, and the pair were still at a point in their lives where they were unaffiliated and unencumbered enough to set out on the road without a care. It was the prospect of the unknown that excited them most.

"Boston," Duncan said. "Sure, why not."

CHAPTER 3

DEPARTING FROM RICO'S house in the BMW, Duncan and Ray went over the specifics of the job. It sounded easy enough. They had a name, an address, and the exact amount of money that needed to be collected. The hardest part, it seemed, would be crossing the country and making it to Boston without distraction.

They drove back onto the highway.

Ray switched on the radio.

It felt good to listen to music for a change – to care about something other than football, baseball, basketball, or hockey scores. The recently found freedom from concern did not go unnoticed. And, though they both still considered themselves fans of sport, the break from obligatory attention came as a welcome respite.

The first leg of the trip plunged the continental travelers into the early hours of the morning. The sprightly enthusiasm that carried them back onto Interstate 15 had conclusively waned by the time they reached the Utah border. The goal was to rest when they reached Colorado in the morning, but achy legs and heavy heads curtailed their ambitious plan. Duncan and Ray instead pulled into a motel not far from Fishlake National Forrest, just outside of Richfield, Utah.

The pair oozed from the car into the arms of the night air.

Duncan entered the motel office and paid cash for a room. He thanked the amiable, elderly woman behind the desk and returned to the car.

Duncan and Ray went up to the top floor of the two-story complex, turned the key and entered room 216. Each threw their bag onto one of the beds in the malodorous lodgings. Duncan slipped into the bathroom to wash his hands and to stash the black money bag atop the moveable ceiling slats above the shower.

Though tired from driving, Ray and Duncan yielded swiftly to the idea of having a cold beer and something to eat before calling it a night. They knew that a watering hole would not be hard to find, even in the small roadside town. After a very brief rest, they got back into the BMW and made for the poorly lit narrow streets.

They came upon a bar not five minutes from the motel along a street with no signs or noticeable markings. Outside the bar rested a narrow, linear fortification of black and silver motorcycles in perfect angular symmetry. Duncan pulled the car into the gravel parking lot.

The inside of the bar was enough to make both of the city-dwelling, opulent-car-driving patrons smirk from ear to cheek. Wooden floors creaking under foot, license plates gilding walls, and loud rock n' roll music assaulting their ears. It smelled of stale beer and smoke.

As they walked through the establishment, the pair could feel eyes following them from every direction. Neither Duncan nor Ray looked the type that had just rolled in on iron horses, and they certainly didn't look like they were from the neighborhood.

They approached the bartender.

Duncan stood with his back to the bar and surveyed his surroundings while Ray waited patiently to place an order. Duncan could feel the palpable tension. Whether reasonable or not, Duncan felt for a moment as though he and Ray were gazelles dropped into a lion's den as some sort of strange sociological experiment.

Duncan endeavored to avoid confrontation at every turn. He wasn't the type that possessed the urge to confirm his manhood by engaging in clashes of primeval fury. But what the leather and denim-clad lions in that particular bar didn't know about Duncan would have served them well to not find out. Duncan was not one to be considered prey. In fact, he was very far from it indeed.

Ray turned around and handed Duncan a bottle of beer. He looked around the bar and took in the environment much in the way Duncan had been doing.

"Those guys are huge," Ray said, referring to the bearded horde surrounding a nearby pool table.

"I think they like you," Duncan said.

"I'm sure they do."

According to urban legend, prison rules stated that if you wanted to prove yourself tough or worthy of respect, on the first day of incarceration you had to find the biggest and meanest inmate and challenge him to a fight. It was most likely a commonly held idea among those never to have been dropped behind tall bricked walls and barbed wired fences.

Duncan reached into his pocket and pulled out a warm wad of change. He looked down into his palm and appraised it. He shook his hand up and down allowing the coins to jingle and spread about in his palm. Duncan then clenched his fist around the pile making a strong fist and began to walk assuredly towards the pool table. Ray followed without hesitation.

The pride that stood guard at the green felt table saw them coming, they clenched their chalky spears and stood upright. One of the biggest took a step forward and positioned himself in the path of Duncan and Ray. Ray leisurely pulled a chair and took a seat at a small table beside the towering man as Duncan came face-to-face with the tattooed goliath. Duncan was close enough to smell the whisky and cigarettes on his breath, but far enough not to insinuate that he was challenging for territory. Duncan said nothing. The bar seemed to come to a hush, though the music still blared and people still spoke in their usual tone. Duncan was eclipsed by the stature of his would-be opponent and stood in the man's shadow.

Duncan looked down to his fist, then back to the face of the man in front of him. He then raised his hand, plucked four quarters from the stack, and placed them on the rail of the table. He then took a twenty-dollar bill from his pocket and placed it beside the quarters.

"Next game," Duncan said.

The extra-large man permitted himself to crack a small smile. The man then nodded once.

Duncan returned the gesture before taking a seat at the table with Ray. The sound of the bar seemed to rise once more. Duncan took a swig from his beer and smiled at Ray.

Duncan lost his twenty dollars to Sam, the bulky man with whose beard he had recently become acquainted.

Ray played Sam in the next game and won the money back.

It wasn't long before both Duncan and Ray had assimilated into the faction that would to others seem frightening. But in truth, there was nothing frightening about them. They proved to be welcoming and jovial and overtly generous. Sam used the twenty he won from Duncan to buy each of them a beer. Ray returned the gesture with his subsequent victory.

Sam's compatriots consisted of a throng of young to middle-aged bikers together on their way from Colorado to Las Vegas. They had names like Burner, Slim, Varr, and Mick. One was a mechanic, one worked construction, and one owned a company that shredded paper documents. Sam never did say what his occupation was, or if he had one at all, but when he held his pool cue against the table it was obvious by his hard, calloused hands that he was not an accountant.

Last call came.

Duncan was embroiled in a conversation with Sam and Varr about the practice of wooing women, while Ray was putting similar theories to practice at a table with two buxom brunettes. Ray had great luck with the softer sex. He was good looking, young, and had plenty of charm to spare. He once had a girl back in Phoenix to whom Duncan thought Ray would one day be married. She was the daughter of a prominent city politician. The pressure from her family to find someone more suiting their elite traditions weighed heavy on the relationship. They eventually broke up, much to Ray's dismay.

Ashley Dupree and Ray still had trouble staying away from one another and there was little doubt for Duncan that they were still in love. Ashley was, and always would be, Ray's first love. He looked for her in every woman he spoke to, kissed, or with whom he made love. Ashley left Arizona a few years prior to continue her education at an Ivy League college. She and Ray continued to exchange emails, text messages, and the occasional phone call, but Ray hadn't heard from Ashley in nearly six months. Duncan was certain that Ray was still looking for a small piece of Ashley in that bar just outside of Richfield, Utah that night.

The sound of a large cowbell rung out from behind the wooden bar signaling the end of last call. The bar had all but cleared out by that time, though Duncan, Ray, and their new comrades remained.

Duncan and a few of the lingering bikers from Colorado made their way out the doors. Sam lit a smoke.

Ray emerged a few minutes later, arms devoid of hangers-on.

"Ask for Carlos at Luxor," Duncan said to Varr, a wild haired, yet seemingly taciturn fellow. "Tell him I said to take care of you. He'll know what that means."

"Thanks, Dunner," Varr said. He raised his arm as if he were preparing to arm wrestle the air. Duncan slapped his hand and held on for a shake. The group that remained took turns bidding similar farewells. The six bikers then mounted their vehicles and roared off, leaving Duncan and Ray in a swirling cloud of dust and smoke.

The two females that Ray had befriended exited the bar in a giggly and slightly unsteady way. Duncan and Ray exchanged a look. Duncan shook his head with a grimace. Ray nodded in agreement. The pair then got into the BMW and slowly pulled out of the lot.

Returning to their room, Duncan's first order of business was to lift the ceiling slat above the shower just to be certain that nothing had changed.

All seemed well. The bag was intact.

Ray flopped onto the bed closest to the humming air conditioner and turned on the TV. Making a concerted effort to stay away from Sports Center, he flipped the channels restlessly.

"Just turn it off," Duncan said, falling onto his bed.

Ray did.

As soon as TV blinked off, what sounded like a commotion not far from the front of their door became audible. "You hear that?" Ray asked.

Duncan got up from his bed and walked over to the window. He pushed back the wall-length curtain and peered in each direction. He saw nothing. The commotion began again and Duncan's curiosity piqued. "What's with all the noise?" he said. He opened the front door and stepped outside.

Duncan's first inclination was to look over the railing. As he did so, a loud bang filled the open-air terrace. "What was that?" Ray asked.

Shoeless, Duncan began to walk toward the loud sound. Ray leapt from his bed and followed his friend.

Duncan was first to turn the corner at the end of the aisle. There he saw a woman slumped on the ground, huddling up to a vending machine. A man stood over the woman, his fists were clenched and his eyes enraged.

"What's going on here?" Duncan asked.

He only needed to look down onto the face of the woman before it became patently clear what had been going on.

Neither girl nor assailant said anything.

"Why don't you back up?" Duncan said to the man.

Ray rounded the corner.

"Hey," the man said. "This is none of your business. Go back to your room."

The man unclenched his fists and feigned calm.

"Don't," the girl pleaded.

She was wearing jean-shorts and a thin white tank top. Ray instinctively leaned over to help her up.

"Hey!" the man yelled, his hands transforming into fists once again. He made a move toward Ray.

That's when Duncan interceded. With stealth and speed, he grabbed the man from the side, swept his legs out from under him and had rendered him immobile on the ground before the man knew what had happened. With a knee in one ear and the cold concrete under the other, the skinny man quickly realized he would be no match for the one on top of him. "What the fuck?" he gasped.

Duncan had the man's arm twisted around and held it up in the air over his body. The man couldn't move in a thousand different ways. "What're you, a cop?" the man asked.

"Why?" Duncan answered, "You doing something illegal?"

"Fuck no. There's no problem here. I got no problems with you."

Ray helped the blonde-haired girl up from the floor. Her young face was red and beginning to swell. "Do you know this guy?" he asked her.

She nodded.

"Boyfriend? Husband?"

"Neither," the girl answered. "He's just an asshole."

"You do have a problem with me," Duncan said to the man under his knee. "I paid $39.99 to the woman at the front desk for a room. So that means tonight, this is my house. You're making noise in my house."

Duncan gave the man's arm an extra little twist. The man grunted in pain.

"I paid too, man. It's my house too."

Duncan gave the twisted arm a pull.

"Okay!" The man howled. "Okay!"

"It's time for you to leave," Duncan said. "I'm going to let you up and then you're gonna get your shit and go."

"I don't have any shit," he said.

"That should make it easier."

As he finished his words, Duncan yanked the man up from the ground almost as violently as he had sent him down.

Ray took a step forward to shield the girl now standing by his side.

Duncan unleashed the man from his control and stood in front of him. The man looked over Duncan's shoulder and peered at the girl.

"You're a real cunt, you know that?" he said, pointing in her face. He might have said something more but thought better of it when he once again met Duncan's glare. The man turned and clomped heavily down the open stairs to the first floor.

All three that stood on the landing above could see the man's grey and red pickup truck peel out of the lot and onto the street.

"What's your name?" Ray asked the girl once the truck was well out of sight.

"Amanda," she answered.

"You live around here?"

She shook her head no.

"What were you doing with that guy?"

"He's just...some guy," she said, tapping her fingertips to her cheek to survey the damage.

"How old are you?"

"Twenty-three."

"Yeah, twenty-three," Ray said in disbelief.

"I am," she insisted. "Why, how old are you?"

Ray didn't answer. "You have somewhere to go?" he asked.

The girl shook her head again.

"What the hell are we supposed to do now?" Ray asked Duncan.

Duncan leaned over and swiped up the girl's bag from the ground beside the vending machine and handed it back to her.

Both Ray and Duncan knew they couldn't just let the girl go off on her own, not after what had transpired. By the way she looked at Ray, it seemed as though she didn't want that either.

"Fuck it, let's go," Ray said.

"Where?" the girl asked.

"Where do you think?"

CHAPTER 4

"YOU CAN HAVE that one," Ray said, pointing to the bed closest to the door.

"I don't even know your names," the girl replied.

"I'm Ray, that's Duncan, that bed's yours."

"Well, where you from?" she asked, gingerly entering the room.

"Phoenix."

The girl paused as Duncan closed the door behind her.

"Thanks for helping me," she said to him.

"Who was that guy?" Duncan inquired.

"His name is Randy. He's just…someone I met."

The girl threw her bag onto the floor and sat down in a chair against the wall.

"That's it?" Ray asked. "Just someone you met?"

"What else do you want to know?"

Ray took a washcloth and soaked it in cold water. He brought it over to Amanda and motioned to her swollen cheek. The girl took the cloth from his hand. She pressed it gently against her face and tilted her head to the side.

"Why'd he hit you?" Duncan asked.

"That's a long story."

The girl took the cloth from her face and touched her cheek softly with her hand. She clenched her jaw and winced in pain. Duncan got comfortable on the bed.

"And you have nowhere else to go?" Ray asked.

The girl didn't answer right away. "Why do you want to know?"

Duncan was curious about the girl and her circumstance, but not as much as he had been five minutes prior. Duncan turned away and lay down on the bed. "It's Amanda, right?" he said.

"Yeah."

"Goodnight, Amanda."

Ray smirked at the girl. "You don't have to tell us," he said.

"Well what about you? Why are you guys here?"

"Just passing through."

"Where you going?"

"East."

"What's east?"

"A lot of things I imagine."

Amanda took the cloth from her face once again.

"You know you're in a shitty motel when there's no ice machine," she said.

Ray smiled.

"Can I use the bathroom?" the girl asked.

Ray nodded.

Amanda threw the cloth into the small sink outside the bathroom and then disappeared behind the door.

Ray let out a sigh and shook his head. He sat down in the chair that had been vacated by the swollen-faced girl. He could hear the water running behind the bathroom door.

"Hey," Ray said.

"Tomorrow," Duncan answered. "It's 3 a.m."

"What are we supposed to do with her?"

"She can stay the night, but we're outta here in the morning. She's on her own."

Ray nodded in agreement.

Without lifting his face from the bed, Duncan reached into his back pocket and removed his wallet. "Take this," he said.

"And the bag?"

"I'll check first thing in the morning before she goes. She won't find it."

The running water turned into the sound of a running shower. The girl popped out of the bathroom to grab her bag, and then disappeared back behind the door.

Ray lifted the mattress upon which his friend laid. He shoved both their wallets underneath it.

"They're under you," Ray said.

"Yeah, I figured."

Ray turned off the lights and sat down on the empty bed. Using a few pillows he propped himself up against the headboard and turned on the TV. He flipped the channels but was concentrating on something else altogether. He was going over in his head the various encounters of the day, starting with the collection route that began while the sun was still new in the sky, and ended in a garage with Martin Bridge. He and Duncan had covered a lot of road in one day.

Ray's eyes began to close.

Amanda emerged from the steamy bathroom clad in two white motel towels. Her wavy hair was straight, wet, and darker in color.

Ray made a motion to get up off the bed, but the soaked girl reached over and put her hand on his shoulder.

"Stay," she said softly. "It's fine."

The room was lit with a bluish tinge from the TV. Ray looked over to the adjacent bed where Duncan was spread out on his stomach like a giant starfish. Without much thought to the contrary, Ray simply allowed his eyes to close once again.

Though he tried to ignore it, the rustling about of Amanda and her bag kept Ray awake. He opened his eyes to see Amanda face-to-face with herself in the mirror, her bag resting on the countertop. He closed his eyes once more.

Ray's eyes opened again a few minutes later; Amanda was in the same spot, brushing her hair. Thinking Ray asleep, Amanda shed her top towel. She was facing the other way, her naked back exposed to him.

The thin girl pulled a pair of underwear out from the bag and stepped into them one leg at a time. She looked at herself again in the mirror and removed the second towel. She then turned around and presented her bare body to Ray as she pulled a small shirt from her bag. She didn't notice that Ray's eyes were open and continued about her business slowly and quietly so not to disturb her two sleeping saviors. She pulled the T-shirt over her head and covered up her exposed chest. Upon the realization Ray was in fact still awake and watching her, Amanda shuddered then smiled, shrugging off any fleeting embarrassment. Ray couldn't help but let out a short and audible blow of air from his nose, the kind made when using one's voice to chuckle is simply too much effort.

Amanda walked over to the far side of Ray's bed and drew back the covers. She climbed in slowly, as if she were still presuming him asleep. Ray remained above the sheets, still wearing his clothes. The young girl leaned over and kissed Ray on the cheek, then turned over and put her head down on the pillow, certain to face opposite Ray and lie on her unharmed left side.

CHAPTER 5

DUNCAN WAS THE first to wake the following morning. A slice of sunlight pierced through the edge of window and stabbed him in the right eye. He tilted his head to avoid the bothersome beam, but it had already robbed him of reaching the conclusion of his dream. Duncan raised his head and looked over to scrutinize his still sleeping cohorts with one eye still closed. Ray had gravitated to a supine position atop the bed. Amanda was nearly undetectable under the bunching layers of off-white motel sheets and yellow and red floral cover.

Duncan moved to a sitting position on the side of the bed. He took a sniff of his underarm to determine if the odor he smelled was indeed emanating from his unwashed body. He concluded that the wanton smell was coming more from his surroundings than from the pits of his arms. Duncan lifted his phone from the bedside table and checked the time. He leaned over and managed to nudge Ray's placid body. Ray awoke with little drama. Duncan got up from the bed and removed his shirt. He used two of his fingers to point to both of his eyes, and then pointed to the slumbering young lady. Ray gave a short nod of understanding and reclosed his eyes. Duncan gave him another nudge. Ray opened his eyes and nodded again.

Duncan pointed to the mattress under which Ray had stashed the wallets.

Duncan moved toward the bathroom and began unbuttoning his pants as he walked. He closed the door behind him.

Ray heard the sound of the levered lock and then the sound of ceiling slats being moved about. He looked over to Amanda. Her head was still on her pillow, but her eyes were now open and facing Ray. Ray's gaze met hers. Amanda reclosed her eyes. For the duration of Duncan's shower, neither Ray nor Amanda did much moving.

When Duncan emerged, fully damp and carrying the black bag, Amanda finally showed signs of life. She threw the sheets off the top half of her body and let out a moan.

"What time is it?" she asked, visibly warm and moderately uncomfortable.

"Almost nine," Ray answered.

"It stinks in here."

Ray lifted his arm to smell himself much in the way Duncan had. "Any hot water?" he asked.

"Yeah," Duncan said.

Ray managed to pull himself to his feet, but gave an elderly man grunt as he did. "Towels?" he asked.

He didn't get a verbal response from Duncan but caught the tail end of what he interpreted as a nod. Ray disappeared into the bathroom.

Duncan grabbed his clothing bag from the floor and dropped it onto the bed. He pulled out a neatly folded shirt and laid it on the bed.

Amanda took notice of Duncan's sculpted torso and upper body. Not remarkably large – standing only about six feet tall and weighing about one hundred ninety pounds – Duncan's impressive physique was usually kept well hidden.

Most that grew up in New Mexico gravitated towards baseball as kids. Duncan, instead, spent his youth fascinated instead by something much different. While most his age were practicing pitching and fielding and batting, Duncan was adamantly studying martial arts. He participated in classes and private tutelage beginning at the age of five. A neighborhood instructor took notice of his enthusiasm and of his aptitude. Not always able to pay for lessons, Duncan would often visit the childless man's home after hours for one-on-one training. The man never expected anything in return from Duncan.

The man's wife, Melinda, was a frail lady, unable to leave the house most days, so Duncan's visits were a welcome reprieve from what would otherwise have become a monotonous routine. Max, the half-Jewish, half-Asian instructor became a valued friend and mentor to Duncan. The relationship cultivated by the pair over the years was reward enough for both.

Melinda passed away the year Duncan left for college. Max began to deteriorate soon thereafter. The steadfast man that Duncan had come to know so well relied more than he had imagined on a ninety-pound caregiver. Max died of cancer quickly and painfully six years after his beloved wife, but only five months after diagnosis. Duncan was at his bedside the night he went. The two had no unfinished business and Duncan looked back on the time with his friend with nothing but love and fondness. Thanks to Max, Duncan could wield a baseball bat better than most in New Mexico, but not in the way that would get him noticed by any professional scouts.

When Ray emerged from the washroom, Amanda arose and took his place inside.

Ray and Duncan were both dressed when she came out, clothes changed and make-up applied. The swelling on her face had all but disappeared and for the first time the pair got a good look at the girl's true appearance.

She was tall, slim, and fit but not overtly muscular like an athlete might be. She had the wholesome pretty face of an innocent, but the look in her blue eyes suggested something much different.

"What?" Amanda asked.

"Nothing," Ray said. "You look different."

"My face. The swelling's gone down."

"It has," agreed Duncan from across the room.

All three organized their belongings and grabbed their bags. Duncan handed Ray his wallet from beneath the mattress and then slung the black bag onto his shoulder. Together they exited the room.

"I'll go check out," Ray said. "I'll meet you at the car."

Duncan handed Ray the room key and he and Amanda walked off in the opposite direction.

"Is that your car?" Amanda asked as she and Duncan approached the BMW.

"Something like that," Duncan said.

"Wow. You guys don't look like the type."

"We're not. It's a long story."

Duncan popped the trunk and threw his bag inside. He made certain to hang on to the black one, though.

Ray began to approach from the far end of the parking lot a few minutes later.

"What's his story?" Amanda asked. "Is that a long one, too?"

"Longer," Duncan said.

"So what's in the bag?"

"You got a lot of questions."

"Ready?" Ray interrupted upon arrival.

Duncan paused. They both looked at Amanda.

"You gonna be okay, Amanda?" Ray asked the girl.

"There's something I should tell you," she said.

Though it was still early in the morning, the summer sun was hot on the back of Ray's neck. He moved into the shadow cast by the building.

"My name's not Amanda," the girl said.

"Uh huh," said Ray.

"It's Ruby."

"Ruby."

"Ruby," she repeated.

"Okay. Well I'm still Ray. And that's still Duncan."

Duncan waved.

"I mean you can't blame me, can you?"

"It's okay," Duncan assured.

"It's just that you guys have been so nice to me…"

For the first time since cowering under Randy's fist, Ruby looked vulnerable. She had one hand in her back pocket and her bag slunk lazily over her shoulder.

"Hey, don't worry about it," Ray said. "It was…an interesting night."

Ruby smiled. Ray thought for a second he saw a tear in her eye, but she looked away too quickly for him to be certain.

"So what now, Ruby?" Duncan asked.

"Now I keep going," Ruby said with renewed confidence.

"Going where?" Ray asked.

"I don't know. But that's the point."

"The point?"

"Yeah, the point. Haven't you ever just wanted to *go*?"

Duncan and Ray looked at each other.

"Actually–" Duncan said.

"You wanna come with us?" Ray asked.

"Ray," Duncan interjected.

"No," Ruby said after a pause. "Thanks though."

"Why not?"

"*Ray*," Duncan said again.

Ruby looked over at Duncan and then back to Ray. "It's okay, Ray, really," she said. "I'll be fine."

Ruby walked up to Duncan and kissed him on the cheek. "Thank you for everything," she said.

Duncan nodded and smiled.

Ruby approached Ray. "It was nice sharing a bed with you, Ray."

She kissed Ray's cheek, though she held it for a fraction of a second longer. Ray said nothing.

He didn't want that to be the end. He couldn't say why, or what it was he wanted from Ruby. He simply knew he didn't want her to just leave.

"We should get out of here," Duncan said, climbing into the car.

"Be good," Ray said to Ruby as he relented and opened the passenger door.

"Always," Ruby said.

Ruby took a few steps back to let the BMW pull backwards out of its spot. Through the tint of the car window, Ruby and Ray came face to face and caught each other's eyes as the car reversed.

Duncan changed gears and began to pull away. At that moment, Ruby got a feeling in the pit of her stomach. It was one of exhilaration, but also of fright.

Ruby left home only two weeks prior and had already encountered one minor run-in with the law, and one major run-in with a fist. She truly didn't know where she was headed, and for the first time that made her feel uneasy. Perhaps it was the daunting experience of the night prior, or maybe it was the fact that for the first time since she left home she had met people that she might have been able to trust, and those people were leaving her standing in the parking lot of a shoddy motel in Utah.

Ruby turned and began to make her way to the motel office. She needed to call a cab to take her to the bus station. She was on her own again.

Ruby made it about thirty paces when she couldn't help but turn her head to see off her new friends. When she did, she was surprised to see that the car had stopped at the far end of the lot.

"You sure?" Duncan asked.

"I'm sure," Ray said.

Ray opened the side door and got out. He leaned against the car and peered across to Ruby. "It's only a two-door," he yelled. "You'll have to squeeze in."

Ruby couldn't help but smile as she looked up at the sky.

"Well?" Ray called out.

"Hurry up," Duncan shouted, his head popping out of the driver-side window.

Ruby sauntered across the nearly empty lot until she stood face to face with Ray. His smile was big and sly.

"East?" she said.

"Boston." Ray nodded.

Ruby smiled. She crouched her head down and slid past Ray into the back seat of the car.

CHAPTER 6

NOT TWENTY MINUTES after leaving the motel, young Ruby fell asleep upon her bag in the back seat. As the BMW crossed the border into Colorado just before lunch, Ruby had still not awoken.

"When did you know?" Ray asked Duncan. He put down his book and looked over to the driver.

"Know what?"

"Did you just decide it one day or did you always think it?"

"This again?"

"Maybe it's just a feeling," Ray surmised. "Like people who think that everything happens for a reason. But you don't think that, do you?"

"I think some things happen for a reason, sure," Duncan said.

"Really?"

"Why would there be a word for fate if it didn't exist?"

"There's a word for unicorns, isn't there?"

"I think there has to be some kind of plan," Duncan said. "You can fall off the path or change direction, but you can't run from who you are."

"What're you guys talking about?" a voice said from the back seat.

Ray curled his head around the over-sized headrest.

"Oh, nothing," he said. "Just something we started a long time ago."

"Unicorns?"

"No. Not unicorns."

"It sounds like you're talking about unicorns."

"Ray's been trying to understand how I can believe in God," Duncan said.

Duncan looked in the rear view mirror to see if he could catch Ruby's reaction. He couldn't even see the top of her head. Though awake, Ruby had slouched down even further and curled across the entire back seat. She rested her head on her bag and shut her eyes once more.

"Arguing whether there is or isn't a God is like arguing whether or not a song is good," she said. "You can never be right and you can never be wrong."

"You believe in God?" Ray asked.

"I don't know."

"You don't know?"

"I'm assuming you don't?"

"Not for a second."

"How can you be so sure?"

"The evidence against it is overwhelming."

"So then what happens to you when you die?" Ruby asked.

"You die," Ray said. "You're dead. End. Over. Bye bye."

"I think I believe in reincarnation," Ruby said, her eyes still closed. "Haven't you ever met someone that you feel you've met before, or that you know from somewhere else? And what about all those people that just seem so new?"

"Well, if there *is* such a thing as reincarnation, I'd come back as a cat," Ray said.

"A cat?" Duncan said. "You hate cats."

"For the same reasons I'd want to be one."

"A cat?"

"A housecat, yeah. I'd lie around all day. Someone else would get my food, rub me down, and no one would give a shit if I ever paid any attention to them."

"Pray on it," Duncan said.

"Don't you want to be in heaven?" Ruby asked. "Don't you want to think that once you die you'll get to be with the people you love? The people you've lost?"

"I think it sounds like a pretty crowded place," Ray said. "And no, I don't think I'd want to be anywhere where I had no purpose."

Duncan shook his head.

"Can we stop?" Ruby asked.

"Yes, please," Duncan said. "We've been talking about it forever and we never get anywhere."

"No, can we stop. I'm a girl, small bladder."

"Oh, yeah, sure," Duncan answered. "I'm hungry, anyway."

"Yeah, a cat." Ray said. "That's the life." He nodded as he looked out the window at the grass whizzing by.

Duncan pulled off Interstate 70 at the outskirts of Grand Junction, Colorado. He screeched into a gas station and Ruby sprung from the car and scurried to the washroom. Ray got out to stretch his legs; Duncan began refueling.

Ruby returned with a look of relief on her face.

Ray went inside to pay for the gas and returned with an armful of drinks, chips, and candy. The three hopped back into the car and drove off in the direction of a nearby family restaurant. They entered the small establishment; they sat, they ate, they ogled the array of patrons.

Once back on the highway, satiated and restored of fervor, the conversation easily turned from Ray's posthumous desires to be a feline, to something more germane to the occasion.

"I left home a few weeks ago," Ruby said, answering Duncan's inquiry as to how she ended up in Utah. "I was heading to California."

"Where's home?"

"Greenbrook, Kansas."

"You leave any family there?" Ray asked.

"My mom."

"You guys don't get along?"

"Actually, we get along fine," Ruby said. "I love my mom. But I don't want her life."

"What's her life?"

"A dead-end job, a shitty new boyfriend every couple of months. I mean she does the best she can, but I saw my life turning into hers and I had to get out."

"Amanda was twenty-three, how old is Ruby?" Duncan asked.

"Twenty-three also," Ruby smiled. "Ruby was a twenty-three year old waitress with one year of junior college, a pot-head ex-boyfriend that liked to hit her every once in a while, and eleven hundred dollars in tips in a shoebox under her bed."

"And now?"

"Now she's a twenty-three-year-old in the back of a BMW on her way across the country. Maybe I'll get a degree from Yale. Maybe I'll go to New York and marry Eli Manning. I can be whoever I want."

"With eleven hundred dollars," Ray added.

"More like eight now," Ruby smiled.

"Sky's the limit," Duncan said.

"So what's your story, then? Ya'll are from Phoenix, and?"

"We both went to ASU, graduated, and now we're driving across the country with Eli Manning's future wife," said Ray.

"You can give me more than that," Ruby said, smacking Ray on the shoulder.

"Like what?"

"I dunno, how about you tell me what's in that bag?"

"Which bag?"

"Which bag? That bag. The black one. The one you two are protecting like it's got a million bucks in it."

Ray looked over at Duncan. Duncan didn't make a move or utter a sound; he just kept his right hand on the wheel and his eyes on the road ahead.

Without much more thought, Ray lifted the black bag from his feet and pulled the two zippers apart from the top. He flashed the contents into the back seat.

"Holy shit," Ruby howled.

"Really, Ray?" Duncan said.

"I was just kidding about the million dollars. How much is that?"

Ray was holding open the two sides of the bag as if he were showing a picture book to a classroom of kids. Inside the bag were wads upon wads of cash. Some wads were bigger than others, but all were held together with things like paper clips, rubber bands, and in a few cases – like the money they collected from Martin Bridge – original bank wraps.

"I've never seen that much money in my life," Ruby said. "How much is it, for real?"

"Not as much as it looks like," Ray said.

"Still…wait, you guys didn't steal that, did you?"

"No, it's ours."

"Wow."

Ruby took a second to drink in the contents before Ray pulled the bag back into the front and zipped it closed.

"Why you walking around with all that money?" Ruby asked.

"We just left Phoenix. What else are we supposed to do with it?"

"You know guys," she said. "If you take that bag into a bank they'll give you a cute little plastic card and you can take it out little bits at a time instead of carrying it around everywhere you go."

Duncan and Ray looked at each other as if Ruby had just revealed to them the secret recipe of how to make toast.

"You can't just walk into a bank with this much cash," Ray said.

"I dunno," Duncan said. "Maybe you can."

It was later that afternoon, just outside of Denver, Colorado that Ray, Duncan, and Ruby sat parked in the lot of a national bank chain and began sorting the money into piles on the back seat. After Ray had given away the secret of the bag's contents, Duncan felt even less comfortable keeping the cash with them.

"I'm up six from that thing," Duncan said, peering at the stacks.

"We settled, didn't we?" said Ray.

Duncan thought for a moment.

"Yes. We did, you're right. But only four. So I'm up two."

"And two more from that guy with the dogs."

"Right, so that's four in total. Let's split it down the middle and then you give me four."

Ruby sat, straight-backed and eyes agape, watching Ray and Duncan swap wads of thousands like they were baseball cards. Ray began to make one-for-you one-for-me piles on the armrest separating the two front seats.

"And you're four up," Ray said as he took four thousand from his pile and handed it to Duncan. Duncan took the extra four thousand and put it into his pocket. "So that's…"

"One hundred sixty seven thousand for Ray and one hundred seventy one thousand for Duncan," Ruby said. Duncan and Ray both turned to look at her.

"What?" she said. "I waited tables for three years. I'm good with numbers."

"We can't just walk into a bank with this much cash," Ray said. "Someone's gonna ask questions."

"There are all sorts of things that happen in cash," Duncan said. He pulled out his phone and dialed a number. You just need to know the right thing to say.

"Marty," Duncan said into the phone. "We need a favor…"

Duncan and Ray exited the car, each with their newly formed mounds of money wrapped in plastic bags repurposed from when Ray had purchased snacks at the gas station.

Ruby waited in the car.

Duncan and Ray stood outside the bank until their conversation with Martin Bridge ended. Confidently, the pair strode into the bank where they remained for the good part of an hour.

Duncan was the first to return. He got in on the passenger side, still reading the paperwork he received inside. He turned his head and noticed Ruby staring at him.

"It's Ray's turn to drive," he said. "I'm taking a break."

Ray returned a few minutes later, apparently uninterested in the printed information he had received inside the bank. He didn't make mention of the seating switch and got in on the driver's side without so much as a raised eyebrow. Duncan handed him the key, his eyes still down on his papers.

"Everything worked out then?" Ruby asked.

"Fine, yeah," Ray answered. "Apparently all you need is a high profile lawyer with a gambling problem and you can accomplish almost anything."

Ray revved up the engine and pulled out of the parking spot.

"We might as well get something to eat while we're here," Duncan said.

"Yeah, sure." Ruby agreed. "Your treat."

CHAPTER 7

ONCE BACK ON the highway, Ruby occupied the front seat which gave Duncan a chance to stretch out in the back. As the sun began to lower across the horizon, though crumpled and less than comfortable, Duncan managed to nod off. Ruby lowered the radio so not to disturb Duncan's seemingly light slumber.

The trio crossed the border into Nebraska on Interstate 76.

"What?" Ruby inquired softly.

"What?" asked Ray.

"Did you say something?"

"No why?"

"Thought I heard you say something."

"Nope."

"Oh."

"Turn the radio off," Ray said.

Ruby followed his direction. Ray turned his ear upward.

"What?" Ruby said.

"Shhh."

Ruby sat and listened closely to the white noise of the highway.

"Canesten."

"You hear that?" Ray said.

"Duncan talks in his sleep?"

Ray contained his laughter as best he could.

"This is awesome," he said. "He does this every once in a while. I haven't heard it for years."

"What does he say?"

"Just random things. Last time he said something about bread crust and chunky peanut butter."

"Wintertime," Duncan mumbled.

Ray and Ruby laughed quietly.

"I've never heard someone talk in their sleep before," Ruby said. "I hooked up with a guy once that said he sleepwalked, but I never saw it."

The silence continued.

"No socks," Duncan exclaimed.

Ray couldn't help but burst out laughing which woke the back-seat orator.

"What's up?" Duncan asked.

"Sorry dude, were you sleeping?"

"I don't think so."

"We crossed into Nebraska," a smirking Ruby informed Duncan.

"Fuck, my head hurts," Duncan said.

"You've been sitting kinda funny," Ruby said. "Straighten up a bit."

Duncan lifted himself on the seat and tilted his head from side to side. "That's it, I need a proper bed tonight," he said.

"We'll be in Omaha in about four hours," Ray said. "Let's do dinner and get a room at a nice hotel."

"I don't think I can afford that, guys," Ruby said.

"The room is on us," Ray offered.

"I'm not a charity case."

"No one said you were, Ruby," Duncan added. "But I'm not sleeping in a stink room again. I'm getting a suite with a giant bed and a proper shower. You and Ray are both welcome to join me."

Duncan closed his eyes and rested his head on the side of the car.

"He's four grand richer than everyone else in the car, you should listen to him," Ray said.

"Good point," Duncan added. "And I know how competitive Ray is. So let's call that extra four K I pocketed our travel fund? Good? Good. Between here and Boston we'll use up the four grand. There. Done. It's a challenge. Now shut the fuck up."

"No socks," Ray said.

"What?"

"Never mind."

Ruby laughed into her arm.

Following instruction from the GPS, Ray pulled up to the Magnolia Hotel near the Old Market in downtown Omaha just a spot over four hours later. With gas tank and stomachs nearly empty, the trio zombied into the lobby where Duncan alone approached the front desk. In a serendipitous turn, Duncan was able to secure the luxurious presidential suite, recently forfeited by means of a canceled stop on an unnamed rock band's tour. The 1,200 square foot, two-level accommodations boasted more opulence than conceivably required, but the young desk attendant won Duncan's favor when she informed him of the private Jacuzzi room within.

Ruby and Ray took heed of Duncan's move away from the check-in desk and carried themselves over to meet him.

"This way," Duncan said.

Ruby dragged her feet behind the boys down a long hallway toward a private entrance. Duncan turned the handle and unveiled the room to his unsuspecting followers.

"I'd say this is an upgrade from last night," said Ray.

"Wow," Ruby agreed.

The three perused the rooms within the suite, each in their own direction. Ruby pulled back the drapes from the floor-to-ceiling windows and gaped at the courtyard below. Ray closed the bathroom door behind him and got acquainted with the facilities. Duncan found his bed of choice and threw his bag upon it.

"Hey Dun, you think Quinton's around?" Ray yelled emerging from the bathroom, the sound of flushing behind him.

"We could try," Duncan yelled back from his room. "Probably should have called before though, given him some notice."

"Who's Quinton?" Ruby asked.

"Old friend from Phoenix, married a girl from Omaha."

"I don't think I've spoken to him in over a year," Duncan said.

"Big deal, he's not your ex-girlfriend. He's a dude from college." Ray said.

"You have his number?"

"Not since he moved. But I'm sure we can get it. How many Quinton Darleys do you think there are in Omaha?"

Duncan lifted the phone and called down to the front desk. "Hi, yeah, I'm looking for a local number, I wonder if you can help me?"

"I'm hungry again," Ray said to Ruby. The pair flopped down on two couches opposite one another.

"I could go for a big steak," Ruby said.

"I could go for anything right now. I'm thinking about chewing on that lamp."

"There's a full kitchen in here, I'm sure there's food."

"Yeah, I know Duncan's on a spending spree but I'm not eating $10 cashews."

Duncan sat down beside Ruby. "She'll get back to me," he said.

"Let's go grab some food," Ray said.

The three exited the room more swiftly than they had entered. Stopping off at the concierge desk, Ray got the name of two steakhouses, both only three blocks away in the same direction. If not for the cab lying in wait just outside the front doors of the hotel they might have walked. But things being as they were – teeth salivating and stomachs growling from neglect – they opted for the speedier means.

After a hearty meal at Sullivan's Steakhouse, the crew returned to their room and to an envelope waiting on their doorstep. The contents of the envelope contained the address and phone number of one, Quinton Darley, local resident of Omaha, Nebraska.

Ruby excused herself into the large shower as Duncan sat down to call his old friend.

"Q!" Duncan said into the phone.

"Yeah," the voice answered, "Who's this?"

"You don't know who this is?"

"Duncan?"

"Yup."

"What's up, brother? Long time no speak!"

"What you doing with yourself?"

"Same shit, trying to scrape out a living, stay sane, you know. What about you?"

"Just doing a little traveling. How's your girl?"

"She's good. Where you traveling to?"

"A few places actually. I'm on the road."

"Are you in Omaha?"

"I am."

"Fuck off. How long you here for?"

"Just for the night."

"You serious? Why didn't you call me?"

"I did. I am. We just got here."

"Who's we? Is Ray with you?"

"Ray's here."

"What's up Q?" Ray shouted from the couch.

"We have to hang out," Quinton said. "Where are you guys now?"

"We're at the Magnolia."

"Fuck, it's late, I gotta work tomorrow."

"Don't worry about it, man."

"Court!" Quinton yelled. "Courtney! One sec, Dun."

Quinton turned away from the phone to chat with his wife. Duncan shrugged to Ray.

"I'm coming there now," Quinton said upon his prompt return. "What room you in?"

"We're in the presidential suite."

Quinton laughed. "Running numbers is treating you well, huh?" he said.

"Something like that."

"I'm on my way."

Twenty minutes later, Ray opened the door to a wide armed, wide smiled Quinton. He greeted his friend with clasped hands and a shoulder-bumping hug.

"What's up Ray?" Quinton said.

"What's it been?" asked Ray. "Two years?"

"At least."

Quinton followed Ray into the room and met Duncan with a similar embrace.

"This is Ruby," Duncan said.

"Hey Ruby."

Ruby said hello and gave the visitor a friendly smile. Quinton sat down on one of the couches and put his feet up on the table.

"So what're you guys doing here?" he asked.

"We're just passing through," Duncan said. "We're heading to the east coast."

"What's on the east coast?"

"Change of scenery."

"Vacation?"

"Relocation."

"For good?"

"Could be," Duncan said hesitantly. "Don't really know."

"What about Phoenix?"

"We were in Phoenix for more than a decade. It's time for something new."

"Okay, alright, I dig it. Nothing holding you down, nothing holding you back, why not go for something different, right?"

"Pretty much, yeah."

"Do you know where you're heading?"

"Boston, for now."

"Boston?" Quinton looked over at Ray who was sitting on the couch across from him.

"I know what you're thinking," Ray said. "That has nothing to do with it. Just a coincidence."

"So you just chose Boston, what, out of a hat?"

"Well, there's some unfinished business to take care of, too."

"Uh huh, that makes more sense."

"How's business with you?" Ray asked.

"It's okay," Quinton said. "Courtney's dad is pretty cool."

Quinton worked for his father-in-law at the family furniture manufacturing company. They produced and distributed wooden furniture like armoires, dressers, side tables, coffee tables, and bed frames. Graduating with a degree in philosophy from ASU, Quinton never saw himself as part of the industrial apparatus, but marriage and responsibility crept up on the idealist post-haste and smothered his once fiery ambition like a cold, wet blanket. When reflective, Quinton credited both Courtney and her father with helping him snap a trend of ambiguity and doubt, and for giving him the uncomplicated direction he never knew he needed. In the dawn of his third decade, the once dissident Quinton was actually relieved to have traded the tribulations of Voltaire, Nietzsche, and Spinoza for those regarding dowels, castors, and knobs.

"And Courtney?" Duncan asked.

"She's good. It's sometimes hard to see her twenty-four hours a day, but I can't complain. Let's just say she puts up more with me than I do with her."

"So nothing's changed."

"Did you all go to school together?" Ruby asked.

"Quinton and me are the same year, Courtney is a year younger, and Ray is a year younger than her, but we were all at ASU at the same time."

"So you met your wife in college then," Ruby said to Quinton.

"Twelve years ago," Quinton agreed.

"Holy fuck," Ray said. "Twelve years."

"How did you get mixed up with these guys?" Quinton asked Ruby. "One of them belong to you?"

"No," Ruby said. "They're giving me a ride to Boston."

"Well look at all you ne'er-do-wells navigating our noble country. Must be nice."

"It's not bad," Ray said.

"Well," Quinton said, reaching his hands into the tubular pocket of his hooded sweatshirt. "Old times?"

Quinton pulled out a plastic bag of weed and a colorful glass chillum.

"Sure," Ray said. "I'm in."

"Not me, but thanks," Duncan said. "I could go for a beer though."

Duncan got up off the couch and headed for the bar in the kitchen.

Ruby didn't say anything, but by the way she wiggled across the couch to get closer to Ray and Quinton, it was obvious she was interested.

Quinton pinched a sample from his bag and loaded the chillum for Ray. "So you guys really leaving tomorrow?" he asked.

"In the morning," Duncan said as he returned to the couches with an open bottle of Heineken.

"Is there anything I could do to convince you to stay one more day?"

Ray unloaded a hefty huff of white smoke from his gaping mouth and passed the chillum to Ruby.

"What for?" Duncan asked.

"I'm having people over tomorrow night, it would be awesome if you guys came."

"I guess we're not in any hurry to leave," Duncan said.

"I'd stay," Ray said.

"Me too," Ruby added after she expelled smoke and ceased her cough.

Quinton loaded the chillum once again and lit up the bowl for himself. He clamped his hands together and sucked back the contents in one extended breath. He held the smoke in his lungs; his back straight and his chest puffed out like a rooster.

He then huffed the contents out into the air with an audible blow.

"Good," he said, smacking his lips together. "Then it's settled. Don't worry, it's not a big thing. Just a few friends coming over for a quiet Friday night."

CHAPTER 8

QUINTON EXCUSED HIMSELF from the presidential suite just before one in the morning and just after his third bowl from the chillum. Ray, being in off-season smoking form, was nearly knocked out from partaking in Quinton's ritual. Ruby – red eyed and giddy – was in better shape having taken fewer hits from the pipe. She was unsuccessful in getting Ray to stay up and "hang out" however. Duncan had retired to his room as soon as Quinton left, and though Ray tried to appease his new female friend by staying in the main room for longer than Duncan, he was no match for the tiring affects of the drug.

The following morning, Duncan found Ruby and Ray in almost the same position as he had the morning before. Ray was asleep in his clothing and Ruby, occupying the same bed, was under the covers. There was a third bed in the suite; it had gone untouched.

One difference Duncan took swift notice of was that Ray's arm was lovingly draped over the sleeping tag-along. Duncan didn't disturb his dormant companions and instead quietly withdrew himself from their room.

Not five minutes later, Ray joined Duncan out on the couches. Duncan assumed that his visit to Ray's room must have somehow woken him. Ruby, however, made no indication that her mummy-like slumber had been disturbed. She lay motionless long after Duncan and Ray had ordered, eaten, and laid their breakfast plates outside the suite door for the maid service. When she did finally wake, she attempted to slink from bedroom to washroom without being detected, but both Ray and Duncan caught the nearly naked girl before she completed the transfer.

"Did she sleep like that?" asked Duncan.

"Underwear and bra? No idea. I think I was out first."

The better part of the morning had passed by the time all three were prepared to declare the day had officially begun. Ray and Duncan were beginning to notice Ruby's ursine-like ability to thrive on varying and unbalanced feedings. The girl showed no signs of hunger though not having eaten a morsel since her indulgence more than fourteen hours prior.

"I need to get some things," Ruby insisted, once dressed and vital. "Anyone have any idea where to do some shopping around here?"

"What kind of things you need?" Ray asked.

"You know, this and that. A few girl things, a few...not...girl things."

"Let's just walk," Duncan said. "I'm sure we'll find what you're looking for."

And with that, the trio set off into the streets of Omaha like scouts on a trail. Duncan led the way down the sidewalks. Ruby ducked into the first pharmacy upon which they came; Duncan and Ray simply followed her in. New toothbrushes, some deodorant, gum, shampoo, and feminine hygiene products decorated the countertop of the only open checkout. Though the deodorant and toothbrushes didn't belong to her, Ruby insisted on paying for the lot.

A brisk wind picked up in the early afternoon. Ruby latched on to Ray's arm while crossing the street, both for warmth and security. She didn't let go once they had reached the other side. They dipped into clothing stores, shoe stores, even an old record store, the likes of which had all but been eradicated from urban landscapes. When they came upon a small bookshop on Jackson Street, they spent some time looking around.

"I haven't read a book in a while," Ruby said.

"Is it thirty years?" Ray said. "'Cause then you'd be tied with Duncan."

"Good one," Duncan said sarcastically.

"I used to read a lot," Ruby continued, walking down a thin aisle of colorful book spines. "I don't know why I stopped."

"What was your favorite?" Ray asked.

"That's like asking someone what they're favorite movie is, or what kind of music they listen to," Ruby said.

Duncan stopped at a pile of hardcover biographies, picked one up, and started thumbing the pages.

"I just meant what kind of books did you read?" Ray said. "Mystery? Sci-Fi? Fuckin', I don't know, romance?"

"I usually read whatever my mom had lying around the house – all those books you were supposed to read in high school but never did – plus some newer stuff. When my mom brought a guy home I would just stay in my room and read. I also had mono one summer and read, like, ten books."

"When was the last time you spoke to your mother?"

"Um, three days ago? Four? I know you think I'm some kind of damaged runaway, but I'm really not. My mom and I get along fine."

"I never said you were damaged," Ray insisted. He pulled a book off one of the shelves. "Have you read this?" he asked.

Ray handed Ruby *God is Not Great*, by Christopher Hitchens. "You'd like that one," he said.

"What about you?" Ruby asked, giving the book a once over. "Where's your family?"

"I have a sister."

"Just a sister?"

"Pretty much," Ray admitted. "I mean, there are some cousins out there, and a great aunt I haven't seen since I was a kid, but my family is not what you'd call close."

"Do you talk to your sister?"

"Umm, I did – I guess I still do – I mean we're on speaking terms if that's what you mean. She's younger than me so we never went to the same school or had the same friends or anything like that. Plus, she's one of those obnoxious hippy types. Not really a lot to relate to, ya know?"

"I had a brother," Ruby said. "He died when he was two."

"How'd he die?"

"He was born sick. He had a hole in his heart. He had, like, six surgeries before he was one. I just remember being alone a lot."

"How old were you?"

"I was six when he died. I didn't really understand what was going on."

"Still…"

"Yeah."

"Bruce Lee," Duncan injected from across the store. He was holding up a book for Ray and Ruby's approval.

It was late in the afternoon and the trio had accomplished all they were going to do on that particular outing. Duncan purchased his book on the life of Bruce Lee, and picked up the tab on the one Ray had recommended for Ruby. Walking further from the hotel than they initially planned, they hailed a cab outside the store and rode silently back. During the trip,

Duncan received a call on his cell from Quinton. The plans were laid. They were to meet at Quinton's apartment at six thirty that evening.

"Can we bring anything?" Duncan asked.

"No, thanks," Quinton said. "We got beer and wine and all that shit."

Back at the hotel, Duncan made no hesitation in taking full advantage of the suite's private Jacuzzi room. He took his new biography of Bruce Lee into the bubbling water and leaned back against the jets.

Ruby began preparations for the upcoming evening, excusing herself into the washroom and into a long shower. Ray opened a beer and turned on the TV. He caught a replay of Sports Center, a one-time ritual turned carefree interest.

When Ruby emerged from the bedroom, dressed and ready to go, she immediately ensnared the attention of both Ray and Duncan – Duncan having vacated the Jacuzzi a long time prior. She was wearing a tight pair of jeans and a form-fitting top. Her hair was up and bedecked with small braids and clips. Her make-up was done with a classy precision that made it look almost as if she weren't wearing any at all. She looked like a different girl, one that wouldn't look unnatural walking out of a presidential suite.

"Wow," Ray said, from the couch.

"I guess I should get dressed then," Duncan said.

Ray looked at the clock. "Me too," he agreed.

The two disappeared and reappeared in less than ten minutes. Not ones to stickle much with their looks, their entire criterion of evening necessities consisted of clean clothing and brushed teeth. They felt that concerning themselves with anything more would entail a change in their common philosophy. If they were the kind to, say, pick out something considered an "outfit", meticulously preen in front of a mirror, wear hair gel, or spray on a tan, they would then be the kind to listen to trendy music, or drink specialty coffees, or watch reality TV. Instead, Ray and Duncan were satisfied with jeans and a T-shirt and a bottle of beer.

A cab waited for them outside the front doors of the hotel.

They arrived at Quinton's apartment building just shy of seven o'clock.

From the outside, the apartment building looked more like a warehouse. It was three stories of brick and glass that took up almost an entire city block. The reddish-brown building stretched far and deep and imposed itself on the surrounding streets.

Duncan drew his finger down the buzzer list and punched in the four digits beside the name Darley. After a few seconds, the heavy black door buzzed and clicked and Ray tugged it open. Consistent with the warehouse look, the ceilings in the foyer were high and the ductwork was exposed. This wasn't the first converted loft space Duncan and Ray had seen, but it was, by far, the largest.

"307," Duncan said as the trio reached the top of the staircase. They followed the wooden floorboards down a long hallway looking for the appropriate door.

Duncan knocked.

"Heyyyyy!" Quinton yelled, answering the door with a beer in his hand. "Come in, come in!"

They followed Quinton into the apartment.

The narrow hallway gave way to a large, open room where almost the entire layout of apartment could be seen. Upon their arrival, Courtney welcomed both Duncan and Ray with a hearty hug. "I haven't seen you guys in forever," she said, holding on to Ray.

"This is Ruby," Ray said, releasing Courtney from his grasp.

"Hi Ruby," Courtney said. She surprised Ruby by pulling her in for a hug, too. "That's Tina, Tim, and the blonde one there is Kennedy," she said, holding on to Ruby's hand.

The guests were all perched atop stools surrounding a fat kitchen island.

"Duncan and Quin lived two doors down from each other their freshman year at ASU," Courtney informed the group. "Tim and Tina live in the building, they're married, and Kennedy is my best friend. Everyone, this is Ray and Ruby."

Everyone made somewhat awkward greetings to one another before Quinton broke the moderate mood by offering drinks to those who didn't yet have one.

"Dinner is almost ready," Courtney said. "Hopefully everyone likes lasagna?"

Everyone looked around and nodded at one another.

"You gonna show us around?" Ray asked Quinton.

Quinton led a small contingent around the apartment pointing out various characteristics. Three bedrooms not encompassed within the large main room were separated from the living area by massive, ceiling-high grey metal doors on rollers. The apartment had three bathrooms (including one attached to the main bedroom), a laundry room, a storage closet, and a walkout terrace that looked like it was once part of the interior of the building.

"Very nice," said Duncan. "Big."

"Thanks," Quinton said. "It is a bit big but the price was right at the time."

Duncan, Ray, and Quinton made themselves comfortable on one of the long couches at the very center of the apartment. Tim and Kennedy both came to join them not long after. Ruby, Tina, and Courtney remained in the kitchen. Ray was impressed by Ruby's attempt to domesticate herself in the unfamiliar surroundings.

"So you went to college with Courtney?" Kennedy asked as she sat down beside Duncan.

"Yeah," Duncan said, tilting his body a bit to face the petite girl. "I've known her since she started dating Quin."

"I've known her since grade school. Our mothers are best friends."

"Did you go to college?"

"I went to art school."

"So you're an artist then?"

"Well, I'm a dancer."

"Okay, that's cool," Duncan said.

"What about you?" she asked. "What do you do?"

"I was in sports," Duncan said, "But now I'm in between things."

"Well, do you know what you want to be doing?"

"I haven't narrowed it down just yet, but I'm in no hurry."

"That's good. It's good to take a breather."

"So do you dance professionally now, or…"

"I have a small dance studio," Kennedy said proudly. "So I pretty much teach little kids how to balance."

"And you like it?"

"I love it," she said confidently. "I never saw myself as a teacher, but I really, really love it. What I love the most is *my* studio, you know? It's just a small little thing, but it's mine."

"No, I get that," Duncan said. "You're your own boss."

"Yes," Kennedy said. She placed her hand on Duncan's arm. "Yes."

"There's something to be said about having your own little business."

Duncan was intrigued, both by the girl, and what she was saying.

"Anyone need another?" Quinton said as he got up from the couch. He was shaking his empty bottle of beer.

"I'll take one, thanks," said Ray.

Duncan and Tim both agreed.

"I could use another too," Kennedy said, taking the last sip of her white wine. "I'll help you."

Quinton and Kennedy ventured off to the fridge to fill the drink order. Duncan caught Ray gazing over at him and did a double take. Ray lifted his eyebrows and pointed his head kitchen-ward, no doubt urging his friend on toward the attractive dancer.

The whole group soon sat down for dinner at a long dining table arranged by Courtney. Perhaps with purpose, Courtney made a point to move Kennedy down one seat to ensure that she took the one beside Duncan. Duncan wasn't at all averse to the shift.

The meal went well. The salad Tina brought was a hit, as was the lasagna and garlic bread prepared by Courtney, who was never one to consider herself a chef.

The entire group sat amongst the unclean plates and bread crumbed tablecloth and continued their conversations long after they were done eating. More than an hour had passed since the last bit of food had touched a fork, and not one person had yet excused themselves. Ruby found fast friends in Courtney and Tina, Ray argued with Tim about various sporting concerns, and Duncan continued to find himself entertained and interested in the cordially receptive Kennedy.

It wasn't until Tina finally had to escape to the washroom that the huddle finally concluded. She sparked an exodus. A few helped to clear the table; others scattered off to share a smoke on the terrace.

Congregating again not long after to partake in store-bought cake and vanilla ice cream, Quinton unleashed a bit of a surprise on his full-bellied guests.

"Does anyone have room for a special desert?" he asked. He pulled a small bag from his pocket and unrolled it as if he was unraveling an ancient scroll.

"Oh, man," Duncan said.

"Are you serious?" Tim jibed.

"I've had these in the freezer for months. I've been waiting for a special occasion," Quinton admitted. "My good friends are here from out of town, and after tonight, I'll probably never see them again – just kidding – so why not?"

Quinton threw the bag onto the middle of the table for anyone and everyone to inspect for themselves. Kennedy was the first to seize it.

"Mushrooms?" she asked rhetorically.

"When was the last time you ate 'shrooms, Duncan?" Quinton asked. "Ray?"

"Years," Duncan said.

"Year," Ray said.

"I'll do it," Ruby said without hesitation.

"Yes!" Quinton pointed, "Ruby's in. Thank you Ruby. Who else?"

"Why not," said Ray.

"What do you think Tina?" Tim said to his wife.

Tina shrugged.

"You don't need permission from me," she said. "It's up to you."

Tim thought for a moment before requesting to see the bag for himself.

"I'm out, by the way," Kennedy said as she handed the bag to Tim.

"Me too," Duncan said.

"What?" Quinton yelped. "Dun, you're out?"

"I did enough in college."

"Dun," Quinton pleaded. "The guy who ate a half-quarter the night before his history final?"

"That was a mistake," Duncan laughed. "We didn't have a calendar."

"I'll try a little," Tim said. He stuck his nose into the bag.

"Yes!" Quinton yelped again. "Timmy's in. Is that everyone? Court?"

Courtney silently waved her husband off.

"Fine," Quinton said. "Ray, Timmy, Ruby, over there. The rest of you, fuck you."

Quinton took the remainder of the chocolate cake from the table and brought it over to the kitchen. He cut small pieces for each participant and put them each on a napkin. "I have a little less than a quarter here," he said, "I'll eye out about a gram for Tim, then the three of us will split the rest?"

"Maybe a little less for me, too," Ruby said. "I've never done it before."

"No problem, Ruby, a little less for you." Quinton began portioning out the contents of the baggie. The beige, white, and slightly blue dried-up fungi looked anything but appetizing.

"That good?" Quinton asked the group after having made little piles beside the cake slices.

Tim took a little piece from his pile and put it on Quinton's. All in all it looked like Tim and Ruby each had about a gram, while Quinton and Ray each had nearly two. Quinton's pile was a little larger than Ray's, which was fine with both.

"Down the hatch," Quinton said. He chomped a bite of chocolate cake and then took a hefty pinch of mushrooms and dropped them into his mouth like coins into a well. The rest of the group, Ruby leading the way, followed in turn until all the foul tasting bits were gone from the countertop.

"Now what?" Ruby asked.

Quinton laughed. "Now we wait," he said, patting Ruby warmly on the shoulder. "Give it about twenty, thirty minutes."

CHAPTER 9

THE RUCKUS WAS long over and everyone congregated on the elongated couches in the apartment center.

"How do I know if it's working?" Ruby asked.

"How long has it been?" Quinton turned to look at the clock on the stove. "About twenty minutes?"

"Should I feel something?" Ruby asked.

"We could do the box test," Ray offered.

"What's that?" Ruby asked.

"Well," Quinton said, scooting down the couch to get closer to Ruby. "Everyone has to be quiet if the test is going to work." Quinton raised his voice a bit and addressed the whole room. His tone was nothing if not friendly and the onlookers took heed soon thereafter and abruptly ended their chatter. A few knew what was about to happen and took a keen interest.

Sitting up straight and facing Ruby, Quinton then placed both his hands out in front of him as if he were holding an invisible box between them.

"This is the box test," he said. "I have a box here in my hands. You can't see the box, but it's there. Imagine it there."

"Okay," Ruby said, smiling.

"Now if the box test works, when I put it over your head," Quinton began to place the invisible box over Ruby's head, "it should drown out the s…"

Quinton's lips kept moving, but his voice ceased completely. He mouthed the words: *Stop. And you shouldn't be able to hear a thing.* His lips were moving, but he made no sound. Ruby's eyes opened wide. Quinton then began to motion as if he were taking the box off Ruby's head. *Then I'm going to take…*, he mouthed, "…it off and you can hear again," he said aloud.

Ruby took a deep breath.

"Do that again," she said.

The room laughed.

"Okay," Quinton agreed. "When I place the box over your h…". The box was on Ruby's head. Quinton finished the sentence in silence. Ray leaned over and mouthed the words, *Can you hear me? Ruby? Can you hear me?*

"…ake it off. And now you can hear again," Quinton said, as he removed the invisible box.

"Oh. My. God," Ruby said as her eyes began to water with glee.

Laughter echoed throughout the spacious apartment once again.

"One more time."

"Okay fine, but I th…". The box was back on.

Ray and Quinton had a short, silent conversation with each other. Quinton turned to lift the box back off.

"…een the thing again," he said aloud.

Ruby felt a rush of adrenaline and was overcome with a mix of fright and utter joy.

"I'm putting the box away," Quinton said. "I think we have our answer. Quinton tossed the invisible box over his shoulder.

Ruby leaned forward and smacked the table in front of her. She stood up abruptly and stumbled a bit when she made contact with Quinton's knee. Ray instinctively reached to stabilize his friend and accidently knocked a bottle of beer off the table and into his own lap. The bottle's contents landed with a splash on the crotch of his pants. He stood, shocked and dismayed with his arms out wide.

"Crap," he said.

"No worries, no worries," Quinton assured.

"I got it," Courtney laughed. She rose to her feet from the couch opposite and snatched a wad of napkins from the dining table not far behind her. She leaned over the short coffee table that separated her from Ray and began patting down his crotch.

"Oh," Ray said. "I like this."

"Settle down," Courtney laughed.

"She so promiscuous," Quinton added.

"Okay," Courtney said. "You do it."

She handed the napkins to Quinton who proceeded to take over patting where she left off.

"Oh!" Ray said. "I like *this*!"

Kennedy burst into laughter and leaned her body into Duncan's lap. Duncan rested his hand on Kennedy's quaking shoulder.

"I'm putting on some music," Courtney said. "That is if everyone is done with their boxes?"

"Yeah, music is good," Quinton agreed.

Kennedy composed herself and returned to her proper position on the couch.

"You okay?" Duncan asked.

"Yeah," Kennedy said. "I think I'm gonna take a break from this though." She placed her wine glass on the coffee table beside her.

As time passed and music played, Ray, Quinton, and Tim were feeling the full effects of their party favors. Ruby, too, was wholly enjoying the new experience. The night had fully enveloped the apartment and Courtney took it upon herself to light a few candles. Tim, still on the couch, found a new appreciation for the hypnotic glow of one particular dancing flame set near him. Quinton and Ray had moved from the group and established themselves on the terrace. They were leaning against the rail overlooking the city street.

"I could really go for a cigarette," Ray said, peering down to the sidewalk below.

"Oh man, me too." Quinton said. "I usually have a couple, but I'm out."

"Bah," Ray winced, picking himself up off the railing. "I could smoke an entire pack of Marlboros right now."

"Let's go get."

"I'll buy if you go," Ray offered.

"I'll buy if you go," Quinton countered.

"Deal."

Ray tailed Quinton into the apartment and followed his friend through the thick music and into his bedroom. Quinton opened a small wooden box on the dresser and pulled out a twenty-dollar bill.

"There's a service station right on the corner," he said. "You can't miss it."

"Which corner?" Ray asked, yanking the twenty from his friend's hand.

"That one," Quinton answered, pointing to the air over Ray's shoulder.

"Got it," Ray said.

"Okay – stairs, door, right, right, walk, walk, store." Quinton acted out the motions as he spoke. Ray then mimicked the same. They high fived and then broke away as if ready to take a football snap. Ray was invigorated by his new mission and walked with purpose past the couches and to the front door. Quinton sat on the couch beside Tim and took notice of his neighbor seemingly mesmerized by a tea-light candle floating in a glass of water.

"Tim!" he yelped.

"Yo," Tim said.

"What's up?"

"Nothin'."

"Totally."

Duncan and Kennedy remained in the same spot on the couch. They were facing each other, enmeshed in what the other was saying.

"I don't know what I'm going to do when I get there," Duncan said. "I have a few ideas."

"What would you do if money weren't an issue?" Kennedy asked. "You know, that question your middle school guidance counselor asks you?"

"I have a few hobbies and I guess that's what hobbies are, right? The things you do for enjoyment on your own time."

"Like what? What are some of the things you do on your own time?"

"Well," Duncan hesitated. He was trying to find a way to say it without sounding pretentious. "I'm a bit of a fighter, I suppose you could say."

"Like boxing?"

"Mixed martial arts. As a kid I studied Muay Thai, kung fu, boxing, Brazilian jujitsu."

"That sounds mixed."

"Yeah," Duncan laughed. "The issue is – what do you do with that?"

"Beat people up?" Kennedy suggested.

"That's one idea."

Ray had made his way to the sidewalk in front of the building. He remembered Quinton's instructions and turned abruptly to his right. He followed the grey concrete slabs until he reached the traffic lights forty paces ahead. He made another right and kept up the tempo.

When he reached the end of the shortened block he could see the gas station his host had promised would be there. It was a brilliant oasis on an otherwise shadowy street. Ray felt around in his pocket for the twenty and clasped it in his palm. When he reached the front of the station, Ray tugged at one of the doors. It didn't budge. Having encountered this issue before, Ray quickly knew how to remedy his trouble. He pushed on the door. More trouble still – the door still didn't move.

Ray looked through the glass at the attendant and threw his arms up in the air. Was this one of those weird stations where you had to purchase gas before you were allowed in? Did they lock the doors when the sun went down because it was an unsafe neighborhood? Ray turned to look at the single car filling up with gasoline and conceived a plan. He was going to wait until the man was done and then follow him into salvation once he went to pay. Brilliant in its simplicity, he thought.

He waited.

When Ray heard the jingle of the service station door, it became apparent that he had made the grave mistake of simply choosing the wrong one of the two to try to open.

"Oh," he said to himself.

A little ashamed, but finding the humor, Ray snuck into the station with his eyes down on the ground. Trying not to make eye contact with the attendant, Ray accidently stepped on the leg of a chip display and the wobbly metal frame tumbled to the floor.

"Whoops," Ray said. "Sorry," he waved. "I'll get it."

Ray lifted the three-legged stand and began to refill it with the contents he had mistakenly liberated. The man who was outside filling his car had completed the task and entered the station. He didn't notice anything out of the ordinary and approached the counter to pay his bill. Ray replaced the chips and excused himself down the candy aisle to peruse its wares. The Sweet Tarts looked good, as did the Whatchamacallits. Ray lifted one of the candy bars to further inspect its ingredients. *I bet I could make one of these at home.*

The door jingled and then jingled again. Ray took the opportunity to approach the attendant.

"Your finest pack of Marlboros, please, sir," he said.

"Which kind," the attendant said, unimpressed.

"Reds please."

"Is that all?" the man said, placing the pack on the countertop.

"That's all," Ray insisted. "Actually, do you have a soft pack?"

The attendant peered upward to where the cigarettes lived and tugged down a soft pack of Marlboro regulars.

"Is that all?" he asked again.

"Yes. That is all."

Ray stuck his hand into his pocket in search of the twenty, but came up empty.

"I just had…" he mumbled as he checked the other pocket. He checked both pockets thoroughly. No twenty found.

Ray returned to the scene of the chip spillage and searched the surrounding area. As he did, another man approached the counter with a steaming cup of coffee in hand.

"Ha!" Ray exclaimed, finding the crumpled up twenty on the floor beside the chip display. He un-crumpled the bill and returned to the counter where he found – as if with perfect poetry – an officer of the Omaha law purchasing his beverage.

Ray smiled at the man in blue. The cop smiled back and nodded to Ray. With no more than a "thank you" to the clerk, the officer excused himself through the working door.

"Found it," Ray said, placing the twenty on the counter. "Sorry about that."

The man behind the counter handed Ray his change and the soft pack of Marlboro reds and told him to have a good night.

Ray exited the station, smacking the fresh cigarettes against his palm. He peeled back the clear plastic and then carefully adjusted the silver foil so not to expose the entire pack, but instead only the section to the left of the white and red paper that ran across the center. Ray popped a cigarette out and placed it in his mouth. Pausing for a moment of reflection, Ray re-entered the station and bothered the attendant for a pack of matches. Quinton had lighters back at the apartment, but it was at least a seventy-five second walk back.

Ray stepped back onto the concrete of the filling platform and thought better of striking a match so close to the pumps.

"You okay, buddy?" a voice said.

Ray looked around. It was his old friend from the counter, coming to check in on his fellow patron.

"Sure, officer," Ray said confidently. "I'm fine."

"Have you been drinking?" the cop asked, approaching Ray.

"I had a couple beers with dinner," Ray answered. "But that was a while ago."

"Just a couple of beers?" the cop asked, looking down at Ray's legs.

Ray followed the officer's eyes down to his crotch. It was still wet from the earlier spillage.

"Oh that," Ray said.

"Is that urine?"

"No, not at all."

"Then what is it?"

Ray hesitated for a second. Was admitting it was beer better or worse than saying it was urine, he wondered.

The cop came face to face with Ray. He looked into Ray's eyes.

"You want to come with me, sir," the cop said.

"Why?" Ray asked. "What's up?"

"Follow me, sir," the cop said again.

Ray did as requested and followed the officer to the side of the station. The officer then looked straight into Ray's eyes once again, this time with the aid of a small flashlight.

"I'm not drunk," Ray said.

"Uh huh," the cop mumbled. "What's your name?"

"Ray."

Ray took the smoke from between his lips.

"Are you from around here, Ray?"

"Actually, no."

"Uh huh."

"Honestly, officer, I'm completely sober," Ray said, perhaps overcompensating a little for how he truly felt.

"Your eyes are bloodshot, you stink of alcohol, and it looks like you pissed yourself."

"That's beer," Ray said. "Look, I'm just going back to that apartment right there. He pointed across the street to Quinton's building. "No big deal, I'll be fine. Everything is fine."

"Do you live there?"

"No, I'm from out of town."

"But that's where you're going?"

"Yes."

"What's the address of that building?"

Ray paused.

"Fuck," he said. He had no idea the street or number.

"Okay, sir, let's go."

"Are you serious?" Ray pleaded.

The cop helped Ray into the back of his cruiser and closed the door behind him.

"We're going to go sleep it off," the cop said entering the driver's side door.

"Look, let me just call my friend," Ray begged. "He lives right there. He'll come out and explain everything."

The cop turned to face Ray through the glass partition.

"What's his phone number?" he asked.

Ray paused again.

"Fuck!"

The cop started up the car and backed out of his spot.

"Let me call my friend's cell," Ray said as they pulled out onto the street.

"You can call him from the station."

"Which station? The gas one? Okay, pull back in."

The cop ignored Ray.

"Fuck," Ray said again, admitting defeat.

CHAPTER 10

"SO YOU JUST met Ruby a few days ago?" Kennedy asked in shock.

"Yeah," Duncan said.

"That's insane. You guys look like you've known each other forever."

"Extreme circumstances, I guess."

"What do you mean?"

Not wanting to get into the story of how they actually met Ruby, Duncan opted for a less intriguing response.

"We're all in the same sort of situation," he said. "Me and Ray left Phoenix, you know, just wanting to get away, to start fresh. Ruby is pretty much doing the same thing. It seemed like a good fit when we met."

"So you guys are just, like, nomads?"

"Something like that. It's a pretty great feeling actually. Right now I have no responsibilities – no bills, no boss, no belongings."

"Isn't that scary though?"

Duncan shook his head.

"I don't think I could ever do that," Kennedy said

"I bet you could."

"Maybe. But I love my life right now."

Quinton, Ruby, and Tim were out on the terrace. Tina and Courtney had turned a corner of the apartment into a club and were entertaining themselves with dance. The three groups spread across the apartment didn't think to question where Ray had gone. Each assumed that he was with the other. The only one that knew that Ray had in fact left the apartment was Quinton, and he had absolutely no perception of time.

Courtney turned the music way up and was putting her best moves on display. Duncan and Kennedy turned to take witness. Tina tried to mimic Courtney's actions as the bass line shook the floor beneath them.

"You wanna go somewhere quiet?" Kennedy shouted, though it sounded like a whisper.

"Sure," Duncan said. He followed Kennedy out of the main room into what looked like a guest bedroom. She closed the door behind them. The music was still audible, but the size and weight of the bedroom door at least made it possible for the pair to hear each other speak. They sat on the bed and continued their conversation.

At about the same time, the officer was helping Ray into the police station. It had been a quiet night and the cell in which Ray was to be detained housed only one other person.

"You can make a phone call if you want," the officer said, sitting Ray down at a desk outside the cell. He pulled the phone closer to Ray. "Make it quick."

Ray picked up the phone. The sound of the dial tone mesmerized him.

"So what's going on with Ruby and Ray?" Kennedy asked.

"What do you mean?"

"They're not...doing it?"

"Doing it? No. Why?"

"What do you mean why? You don't see it?"

"See what?"

"Men." Kennedy sighed. "She's totally into him."

"How do you know that?"

"The way she looks at him, the way she sits when he's beside her, the way she kind of said something when we were in the kitchen."

"Ohhhh," Duncan laughed. "I see. What did she say?"

"She didn't have to say much. Girls just know."

Duncan's phone rang in his pocket.

"Sorry," he said. "One sec."

Duncan plucked the phone from his jeans. "617? Where is that?"

Ray had finally dialed a number and the phone began to ring on the other end.

"Hello," a female voice answered.

"Hey," Ray said.

"Hang on a sec," the girl said.

Ray could hear talking in the background. When the sounds began to dull, the voice on the other end came back. "Ray?"

"Yeah."

"Um, hi?"

"What're you doing?"

"I'm just with some friends."

"That's cool," Ray said.

"You okay, Ray? You sound weird."

"No, yeah, I'm fine," Ray assured. "I'm in jail in Omaha."

"What?"

"The cops think I'm drunk so they brought me to jail."

"In Omaha?"

"Nebraska."

"Yes, I know where Omaha is. Why are you calling me from a jail in Omaha?"

"'Cause you're a lawyer," Ray said confidently.

"Are you in Omaha alone? Wait, why are you in Omaha?"

"No, Duncan is here too...and Ruby."

"Okay, Ray," she said calmly. "You need to call Duncan so he can come get you. There's nothing I can do from here. Did they say how long they were going to hold you?"

"I don't think so."

"Well they might want to keep you for the night if you're drunk, but if you can get Duncan down there to get you before they process you they may let you go."

"Okay, buddy," the cop said, returning to the desk. "Time's up."

"I gotta go," Ray said.

"Is that the cop that brought you in?" the girl asked.

"Yeah."

"Put him on for a second."

"She wants to talk to you," Ray said, holding out the phone. The police officer took the receiver.

Duncan answered his phone. "Hello?" he said.

"Duncan?"

"Yes?"

"It's Ashley."

"Ashley?"

"Yeah."

"What's up Ash?" Duncan was caught off guard.

"You need to go get Ray," she said.

"Did you try his phone? He'll answer."

"No, I don't mean get him on the phone. I mean go pick him up. He's at the police station."

"Wait, wait. What are you talking about?"

"You're in Omaha, right?"

"Yes," Duncan said, even more confused.

"Yeah, Ray just called me, he's at the police station there."

"One second."

Duncan took the phone from his ear. "Ken," he said, "Can you go get Quinton for me, please? Quickly?"

"Is everything okay?" Kennedy asked.

"I think Ray is in jail."

Kennedy shook her head as if she was trying to shake off a fly. "What?" she said.

"I have no idea."

Kennedy tugged at the massive door and disappeared into the main room.

"Hey," Duncan said into the phone.

"Listen," Ashley said, "I'm at a dinner party here. I can't deal with this. I spoke to the cop that brought Ray in, if you can get down there in the next few minutes he'll let you take him home."

"What's up?" Quinton said, popping into the room.

"Where's Ray?" Duncan asked.

"He went to get smokes."

Duncan couldn't help but laugh.

"Ash?"

"Yeah?"

"He called *you*?"

"Yeah," she said. "He said it's because I'm a lawyer. What's wrong with him anyway? He sounds drunk."

"Don't ask," Duncan said, still laughing.

"Go get him, Dun," Ashley said, giggling herself. "It's not funny."

"Well, good talkin' to you, Ash. You doing okay?"

"I'm okay. You okay?"

"I'm okay."

"Go get him, will ya?"

"Which station?"

Duncan wrote down the information on a tissue box beside the bed and hung up the phone. He got up and immediately punched Quinton on the shoulder.

"Ow!" Quinton cried. "What was that for?"

"How long ago did Ray leave?" Duncan asked.

"I don't know…ten minutes?"

"That's impossible."

"Fifteen?"

"You're an idiot," Duncan laughed. "Courtney!"

"Yeah," Courtney shouted from the other room. Kennedy got the girls to lower the music when she went to find Quinton. She informed the rest of the party of Ray's supposed predicament.

"Will you come with me to get Ray?"

"You okay to drive?" Courtney asked, entering the room.

"Oh yeah," Duncan said confidently. "Absolutely."

"I'll get the keys," Courtney said.

"I'm coming," Quinton said.

"No chance," Duncan insisted.

"But I want those smokes."

Duncan punched Quinton in the other shoulder.

"Ow!" he shrieked. His hands crossed over his body and he was holding his shoulders like a diver about to roll back off a boat into the sea. "Stop doing that!"

"What's going on?" Ruby asked, peeking into the room.

"Ray's in jail," Quinton said.

"What'd he do?" Ruby asked.

"He bought smokes," Quinton said.

"And they put him in jail?"

"Can you believe it?"

"Are you going to get him, Duncan?"

"Yeah."

"Can I come?"

"No!" Duncan laughed. "No one's coming. Ruby, you stay here. Quin, take her away."

"Away!" Quinton shouted with a swoop of his hand. Ruby turned and left the room.

"Ready," Courtney said with keys in hand.

Duncan and Courtney arrived at the station in a matter of minutes. The local precinct was only three blocks from the apartment and two from the gas station where Ray was nabbed. Standing at a waist high desk that separated citizens from the inner workings of the police station, Duncan and Courtney could see Ray in the holding cell. Ray had apparently made friends with his sole cellmate, and the two – one clearly drunk, the other on a known hallucinogen – were trying in vain to remember the lyrics of Simon and Garfunkel's *America*.

"Courtney?" one of the officers said from behind the barrier.

"Hey, Matt," Courtney said as the man approached.

"What're you doing here?" he asked. The officer lifted a bar-like section of the counter top and embraced Courtney with a friendly hug.

"Oh, just picking up a friend," Courtney said, pointing to the two in the cell.

"Really?"

"Duncan, this is Matt."

"Matt," Duncan offered, shaking the officer's hand.

"Matt is married to my cousin Lacey," Courtney said.

"Nice to meet you," Matt said.

"We're supposed to ask for Officer Partin?" Courtney said.

"Yeah," Matt said, "Tony. I think he's still here. Let me go check for you."

"Thanks."

Matt disappeared back behind the counter and returned soon after with the good officer that had picked up Ray.

"Are you here for Ray?" Officer Partin asked.

"That's my cousin," Matt informed him.

"Hi," Courtney said with a wave.

"If you guys want to take him home I'd be okay with that," he said.

"That would be great," Courtney said. "We'll take him straight home."

"Okay," Officer Partin said. "Come around this way."

Courtney followed his direction and was buzzed through a glass door beside the desk.

"So how do you know Courtney?" Matt asked Duncan.

"We're friends from college actually," Duncan said. "I'm good friends with Quinton."

"You went to ASU then."

"Uh huh."

"That's good."

"And you went to…"

"The Police Academy."

"Sure, sure, that makes sense. And that was good, yeah?"

"Yup," Matt said, followed by a prolonged silence. "So I'm gonna go back there now," he added.

"Cool," Duncan said, relieved. "Nice meeting you."

Out from behind the glass door came Courtney with Ray in tow. Ray was doing his best to play sober, and to his credit, was doing quite well. Years of smoking marijuana in school afforded him much practice.

Without so much as a word of hello from Ray or a mention of goodbye to Matt, the three exited the police station in complete silence. As soon as they smelled the fresh air of the Omaha night, Ray pulled out his pack of cigarettes and lit one up.

"Happy now?" Duncan said.

"So good," Ray replied.

"Finish that before you get into the car," Courtney said.

"No problem."

Ray took a few long pulls from the smoke before crushing it out under his foot.

"Thanks for coming to get me C," Ray said, getting into the car.

"No problem, *R*. This isn't the first time I've picked you up at a police station."

"It isn't?"

"You don't remember me getting you and Quinton?"

"Ohhhh yeeeaaaah," Ray sung. "But that doesn't count."

"They all count," Courtney said.

They returned to the apartment and to a resounding ovation led by Quinton. "The prodigal son returns," he yelled above the applause.

Ray took a bow.

"Did you get the smokes?"

"Yes," Ray said, displaying the pack.

Quinton and Ray escaped to the terrace together and lit up their cigarettes. Ruby soon joined them.

Duncan took a seat on the couch beside Kennedy.

About two hours passed by with minimal incident. Tina and Tim finally decided to take their leave from the party when Tim began to show signs of becoming one of the undead. The effects of mushrooms last for about four hours. Tim's diminished dose paired with his larger size saw him descend from his high a fraction earlier than the others.

When Quinton, Ray, and Ruby finally returned indoors, they too had begun to show signs of waning effects. Kennedy, Courtney, and Duncan were quietly enjoying each other's company and had almost forgotten about the medicated triumvirate outside. The tone of the gathering had long since reached its crescendo.

Duncan joined Kennedy on her quest to locate her cell phone and the two returned to the privacy of the room in which they were interrupted earlier. Kennedy conveniently found her lost Blackberry in her pocket soon thereafter, though the two remained alone in the room for some time.

Two a.m. had come and gone when Kennedy and Duncan finally re-emerged. To Duncan, it quickly became obvious that Courtney was playing the part of an overly cordial yet very tired hostess.

"You guys wanna get going?" asked Duncan.

"We were just waiting for you," Ray insisted.

"I'll call a cab."

Duncan and Ray said goodbye to their old friends, and along with Ruby, made their way from the apartment. Kennedy was staying over and was sure to supply Duncan with more than one hug before he left. The last of their exchanges lingered significantly longer than would a typical friendly goodbye. The two made a promise to stay in touch.

Returning to the presidential suite at the Magnolia, Ray and Ruby found themselves of a very unique mood and mind. Coming down from the effects of mushrooms always affords its participants a unique sensation; a perspective unlike anything one would otherwise experience. The seemingly matchless clarity of thought and visceral perception of the entire world is shared only by those in a similar physical and mental state. To say that sharing that frame of mind is a bonding experience is to not give it nearly enough credence; it is a shared experience that cannot be rivaled, nor forgotten. Two people will connect on an entirely new plain of consciousness and understanding when finding themselves in such a situation. The high is gone, but participants are left with a soothingly warm and comfortable feeling.

When Duncan excused himself to enjoy the pleasures of his lavish bed for one more night, Ray and Ruby were left in a world that occupied nothing but themselves, and their compellingly lucid dispositions.

They lay on Ruby's bed facing one another, talking in a manner to them so deep that philosophy students would do well to listen.

"Yes," Ruby said, mid-conversation. "I completely get that, so that's why you left Phoenix?"

"Yes and no," Ray said. "I mean, as long as I stayed there I wouldn't be able to escape the life I had, but that's not the only reason."

"So what's the other reason?"

Ray thought. "When me and Duncan first talked about it, he said something that really made sense. He said he was tired of waiting for his life to really start. He didn't have to explain what he meant, I got it right away."

"Like, what you really want to do with your life?"

"Kind of, yeah. It's like...how can I describe it? It's like when I was a kid, and my mother would buy me clothes that were too big for me, you know? She would always say 'you'll grow into them, you'll grow into them'. Well, that plan never worked out because by the time they would fit me properly I didn't like them anymore, or they were ruined with grass stains, or lost, or I grew right past them. Whatever the case, it just always seemed like I was wearing clothes that didn't fit me properly. I never felt comfortable cause I was always *waiting* for them to be right – looking ahead to a time when it all came together. When I was in high school, I was waiting to go to college to start my life. When I was in college I was waiting to graduate so I could *really* start my life. I guess what I'm trying to say is – I'm tired of waiting for what comes next to be the *right* thing, the thing I feel comfortable with. I just want my clothes to fit me now, you know?"

"Totally," Ruby said. "I feel that too."

"Is that why you left home? To start your life how you want it?"

"You're gonna laugh at me," Ruby said, shyly.

"I won't laugh," Ray said stoically. "I swear."

"I left because there are no condos in Greenbrook."

"Condos," Ray repeated.

Ruby nodded.

"I don't get it," Ray said.

"When I was a kid, my mom took me out of school to go see my grandmother. I didn't know it at the time, but it was because she was dying. She had cancer and my mom wanted to spend time with her before…you know. She lived near Atlanta on the thirty-first floor of a condo building. For three weeks, every day, my mom, my grandmother, and me would sit at the window of her bedroom and watch the sun go down. My grandmother said to me that nighttime was her favorite time. Watching the sun go down meant that the day was ending, which meant she could do what *she* wanted to do. She said that during the day, you have to go to work, pay your bills, dress in proper clothes, talk to strangers you don't know – but at night, when the sun was gone, you could be yourself. You could wear what you wanted, watch whatever TV shows you liked or read whatever book. You could talk to your friends, go out for dinner, go to sleep early. You didn't have to worry about the little things until the sun came up again. I liked how that sounded, even as a kid. When she died, and I went back to Greenbrook, I tried to watch the sun go down every day, but the best I could do to get high enough was climb up into a tree.

It wasn't the same. There are no tall buildings in Greenbrook and we certainly don't have condos."

"Wow," Ray said. "When was the last time you saw the sun set?"

"I think it was the day my grandma died," she said.

Ray shifted closer to Ruby. He put his arm around her and pulled her in close. Ruby turned herself just enough so that they were face-to-face and her nose was nearly touching his. They could feel each other's breath.

Ruby smiled at Ray. He leaned in and kissed her on the lips.

"I could fall asleep like this," Ruby said, resting her head down on a pillow.

"No," Ray said. "Don't go to sleep yet."

Those were the last words either of them spoke that night.

CHAPTER 11

"YOU GUYS READY?" Duncan said, poking his head into the room the next morning.

Ray had shifted in the night and lay on his stomach on the left side of the bed. Ruby remained in the same position in which she fell asleep with Ray's arm barely reaching her.

"What time is it?" Ray asked.

"Ten-thirty," Duncan said. "I'm hungry."

"A few more minutes."

"Shhhhh," Ruby added.

"Whatever," Duncan said. "I'm getting food."

Duncan disappeared from the room. Ray tried to fall back asleep but his throbbing bladder had other plans for him. Rising to his feet, Ray felt lightheaded and his mouth was dry and raw. He made his way into the washroom and experienced the joyous relief of releasing the pent-up fluids. Ray smacked his tongue against his lips. It felt like leather. Still in the same clothes from the night before, he pulled the soft pack of Marlboros from his pocket to find that only a single crushed yellow and white stick remained. "Gross," he said to himself. He threw the worn pack somewhere in the general vicinity of the trash bin.

Ray finished his business, immediately unwrapped a complimentary toothbrush and smeared it with a heaping gob of toothpaste. Brushing his teeth and removing his clothes at the same time was a bit of a chore. With the toothbrush still in his mouth, Ray got into the shower and blasted the warm water. His eyes began to burn from the steam, but it was a good kind of burn.

Through the foggy glass door Ray saw a figure enter the bathroom and drop the seat on the toilet.

"Ruby?"

"Pretend I'm not here," the girl said as she took a seat. It didn't bother Ray at all that Ruby already felt comfortable enough to do something like that in front of him, even though they could both only make out blurry shapes through the steam.

"There's plenty of room in here if you want," Ray said in jest.

"Is that an invitation?"

"Yes?"

"Another time," Ruby said.

"Open invitation."

Ruby finished up and left Ray to his shower.

Duncan returned to the presidential suite sometime later. With a full belly he dropped down on the couch to wait for his friends.

Ray had finished dressing and emerged from the bedroom with bag in hand.

"Ruby ready?" Duncan asked.

"She's coming."

"What's that smell?"

"I used that fucking fancy soap in there. I smell like a flower pot."

"Did Ruby shower?"

"Yeah, in your bathroom. I almost got her to come in with me, but, no go."

"Maybe next time."

"That's what she said."

Ruby came out a few minutes later looking preened but still tired. Her hair was wet and her eyes drooped.

"Rough night?" Duncan asked.

Ruby shot him a facetious smile.

"So let's go," Ray said.

Duncan took the first leg of the drive. The crew made their way onto the I-80 where it was a straight-shot two-hour drive to Des Moines. Duncan remained behind the wheel after a quick food stop, and they hit Davenport on the Illinois border just under three hours later. Ray took over behind the wheel and by the time they passed through South Bend, Indiana, Duncan suggested a dinner break and Ruby pleaded for a washroom. Ray pulled into the next rest stop along the route. The entire exit seemed to consist of nothing more than a two-pump gas station and a small diner someone had plucked out of the sixties. Pulling up to the diner, Ruby dashed from the car and sprinted for the washroom inside.

"I guess she has to pee," Ray said.

The day had been a somber one. Both Ray and Ruby had used it to recover from an event-filled evening, while Duncan had spent much of the drive thinking intently about the things he and Kennedy had discussed. Ideas had begun to surface to the top of his mind, though he wasn't ready to share his thoughts with anyone just yet.

The boys made their way through the jingling door of the diner and what they saw further stoked their apprehension. Not only did the diner look like something out of a bad horror movie from the outside, but more than half of the already small, dank shop was cut off by means of a floor-to-ceiling plastic sheet on the inside. On the plastic sheet was a sign that read: Please excuse the mess, we're renovating to serve you better.

What remained of the diner counter was fully occupied by only five people. Likewise, the two tables and three window-side booths were also in use. Duncan and Ray stood by the entrance and took it all in.

"No maitre d'," Ray said.

"He's doing the drywall," said Duncan.

"What the…" Ruby said, returning from the washroom.

"Feel better?" Ray asked.

"Nowhere to sit," Duncan said.

"Let's just do take out," Ruby offered.

"We've been sitting in a car all day, let's take a break."

"So what do you suggest?" Ray asked.

"Would you like to sit with me?" a small voice offered.

Turning to their left, Duncan, Ray, and Ruby noticed a small old man taking up barely a fraction of one of the diner booths. "Lots of room," the man gestured.

The three looked to one another, waiting for someone to take the lead.

"Thank you." Duncan said. "That's really nice of you, but we can wait."

"If you vant to," the old man said, revealing an accent. "But I only have a coffee and your girl looks hungry."

"Are you sure?" Ray asked.

"Of course," the man insisted. "Sit, sit."

Like good grandchildren, the three carefully squeezed into the booth with the old man. The closer they got to him, the smaller he looked. His hair was white and barely formed a horseshoe around his head. His short legs wouldn't have touched the ground if he hadn't propped himself right up against the table, and by the looks of his worn, crinkled hands, one of them alone had a lifetime of stories that could outdo those of the three newcomers combined.

"I'm Duncan, this is Ruby, and Ray."

"My name is Abe."

"So do you live around here, Abe?" Duncan asked.

"Oh, no. I live in Long Island, New York."

"You guys eating or just the coffee?" A waitress asked, appearing from nowhere.

"No, we're eating," Ray said. He looked up over the open kitchen to see the entire menu up on boards. "How about just a burger with fries?"

"Two," Duncan said.

"Three," Ruby added.

"Three burgers," the waitress repeated. "Anything to drink?"

"Water is fine," Ruby said.

Duncan and Ray just nodded.

"You're a long way from Long Island," Ray said to Abe.

"I'm driving to Chicago."

"Alone?"

"Alone, yes."

"Where is your accent from?" Ruby asked.

"Poland," Abe said. "But dis is not a Polish accent. Dis is a Yiddish accent."

"Yiddish?" Ruby said.

"Max's father spoke Yiddish," Duncan said. "I've heard it before. It's like Hebrew."

"So you're Jewish," Ruby said.

"Sure," Abe said, as if she should have known.

Ruby thought to try and hide her interest. She had never met a Jewish person before. She only knew of them and seen them on TV and in the movies. Ruby wished in that moment that she could go back to the bookstore to tell Ray that her favorite book of all time was *The Diary of Anne Frank*. Never before or since had a book make Ruby cry. She had read it as a fourteen-year-old girl and felt closer to young Anne and her isolation than she did to many of her friends at the time. "When did you come to America?" she asked.

"I came after deh war, to America."

"We can talk about something else," Duncan offered.

"It's okay," Abe said. "With such a shayna maidel, it's good for an old man to talk."

"We don't want to pry," Ray said.

"I belong to a group of survivors," Abe said. "We go to deh schools, to deh children, and we tell dem deh stories so no one will forget. I don't mind to talk about it."

"The Holocaust?" Ray asked.

"Yes. Vat happened. It's important to talk about dis. Dare are very few people left, you know."

It was when Abe went to pick up his coffee cup that Duncan saw the numbers tattooed on his arm.

"You were in the camps," Duncan said.

"Yes. You see," Abe displayed his tattoo to Ray and Ruby. "I was in deh camp Belzec, and den dey put me to Auschwitz."

"And now you're in a diner in South Bend, Indiana."

"If you say," Abe shrugged. "I am by deh highway. Dis is what I know."

"What's in Chicago? Family?"

"I go to see my cousin."

"How did you survive the Camps, Abe?" Ruby asked.

"I jumped off from a train," Abe said.

"You jumped from a train?" she repeated in surprise.

"I was very young and very strong," Abe insisted. "Like an ox."

"And you jumped from a train to get away?" Ray asked.

"I was in deh camp Auschwitz II. Dey wanted to put me to Auschwitz III to do work for dem, because I was young and strong, like I said. Deh day came and dey put me on deh train." Abe spoke with confidence; as if he had told the story so many times that it almost didn't seem real anymore.

"A Jewish officer came to me. He took me to deh side and told me in secret dat when I hear deh noise, deh squeaking noise from deh train for more den I count to ten seconds, dis means deh train is going around a big turn." Abe made a circle with his hand. "I'm in a car in deh middle of deh train. When we go on da big curve, deh train makes a U, yes? Dare are Nazis in deh front, and Nazis in deh back, but in deh middle, just we are dare. Deh Jewish man didn't lock our door on deh train, and he told me when we make deh U, no one will see us. Deh door is on the outside of the turn. Deh man told me, jump from deh train and run away."

"Wow," Ray said.

"When I hear deh noise, I pull deh door with deh men, and we see deh forest."

"And you jumped out," Ruby said.

"I jumped out from deh train with my friend Yosle, and wit my sisteh."

"Your sister was on the train with you?" Ray said.

"Yes, my sisteh too. I took her by deh hand, and we jumped. My sisteh, she was only tvelve, she was not very strong, she did not survive. She hit her head on the ground when we make deh jump. Her hand came away from mine and she banged on her –" Abe pointed to the back of his neck.

"Neck," Duncan offered.

"Neck – on her spine. My friend Yosle, he landed wit his foot – how you say it – on a tree hump and was hurt."

"But you were okay?" Ray asked.

"When I land in deh forest, I fall forward, and roll down a hill. My arm falls on a rock by deh stream and is bleeding." Abe revealed a long scar on his arm that ran from the ball of his elbow to his wrist. "Dis arm was broken, but how do you put a cast in deh forest? I wrapped it in some clothes and I run."

"What about your sister and your friend?"

"When deh train was gone, we take my sisteh and put her by deh water. We cover her body wit leaves and sticks. I give her a kiss on the cheek and say goodbye.

Ruby shook her head in disbelief.

"I take two sticks, and I take deh string from a shoe, and we make a strong – em – leg for Yostle, and we go into deh forest."

The waitress came by with the food and filled up Abe's coffee cup. The trio began to eat as Abe continued his story.

"Yosle wanted to go to deh border, to run away. But I, I wanted to go to my home, to my farm. I wanted to see if I could find my family. Any."

"Did you have a big family?" Duncan asked.

"I had four brothehs and tree sistehs."

What Ray didn't want to point out was at that point in the story Abe had only two sisters remaining. It seemed an unnecessary observation.

"In a week's time, I ran up to my house in deh night by myself. A man was living dare. Dis man was called Jozef. I told him who I was. He brought me into deh house and I hid in deh basement, in a big oven."

"How long?" Duncan asked.

"Like an oven you make deh pizza," Abe said, spreading his arms out wide.

"No, I mean how long did you hide in there for?"

"One year, two months."

"You hid in a pizza oven for over a year." Ray said.

"In deh night, I go out from deh oven and look for what to eat."

"Unbelievable."

"One day, I come back in deh night, and I see people in the house wit Jozef. So I run away."

"You just ran away?" Duncan asked.

"I run away," Abe said again matter-of-factly, as if he were running away from a bumblebee.

"Where did you go?"

"I went to a town near deh farm. And den I stay under a toilet."

"What do you mean?"

"Not all deh toilets were in deh house. Some toilets were in deh outside. I climb down into deh bottom and I stay dare during deh day."

"Are you serious?"

"At night, I go out and look for what to eat."

Ruby barely touched her food. She was enveloped in Abe's story, drinking it in as he did the coffee in his cup.

"One night, I'm out in deh town, and a man in a German uniform comes up to me, he stops me and puts his gun on my head."

Abe held his finger to his temple. "Deh German yells, 'Juden, Juden'. Jew, Jew."

"What did you do?" Ruby asked.

"He turns his head when he yells to deh others to come get me, and I smack deh gun from him and I run."

"You smacked the gun from his hand?"

"I smack deh gun from his hand," Abe said. "What else I should do?"

"How?" Ray asked. "How do you smack a gun from someone's hand?"

"Like dis?" Abe said. Abe smacked his own hand away from his head. "In a few more weeks, deh Russians came to deh town and deh Germans vent away."

"And what happened to you?" Ruby asked. "What happened to your family?"

"Dey took me to a DP camp in France."

"What's a DP camp?"

"Dis is a Displaced Person Camp."

"Did anyone in your family…"

"No one in my family lived. Aunts, uncles, cousins, all did not live."

"How did you get to America?"

"When I was in France, dare was nothing to do for work. So dare was a big – how do call it – market for trading."

"A black market," Duncan said.

"A black market. One night, I was out in deh square, I came to a man to trade wit him for some bread. He was a big man. I didn't have what to give him enough, but he brung me home wit him, to where his family was in deh camp. He said he liked me; he wanted to give me food. Dare, where he stayed, he showed me his wife, and his sister, Rebecca. I was alone, wit nothing. Deh man let me stay wit his family. Later, Rebecca became my wife. In a year, Rebecca's uncle in America saw her name and deh name of her brother on a list of people, a list from deh Red Cross. He lived in Brooklyn. So he brung us to America."

"That's some story," Duncan said.

"If I could only tell you about deh parts I didn't say. You couldn't believe it. My wife would say dat if you took all deh paper and all deh pencils in deh whole world you still couldn't write it down to make people understand."

"Where is your wife now?" Ruby asked.

"Well," Abe stalled. His eyes lowered. When he spoke again he did so with a rasp in his voice. "Rebecca has died."

"I'm sorry," Ruby said.

"When did she pass away?" Duncan asked.

"Tree weeks Tuesday," Abe said.

"Oh," Duncan said, at a loss for more words.

"Is that why you're going to Chicago?" Ray asked. "To see your family?"

"I go to Chicago to live wit my cousin," Abe said, collecting himself. "I don't have where to live in Long Island."

"You sold your house?"

"Deh bills for deh hospital were very big. Very big."

"And you had to sell your house."

Abe nodded.

"She died very slowly. She stayed at deh hospital eight months. I was a just a tailor in my work, I didn't have what to pay dem with."

"So now you're going to live with your cousin in Chicago," Duncan added.

"When I go to Chicago, I sell my car. Dey give me maybe a few tousand and I live. I don't work anymore. I have diabetes, and arthritis in my hands."

Abe held up his weathered hands for all to see. His fingers were curled and his knuckles were big, and swollen.

"You didn't have any children?" Ruby asked.

"We had a little girl, yes," Abe said. "She was born with a bad heart and didn't live very long."

Duncan, Ruby, and Ray had little left to say. What started out as a simple stop for a burger had brought them face-to-face with the kind of life story none of them could imagine. Each felt a special kind of kinship with the old man. Not lost on them was that he too was heading out to start a new life. One at the dawn of what seemed to be a saga of sadness and pain.

Ruby's eyes were full of water. When she heard of the child with the bad heart, it reminded her of her brother, and the tears fell down her face. She wiped them with her sleeve.

"Which car is yours?" Duncan asked, peeking out the window.

"Deh blue one," Abe pointed.

"What is that?" Ray asked. "A Grand Marquee?"

"A Fifth Avenue, a Chrysler," Abe said proudly.

"That's a nice car," Duncan said.

The waitress came by to fill Abe's coffee cup one more time. She cleared the half empty plates and asked if there were any final orders. She got no response and dropped two checks on the table and moved along.

"Just the coffee?" Duncan asked Abe.

"I had a piece of cake," he said.

"In exchange for that story, I insist on paying."

"Oh, tank you, you don't have to."

"You're not going to stop him, Abe," Ray said.

Duncan took out a few bills and placed payment on top of both chits.

"Can I take a look at that Chrysler?" Duncan asked.

"Shuweh!" Abe said happily.

Abe followed the others out of the booth. He stood with a little hunch in his posture, leaning forward just a bit to help keep his balance. When he walked, he did so with short, sputtering steps, his hands clasped together behind his back all the while.

The old man led the group out to the parking lot and up to his car. Abe fumbled a bit with his keys before opening the door for Duncan. On the driver seat was a circular couch pillow resting on top of two hardcover books. Abe moved the books and the pillow aside and motioned for Duncan to climb in.

"What's the pillow for?" Duncan asked.

"I'm shrinking," Abe smiled.

Duncan slid in and got comfortable in the big leather bucket seats. He took the wheel in both hands. "Only fifty four thousand?" Duncan said, looking at the number on the odometer.

"Where I have to go?" Abe admitted.

"This has to be, what? Early 80's?"

"What do you mean?"

"The year. What year did you buy the car?"

"Oh. I bought deh car…" Abe looked up to the sky. "Maybe…1986?"

"Can I turn it on?" Duncan asked.

Ray smiled to Ruby. Ruby looked puzzled.

"Of course!" Abe said.

Abe handed Duncan the keys and pointed out the correct one to use in the ignition.

Duncan started up the car.

The large boat-like automobile started up without hesitation, and the powerful engine roared with a healthy groan.

"It's in good condition," Duncan said.

"Oh yes. I take care of my car."

"Ray," Duncan nodded.

Ray walked around to the front of the car and lifted the hood in almost perfect timing with Duncan's tug of the lever to unleash it. Ray stuck his head down to take a closer look. Duncan stomped on the gas pedal a few times. After a few moments Ray slammed the hood down and nodded to Duncan.

"Abe," Duncan said, turning off the car. "Can I show you something?"

Duncan led Abe, Ray, and Ruby across the parking lot to the BMW. He tweeted the alarm and opened the driver side door.

"Dis is your car?" Abe asked, impressed.

"Get in," Duncan said.

Abe did as he was told and sat in the driver's seat.

"Dis is beautiful," Abe said, stroking the dash above the wheel.

Duncan bent down beside the seat and put his finger on the mechanical controls. Then, with a tiny flick of Duncan's index, the seat in which the dwindling man sat began to rise. Abe took hold of the wheel and his eyes opened wide. When Duncan had positioned the seat at an appropriate height, he flicked the next button and Abe began to move closer to the wheel until he was in an ideal driving position.

"How does that feel?" Duncan asked.

"Dis is a beautiful car. A beautiful car."

"Abe," Duncan said, rising to his feet. "I have a proposition for you."

"Okay?" Abe said.

"See, there are three of us; me, Ray, and Ruby. We're in need of a little more room and, well, your car is much bigger than ours. And, since you were planning on selling it anyway, I was hoping maybe you would consider taking this car instead and letting us have yours."

"You want to take my car?" Abe said, a little confused.

"I want to trade with you. You take this car and we take yours. You can sell this car when you get to Chicago. But if I were you, I wouldn't take less than 80 thousand for it when you do."

"80 tousand?" Abe exclaimed.

"Would that be something you would consider?"

"But my car is only–"

"We could really use the room, Abe," Ray said.

"No, I can't let you do dis."

"You can't, or you won't?" Duncan asked.

Abe paused. "Why do you do dis for me?" he asked.

"We're doing it for each other. Like I said, we'd be much more comfortable in your car. Do we have a deal?"

Abe thought for a second. Again his voice became raspy and small. "Will you help me move deh bags?" he asked.

"Of course," Duncan said. "Let's shake on it."

Abe got out of the car and shook Duncan's hand.

"You're a real mensch," Abe said.

"Let's get your bags," Duncan said.

Ray followed Abe back to his car and removed all of his belongings. The old man had but one suitcase and one large laundry bag. Abe poked his head into the glove box and removed a few cassette tapes, two pens, and some papers, including his insurance and personal information.

"I should make it clean first," Abe insisted.

"Don't worry about it," Ray insisted. "It's clean enough."

Ray put Abe's belongings into the emptied trunk of the BMW. Duncan handed him the key in a ceremony that nearly mirrored the one with Martin Bridge only a few days prior.

"The pink slip is in the glove box," Duncan said.

He could see that Abe was overwhelmed with gratitude and wouldn't let him try to speak.

"We better get going," Duncan said to the others.

Ruby walked over and wrapped her arms around Abe. "Take care," she said.

The man nodded and touched the back of his coarse hand to Ruby's cheek.

And with that, the old tailor with tales from the Holocaust got into his new car, turned it on, and backed out. He put the car in drive and pulled onto the street very, very slowly. And as if the generous deed weren't enough to fill their hearts, Duncan, Ray, and Ruby were treated to even more jubilation as they watched Abe drive away down the rural road, with his left blinker still flashing.

CHAPTER 12

"NOW THIS IS a car," Ray said, getting into the back seat of their new acquisition. The amount of space the once-premium automobile afforded surpassed that of the BMW. The large back seat was enough for two of them to stretch out upon. Ruby took the front and Duncan took the driver's position.

"I can't believe what you did for him," Ruby said.

"That car wasn't us," Duncan said.

"Come on, still."

"He needed the money more than we do," said Ray.

"You guys are nothing like the guys back home."

"A few months ago and who knows if I woulda done it," Duncan said. "There's something about being on the road. And, there was something about his story. I figure if I could give the guy even a little break, why the hell not?"

"It felt good," Ray added.

The sun had completely vanished by the time they were back on the I-80. They were heading for Cleveland, Ohio.

"So how do you account for all that happening," Ray said. He was laid out, spread across the back seat with his feet up and plenty of room to spare.

"What?" Duncan asked.

"The story that Abe told us. How could that happen?"

"You mean how could God *let* that happen?"

"Yeah. Wouldn't that be proof enough?"

"Not at all."

"So then why didn't he stop it? If he's all-powerful and capable of working in mysterious ways, why did it go on for so long? Why was there so much suffering? Not only that, why was there so much suffering of *innocent* people, who, if they're still alive like Abe, are probably still suffering?"

"You know there's no good answer for that, Ray."

"Well isn't that a problem? How can anyone believe in something that is supposed to make their lives better, when there is so much evidence that it just doesn't?"

"So you're saying that if bad things happen, that must mean there's no God?"

"No. I mean, I'm not talking about a car accident or someone getting sick, I'm talking about ten million people dying. And more than half of those people weren't fighting back. They were kids and mothers and grandparents. Look, all I'm saying is that religion and God are there to supposedly make people's lives better, right? So why does it seem like all these people that believe in that stuff simply aren't any happier because of it?"

"My grandmother went to church every Sunday," Ruby said. "She seemed pretty happy."

"Okay, but was she happy because she went to church? Would she have been any less happy if she didn't?"

"I don't know."

"All I'm saying is – okay look, we met this random guy who has obviously suffered more than we could ever imagine in one lifetime. Now, I didn't ask him if he believed in God, but I'm pretty sure that if he did, it was in spite of his life."

"How do you know that believing in God or in his religion didn't help him survive?" Duncan asked. "Maybe he wouldn't have survived if he didn't have that hope, or that belief that there was something out there looking out for him."

"Maybe," Ray said, conceding the point. "But being removed from it, I mean us, here, now, how can you say that there was a purpose to all that?"

"How can you say there wasn't? It happened, and of course people suffered and it was an absolute disgrace, but it happened, and now here we are. Maybe it had to happen for humankind to progress. Think of all the technological, medical, scientific advances that were made during that time. Was the trade off worth it? Of course not. No one would argue that all killing and suffering was worth – I dunno – learning how to split the atom, or whatever, but it's not our place to judge."

"Why not? Why isn't it our place? I say it is our place. That plan was shit. If there was an all-powerful being that could have done something then he should have done something, period. The fact that nothing was done means to me that God is either completely uncaring, completely cruel, or that he doesn't exist at all."

"What if God created the world, but then just left it for people to live on their own? You know, like free will?" Ruby said.

"So you're saying there's a God but he doesn't care what happens to us?"

"I'm just asking," Ruby said.

"Well, for one thing, it would mean that all religions are bullshit," Ray said. "If there is a God and he doesn't care what happens to us then what's the point of all the rules, or the prayers, or the holy books that tell us what he wants us to do?"

"You can believe in God and not in religion," Duncan said.

"So what's your idea of God then?"

"Something that started the universe; something much bigger than us. I never said it was a man sitting up on a cloud writing names of good and bad people down in a book. I never said it was someone that cared if we used condoms or were gay or ate meat on Fridays. You're just assuming that stuff."

"Okay, maybe you don't believe that, but there are millions of people that do."

"Then take that up with them," Duncan chuckled. "What do you want from me?"

"I want to know what makes you believe in it? I'm not saying you shouldn't, I'm just trying to figure out how you can believe something that has absolutely no evidence."

"Because there is evidence."

"Like?"

"The sun, the moon, gravity, birth, death, trees, Mars, ants, whales, cold, heat…"

"You're just naming random things."

"That's right. Where did they come from?"

"Science."

"No," Duncan said confidently. "Science is what we use to explain those things, but where did they come from? How did they get here? How did we get here?"

"The Big Bang."

"There had to be a cause, Ray. Something had to start it all."

"So you believe that the world was created by something, but that something isn't around anymore."

"I didn't say that."

"So it is still around."

"Okay look, I'll make it easy for you," Duncan said. "I believe in God. I believe that *something* created the universe. I think that certain things happen for a reason, but not all things. I think humans and animals and aliens – if there are any – were created with their own consciousness and *God* doesn't try to control those things. I don't really think that Jesus was the Son of God, or that any religion is a hundred percent true, but I think that using only science to explain how and why we're here isn't enough."

"You don't believe in Jesus?" Ruby asked.

"I believe there was a Jesus," Duncan said. "But I don't think he was God. He was probably a cool guy that meant well and said good things, but God is God. He wouldn't come for a visit as some dude."

"But what about all his miracles?" Ray asked.

"Now you're talking about religion again. I didn't say I believed the Bible was true."

"So you can believe in God and not the Bible," Ruby said.

"Yes," Duncan agreed. "That's what I've been saying. I don't think the Bible is true, I don't think the Koran, or the Torah, or the Hindu books are *true* either. I know what I know, and what I believe from my life experience."

"Well you can't argue with that, then, can you?" Ray said.

"Why are you so against it, Ray?" Ruby inquired.

"Where would I even begin?" Ray said.

"Ray's more than against it," Duncan said. "He thinks people that believe in God are stupid."

"I never said stupid, Dun. Do I think you're stupid? I think you know that's not true. I said delusional, there's a difference."

"Oh, sorry, delusional. That's much better."

"Sure it is," Ray said. "You're plenty intelligent, you just believe in ghosts and fairies and shit."

"I do?"

"You know what I mean. Okay look, how about this: If nobody ever told you about the idea of God, or explained to you religion or anything like that, do you think you would have figured it out yourself? Do you think you would have come to that as an answer? Or do you think it's just something that has been around for so long that it gets passed down?"

"That's an unfair question," Duncan said.

"Why?"

"Why?" Duncan repeated. "Because you can't say that. That's like saying if no one taught you math would you figure it out on your own – or science, or how to throw a football, or whatever. I wouldn't have figured out gravity on my own but that doesn't mean it doesn't exist."

"Good answer," Ruby said.

"Thank you."

"I don't know, man, I think it's a little bit of brainwashing."

"You think because someone thinks something different than you they've been brainwashed?"

"Yes," Ray said quickly.

Duncan and Ruby laughed.

"Whatever, man," Ray added, "You're free to think whatever you want. My problem is more with the religious people that think God makes decisions for us, and that they know what he wants, and what I should do, and who is going to heaven, and all that bullshit."

"You don't believe in heaven?" Ruby asked.

"Me?" Ray said. "Nope. I'm coming back as a cat."

"Oh, right," Ruby said. "I almost forgot."

The four-hour haul to Cleveland went by quickly and the trio decided to drive right through. They kept going until they crossed the New York State border and reached Jamestown. It was approaching the early hours of the morning when they pulled off the highway and into a gas station. Ray was given the mission to go into the station and buy three six packs of beer without getting arrested. He pulled it off without ordeal and returned to the car to a round of applause. Along with the beer, Ray purchased a road map, because without the assistance of the BMW's GPS, they were on their own to find the best route to their destination. Ray also bought a couple of gas-station-special roast beef sandwiches, against his own better judgment.

The gang set up camp at a roadside motel and retired to their room with their bags and still-cold beer. Ray found a commercial-ridden version of *The Big Lebowski* on TV and – as was becoming custom – shared a mattress with Ruby. Duncan sat on the other bed with his book, though the ramblings of Jeff Bridges and John Goodman kept him away from it for long stretches.

"What time are we going to get to Boston?" Ruby asked during one of the commercial breaks.

"We should get in around dinnertime," Duncan said. "We'll have to find somewhere to stay for the night."

"Do we have any idea what comes next?" Ray asked.

"You mean once we find Franklin?"

"Well that," Ray said. "But also what comes after Boston."

"Let's find Franklin and then we'll worry about it."

"Who's Franklin?" Ruby asked.

"We have to find this guy and get something from him. That's why we're going to Boston," said Ray.

"I thought we were just going east for the hell of it," she said.

"We are," Duncan said. "We just have to do something first."

Ruby got up off the bed, put on her shoes, and left the room without another word.

"What's wrong with her?" Duncan asked.

Ray got up and followed Ruby out the door. He caught up with her halfway down the hallway.

"Where you going?" he asked.

"I don't know. Out."

"What's the matter?"

"You lied to me."

"No, we didn't," Ray insisted.

"I thought we were just going where we felt like; doing what we felt like. But you guys knew all along you were going to Boston to find this guy."

"So?"

"So? So? So it's a lie," Ruby said. "And what happens after you find this guy? Are you going back to Phoenix?"

"No," Ray insisted. "I don't know why you think it's a lie. A friend asked us if we could do him a favor in Boston and we said we would. We just have to find this guy, make a quick collection, and then we're done."

"Done? Done what?"

"Done the job. It's just a collection."

"What kind of collection?"

"Some cash."

"You have to go to Boston to pick up cash? Why couldn't this guy send it to you?"

"He doesn't know we're coming. Look, it's a long story, Ruby."

Ruby folded her arms and glared at Ray. Ray got the message right away.

"This guy Franklin owes us twelve grand. The guy in Boston that was supposed to get it died a while ago and now no one can find Franklin. It's a simple pick-up. No one is going to get hurt, nothing crazy is going to go down. This guy is in his fifties or sixties or something like that. It's really not a big deal."

"So why didn't you tell me about it?"

"It just never came up," Ray said. "It's really not a secret."

"So we're not staying in Boston?"

"I don't know, we could, we could not. What's the difference?"

A fat man in an undershirt poked his head out from one of the doors near the elevator to see what all the commotion was about. Ray assured him that everything was fine. The man's head disappeared like a turtle escaping back into its shell.

"I don't want to drive forever," Ruby said a little quieter. "I thought we were going to Boston to–"

"To what?"

"I don't know – live? I mean, I know we're out here having a good time but I want to *go* somewhere," Ruby said, throwing her arms up in the air.

"I don't want to drive forever either," Ray said. "We could stay in Boston, who knows? The point is, we haven't thought that far ahead, Ruby, so it's not a lie. We never lied to you."

"So we might stay in Boston then?"

"Sure, why not? Let's see what happens when we get there."

"Okay," Ruby said after a moment of silence.

"Okay?"

Ruby nodded and even allowed a smile to squeak out. Ray took her by the hand.

"What did you get so upset about?"

"It's not easy, Ray. I'm a girl, driving across the country with two guys I just met."

Ray led Ruby back to the room, holding her hand the entire way. It was when they sat back down in silence to watch the movie that Ray tried to piece together Ruby's words. At first, she was upset that he and Duncan apparently did have a plan and were not in fact traveling without care for location or destination. But her argument quickly changed once she found out that they might not be staying in Boston for long once they got there. Ruby, in reality, wanted for a destination. She wanted a plan and perhaps glommed onto the boys because they indeed had one, and not the opposite. Ruby may not have been running from anything in particular, but she did want something to head towards. The feeling that she had no purpose at all was beginning to frighten her, at least in Ray's estimation. She didn't become upset because they were no longer heading out into the great unknown; she became upset for a time because she feared they were.

CHAPTER 13

RAY TOOK THE first leg of the drive the next morning. Ruby sat up front along with him; Duncan stretched out in the back with his book.

"We're driving through Schenectady?" Ruby said, flipping through the road map.

"I always thought it was pronounced Schenectany?" Ray said.

"Schenectady," Duncan said. "With a D. Schenectady."

"Schenectady," Ray said.

"Schenectady," Ruby agreed.

"I like my way better," Ray said.

"Yeah," Duncan said. "Maybe when we get there you can talk to someone about that."

"When we get to Schenectany?"

"Schenectady," Ruby corrected.

"Schenectany."

"We're only ninety five miles from Niagara Falls," Ruby said, still looking at the map.

"And?" Ray said.

"Niagara Falls? Hello?"

"Hi, Ruby."

"Let's go!"

"Are you serious?" Ray asked.

"Why not? Have you ever been there?"

Ray looked in the rearview and caught Duncan's look of ambiguity.

"I don't care," Duncan said. "They have a casino on the Canadian side."

"You know what else they have there?" Ray said.

"What?" Ruby asked. "The actual falls?"

"Well that, but also…"

"What?" Duncan asked.

"Come on Dun, You should know this."

"I do not."

"Just say it, Ray," Ruby said.

"The Sundowner," Ray said.

"What's The Sundowner?"

"It's a strip club," Duncan said.

"A strip club?"

"Not just any strip club," Ray said. "Only one of the best strip clubs in the world."

"According to who?"

"Everyone," Ray insisted. "They talk about it in Vegas."

"Ninety five miles?" Duncan said. "That's less than two hours."

"Well you'll have to get on the 62 now if we're going to go," Ruby said.

The off ramp to Highway 62 was fast approaching. Ray had to make a quick decision.

"What do I do?" Ray yelled.

"Up to you," Duncan said.

"Ummmmmm," Ray sung as the ramp arrived.

With a near violent swing of the wheel, Ray veered the car onto the ramp. Each occupant of the vehicle offered his or her own version of a scream. Duncan swore his was one of excitement, but it sounded like a little bit of fright mixed in. Ruby clutched the dashboard in front of her and was clearly screaming because of the drastic motion and screeching wheels of the old car. Ray screamed just for the hell of it, but the shriek quickly turned into laughter once the car had safely cleared the sand-filled barriers of the road transfer.

"Maid of the Mist, baby!" Ray yelled, pulling the car to a normal pace and line.

"Holy shit, Ray," Ruby said.

"What? You said–"

"I didn't say to try and kill us!"

"You didn't?"

"I guess we're not going to Schenectady," Duncan added.

"Not today!"

"I'm excited," said Ruby. "This will be the first time I've ever been outside the U.S."

"Really?" Ray asked.

"You may be a little disappointed," Duncan said. "From my experience, Canadians are pretty much the same as Americans – only with more thank-yous and fewer guns."

"And more hockey players," Ray added.

"Still," Ruby said. "I'm excited."

"Good. You should be. It's gonna be fun."

"Canadian beer is awesome," Duncan said.

"Is it different?" Ruby asked.

"Well, it's more or less the same, but they have kinds we don't and the alcohol content is higher."

"What kinds do they have?"

"Molson," Ray said.

"Molson, Labatt…what was that one I had? Duncan said. "I went to see my sister in Vancouver and I had a few good ones. Moosehead I think."

"And they're stronger?"

"I think their light beer is like our regular beer."

"Do they have Bud?"

"Yeah, sure, and Miller and all that. But they have a bunch that we don't. It's like if you go to Mexico or England or wherever, there's always different kinds of beer."

"Molson Canadian," Ray said.

"How far are we from Toronto?" Ruby asked, looking down to her map.

"What's in Toronto?"

"I don't know? The Blue Jays? Looks like only another two hours from Niagara Falls."

"Why stop there?" Duncan said facetiously. "Why not Ottawa, or Montreal?"

"Okay, okay, never mind," Ruby said.

"Sorry, Rube," Duncan said. He squeezed her shoulder from the back seat. "I'm just screwing with you."

"I know. It's okay."

"We'll probably be there in time for lunch," said Ray.

They arrived at the Peace Bridge in Buffalo, New York a little after lunch. They had hit some construction along the way and decided to take a short cut that turned out to be nothing of the sort. They didn't let a little misfortune ruin their mood, though, and with papers in order and friendly smiles on their faces, the Chrysler Fifth Avenue shuffled through the line at the border check without a hint of trouble.

After a mildly scenic twenty-minute zip northerly, they pulled off the highway and onto Fallsview Boulevard. The mist from the falls could be seen in the distance; Ruby shuffled forward in her seat. Ray followed the signs and eventually pulled the car into a lot, directly beside the great falls.

Ruby and Ray were the first to reach the viewing platform. They both hugged the waist high rails and leaned over to feel the cool mist on their faces. Duncan joined the pair and marveled at the seemingly endless array of tiny rainbows and shards of refracted light that cascaded across the gushing water.

"It's so trippy," Ruby said. "If you stare at the water, it hypnotizes you."

The three travelers hung on to the rails in silence and watched the phenomenon as it rumbled and roared. Parents came with their children, elderly couples strolled by, two teenage girls shared a soggy cigarette a few steps behind them.

"There's the boat," Ruby noticed.

In the distance, the Maid of the Mist tour boat could be seen approaching on the water. The matching hooded water shields worn by its occupants made them look like a group of blue bowling pins. The boat approached slowly and hovered in the large wading pool at the bottom of the white rapids.

"It's a lot louder than I thought," Ray said.

"It's pretty cool," Duncan added.

"You know they move back by close to a foot a year?" Ray said. "Ten thousand years ago, the falls were like a mile down the river that way."

"Is that true?" Ruby asked.

"Yup. In a few hundred years all these viewing places will be in the wrong spot."

"I think it will take a little longer than that," Duncan said.

"Probably, but I'm just trying to make a point."

"Let's get one of those rooms," Ruby said, pointing up at the windows of a large hotel that hovered above the falls.

"That's the casino," Duncan said. "Wanna go check it out?"

"Sure, Ruby?" Ray said.

"Yeah, I'm ready."

The crew peeled themselves off the black rail and made their way back to the car. The casino hotel was only a few hundred yards away and Duncan pulled the Fifth Avenue up and around its circular drive. He rolled down the window to speak to the valet that greeted them.

"We're going to see about a room," Duncan said.

"No problem, sir. The front desk is straight through the main doors."

"Can I just leave the car here?"

"Just go ahead and pull up a bit and leave it there for now," the attendant offered.

Duncan did as he was directed and pulled the car over to the side of the massive drive and parked it behind a line of waiting taxis.

Leaving their bags in the car, all three entered through the glass doors of the hotel. In the middle of the foyer was an ornate fountain surrounded by guests exchanging war stories from inside the casino. Behind the fountain was the entrance to the gaming floor, and the front desk for the hotel. Two young women in evening gowns passed by in the opposite direction and gave Duncan and Ray a second look. Ray and Duncan looked back.

Contrary to the routine at the Magnolia, all three approached the front desk together.

"Good afternoon," a young woman greeted.

"Hello there, Kathy" Ray said, eyeing her nametag. "We are interested in one of the rooms overlooking the falls."

"Okay, sir, will that be for all three of you?"

"Yup, one room, three adults."

"Okay, let me just have a look here."

The attendant clicked away on her mouse.

"Ohhhh," Kathy grimaced. "It looks like all the rooms with a fall's view are booked. We do have a few rooms available on the other side though."

"They're all booked?"

"We have a dental convention coming in later today and tomorrow. They've booked the majority of the rooms."

"Well we're only here for one night, is there any way we could get one of the rooms that are booked for tomorrow?"

Kathy clicked. Then she clicked some more.

Ray reached his hand into his pocket pulled out a crisp Benjamin Franklin and slid it slyly across the counter. Duncan gave Ruby a tug and the two of them turned their backs to Ray and did their best to shield both him and Kathy from lobby onlookers.

"We'll only be one night," Ray said again.

Kathy took a look around. She was one of three attendants at the front desk. An older gentleman was completely occupied by a guest, and a younger man was busy on his computer at the end of the row. Neither seemed to care about Kathy's conversation.

Kathy reached her arm out pulled the bill along the counter and placed it quickly into her pocket.

"Well, sir," Kathy said, clicking a few more times on her mouse. "It looks like you're in luck."

"Excellent," Ray said. "Something high up, if it's not too much trouble."

Duncan went out to the car to relocate it into the guest parking and to obtain everyone's bags. He was to meet Ray and Ruby up on the twenty-first floor, which he did, overloaded with a surplus of bags and straps. The doors of the elevator opened and Duncan was face-to-face with a twenty-something couple waiting to enter.

"Wow," the young man said. "Can I give you a hand with those?"

"It's okay," Duncan said, "I'll be okay."

The man didn't wait to argue with Duncan and relieved him of one of the bags from his shoulder. Duncan wouldn't have looked so overwhelmed if it wasn't for the awkward manner in which a six pack of beer dangled from his fingers. He had to adjust his original posture to press the button in the elevator and the beer shifted downward. Duncan figured he would muscle out the strange grip. He wasn't able to test that premise thanks to the unnecessary hero who took the beer along with one bag from him.

"Thanks," Duncan said. "I'm in 2112"

"We're neighbors!" The man said. "We're in 2114. I'm Kevin and that's Sara."

"Hi," Sara waved.

"Duncan."

Kevin led the way around the bend toward their rooms. He was only about five-foot-nine, but he was built like a brick wall. He was almost as wide as he was high. Sara was a little smaller in height and much smaller in figure. She actually looked a lot like Ruby; only her hair was darker and shorter.

"Where you guys from?" Duncan asked.

"St. Catharines," Kevin said. "What about you?"

"Where's St. Catharines?"

"It's about twenty minutes north of here, on the way to Toronto."

"Oh, that close?"

"Yeah. We come down here for a vacation every once in a while."

They arrived at the door of room 2112. Sara had relieved Kevin of the six packs, if only to become useful. Duncan knocked, Ray answered.

"Oh," Ray said, surprised to see Duncan accompanied.

"Kevin, Sara, this is Ray," Duncan said. "They're our neighbors."

"Hey," Ray said. He took the beers and bags from their new acquaintances.

"Thanks for the help," Duncan said.

"No problem. We were just going down to the casino."

"You guys should come by later and have a drink with us," Duncan offered.

"Yeah, sure, thanks."

"You carried it here, after all."

Duncan and Ray transported the bags into the bedrooms and claimed their sleeping quarters. Ruby had already moved a chair over to the window and was sitting with her feet up staring at the tumbling falls when Duncan and Ray came to join her.

"You can almost hear them rumbling," Ray said.

"The window's open," Duncan said. "You can definitely hear them."

Duncan replaced the contents of the mini bar with the beers that Kevin and Sara helped him transfer. They had warmed up in the car and weren't yet drink-worthy. "Let's go check out the casino," he said.

"Yeah, cool," Ray agreed.

"Ruby, you coming?"

"Nah. I think I'm gonna stay here."

"You sure?"

"Yeah. I want to call my mom and I'm not much of a gambler."

"Okay," Ray said. "You got our number if you need anything."

"Have fun."

"We won't be that long," Duncan said. "I'm not getting into anything serious now. I want to check it out and maybe get a drink or something."

"You got a key?" Duncan asked Ray.

Ray patted his front pocket.

Ruby heard the front door of the suite close with a bang and turned her attention back out the twenty-first floor window. She pulled her phone from her pocket to have a look at the time. The sun wouldn't be setting for hours.

Duncan and Ray stood on the floor of the casino.

"It's a lot bigger than I thought," Ray said.

"Me too," Duncan agreed.

Ray led the way through the labyrinthine maze of people and noise and blinking machines.

"Blackjack?" Ray asked.

"Sure."

Ray followed the ceiling signs and the pair found a cache of blackjack tables. They walked along the line of green felt, half-moon tables looking for one that met their fancy. They came upon a $25 minimum table near to the end of the row. Not only were only two seats occupied at the table, but the gamblers were none other than their new friends, Kevin and Sara.

"Hello again," Duncan said, taking a seat beside Kevin.

"Hey!" Kevin said.

"That didn't take long," Sara said as Ray took the end seat beside her.

"How you guys doing?" Ray asked.

"Awesome," Kevin said. "Mary is up $150 already."

Mary was the dealer.

"Changing 500," Mary said as Duncan dropped a fan of cash in front of her. She took the money and replaced it with chips. She did the same for Ray.

"Can I get you anything?" a waitress asked Ray from over his shoulder.

"I'd love a beer," Ray said. "How about a Canadian?"

"No problem, sir."

"One for all of us," Duncan said.

"Sounds good," Sara agreed.

All four stool-sitters put $25 onto the live squares in front of them. Ray threw another $25 on top to make his $50. "First hand's lucky," he said.

Mary started to deal the cards.

"You guys gamble a lot?" Kevin asked.

"A little," Duncan said. "We go to Vegas every couple of months."

"Where you guys from again?"

"Phoenix," Duncan said.

"Really? What you doing all the way up here?"

"Just traveling. We were on our way east and took a little detour."

"You like it so far?" Sara asked.

"Sure, what's not to like?"

Duncan busted. Kevin pushed. Sara and Ray each won with 20.

"I'm sure Vegas is much better," Sara said. "I really want to go."

"This is a pretty big casino," Ray said. "I wasn't expecting something like this. It's bigger than a lot of the places in Vegas."

"Why don't you take your girl to Vegas?" Duncan asked Kevin.

"Well, mostly 'cause it's too expensive, but also 'cause she's my sister."

"Your sister?"

"Don't we look alike?" Sara asked, leaning forward so Duncan could get a good look.

The waitress came with the drinks and Duncan insisted on taking care of the tab.

"So what do you guys do?" Ray asked.

"I have an excavating company, and she's still in school," Kevin said.

"What're you doing in school?"

"Finishing my master's in early childhood education," Sara said.

"Oh, so you're a smart one."

Sara smiled.

She won her hand again. Everyone else lost.

"Mary, you're killing me," Kevin said.

Instead of sipping his beer, Kevin drank down nearly half of it in one shot. "That's good," he said.

"So what do you guys do?" Sara asked.

"We owned a bar, but we just sold it," Duncan said.

"Right on," Kevin said. "What kind of bar?"

"It was a sports bar."

"Right on," Kevin said again.

Up in the room, Ruby was getting off the phone with her mom. She called to check in and to let her know that she was doing well, and that she was with friends.

"I'll call you when I get to Boston," Ruby said. "Okay. Love you too. Bye, mom."

Ruby took advantage of her first moments alone in days. She took off her bra from under her shirt and slung it onto the bed. She flicked on the radio on the bedside table and removed her jeans. The girl couldn't help but dance in front of the mirror to an unfamiliar but catchy tune. When the next song came on, by Huey Lewis and the News, Ruby found herself atop the bed, bouncing, dancing, and singing. She wasn't a big fan of Huey Lewis, but it didn't seem to matter – in that moment, she loved everything about him. Ruby opened one of the noticeably cooler beers and started a little party of her own. She even managed to eat one half of one of the roast beef sandwiches Ray had purchased at the gas station. It wasn't the tastiest treat, but it filled her stomach nonetheless.

Ruby wasn't trying to put on a show when she continued to dance in front of the window to Aretha Franklin. Nobody could see her, though the thought that someone might filled her with warm excitement. It was then that Ruby noticed that something was missing. The falls were there – spellbinding as ever – but Ruby had to consult the road map to decipher the absence of something else. Ruby dug into the plastic bag that Duncan brought up to the room. In it was the map along with the snacks and drinks they had collected along the way. Ruby unfolded it upon the bed and with her finger, pinpointed her location. She immediately felt a wave of disappointment. The Niagara Falls were to the right of where she was, which meant that Ruby – though delighted with the view – was in a room that was facing due east, and not to the west.

CHAPTER 14

A DEALER NAMED George replaced Mary and everyone at the table was enjoying his early losing streak. Kevin had won all his money back and was beginning to turn a profit; Ray and Duncan too, were building nice sized stacks. But the big winner at the table was Sara, who had collected more than triple the money she had when she sat down. At the end of George's second shoe, Mary returned, and along with the new dealer came a quiet, smiling Asian couple to the table.

"I think I'm gonna quit for now," Duncan said during the break.

"Really?" Kevin said.

"Yeah. I'm starting to get hungry and I want to use the gym for a bit. We've been playing for two hours."

"Maybe I'll join you."

"You should," Duncan encouraged.

"I could take a break too," Sara said.

"I'm staying," Ray said. "I'm gonna ride it out. Take one for the team."

Kevin, Sara, and Duncan waited in line at the cashier to exchange their chips. The line moved slowly because of a dispute between security and a clearly intoxicated man at one of the windows. After finally receiving their funds, the trio made their escape from the maze-like casino floor and arrived back on the twenty-first floor.

"You should meet Ruby," Duncan said.

"Who's that?" Kevin asked.

"Ruby's with us, she's in the room."

"Oh," Sara said. "There's three of you?"

Duncan slid the key card in and out and shoved the door open with his shoulder.

"Ruby?" He yelled into the openness.

Ruby was sitting in the chair by the window. Her hair was wet and she was wearing different clothes. Her hand was under her shirt and she seemed to be rubbing her side.

"What's up?" Duncan said.

"Nothing," Ruby said.

"This is Kevin, and Sara. They're staying next door."

"Hi," Ruby said pathetically.

"You okay?" Duncan asked.

"Yeah," Ruby said. "I think so."

"You sure?"

"I have a cramp or something," She clutched her side with her hand.

"Well we're going to go to the gym, I just wanted to introduce you."

"Sorry. I think I'm just not feeling well."

"That's okay," Sara said.

Ruby forced out a smile.

"I'm going to go get changed," said Kevin. "I'll meet you back here in five."

Kevin left the room but Sara remained. She sat on the end of the bed near to where Ruby was sitting.

"Is it your side?" Sara asked.

"It's right here," Ruby said. She placed her hand over the right side of her midsection. "The whole side hurts. I'm sure I'm fine, though."

Duncan began to prepare for his gym visit and left the two girls to themselves. When he returned a few minutes later, Ruby was hunched over in the chair and Sara was rubbing her back. "You sure you're okay?" he asked again.

Ruby nodded, but then shot up from her chair and darted into the washroom. Sara began to follow but stopped when she heard the unmistakable sound of vomiting. Kevin knocked on the door and Duncan ran to answer it.

"Ready?" Kevin asked.

Sara was perched outside the bathroom door. Ruby was still inside.

"Ruby's sick," Sara said.

"Rube," Duncan said to the door. "Can I do anything? You need water or something?"

"Shh," Ruby insisted. "I'm fine. Just...go away for a minute. Stop talking."

Duncan did as was asked. Kevin and Sara followed him over to the window. The sun had begun to set on the other side of the hotel and colored lights began to illuminate the falls.

Ruby emerged from the washroom, still tilted in pain.

"Here," Sara said, rushing to her aid.

Sara helped Ruby onto the bed where the injured girl laid curled up on her side.

"She doesn't look good," Duncan whispered to Kevin.

It wasn't long before Ruby once again darted into the washroom and slammed the door.

"You should take her to a doctor," Kevin said. "Could be her appendix or something."

Duncan changed out of his workout clothes and returned to the room. Ruby was back on the bed.

"I'm gonna take you to the hospital," Duncan said.

"No," Ruby said. "I just need to sleep."

"Ruby—"

"I'll be fine."

"We gotta get you checked."

"I don't have insurance."

Duncan took a seat on the side of her bed.

Sara joined Kevin by the window and the two began to whisper.

"You're boiling," Duncan said, touching Ruby's arm in an effort to comfort her. He placed his hand on her forehead to be sure.

"Okay," Kevin said taking something from Sara. "Come on, let's go to the hospital. Sara will go find Ray."

"No," Ruby said again.

"It's not a big deal," Kevin said. "Just trust me, okay?"

Ruby, too weak to fight it, allowed Duncan to lift her off the bed. Sara handed Kevin the wastebasket she had placed beside the bed to take for the journey. Sara followed them into the elevator and ran ahead once the doors opened on the main floor. When Duncan and Ruby reached the outside, an attendant had a cab door open and waiting.

They were off to the hospital.

Sara found Ray right where they had left him. His stack was significantly lower, but that was of no concern once Sara informed him of the news. Ray collected his chips and returned to the room with Sara without bothering to cash them out.

Once in the privacy of the room, Ray called Duncan's cell phone.

"She's just walking in there now with Kevin," Duncan said. "I'm waiting outside."

"What's wrong?"

"She's a thousand degrees and her side is hurting her."

"And she's throwing up?"

"Appendix maybe?" Duncan offered.

"Why aren't you in there with her?"

"It's all under control, Sara will explain."

"Okay," Ray said, a little confused. "Call me when you know what's up."

Ray hung up the phone. "I guess we just wait," he said.

Kevin came out of the emergency entrance about twenty minutes later. Duncan was sitting on a bench by the doors.

"They took her right in," he said.

"Everything work out?"

"No problems at all."

"What did they say?"

"Nothing much, they took her blood pressure and temperature and then rolled her in on a gurney."

"Dude," Duncan said, "I really appreciate this."

"No worries, bro," Kevin said. He took a smoke out of his pack and lit it up. "We can wait inside after, there's a baseball game on the TV."

Duncan waited for Kevin to finish his smoke and followed him through the sliding doors into the waiting area. As mentioned, there was a Blue Jays baseball game on TV. The waiting area was sporadically filled with all sorts of people. Duncan wasn't a hypochondriac, but was uncomfortable among the sick nonetheless.

Two full innings passed when a nurse came out to find Kevin.

"Mr. George?" The nurse said. "You can go in now, the doctor is with her."

Kevin and Duncan followed the nurse through two big silver doors. She pointed out a small stall separated from others of its kind by a long blue sheet on rollers. Ruby was sitting in a propped-up bed with a doctor beside her.

"Hey," Duncan said to Ruby. He put his hand on her leg.

"We put her on a drip with some Gravol, so she should be feeling a little better soon," the doctor said. "We're doing her blood work now to double check everything." She looked down at her clipboard. "But, it looks like you just have a case of food poisoning, my dear."

"So she'll be okay?" Duncan asked.

"Oh sure," the doctor said. "From what she tells me, it sounds like she's probably vomited most of it out of her system already. Doesn't she look better?"

"How you feeling?"

"Tired," Ruby said.

"That's the Gravol," the doctor said. "But the pain is gone?"

"Yeah," Ruby said quietly. "I'm still really nauseous though."

"That's normal. It'll pass soon. We're going to keep you here until your blood work comes back to rule everything else out, so sit tight, okay?"

"Thanks doc," Duncan said.

The young doctor smiled and moved on to a patient on the other side of the blue curtain.

"So that's good," Duncan said.

"I already feel a bit better," Ruby said lethargically. "I threw up like three more times."

"You don't have to stay, Kev," Duncan said. "Why don't you go back to the hotel and tell Ray and Sara what's up. I'll wait here with her."

"Okay, cool," Kevin said. "Feel better, Ruby."

"Thanks so much, Kevin," Ruby said.

"No worries. See you in a bit."

Kevin left Ruby and Duncan alone to wait for the results of her tests. Upon arriving back at the hotel, he found Sara and Ray in his room, sitting by the window and chatting.

"So?" Ray asked.

"Food poisoning," Kevin said." She'll be fine."

"Food poisoning? What did she eat?"

"She said she had a roast beef sandwich or something?"

"Fuck off," Ray said.

Ray returned to his room with Kevin and Sarah in tow. He opened the plastic bag and pulled out the one remaining sandwich.

"We got these at a gas station," Ray said, displaying the culprits' twin. He threw the sandwich in the trash. It hit the bottom with a thud.

"No wonder she got sick," Sara said.

"But she's okay now?"

"They're just waiting for her blood tests and they're sending her home," Kevin said.

"Okay, good."

Ray looked into the bag and whirled his hand around inside. "Wanna hear something weird?" he said.

"What?" Sarah asked.

"In spite of all that, I'm fuckin' starving. I can't stop thinking about food."

"Me too," Sarah laughed.

"Wanna grab something?" Kevin asked. "There's a good place downstairs."

"Yes, please," said Ray.

Kevin and Sara introduced Ray to *The Famous*, an art-deco diner in the lobby of the hotel. The crowd was almost as eclectic as the menu and the turnover at the tables was breaking records. It seemed as though more people came in and out of that place than the casino itself.

After they ate, Kevin retreated to the poker tables while Sara and Ray went up to Ray's room to wait for Ruby's return. Ray was in the middle of telling Sara the story of how he had managed to get arrested in Omaha when Duncan returned with Ruby. Ruby immediately flopped her weary body onto the bed and shut her eyes with a smile of relief.

"How you feeling?" Ray said, taking a seat on the bed beside her. Ruby just nodded.

"Tired more than anything," Duncan said.

"Okay. Then let's let her sleep."

"We can go to my room," Sara offered.

The three of them slunk out of the room, but not before Ray peeled back the blanket from the other bed and laid it over Ruby's body.

"How was the hospital?" Ray asked.

"Delightful," Duncan said.

"I'm sure."

"This belongs to you," Duncan said, handing Sara a card. "I hope your hospital visit wasn't too stressful."

"Thanks," Sara said.

"What's that all about?" Ray inquired.

"Ruby wasn't in the hospital," Duncan said.

"I don't get it."

"Sara was in the hospital."

Sara flashed the card that Duncan had just returned to her. It was an Ontario Health Card with Sara's name and photo on it.

"I still don't get it."

"She used my Health Card," Sara said, flashing it once again. "The government covers her visit. She looks enough like me, don't you think?"

"I guess they did," Duncan said. "It probably helped that your brother was the one with her, too."

"So it was free?" Ray asked.

"Hospital is always free."

"Even if you don't have insurance?"

"This is our insurance," Sara said.

"Hang on," Ray said, "I knew you guys had universal health care, but that means it's completely free?"

"Yeah. I mean we still pay for prescriptions and stuff, but that's what we get insurance for. But going to the hospital or the doctor or whatever, that's free. No bill."

"So if I have a heart attack and go to the hospital for bypass surgery…"

"Free."

"Broken arm?"

"Free."

"Boob job?"

"Why, what's wrong with them?" Sara said, sticking out her ample chest.

"Boob jobs aren't free," Duncan said.

"Elective surgery isn't free," said Sara. "It's fucking expensive."

"So if you have a sore throat and want to go to the doctor, he doesn't need to contact your insurance or anything?"

"Just gotta show them this card."

"And it's free?"

"What part are you having trouble with?" Duncan asked.

"That's fucked," Ray said. "I had to pay close to $2,000 for stitches and a cast."

"Well, it's not perfect," Sara said. "Sometimes you have to wait a while 'cause people abuse the system."

"What's a while?"

"My dad had to wait four hours to get a simple x-ray."

"But it was free?"

"It's part of our taxes."

"Okay," Duncan said, "You explain this to him, I'm gonna go get some dinner and play some poker."

"You want to just, I dunno, hang out or something?" Ray asked Sara.

"Sure."

Duncan left the room and did as he said. He stopped at the take out counter of *The Famous* and got a turkey club before putting his name down for a 10/20 poker seat. He saw Kevin at one of the other tables already involved in a game and shot him a nod. Kevin returned the stoic gesture.

Upstairs, Ray had retrieved a few beers from his room while Sara began rolling a joint for her and Ray to share.

CHAPTER 15

DUNCAN AND KEVIN returned to Kevin's room together nearly three hours later. Sara and Ray had polished most of the beer and had partaken in enough weed that the sweetish smell still lingered in the room. Ray and Sara had gotten quite familiar with each other, and their affinity was evident to the returnees.

"Have you guys been up here the whole time?" Kevin asked.

"Yeah, so?" Sara giggled.

"So nothing."

"How's Ruby?" Duncan asked.

"Last time I went in she was still asleep."

There was a knock at the door. Kevin went to answer it. He returned with a blanket-clad Ruby following behind.

"Speak of the devil," Ray said.

"How you feeling?" Duncan asked, putting his arm around the clearly worn girl.

"Better," Ruby said, looking to Kevin and Sara. "Thank you guys so much for helping."

"No problem," Sara said.

"You need anything?" Duncan asked.

"Water," Ruby said.

"There's a bottle in the mini-bar, just take it."

"I'm gonna go watch a movie or something."

Ray got up from bed and wrapped his arms around Ruby.

"Feel better," he said.

Ruby left as quietly as she came.

"So now what?" Ray asked.

"Well," Kevin said, looking at Duncan. "We were talking about going to the Downer."

"Are you serious?" Sara asked.

"We don't have to," Duncan said. "I'm not usually into that stuff anyway."

"I'd go," Ray said.

Sara lifted the phone and punched a few numbers.

"Hey," she said into the receiver. "It's Sara. What movie you gonna watch?"

The faint squeak of Ruby's voice could be heard through the phone.

"Want some company?"

"We don't have to go," Ray said.

"It's fine," Sara assured. "We'll be here tomorrow night too. I don't mind staying in. And we shouldn't leave Ruby alone."

"Now I feel bad," Ray said.

"Don't. I honestly would rather stay in."

"Who are you people?" Ray said, looking at Kevin and then back at Sara. "You're too fucking nice."

"Not really," Sara said. "Anyone would do the same."

"Alright," Kevin said. "Boys night out!"

The Sundowner was only about ten minutes away from the hotel. The cab ride over took the guys through the innards of Niagara Falls. A smattering of fast food restaurants and a couple outlet malls made it look like any other small city they were used to seeing.

Having been to some of the better establishments in Las Vegas, neither Ray nor Duncan was completely impressed by the exterior of *The Sundowner*. The inside wasn't anything to begin a poem about either. But once they took a seat at one of the horseshoe tables beside the main stage, their opinion began to change. As if they were a lone bulb of light in an otherwise blackened night, girls, like moths, encircled them. There must have been close to fifty dancing girls just within eyesight. Within five minutes of taking a seat, Kevin had one of the barely dressed ladies sitting in his lap. She wore a pink and purple bikini that was purposefully too small for her slender but buxom frame.

"What's your name?" she asked.

"Jim," said Kevin.

"I'm Monica."

"Hi Monica."

"So where are you guys from?"

"Buffalo."

"That's cool."

"Yes, it's very cool."

At the table beside them sat one of the only female club attendees. She was tall, skinny, and black haired, and accompanied by two strange looking men with big fuzzy beards. Her companions more resembled Hasidic Jews than strip club regulars, but nevertheless, they sipped their beers and took in the show.

A waitress came around and Duncan ordered three beers for the table. He was surprised by the expediency in which she returned. Duncan took care of the first round.

Over the loud speaker, the house DJ made his announcement.

"Please welcome to the main stage, Chrrrrristie," he said.

The black-haired girl at the next table perked up in her chair. She leaned forward and placed her hands on the edge of the stage as Christie came sauntering out in mountainous, silver high heels and a red bikini.

The girl let out a shrieking cheer as the song began and Christie's dance commenced.

Ray, sitting across from Kevin, couldn't hear the conversation between him and his new lap-laden friend, but he could clearly see that Kevin's hand was examining one of her breasts with his hand. More a friendly exploration than sexual gesture, Ray was still shocked by the seeming banality of it all.

"They're real," Kevin said to Duncan, who occupied the tip of the horseshoe between Kevin and Ray.

Monica lunged her ample chest forward in an obvious invitation for Duncan to confirm the assertion for himself. Hesitant at first, Duncan obliged.

As if that sight weren't enough to endear Ray to the club, he turned around to see that the black haired girl from the next table was now lying on her back on the stage with a bill clenched between her teeth. Christie, now topless, straddled the girl and removed the bill with her breasts. But it didn't end there. Once the bill was removed, Christie then lifted the T-shirt of the stage-crasher and licked her belly from navel to breast.

"This place is alright," Ray said.

"Right?" Kevin agreed.

After a few bodily caresses from Christie, the girl returned to her seat, flushed, and with a giant smile on her face.

"You're a fan," Ray said to her.

"I love her so much," the girl said. "I come at least once a week to see her."

"Really?"

"Yeah, I drive in from Lewiston. She's worth it."

Ray took a second look at the girl on the stage. She looked a bit older than most of the others working that night. Upon closer inspection, Ray couldn't help but notice that she and the black-haired looked somewhat similar. The black-haired girl was younger, most likely in her early twenties, but their facial features were alike in many ways.

"Isn't she perfect?" the girl said.

"She's something," Ray agreed.

"And she's really cool, too."

"So you know her?"

"Oh yeah, one time I drove her home. We're friends. Can you believe she has four kids?"

"What?"

"Yup. And she's the best mom."

"I bet," Ray said. The Hasidic Jews sitting at her table still seemed uninterested in the conversation.

"Hey," Kevin said. Ray turned his attention back to his compatriots. "I'll be back in a bit."

Like moving from business to first class on a plane, Kevin's new lap friend led him by the hand though a curtain at the side of the club. He disappeared into the dark abyss like so many others before him. Ray and Duncan didn't speak of it, but having seen what they'd seen already, they were both curious about what went on behind that curtain.

Neither Ray nor Duncan was a frequent patron of strip clubs. With complete access and open invitation, they often passed off similar opportunities in lieu of more fruitful endeavors. They both shared in the opinion that while strip clubs could be fun for events like a stag party once in a while, they much preferred attempting to close a deal with a civilian at a regular bar.

Christie finished her on-stage do-si-do and was cheered off stage by her biggest fan.

"Up next on the main stage," the DJ announced. "Siiiiiren."

Along with the main stage that ran down the middle of the fair-sized club, there were two other smaller stages on either side. Both were circular with a silver pole in the center; on stools, oglers surrounded both.

Kevin returned, alone, midway through Siren's performance.

"What happened?" Duncan asked. "She dump you already?"

"Are you kidding?" Kevin said. "She loves me."

After Siren came Trish. After Trish came Vixen. After Vixen, Kevin's new girlfriend, Monica, took to the stage. Throughout the on-stage rotation, girls came and went from the tabletop and the laps of Ray, Duncan, and Kevin. As soon as eye contact was made, the girl was reeled in. Some girls traveled about the club in pairs, some on their own. Some came from far off places and had accents, some claimed to be from the area. No matter what their story or made-up name, they all had an uncanny ability to make each of the guys feel like they were their one-and-only favorite in the whole place, ever.

In the spirit of carefree experience, and with the aid of more alcohol, both Ray and Duncan relented and disappeared from the table at varying times into the mystery that lay behind the purple velvet curtain. It started when a tall, leggy blonde with a fake tan and faker breasts took a liking to Duncan and Ray insisted she take him for a private dance. He handed her three twenty-dollar bills and sent her away with his friend. Upon his return, Duncan returned the favor, handing the same amount of money to a French Canadian brunette sitting on the table with her legs propped up on Ray's shoulders.

Ray's return to the table seemed to signal a turning point in the night. Kevin was on his sixth beer, Duncan had heard enough classic rock, and Ray's eyes wanted for something other than black light.

The trio entered the fresh air of the night and sucked it in as if they were coming up from underwater. There was a fair contingent of people loitering by the front doors, including a short line-up waiting to purchase a hot dog from the vendor situated there.

Kevin lit up a cigarette and handed one to Ray.

"I can't believe I'm saying this," said Duncan, "but I'm getting a hot dog. Anyone want?"

Kevin and Ray both dissented so Duncan joined the queue on his own.

Kevin and Ray were standing beside a throng of young men speaking a foreign language. Both tried to make out the origins but came up short. One of the guys then asked for a light from Kevin in English, which prompted Ray to satisfy his curiosity.

"What language are you guys speaking?" he asked.

"Oh, that's Italian," the young man said in perfect English. "They're here visiting."

"So you're from here then?"

"I'm from Hamilton, they're from Italy."

"What do they think of the Downer?" Kevin asked.

"They love it," he said. "In Italy they have places like this but the girls don't take off their pants. They're just topless."

"Really?"

"Yeah, but you can fuck them there. Here they just tease you for more money."

The doors to the front of the club swung open and a clearly distraught bloke clomped out. He was a large fellow, dressed in black with tattoo sleeves. One of the bouncers took position at the door.

"Just relax, Tony," the bouncer said.

"Fuck you D," the large man replied. "You saw what happened, he put his hands on me."

"I didn't see anything. But you know if you start trouble you have to go."

"I didn't start shit!"

"Tony—"

A second man pushed past the bouncer and stood facing the man the bouncer called Tony.

"This fucker started shit," Tony said. "He put his hands on me."

"Dude," the second guy said. "It's over. It was a misunderstanding."

"Fuck you, buddy."

"Asshole," the second guy said as he turned away.

Tony lunged at the man, grabbing his neck and putting him in a headlock. The crowd dispersed and gave them room, including Kevin, Ray, and the Italian contingent.

The bouncer got involved and the direction of the entangled lump of testosterone made a drastic shift in momentum and the three took out two onlookers like bowling pins. One of the onlookers was Ray. Kevin had jumped out of the way; Duncan didn't even move. He remained beside his friend and looked down at him while calmly chewing on his hotdog. The collision had jarred loose the original captive, leaving only the bouncer clutching Tony.

"It's over!" the bouncer yelled. "Tony, it's over!"

One of the newly arrived bouncers whispered a few quiet words in Tony's ear, and helped the now calmer combatant into a cab and saw him off. The man Tony had in a headlock was allowed back into the club with a warning, and the crowd outside was restored to a normal buzz.

"Well, that happened," Duncan said, taking another bite of his hotdog.

"Funny," Ray said, brushing dust off his pants into a disseminating cloud.

"Now what?" Duncan asked.

"That was fucked," Kevin said. "I've never seen a fight here before."

"Really?" Duncan said. "How many times you been here?"

"I been coming here since I was seventeen."

"Wanna go back and check on the girls?" Ray asked.

"Sure," Kevin said.

"I may hit the poker tables," Duncan said.

"I might join you."

They took the quick cab ride back to the hotel where Duncan and Kevin disappeared into the belly of the casino and were swallowed up by the crowd. Ray went back to the room to see how Ruby was feeling.

Along with two sleeping girls, Ray found a "thank you for ordering" TV screen and a couple joints in a makeshift ashtray by the window. He didn't want to wake the pair so he began to make his way from the bedroom as quietly as he came in. Sara whispered his name and Ray turned. The slightly disheveled girl tiptoed over and tugged him from the room so not to wake Ruby.

"How's she feeling?" Ray asked.

"Much better. She was even getting a bit of an appetite back."

"When did you guys fall asleep?"

"No idea," Sara admitted. "Ruby was out before me though, I know that for sure. Where's Kev?"

"They're playing poker."

"Let's go do something."

"Okay, like what?"

"We'll think of something."

CHAPTER 16

THE MORNING SUN was peering through the open drapes when Ray returned to the room. He crept in and slid into bed with Ruby, who was on top of the sheets with the blanket from Duncan's bed.

"Hey," Ruby whispered.

"Hey," Ray returned.

"What time is it?"

"Almost ten. How you feeling?"

"Fine, I think," Ruby propped herself up on her elbows and looked around the room. "Yeah, better. I'm hungry."

"Shut up, you two," Duncan grumbled. "And close the drapes."

Ruby got up out of bed and disappeared into the washroom. She was in there long enough for both Ray and Duncan to fall back asleep before she returned. When she did, she crept over to the big window and took her seat overlooking the falls. The sun blazed in the cloudless sky, and though Duncan requested the shades be drawn, Ruby ignored the plea and instead made entertainment of the view.

Ruby eventually escaped back into the bathroom and into the soothing confines of a warm shower. When she came out, she was feeling even better. The warm water and fragrant soap aided in her recovery from a long but necessary sleep. Her stomach had reached the point where it was so blatantly empty that it felt like it was beginning to feed on the rest of her body. She dressed in silence and left the room on her own to look for somewhere to eat in the upscale hotel lobby.

When she returned, satiated by a meal of toast, tea, and oranges wedges from a diner downstairs, she resolved to wake the boys. For as much as Ruby enjoyed the falls, she was ready to leave Niagara behind her.

Ray was easier to rouse; Duncan was brazenly cantankerous.

"It's almost noon," Ruby pleaded. "We have to get out of the room."

"We need to do laundry," Ray said, smelling the clothes from his bag. "I'm out of underwear."

"I ran out yesterday," Duncan said, his head still on a pillow.

Ray threw his grubby shirt to the ground. "There are stores in the lobby, let's go buy some new shit."

The notion of new clothes and fresh underwear was to Duncan like a slap in the face. The crankiness seemed to be instantly purged from his system and he rolled off the bed and to his feet.

After packing their bags, all three made for the elevators. Before leaving the floor, they knocked on the door of their neighbors and new friends, but Kevin and Sara didn't answer. Duncan wrote a short letter and included each of their phone numbers and email addresses. Ruby left a special note for Sara, and refused to let the guys see it before sliding it under the door.

The mall-like section of the casino resort wasn't overly extensive, but would suit the needs of the trio just fine. Ruby was still a little weak from her past day's ordeal, but she too perked up once the shopping began. They moved from store to store as a unit.

Ray and Duncan were only interested in socks and underwear and comfortable things like T-shirts and jeans. Ruby, alternatively, seemed engaged by things like fashion, price, and usage occasions.

"I think the fundamental difference between men and women becomes painfully obvious when shopping," Ray said, as he and Duncan stood motionless against a wall in a store. It took only ten minutes for the boys to pick up clean under-things. Ruby's adventure had already tacked on thirty extra minutes to the outing and she had only yet purchased of what she had called "cute" underwear.

"What's that supposed to mean?" Ruby said, overhearing Ray's comment from inside a dressing room.

"When guys go shopping they look for things they can wear as often as possible, like a uniform. Chicks like to buy things to wear that one perfect time."

"That's ridiculous."

"Tell me you don't think about where and when you're going to wear each thing you're looking at right now. You're already creating outfit ideas in your head."

"So? That's just smart planning. Why should I buy something I won't wear?"

Duncan was staying out of the quarrel, though he was enjoying the exchange.

"I'm just saying," Ray pleaded, "there's a difference between how guys and girls shop for clothes. You know why they put benches in malls, right? It's not for picnics. They even put chairs in women's stores for guys that have to follow them around all day. Guys go in, get what they need, and get out. Simple."

"Are you in a hurry, Ray?" Ruby asked calmly.

"No, but–"

"What do you think of this?"

Ruby emerged from the dressing room wearing an extra thin white tank top with no bra, and a sample of her new, white cotton underwear. Ray said nothing. He looked, but he said nothing. The view left him speechless. Even Duncan's eyes popped briefly from his sockets. Ruby was on display.

The young seductress was thereafter able to shop without hassle from Ray for as long as she pleased.

Back in the car, Ray took the first stretch of the quiet drive. The New York leg of the trip proved mostly uneventful, though Ruby took her first turn driving between Rochester and Albany. Duncan slept most of the way in the back seat.

It was just before dinnertime that they crossed the border into Massachusetts, and approaching 8 p.m. they finally reached their destination with Duncan back behind the wheel.

Ray and Duncan had made it to Boston.

They were in a different car, with an extra body, and had arrived days later than they had originally planned, but they were nevertheless relieved to have the driving behind them.

Ray let out a victorious shout as they drove past the sign marking Boston's city limits. Ruby clapped and Duncan rapped on the wheel. The Fifth Avenue had treated them well, perhaps even better than the luxurious but cramped BMW.

"Now what?" Ray laughed.

"I guess we find a place to stay," Duncan said.

"Do we have any idea where Franklin is?"

"Yes and no. We have an address but hell if I know what part of town it's in."

Duncan had plugged their ultimate destination into the GPS in the BMW. Without the car, they were left with only a jotted address on a scrap of paper and no idea how to navigate the streets of Boston.

"No sense in trying to find him tonight," Ray said. "Follow the lights. Let's find a hotel."

Duncan stayed on the I-90 and followed the signs that led them downtown.

"How much of the 4K do we have left?" Duncan asked.

"About twelve hundred," Ruby said, calculating the sum in her head.

"Then let's find a nice place to stay."

Stopping for gas in the downtown core, Ray approached a man filling up a black Porsche. The man was keen and courteous and directed Ray to the nearby Boston Common area where he would find both the Hyatt Regency and The Ritz-Carlton Hotel.

The only reason the crew ended up at the Hyatt was because it was the first one they came upon. The man's directions weren't perfect, but nevertheless, lodgings for the night were easily procured.

"This is exciting," Ruby said, looking out on the city from their room. They were only on the sixth floor but she could see far down the busy street below. "I'm not used to big cities."

"I need some exercise," Duncan said. "I'm going down to the gym."

"Hurry up, we'll go for dinner when you get back," Ray said.

Duncan hustled into a pair of shorts and left the room with nothing more to say. Ray flicked on the TV and left it on a re-run of *The Simpsons* he had seen ten times before. When the cartoon ended, Ray argued with Ruby about what channel they should next choose. Ray wasn't content to leave it on just anything, and Ruby couldn't decide one way or the other. In the end, Ray shut off the TV and threw the remote across the room. Ruby, in an attempt to pacify her frustrated roommate, came over to the bed on which he lay and cuddled up to him.

It was a pleasant surprise for Ray, and one that served its intended purpose. The pair lay there, quietly.

"I had the weirdest dreams last night," Ruby finally said, with Ray's arms around her.

"I'm sure," Ray said. "Do you remember any?"

"Parts. But they were so fucked up."

"Do you ever have any recurring dreams?" he asked.

"Since I was a kid I've had this dream where I'm running but not going anywhere. You know what I mean? Like, my legs are going but it's like I'm running into the wind or something 'cause I'm not moving forward. I'm pushing and pushing but staying in the same spot. I know in the dream that I'm in a hurry to get somewhere. I never know where it is, I just know I can never get there. That happens a lot, actually."

"My recurring dream is always different, but the situation is the same. I'm trying to get to school – to class or whatever – and I can never remember where I'm supposed to go. I'm confused about the day, or the location of the class, or I forget what classes I'm taking. It's always high school, too, which is weird, 'cause in the dream I know that I've already been to college."

"That is weird."

"I can't explain it properly."

"Me either," Ruby said, "Let's talk about something else."

"Like what?" Ray asked.

"Like where you slept last night?"

"What?" Ray chuckled.

"What do you mean, *what*?"

"I don't know what you mean."

Ruby tilted her head to face Ray, and perhaps accidently, came nose-to-nose with him. Ruby instantly forgot what she was hoping to say. They held their position in silence for longer than was typical for a friendly situation. Neither could say who made the first movement, but after a few more silent moments, they began to kiss. Ruby pressed her body onto Ray's. Ray clutched the slender girl and pulled her tightly up against him.

"Yo," Duncan said, entering in the room.

Ruby and Ray, though not ashamed, instinctively separated. Duncan was at the front door and could still not see the pair.

"I'm gonna take a quick one, then we can go for food," Duncan said, poking his head around the corner.

Ruby remained cuddled close to Ray, but it was nothing that Duncan hadn't seen before so he wasn't surprised and reacted as such.

Duncan got into the shower. Ruby rolled away from Ray and got up off the bed in one single motion. "I should get changed if we're going out," she said.

"Me too," Ray agreed.

The pair didn't mention what had happened before Duncan walked in, but they weren't trying to avoid it either. Neither was flustered, or embarrassed, or felt the least bit awkward. They were just going about their business as if their encounter was not a surprising occurrence.

"I could go for some pasta," Duncan said, emerging from the steamy washroom.

Ray and Ruby had both changed into new clothes they had purchased that morning.

"We can send our laundry out through the hotel," Duncan said. "I want my shit cleaned."

Duncan searched for a laundry bag that sometimes hid in the closets of a hotel room. He found one, but it was too small to fit all of their dirty garments. "We'll need to get more than this," he said.

"I'll run down to the lobby," Ray offered.

"Ask them about restaurants," Duncan said.

"Italian," Ruby added.

Ruby filled the bag Duncan had found with her things and left it near the front to take out when they left. Ray returned soon thereafter with two more bags; he threw one to Duncan and began to fill the other.

"Did you ask about restaurants?" Duncan asked.

"Yeah. One of the girls said to go to a place called Bina. She said it's really good. I got directions."

"Okay. Laundry's ready."

The long and lingering dinner made for an ideal conclusion to the extensive road trip. Not normally drinkers of wine, Duncan, Ray, and Ruby took the advice of their server and indulged in more than one bottle of the house's recommended red. They had, after all, hundreds of dollars to blow through from Duncan's original pot of four thousand. The generous dinner didn't exhaust the total of the remaining funds, but it did help to dwindle the sum.

The one block walk home did nothing to relieve their swollen bellies, nor the wobbling effects of the alcohol. Perhaps ill advised to try and keep up with her tablemates, the wine hit the still-recovering Ruby the hardest. Upon her return to the hotel, she was able to do little more than fight the spin of the room.

Ray turned on Sports Center and caught up on information once much more critical. Ruby fell asleep somewhere between baseball highlights and NHL training camp updates. Once their bodies better processed the abundance of food, Ray and Duncan even managed to grow enough of a thirst to visit the hotel bar and partake in a beer before calling it a night.

"Tomorrow we find Franklin," Duncan said, sitting on a barstool beside Ray.

The bar was mostly empty, save for one table of two far away from the pair.

"You think it will be that easy?"

"Don't know. But at least we have a place to start."

"What's the hurry?" Ray asked, sipping his pint.

"Why not get it over with? No sense in drawing it out. I'm sure Rico is waiting to hear from us anyway, we're a few days behind."

"We have to find a place to stay, too. If we're going to hang out here for a while there's no sense in wasting money on a hotel."

"I guess," said Duncan. "But once we find Franklin, there's really nothing keeping us in Boston, is there?"

"Not really," Ray said, though his thoughts floated elsewhere.

Duncan tilted his glass and clanked it against Ray's.

PART II

CHAPTER 17

RUBY AWOKE EARLY the next morning. She was feeling surprisingly good, even invigorated by the absence of any residual effects of her Niagara Falls ordeal. Not wanting to wake the boys, Ruby sidled out from under Ray's timid grasp and dressed herself in silence. She took a seat on the couch in the small adjoining room and pulled out her cell phone. Her first text was to her mother, a short note to inform her of her arrival in Boston. Her second was much longer. It was a hello and heartfelt thank you to Sara George. Sara responded almost immediately, which struck off a back and forth between the girls. Sara was still in Niagara and mentioned her sorrow for not being in her room to wish her new friends goodbye and good luck.

Ray was next to wake. He stumbled to the shower with only a short wave to acknowledge Ruby. He stayed in the shower long enough for Duncan to get up, get dressed, and order room service for all. The trio sat around a small table and shared in a hearty morning meal.

It was approaching noon when Ray and Duncan ventured out. Ruby stayed behind to explore the city, as she put it, which was a serendipitous turn for Ray and Duncan. It's not that they didn't like having Ruby around – they had gotten both used to and comfortable with it – but for this particular piece of business it was better that she wasn't there. Their first and only stop was a bar called O'Keefe's.

They entered the bar.

O'Keefe's was situated at the corner of a two story city block. It was a traditional Irish pub in many ways, one of them being that it looked like it hadn't been updated since the potato famine. It was dark and dank and wooden, like the hull of an old ship. It smelled of things like mold and old beer. The patrons on that particular day looked as natural as the pictures on the walls. They were worn and ragged and thrown together from bits and pieces that were perhaps once finer. They sat with their heads in their beers or mumbling to one another as they tried to avoid the shards of sunlight that stabbed through the darkened windows.

If one thing looked out of place at O'Keefe's, it was the woman behind the bar serving drinks. She was younger than the average patron and looked as though she was the only person in the establishment with a smile on her face. Tall and thin with curly red hair, she introduced herself with a nod – her name was Charlene.

"Two pints, please, Charlene," Ray said.

Charlene poured the pints from the tap to which Ray had pointed.

"You guys haven't been in here before," she said.

"That's true," Ray said. "We're new in the neighborhood."

Ray hadn't planned on broaching the subject so early into the visit. "Actually, a friend of ours told us about it," he said.

"Oh, yeah? Who's that? Would I know him?"

"Don't know. Do you know Willy?"

Charlene placed the pints down on the bar in front of Duncan and Ray.

"Can't say I know anyone named Willy," Charlene said.

"Oh."

"What was Willy's friend's name?" Duncan said, feigning concentration.

"Oh yeah," Ray said. "What was his name?"

"Franklin?"

"Franklin," Ray said. "That's it."

"Oh, Franky?" Charlene said, emptying out the small glass washer behind the bar.

"Rice, I think his last name was," Duncan added.

"Okay. You're talking about Franky and Bill."

"Bill?" Ray asked.

"If you're talking about Franky Rice, you're talking about Bill."

"Bill. Yes. That's right. But we know him as Willy."

"And how did you say you knew them again?" Charlene asked.

"We've known Willy, Bill, for years," Ray said.

"Uh huh," Charlene said. "Well you guys don't look like Bill's typical friends."

"Bill's dead you know," a voice from down the bar said.

"Yeah, we know," Ray said. "We heard. We were in Vegas with some of Bill's other friends. They told us he passed away."

The man who informed them of Bill's demise shuffled a few seats down the bar and took a seat beside Ray and Duncan. He was an older man and his age showed heavy on his face. "And you know Franky?" the man asked.

Ray nodded.

"He hasn't been in for a while," Charlene interrupted.

"Oh," Ray said with a smile. "Oh well."

Ray put out his hand to the man that came to sit with them. "Ray," he said. "This is Duncan."

"Terry," the man said, shaking Ray's hand.

169

"Hi Terry."

Charlene moved her way down the bar to attend to a quiet man sitting in a shadowy corner.

"So you said you know Bill from Las Vegas?" Terry asked.

"That's right."

Ray took a sip from his beer.

"You guys here tooooo…"

"To what?" Ray asked.

"You know," Terry said, wiggling his hand about. "Take over where he left off."

"You know Terry," Ray said, "I'm not really sure what you mean."

"Okay," Terry said, chugging his beer. "Never mind. Forget I said it."

"You guys live in Vegas?" Charlene asked, rejoining the conversation.

"No," Duncan said. "We're from Arizona."

"What brings you in here?"

"We're on vacation," Duncan said.

"Well don't let this guy put you off," Charlene said, thumbing at Terry. "Most of our customers are decent folks."

"Very funny," Terry said.

"Where is Franky, anyway?" Charlene asked Terry.

"Fuck if I know. Now that Bill's gone, doubt we'll see him in here again."

"They were close?" Ray asked.

"You could say that," Terry said with a chuckle.

"They were close," Charlene said.

"Close, ha!" Terry said.

"Am I missing something?" Ray asked.

"Those two were f–"

"Terry," Charlene interrupted. "You don't know that."

"Oh, I know Charlene. I know."

Duncan and Ray exchanged a glance.

"Are you saying that Bill and Frank were...you know?" Ray said.

"As the day is long," Terry said. "They'd never admit it, but those two were queer together, sure. Queer as two fifty-cent pieces. Don't get me wrong now, I got no problem with the gays, fuck if I care what they do."

"Wow," Ray said. "I never would have guessed."

"That Terry?" a voice shouted from behind.

"Who's askin'?" Terry shouted back, turning in his seat and looking to the man walking into the bar.

"That's none of your fucking business, old man," the short, rotund man said as he approached the bar.

"Hi Vinny," Charlene said.

Vinny sat down beside Terry at the bar and graciously accepted a pint from Charlene.

"Why you sittin' at this end T?" Vinny asked.

"Just talking to these guys here," Terry said. "That's Ray and that's...I forgot your name."

"Duncan," Duncan said.

"Friends of Bill," Terry added.

"You don't say," Vinny quipped. "Well that fat bastard's dead."

"We know," Ray said.

"Good guy, Bill," Vinny said, licking beer foam from his upper lip. "How you know him?"

"They know him from Vegas," Terry said.

"You guys know Franky, too?"

"Not well," Ray said.

"Frank doesn't come in here no more, does he?" Vinny said to Terry, as if he were just coming upon the realization himself.

"Nope," Terry said.

"Uh uh," Charlene agreed.

"How long's it been? Haven't seen Franky in, what? Two, three weeks?" Vinny said. "You two want a shot? First one's on me."

"Um, sure," Ray said. "Why not."

"What we drinking?" Duncan asked.

"Jager," Charlene said.

"Yuuuuup!" Vinny shouted.

"Always Jager," Charlene said, pouring four shots.

"And one for you, sweetheart," Vinny said.

"Not this early, hun."

"Oh come on now, Char," Terry said.

"Yeah Char," Ray added.

The four sitting at the bar goaded the female bartender until she relented and joined them in a shot of Jagermeister.

"Why doesn't anyone go by to check on Frank? Or call him?" Duncan asked.

"'Cause no one knows where he lives," Terry said.

"Bill did," Vinny laughed. "You can try and ask him."

"Not funny, Vinny," Charlene said. "And someone should call Franky. He must live nearby, never took him more than a minute to get here."

"Hey, put the Sox game on," Vinny ordered.

"They're playing tonight," a voice yelled from behind. "Afternoon game's tomorrow."

"Who is that? Mikey?" Vinny said, turning on his stool.

"Yeah."

"You mother fucker. You laid off again?"

"Not yet."

It was easy to say that Ray and Duncan liked O'Keefe's right away. They were seduced by the lack of pretention, and by the blue-collar attitude that seemed to permeate even the stagnant air. Ray and Duncan always considered themselves to be of blue collar standing, even if through other's eyes their shirts might have had a lighter hue. They never got on with the richer set, and didn't aspire to join them. Throughout their lives, with money or without, Ray and Duncan better suited the proletariat.

Though Frank had somewhat disappeared from O'Keefe's, the guys had much more to go on. Finding Frank sitting atop a stool on first attempt to find him would have been a pleasure, but neither expected as much. Without discussing it, both knew that to find a man called Franklin Rice within a one or two mile radius of the bar couldn't be terribly difficult.

"You guys in town on business?" Vinny asked.

"Nope," Ray said. "All pleasure."

"Then what the hell you doing in this place?"

Vinny laughed at his own joke.

"Just enjoying the company."

"Oh, all right then. Next rounds' on you."

"No problem," Ray agreed.

"Oh, generous. You sure you're friends of Bill?"

"Why? Bill was tight?"

"Never spent a dime," Terry said. "Must have died a millionaire."

"Didn't drink much either," Vinny added. "Smart though. Smart like a whip."

Ray took a swig of his beer and turned to Duncan.

"Want to get something to eat?" he asked quietly.

"Here?"

"Yeah."

"You kidding?"

"No. Why?"

"Ray," Duncan said, leaning in closer to his friend. "I'm pretty sure even the cockroaches would order for delivery."

CHAPTER 18

LATER IN THE day, Ray and Duncan took their leave of O'Keefe's and counted the visit a success on their path to locating Franklin and the money he owed Rico. Duncan returned to the hotel. Ray had other plans.

Ray sat by the window in a Starbucks downtown and watched the people as they exited a building across the street. The building had to be fifty stories, if not more, and would have been more impressive if not for the hundred-story building that towered beside it, dwarfing the otherwise massive structure. Most of the people that littered the street were dressed in business suits – even the women. It was approaching 6 p.m. and the street was abundantly busy. Ray often had to maneuver his head around crowds to maintain a proper view.

Not normally a coffee drinker, Ray decided to be adventurous and tried his luck with a similar order to that of the man in front of him. He was overly surprised by the hefty price tag on the warm cup of water and beans, but paid it without a word.

Ray waited. Ray watched.

A woman exited the building across the street. A man followed her out; Ray got up from his stool but sat back down before his second foot hit the floor. It wasn't the person he was looking for.

His phone buzzed and he yanked it from his pocket. It was Duncan. Ruby had returned to the hotel and they were wondering if Ray would soon be back. Ray sent a quick text reply and returned his phone to the depths of his pocket.

People continued to pour from the big grey building. Ray sipped his coffee. A small group came out of the revolving door one at a time and convened beside the curb for a few parting words.

Ray's coffee remained on the counter in Starbucks, but he had vanished from the establishment in haste. The group across the street shared their last words and broke off in various directions. One of them got into a cab, two walked one way down the street, and one walked the other way, alone. Ray dodged his way through the traffic and made it to the other side of the street unharmed. He began to follow the lone walker.

About a block down the city street, a traffic light turned red halting the progress of his pursuee. Ray maintained his pace and soon came face-to-back with his target.

"Funny thing, these lights," he said. "Why does it seem like sometimes everything is working against you?" It sounded like a mundane observation, but in fact, it was a comment that would sound familiar to at least one other person.

The person Ray was tailing turned abruptly, eyes opened wide.

"It's you," the girl said.

"Hi Ashley."

When the light turned green, everyone but the two of them began to cross. It's often easy to decipher someone's initial reaction to surprise solely by the way their face does or does not contort. On this particular occasion, Ray couldn't make out a clear response.

"Surprise?" he said, in an attempt to be charming.

Ashley shook off her astonishment and embraced Ray as if it were an overdue reaction.

"What are you doing here?" she asked, standing on her toes, her chin resting on his shoulder.

"What," Ray said, letting her go. "Can't a guy just drop by?"

"Ray. A few nights ago you were in a jail cell in Nebraska. I just…I can't believe you're here."

"Yeah, well…"

The two of them took a silent moment to take each other in. Ashley looked great. Her hair was longer than Ray remembered, and in her sharp business attire she fit well with the other elite-looking figures on the sidewalk. Her black leather bag, surely filled with briefs and legal documents, hung from her hand like a natural accessory. Ashley broke the gaze and looked at her watch.

"You want to go get a drink or something?" she asked. "I have some time."

"Yeah. Sure."

Ashley led Ray to a small cocktail bar in the lobby of a hotel only a short walk away. They sat down at a secluded two-person table and were immediately greeted by a server in a black vest. Ashley ordered a Vodka and soda; Ray did the same.

"So really," Ashley said. "What are you doing here?"

"You're not happy to see me?"

"I didn't say that."

"I know, I was kidding."

"So then?"

"I left Phoenix."

"What do you mean you left Phoenix?"

"For good. I left Phoenix for good."

"I don't understand."

"It was time to move on. Me and Duncan left Phoenix and started driving."

"And you ended up here."

"How's work?"

"So you just started driving with no place to go?"

"Something like that."

"Ray, that doesn't add up. I know you better than that. And, I know Duncan, too. That doesn't sound like him."

"Okay, we came here for a reason. But it's not the reason we left Phoenix."

"What's the reason you came?"

"Wow, you're going right for it, aren't you counselor?"

"Ray."

"Why are you turning this into an interrogation?"

"I'm not interrogating you. But you show up outside my work, out of nowhere, unannounced, and yes, I'm happy to see you, but it's just a little out of the ordinary. Don't you think?"

"I was in the area and I wanted to say hi. Why is that so strange?"

"*Ray.*"

"*Ashley.*"

The waiter showed up with the drinks. He placed them on the table in between the two now-silent patrons.

"I just wanted to have a normal conversation," Ray said, finally breaking the silence.

"We are," Ashley said.

"Yeah, right."

"So it's my fault? I'm the bad guy?"

"No one's the bad guy, Ashley. Why does there have to be a bad guy?"

"You know what, I can't do this now," Ashley said. She got up from her chair and grabbed her bag.

"Where're you going?"

Visibly upset, Ashley just looked at Ray.

"Sit down," Ray said. "Ashley. Sit down. Please."

"I can't," Ashley said.

Ashley stormed off.

Ray got up and followed her out of the hotel. Ashley was walking quickly enough that Ray didn't catch up to her until they were both out on the street again.

"Stop," Ray said, still a few paces behind.

Ashley kept walking.

"Ashley, stop!"

Ashley stopped in her tracks. Ray circled around her and the two came face to face. There were tears forming in Ashley's eyes. "Why did you come here?" she asked. "Don't give me one of your bullshit answers. Why did you come?"

"I came here for you," Ray said.

Ashley dropped her bag to the ground and threw her arms around Ray. Onlookers passed by as the pair stood on the city street, kissing like long lost lovers.

Ashley opened the door to her apartment. Ray didn't wait until they were completely inside before attacking her lips once again. The two clumsily made their way from the front door to the bedroom, bumping and smacking into furniture along the way. Once in the bedroom, they started to tear clothing from one another with unmitigated fervor. Ray and Ashley crawled onto the bed. They made love for the first time in more than two years – their longest span apart since the day they met.

"How did you find me?" Ashley said, lying on her back in bed, her warm body covered only by a thin white bed sheet. Their love making session robbed her of the energy to move more than her lips.

"It wasn't hard," Ray said. "There aren't many lawyers in the city named Ashley Dupree."

"Are you staying?"

"In Boston? For now."

Ashley paused. "Ray," she said.

"Yeah?"

Ray tilted his head and met Ashley's eyes.

"We left without paying for our drinks."

CHAPTER 19

WHEN RAY RETURNED to the hotel, he mentioned nothing to Ruby and Duncan of his encounter with Ashley. As far as they knew, he was simply out exploring the town, much as Ruby had done. At least it was not a lie, simply an omission of the entire truth.

The three of them went for a bite to eat and were coerced by Ruby to catch a late movie. When they got back to the room, all three fell into bed with equal amounts of gusto.

As usual, Ray and Ruby shared a bed. For the first time since the pair had met, Ray's arm was nowhere near Ruby when they awoke the following morning. Ruby took notice of the absence first. She took Ray's arm and placed it across her waist and tried to fall back asleep.

"You guys ready?" Duncan said, emerging from the washroom.

"What time is it?" Ray asked.

"Let's go, lovebirds."

Ray and Ruby eventually rolled out of bed and got ready. Duncan already had a plan for the day.

The Fifth Avenue pulled up alongside the curb of a street in Somerville. Duncan and Ray were in the front seat. Ruby was in the back.

"Is that it?" Ruby asked.

Duncan nodded. "That's the one," he said, lifting his chin to a white house on the other side of the street. "Stay here."

Duncan got out of the car and approached the old, white, colonial home. He looked around to see if anyone was approaching. The street wasn't vacant, but there was nothing to rouse concern.

Duncan knocked on the door of the house.

There was no answer.

He knocked again.

Again, no answer.

Duncan gave it a few minutes before he leaned over the banister and peered through the partially uncovered window.

Seeing nothing to his liking, Duncan returned to the car and got in. "Not home," he said. Duncan's attention was still focused on the white, two-story house across the street. "I guess we should wait a bit," he said.

"Look," Ray said, peering into the passenger's side mirror. "Check that out."

Duncan turned his head and looked out the back. Ray pointed out a lawn sign a few houses behind the car; the words "FOR RENT" were printed on each side.

Duncan paid it little mind.

After two hours of waiting, Ray's stomach made an audible plea, and the boredom on Ruby's face seemed almost as loud. Duncan relented and turned the key in the ignition.

They found a local restaurant and headed inside for a well-deserved meal. Ruby's curiosity would no longer hold and she grilled the guys about Franklin, and about the house they had just waited outside. Duncan and Ray saw no reason to keep her in the dark on the details any longer.

"He's probably at work," Ray said across the table. He was stuffing a sandwich into his face.

"Maybe," Duncan said.

"Then we still need to kill a few more hours."

"We should talk about what's next," Duncan said.

"What do you mean?"

"After we find Frank. What comes next?"

"I'm going to look for a job," Ruby said. "I'm happy to stay here for a while."

"I could stay," Ray shrugged.

"You gonna look for a job too, Ray?" Duncan asked.

"I haven't figured that part out yet."

"I'm not sure there's much you can do with a degree in philosophy and zero work experience."

"Then I'll do my own thing. And you're in the same position, Dun. What're *you* gonna do?"

"Find Frank."

"I couldn't see either of you working a regular job," Ruby said.

"Why not?" Ray asked.

"I just couldn't. I dunno. You seem too…independent."

"And you're not?"

"Not like you guys. Don't forget, I waited tables for years. I know how to work for someone. It's not as easy as you think. You have to swallow your pride a lot when you have a boss. I just can't see you guys doing it, that's all."

"If I didn't know any better I'd say she was insulting us, Dun."

"It's not an insult, Ray."

"I know," Ray said, leaning to the side and giving Ruby a playful shoulder bump.

"If we're going to stay, we'll need to find a place for a while," Duncan said, giving in to the obvious popular sentiment. "I like the hotel and all but we're wasting cash by the day there."

"What are we looking for?" Ray asked. "House? Apartment?"

Ray looked down at Ruby whose head was resting on his shoulder.

"Am I being invited to stay with you guys?" she asked.

"You have any better offers?"

"I'm serious. I didn't know if I was part of your plan. I can find my own place you know."

"It's up to you," Duncan said. "You're welcome to stay with us if you want."

Ruby sat up in her seat and looked at Ray. Ray nodded in agreement.

"Okay," she said, happily.

"What about that place on Frank's street?"

"I don't think that's a good idea," said Duncan.

"It's worth a look. What's the difference?"

"I want to go by Frank's again after we eat," Duncan said. "But we should grab a paper or get online and start looking for a place if we're going to stay for a bit."

"Fuck the paper," Ray said. "We need a computer. I'm tired of checking e-mail on my phone."

Duncan relented and after lunch the trio found an Apple Store not far from Somerville near the MIT campus. It was Ruby's first time in a store of its kind. She was impressed and excited by all the cool gadgetry she had only previously seen on TV. Duncan picked up a MacBook Pro and Ray decided that Ruby needed an iPod. It was his gift to her for no other reason than the minor twinge of guilt he felt for what had happened the day before with Ashley.

With time still to spare, Ray suggested that he and Duncan introduce Ruby to yet another new Boston experience. They arrived to O'Keefe's with a warm welcome from both Charlene and Terry, who looked like he hadn't moved since they left him.

Terry looked a little more somber than he had the day before. It was later in the day, which meant he had been drinking for longer, but there was something in his face that suggested otherwise.

"You okay, Terry?" Ray asked, the lone of the three to approach the bar. Duncan and Ruby found a table in the innards of the establishment.

Terry just nodded as if to shrug off the question.

"Three pints," Ray requested.

Sitting at the far corner of the bar, at a small table in the shadows and cobwebs, Ray noticed the same man that occupied the seat the day before. He drank with his head down, and hidden underneath a black baseball cap.

"Hey Charlene," Ray said. He leaned in close as the attractive bartender poured the pints. "What's the deal with that guy?"

"Who, Pete?" Charlene said. "No deal. He's a sweetheart."

"What's with the secret agent pose?"

"Ask him yourself," Charlene said. She placed the beers down on the bar and then filled up Terry's rock glass with whisky.

Ray ignored Pete for the time being and took the beers over to his table.

All three were enjoying their lagers with no particular agenda when they each took notice of a pair of men that walked into the bar. The men looked a little younger and rougher than the clientele they had encountered in their limited experience. One of the men was bear-like. He had a bald head and arms covered in tattoos from shoulder to wrist. The other was taller, and skinnier, and carried a nasty scowl on his face. He had only one visible tattoo, but the spider's placement on his neck made it look more menacing than his friend's. The big guy followed behind the taller one as they approached Terry at the bar. Charlene saw them come in and conveniently attended to business at the other end of the wood. The men sat down on either side of Terry. Duncan and Ray were facing that direction and watched without staring. They couldn't hear the low conversation, but it was easy to see that Terry was not amused. Terry discreetly handed the big man something just out of sight underneath the bar. The skinny man patted Terry on the back and the two of them got up from their seats and left the bar as casually as they had entered.

"Whadda you think that was about?" Ray asked.

"Don't know," Duncan said. "None of our business."

"Drugs?"

"Could be."

Charlene returned to Terry's area and offered him a smile. Terry took down the shot of whisky that remained in his glass.

Finishing their beers and saying goodbye to Charlene, Duncan drove back to Frank's street and pulled up alongside the curb.

Duncan got out of the car to knock on the door once again. He was met with the same result. Frank wasn't home.

Instead of returning directly to the car, Duncan hesitantly walked over to meet Ray and Ruby who were standing in front of the house with the FOR RENT sign.

"Fully furnished," Ray said as Duncan approached.

"Oh yeah?"

"There's a number on the sign. Is it worth a call?"

"I don't know yet," Duncan said. He joined the pair on the front porch. They peered through the long narrow windows beside the door.

"Looks nice," Ruby said.

The two-story house fit in well with the others on the street. It was a middle class neighborhood with single-family homes. Not a new area by any means, but certainly not run-down or dangerous.

Ray logged the phone number and returned to the car with Ruby. Duncan decided to further explore Frank's house. He walked around the side and disappeared behind it. He emerged around the far end soon thereafter and returned to the car.

"We'll give it a little while longer," Duncan said, taking the driver's seat.

"See anything interesting back there?" Ray asked.

"Don't know yet."

A car approached from behind. Duncan put his hand on the door handle when the car nearly came to a stop in front of Frank's driveway; he let go of the handle when the Ford pulled into the house next door.

It was getting dark. There was still no sign of Frank.

"This is stupid," Duncan said. "Ray, call that number."

"Which?" Ray asked. "For the rental?"

"Why the hell not. We're already sitting here."

Ray did as directed and left a message for a man named Mark. His phone rang back less than two minutes later.

"Hi," the voice said. "Sorry, I'm screening calls. I've been getting a lot of jokers since the sign went up."

"No problem," Ray said. He put the phone on speaker so everyone could hear.

"You said you're interested in the house?"

"Yeah, could you tell me more about it?"

"Sure. Long story short, it's my brother's place. He lived there with his fiancé but they moved to New York 'cause she got a placement. They wanted to keep the place 'cause they eventually plan on coming back, but that won't be for at least a year or two. Three bed, two-and-a-half bath, walk out to the yard…"

"Okay," Ray said. "And how are you doing the rental? Month to month?"

"First and last and you can stay as long as you want," Mark said. "If you're interested I'd have to meet you first though."

"Can I put you on hold for a second?"

"Sure."

Ray hit the mute button on his phone.

"Wanna look at it?" he asked.

"We're just sittin' here," Duncan said.

Ruby was a little more enthusiastic, but contained her excitement well. She considered herself vote number four in a three-vote count, even if the guys didn't think of it that way.

Ray unmuted the phone.

"Mark?"

"I'm here."

"When can we see the place?"

"Evenings work better for me," Mark said. "I only live a few blocks away so I can be there in no time. What works for you?"

"Ummmm," Ray said, looking at Duncan. Duncan nodded. "How about now?"

"Right now?"

"Sure."

"That could work. Hang on." Mark disappeared for a few moments. "How's twenty minutes? I'm just feeding the kids."

"We'll see you there in twenty."

"Great. See you there."

It was more like thirty minutes, but Mark arrived as promised and even brought his son along for the ride.

"Ray?"

"That's me," Ray said.

Ray and Mark shook hands outside the house.

"This is Tyler."

"Hi Tyler. This is Duncan, and Ruby."

"So let's go in."

Mark led the group inside and took them on a tour. The house, though old, was well maintained. All the furniture was in good shape and the house was fully equipped with all the appliances. The couple even left a set of plates and cutlery and a big TV. The main bedroom was fully furnished, as was the guest room. The third bedroom was more of an office, though it did have a futon that could easily be converted into a bed. In the unfinished basement was a low ceiling, a set of dumbbells, and a washer and dryer.

"So how much are you asking?" Duncan inquired.

"$2,000 plus utilities," Mark said. "Right now the cable is shut off so you'll have to take care of that yourselves."

Duncan and Ray looked at each other. They were paying $1,800 in Phoenix for their apartment, so they both knew the house was a good deal. Considering the fact that they needed no furniture if they took it, it was almost a no-brainer.

"And when can we move in?"

"Well," Mark said. He gave Duncan, Ray, and Ruby a good look-over. "We're trying to keep this pretty low-key, if you know what I mean."

"We can pay cash," Ray said.

"And you guys aren't partiers or drug dealers or anything like that?"

"God, no," Duncan said. "We're all college grads just looking for a place. These two are a couple, and I'm too old to do drugs."

Mark laughed. "Well," he said, "when do you want it?"

"ASAP," Duncan said. "We're living in a hotel right now."

Mark thought for a minute. "I'll need first and last."

"Of course," Duncan said.

Mark looked at his watch. "How's tomorrow morning?"

"That works."

"Okay, great!"

Mark shook all of their hands one at a time. Little Tyler did the same. "I can meet you here around 8:30 tomorrow. Does that work?"

"We'll make it work," Duncan said.

It was settled.

Mark drove off with Tyler and left the trio on the curb.

Before leaving to return to the hotel, Duncan took one more walk around Frank's house. All the lights were off and there were no signs of life inside.

"Maybe he's out of town," Ruby said as Duncan returned to the car.

"Something's up, Ruby," Duncan said. "That's for sure."

CHAPTER 20

THE NEXT MORNING, Duncan and Ray met Mark in the driveway of the house. Ruby stayed behind. She was lollygagging and they didn't want to miss the meeting. She agreed to pack up the hotel room and the guys would come back to get her once the transaction was complete.

Without a hitch, the money and keys were exchanged. Mark wished the new renters good luck, and phone numbers were swapped.

Duncan and Ray took one more tour of the house in the daylight before fetching Ruby and bringing her back to their new digs.

Having almost no belongings made it conspicuously easy for all three to unpack. Duncan won the coin toss and took the master bedroom. Ruby got the guest room and Ray was fine with taking the futon in the office, or at least he claimed to be.

Sitting at the kitchen table, Duncan opened the new computer and found not one, but multiple, unsecured Wi-Fi signals in the area. He connected to the strongest one and was online in seconds.

His first order of business was to respond to an email from Kennedy that had been waiting in his Gmail inbox. His second order was to send an email to family and friends informing them of his landing in Boston.

Once done with personal matters, Duncan looked up the phone number of one Mr. Franklin Rice, resident of Somerville, Massachusetts. He found the number easily and placed a call to the missing man. The phone rang, and rang some more. An answering machine picked up. Frank identified himself on the message. Duncan hung up the phone and returned to the computer.

"I guess we should buy groceries," Ruby said, parading down the stairs.

"Why not," Duncan said, his eyes still on the screen.

"I'll go," Ruby said. "Keys?" Ruby stood in front of Duncan and held out her hand.

Duncan pulled the small key ring from his pocket. "Make two copies of the house key," he said.

"K. Want anything special?"

"Take Ray with you. He knows what I like."

"He's on the phone," Ruby said.

"With who?"

"No idea, but he shut the door. I guess it's private."

"I'm off now," Ray said, appearing on the stairs. "What's up?"

"Groceries," Ruby said. "Wanna come?"

"Not even a little."

"Really?"

"Go with her, Ray," Duncan said. "She doesn't know what we get."

"So, you go with her."

"Is it really a big deal? You have anything else to do?"

"Come with me, Ray" Ruby said, holding out her hand.

Ray said nothing, but the look on his face implied surrender.

"Get me protein powder," Duncan said. "But only if they have the good one."

"Anything else?" Ray asked.

"Have fun, kids."

Ruby and Ray left the house, bickering about who should drive and how long they were going to spend inside the store. As soon as Duncan heard the car leaving the driveway, he shut the lid of the computer. After a few pensive moments alone, he got up and headed straight down into the basement.

Duncan located the box marked "tools" he had spotted when Mark and Tyler were giving them the tour. In the box Duncan found what he needed: a screwdriver, a putty knife, and a pair of gloves. The gloves were of the gardening ilk but would do just fine for the job he had in mind.

With tools in hand, Duncan walked out the front door of the house, casually crossed the street, and circled around into Frank's backyard. Beside the back door was a window that Duncan took quick study of on his first wander behind the empty house. He had noticed a latch and base sash lock that was anything but flush. The old wood of the window had buckled just enough so that the arm of the lock was sitting outside of the base. If not for the storm window the house would have been accessible to anyone with the notion to go in. It would have simply taken a good wiggle and tug to jar the window enough to be able to reach an arm in and unlock the back door situated only a few feet to the right.

Even with gloves on, Duncan had the screws of the metal storm covering off in no time. He placed them carefully into his pocket so he could reach them when needed. Once it could be removed, Duncan nudged the small outer window clear and laid it down on the ground. Using a sharp corner of the putty knife, Duncan traced the outline of the interior window. Before placing the storm window on, someone had painted the windowpane behind it, sealing it with a thin layer of white paint. When he had completed tracing the entire bottom section of the window, Duncan took a moment to look around to see if any of his new neighbors were looking his way. Upon inspection, it seemed that no one was.

Duncan wedged the putty knife in the area between the upper and lower windows; separating the two just enough to completely extricate the lock arm from the base. With a little wiggle of the knife, and a tug upwards on the handle, Duncan managed to open the window a few inches from the frame. Another tug opened it even more, enough for him to stick his arm through. Duncan reached in with his left hand and unlocked both the handle and the deadbolt of Frank's back door. He made certain the door was indeed open before beginning the operation to undo the work he had completed on the window.

The door was open. Entrance was assured.

Short of repainting the frame – which was done in error to begin with – Duncan reversed his speedy work and returned the window and its storm covering to its original position.

With one last look around to detect unwelcome eyes, Duncan turned the knob of the door and quietly entered Frank's house. He locked the door behind him.

It was Duncan's promise to Rico that brought him to Frank's back door. It was his precipitous curiosity and determination that impelled him to enter without permission.

The first thing Duncan noticed upon reaching the main floor was that even though the house was immaculate, it didn't smell as such. Duncan entered the main room and stopped by a table heaped with black and white and sepia photographs. The framed pictures consisted mostly of army photos; young men in uniforms posing for the camera in an antiquated decade. Duncan lifted a few of the photos one at a time to get a closer look. On the back of one of them was a note written in pencil. It read: "Bill, Frank, Perry, Naval Infantry 1974". Duncan didn't know Franklin Rice, but he could pick out Willy Dublowicz's unique look in many of the pictures. It seemed that Willy and Frank spent a lot of time together during the war, at least whenever a camera was around.

Duncan replaced all the photos to their original positions on the table. His gardening gloves made fingerprints a non-issue, but they were anything but ideal for handling more delicate items.

Duncan made his way to the narrow staircase at the front of the house. At the bottom of the flight was a row of hooks, upon which keys hung. There were several key rings, none of them marked.

Duncan went up the stairs.

The first door he came to opened onto a bedroom that looked as though it hadn't been slept in for years, if ever. The bed was made meticulously, and there wasn't a shred of clothing to be seen. The second bedroom Duncan found was definitely Frank's. Though still tidy beyond the pale, several clues suggested someone had recently been there. On a dressing chair by the right wall, a pair of men's pants was folded neatly. A shirt hung from a hanger on the handle of the door beside it. A pair of brown shoes sat on the floor at the foot of the chair. There were two doors in the room, one on either side. Through the tiny crack it left, Duncan could see that one of them was a bathroom. Duncan left that one alone but couldn't help but to peek inside the other. It was a walk-in closet.

Duncan flicked on the light.

Just like the rest of the house, Frank's closet was spectacularly organized, right down to the perfectly stacked columns of shoeboxes that lined its walls. Duncan was about to flick off the light and continue his exploration when something caught his eye. As far as he knew, Frank wasn't a married man. If rumor suited, he had little affection for women at all. So why then were there so many female shoeboxes, Duncan wondered.

Duncan reached to the top of one of the shoebox pillars and lifted off the lid. Inside he found a red pair of women's pumps. Duncan opened another, and another, and then one more. He had uncovered a very large collection of very expensive women's shoes. In fact, every box he ventured to open contained the like. Until, that is, Duncan got to the bottom box of one of the stacks. There were no shoes inside that box. Instead, Duncan found more of Frank's pictures. The first few mirrored those that Frank had displayed on the table beside his couch. They were pictures from the Navy, of the war, and of Frank and Bill in uniform. A little deeper in the box, a new tale was developing. If ever Duncan was curious about what his one-time acquaintance, Willy, looked like naked, or what a dress would look like on the body of a pudgy middle-aged man, he now had the Polaroid pictures to satisfy it. He had never met Frank, but with those pictures, he now knew him intimately. The most interesting pictures Duncan found were of both Willy and Frank together. Interesting, because they were clearly performing acts still illegal in many states, but also because they begged the corollary question – if both of men are in the pictures, who took them?

Out of nothing more than morbid curiosity, Duncan continued to explore the boxes. He found shoes, shoes, and still more shoes.

Until, he didn't.

Two of the boxes at the very bottom of their piles contained something much different inside. They were the only two red shoeboxes among the bunch of blacks and whites and silvers. Duncan examined the contents with acute interest. He thought for a few seconds, hard, but eventually resigned to reset them back in their proper place at the bottom of the stacks. After looking through each and every other box, Duncan rebuilt all the towers to their original height. He rose from his knees, and left the closet alone.

Frank's room smelled especially rank. Duncan assumed it was the smell of an aging man that lived alone.

Peeking his head into the bathroom, Duncan saw nothing of interest or suspicion, though the foul smell became even worse. Duncan's first inclination was to peer innocently into the toilet to see if someone had forgotten to flush, so he did just that. He took a few steps forward into the washroom, but the toilet was clean. In the spirit of his endeavor, Duncan took the opportunity to peek inside the drawers under Frank's sink. If ever there was something exceedingly interesting in someone's washroom cabinets, it was not in Frank's. Duncan stood up and caught his reflection in the mirror.

It was then that he was hit with a violent jolt of surprise. Instinctively, Duncan turned and snapped into a defensive pose. It took him only a moment to loosen his muscles and relax his heart. He had processed what he was seeing, and he was certain it wasn't about to put up a fight.

"Wow," Duncan said aloud, taking in the sight.

Duncan escaped the bathroom and intended to vacate the upstairs of Frank's house altogether, but something stopped him.

Duncan stood like a statue in the doorway of Frank's room.

A few seconds passed. Then a few more seconds went by. Finally, Duncan turned like a top and headed straight to the back of the closet. He flicked on the light, grabbed the only two red shoeboxes, and fled the room entirely.

With boxes under arm, Duncan strode down the stairs. Once at the bottom, he snapped up all the keys from Frank's key rack. Instead of walking back to the rear door through which he arrived, Duncan simply exited through the front of the house. Before retreating back across the street, Duncan tested the keys he had just nabbed in search of the one that would lock the door behind him. He found the one he was looking for, did the deed, and escaped out into safety without so much as a sideways look.

CHAPTER 21

RAY AND RUBY were still bickering when they returned home with bags of food. Duncan was sitting at the kitchen table where they had left him. The only difference was that there were two red shoeboxes sitting in front of him. Duncan was feverishly typing and clicking away on the computer.

Ruby and Ray put the food away without noticing anything out of the ordinary. Ray sat down at the table across from Duncan and took a bite of an apple. "What's up?" he said, slurping the juice.

Duncan didn't answer. Ray tried to peer at the computer screen. "What you doing?" he asked.

"Just checking something," Duncan said.

Ray ate his apple. Ruby joined the pair at the table.

"Chanel?" Ruby said, taking notice of the boxes.

Duncan looked up from the screen. "It's not what you think it is," he said.

"Shoes?" Ray guessed.

"Exactly," Duncan said.

"I don't get it."

Duncan shoved one of the boxes over to Ray without saying a word. The box slid heavy across the table and came to rest in front of Ray. "For me?" he said. "They'd probably fit Ruby better, but thanks."

Ray removed the lid.

"Holy shit," he said.

"What?" Ruby asked. She got up from her seat at the other end of the table and walked over to Ray. "Holy shit," she echoed.

"Well these aren't shoes," Ray said.

Ray tilted the box in order to give Duncan another look, as if he had forgotten what was inside. There, inside the box, piled from bottom to top, were thick bundles of cash.

"What about that one?" Ray said, pointing to the other red box. Duncan slid the second box over to Ray.

The second stash of money only filled to about three-fourths of the volume of the box, but was impressive nonetheless. The rest of the box was occupied by what looked to be Frank's military service pistol. It was black, and heavy, and upon further inspection, still loaded. Ray held up the gun as if he were posing for a movie poster.

"There has to be thousands in here," Ruby said.

"Eighty six thousand, four hundred and eighty," Duncan said.

"You counted it already?" Ray asked.

"Twice."

"Okay," Ray said, placing the gun back atop the cash in the box. "Now the question is, where did it come from?"

Duncan closed the lid of the computer and focused his attention on his friends at the other end of the table. "Now that's an interesting story," he said.

Ruby took a seat in anticipation of Duncan's tale.

Duncan began to describe the events that had recently unraveled, starting from the time when the car pulled out of the driveway. He began with his trip to the toolbox in the basement and led them right through Frank's back door, leaving out little detail. The story halted for a moment at Duncan's discovery of the boxes in Frank's closet.

"Now listen closely," Duncan said, "There's more. And Ruby, I need your help."

Once the full story was told, Duncan began spelling out a plan that pertained to what was to happen next. Ruby was to play a key role.

Once each aspect of the scheme was discussed in detail and understood by all, Duncan took a single key from his pocket and slid it across the table. Ruby took the key and put it on her key ring with a copy of the key she had just made for their new house.

"Make sense?" Duncan asked.

"Sure," Ruby said. "I think so."

"Ray?"

"No problem."

"Okay then," Duncan said. "Let's do it."

"Wait," Ray said. "There's something I need to do first."

"What?" Duncan asked.

"Really?" Ray said. "After all that, you can't figure it out."

Duncan thought for a second. "Do it quick," he said.

Ray got up from the table. "You coming?" he asked Ruby.

"Where?" Ruby asked.

"I have to see it for myself."

"Okay," Ruby submitted. "Wait...okay."

Ray and Ruby skulked across the street as if they were running through thickets. Using the key Ruby got from Duncan, the pair quickly entered through Frank's front door and clambered up the stairs.

"This is it," Ray said, poking open the door to Frank's room.

Ray and Ruby walked slowly into the room's ensuite and gave the door a little shove.

"Wow," Ray said, standing at the back of the bathroom near the tub.

Ruby said nothing. She just stared.

There, dangling behind the door as limp as a wet noodle, was Franklin Rice. He was wearing a black corset, red lipstick, and red high heels to match. There was a leather belt around his neck connected at the other end to an attachment on top of the door that held his weight. Interesting still, Frank's lifeless hand still had a tender grasp of his man-parts, and if Ruby and Ray had to confess it, they would both have said it looked like Frank was still smiling.

"Hey, if you're gonna go…" said Ray.

"Oh, real nice."

"He must have really missed Willy."

Ruby smacked Ray across the shoulder.

"What?"

"Everyone's entitled."

"To tugging one out while strangling yourself?"

"Isn't there a word for that?"

"Yeah – risky."

"Okay," Ruby said. "I've seen enough."

Ray followed Ruby out of the bathroom. "Did you like his shoes?" he asked.

"You're going to hell."

"If there was a hell I'd probably agree with you. But, no, I'll be just fine."

When they returned to the house, Duncan was back on the computer. "You guys ready?" he asked.

"Sure," Ray said.

"Okay. Let's do it."

As planned, Ray went outside, got in the car, and drove off.

"Ruby," Duncan said.

Ruby left the house too. She walked back across the street and re-entered Frank's alone. She went straight up to Frank's room and dialed 911 from his phone.

Ruby sat on the front steps and waited for emergency vehicles to arrive. The first to show up was a fire truck, stocked to the brim with firefighters.

"Are you the one that called?" one of the firefighters asked.

Ruby nodded, clearly distraught. "Upstairs," she said. "In the bathroom."

The firefighters vanished into the house one at a time.

The next to arrive was a police cruiser, followed by another. An ambulance came soon thereafter. One of the police officers came directly over to Ruby.

"Are you okay to talk?" the officer asked.

Ruby nodded.

"I'm Officer Bennett. And you are?"

"Ruby."

"Hi Ruby. Do you want to come have a seat in the car for a minute? It's more comfortable there."

Ruby followed the officer to his car still parked by the curb. The man in blue opened the passenger door and helped her in. He left the door open and stood above her. "I'm just going inside to have a talk with my partner," he said. "Can you wait here for me?"

Ruby agreed. The officer made his way into the house, but not before nodding to a fellow policeman on the scene who nodded back. He was going to keep an eye on Ruby.

A white van pulled up a few minutes later and parked in Frank's driveway. Two men with a gurney and a body bag wheeled their goods into the house.

Frank's wrapped body was carried out of the house less than twenty minutes after Ruby had placed the call. The police officer that placed Ruby in his car followed closely behind and joined her in the cruiser.

The van pulled away with Frank's dead body in its belly.

"I'm going to take a few notes, is that okay?" the officer asked, pulling out a notepad.

"Sure," Ruby said.

"Just relax," he said. "I just have to ask you a few questions and then you can go."

"Okay."

Before the officer could begin his questions, a blue Fifth Avenue came screeching up to the curb. Ray popped out and made a beeline for Ruby.

"Are you okay?" he said concerned, hugging the girl who got out of the cruiser to meet him.

"I'm okay," Ruby assured.

The officer gave the pair a moment to embrace before getting out of the car and introducing himself.

"I'm Officer Bennett," he said to Ray.

"Ray. I'm her boyfriend."

"Hi Ray. I just need to ask Ruby a few questions. You can join us if you like."

Ruby got back into the car and left the door open again, Ray sat on the curb beside her and held her hand. Officer Bennett reentered the driver side.

"Okay Ruby, do you know the full name of the occupant of the house?"

"Frank Rice."

"And how do you know Frank?"

"He's my neighbor."

"You live next door?"

"I live there," Ruby said, pointing to the house they just rented. "That one."

"Can you walk me through the events of how you came to find Frank?"

"Well, I hadn't seen him in…I don't know, days. I have a key to his house, you know, to get his mail and things when he's away, or for when he leaves his at the bar. I didn't see his car or see any lights turn on for a while. I knocked on the door yesterday, but no one answered. I thought maybe something was wrong 'cause Frank is always coming and going – and if he went away he would have told us. I got worried so I used the key and went inside just to make sure. That's when I found him."

"And you called emergency response as soon as you saw him?"

"Yeah."

"Did you enter the house alone?"

"Yes."

"Did you see anyone else coming or going from the house in the past few days?"

"No," Ruby said. She thought for a moment. "Nobody."

Officer Bennett scribbled on his pad.

"Is there anything else you can think of that you can tell me? Anything at all?"

Ruby took another moment. "Not really," she said. "I came in, I saw him, and I called 911."

"Well," the officer said. "Thank you Ruby. I think that's it for now. You can go back home if you want."

"Okay."

"If I have any more questions, would it be okay if I contacted you?"

"Sure."

"Here's my card. If you think of anything else, just give me a call."

Ruby took the card and then she and the officer got up and out of the car.

"Sorry for the loss of your friend," Officer Bennett said.

"Here," Ruby said, walking over to the man. "This is Frank's key." She began twisting the old key off her ring. "I guess I don't need it anymore."

"Thanks," Officer Bennett said, taking it from her.

Ray walked with Ruby back to the car and the pair took the short drive to their house only a few doors down on the other side of the street.

Duncan was upstairs, out of sight.

"We're back," Ray yelled, once inside.

Duncan sheepishly peered down the stairs.

"All good?" he asked.

"All good," Ray said.

"I was nervous," Ruby said.

"You did good," Ray assured.

"I didn't really love lying to the cops."

There was nothing Duncan or Ray could say to that. They weren't big proponents of the idea either, but it was the only way to cover up for Duncan's actions that had begun innocently enough, but that had ended in a substantial burglary. Even though Frank was already dead at the time, that wouldn't have mattered to the cops, and no one wanted to get the law involved with the true details of the story, including how Duncan got in to find him.

"It's over now," Ray said. "Let's put it behind us and forget about it."

Duncan then chugged back up the stairs and disappeared into his room for a minute or two. When he sauntered back down, Ruby and Ray were at the window observing the scene still going on at Frank's.

Duncan went directly over to the kitchen table and laid out three different stacks of cash.

"Me and Ray will split Rico's twelve," he said. "After that, I split it up three ways, even."

Ruby and Ray came over to join him.

"Are you serious?" Ruby asked.

Ray simply took his share and said nothing more of it.

"You're in it, Ruby," Duncan said. "Might as well get something out of it. Go ahead. Frank doesn't need it anymore. And even if he did, there's no way to give it back now."

"I guess," she said. "But I don't know."

"I don't either," Duncan said. "But like I said, there's no way to give it back now."

Ruby thought for a moment.

"Only because no one's getting hurt."

Ruby took the mound of cash.

"We wouldn't do it if someone was getting hurt," Duncan said. "I promise you."

"We need to get new SIM cards for our phones," said Ray. "If we're going to start reporting dead bodies all over the place we should really be calling local."

"We'll do that," Duncan said.

"I've never held this much cash," Ruby said.

"You know," Ray said to Ruby. "If you take that into a bank they'll give you a cute little card and you can take it out little bits at a time. They have them all over now."

Ruby laughed with fake, mocking laughter. Ray joined in with mimicry.

CHAPTER 22

THE FOLLOWING DAY, Duncan made the call to Rico and informed him that the situation with Frank had met its end. Rico was satisfied and he made one more attempt to convince Duncan to take over in Boston where Willy had left off. Rico used the silver-plattered twelve grand as a bargaining chip, which was most likely his plan from the start. Duncan felt a little silly for not seeing that from the beginning. Duncan was adamant in his rejection, and Rico, being of fair mind, let it go soon thereafter and wished his old accomplice well in his new endeavors.

It was late in the day. Flush with funds, Ruby decided to take herself on a small spending spree. Never before did she have the opportunity to spend wastefully, and though she didn't take it to extremes – something she had the inclination to do – she did spend a fair cent on clothing to fill her new closet. She had, after all, been traveling with only one small bag of wearables.

Ray, still practicing mute, longed for another meeting with a certain young attorney and ventured down to the coffee shop once again to stake out her building. He thought the gesture exciting, if not romantic, but the notion was quickly thwarted upon his second sneak approach of Ashley on the sidewalk.

"You can't keep showing up like this, Ray," the startled barrister said. She looked around inquisitively and lowered her voice. "I work here."

"So?" Ray said. "I wanted to see you."

Ashley began to walk down the sidewalk.

"You could have called," she said.

"Where's the fun in that?"

"Sometimes I can't afford your fun, Ray. We're not in college anymore."

"Not in college?" Ray said, more following than walking with Ashley down the street. "What's wrong with–"

"I'm seeing someone, okay," Ashley confided in a hushed voice as she came to a stop. "I'm seeing someone."

"What do you mean you're seeing someone?"

"I'm…involved, Ray. I can't just drop everything 'cause you showed up."

Ashley began her spirited walk again.

"I'm not asking you to drop everything," Ray said. He too picked up his pace. "So who's the guy?" he asked. "Lemme guess, someone from work?"

"What's the difference?"

"I'm right, aren't I? It's someone from work."

"So what if it is? Does that make it a joke to you?"

"I didn't say that."

"You implied it."

"I didn't imply anything."

Ashley stopped.

"Ash," Ray began.

"No."

"Ash, it's me. It's us."

Ray put his hands on Ashley's shoulders. Ashley looked around. "Can we go somewhere else and talk?" she asked.

Ray and Ashley returned to the scene of their previous crime. They hoped that no one would remember them or the fact that they had ordered drinks and then simply vanished without a word. To their luck, the server was an unfamiliar female and made no mention of the scandal. She took their order and filled it with expediency.

"His name is Davis," Ashley said. "And yes, he's a lawyer in my office. He asked me out a long time ago and I said no because I was still new there and I didn't want to get involved with someone at work, especially because I'm still one of only, like, five women there. But he kept on asking. Eventually I said yes just to get him to stop. Sounds stupid, I know. I even tried to have a bad time when we went out. But, what can I say? He was persistent and charming and he made me feel…good. That means a lot when you're new somewhere, you know."

Ray tried to be objective, and he let Ashley get it all out, but his stomach turned more and more with each word she spoke. In every relationship there's always one that loves the other just a tiny bit more. It's never really spoken about, it's just something that's more or less known and accepted. Ashley was always the one that loved Ray that little bit extra, which made it even harder for Ray to swallow what she was telling him.

"I've only been seeing him for a few months, so it's not serious or anything," she said. "I don't want to make it seem like I'm in *love* with him or anything." Ashley whirled her head as if she were still wrestling with the meaning of the word. "But I think I want to see where it goes. I don't want to just give up. I owe him that. I owe that to myself. I can't just end everything 'cause you're here now."

"So what was that all about? Last time? Why did you sleep with me?"

"I don't know, Ray," Ashley struggled. "Like you said, it's us, you and me. You know?"

"I know," Ray said.

He didn't really get it, but he wanted it to seem to her like he did. He wanted it to seem like they were on the same page, that they would always understand each other, that they *got* one another, no matter what. It was his only card to play.

"I shouldn't have done it," said Ashley.

"Don't say that."

"No. I shouldn't have. It's not fair to you."

"Don't worry about me. I can handle it."

"Really, Ray? You can handle it? It's just that easy?"

"That's not what I meant, Ash. I meant I can handle the sex. I'm not talking about the whole situation with your Davey."

"Don't do that."

"Do what?"

"Don't try to belittle him by saying things like 'your Davey'. It's not going to work, and it's not you. It's not like we're teaming up against you, Ray. This isn't a competition. I'm not picking him over you."

"You're not?"

"We weren't together anymore. I was out here, alone. We hadn't talked in months."

"I bet your parents would approve," Ray said.

"That's not fair."

"I'm just saying—"

"You know that's not fair. And if you want to talk about taking sides, I was always on your side, Ray. I never let anything my parents said get between us."

"But it still did."

"No it didn't."

"Really? You could have gone to school anywhere in the country. Why did they push so hard to send you out here? Why was it so important that you got away from me?"

"Because they wanted to me go to Harvard, Ray. It wasn't about you. It was about *me*. It was something good for *me*."

"It was about them, too, you have to admit that."

"Okay, yeah – I'm their daughter. My brother's been in and out of rehab since he was fourteen. Are you surprised they pushed me to succeed? Are you surprised that I wanted to?"

"No," Ray said calmly. He was trying to slow the pace of the escalating conversation, one that had begun to wobble off the rails. "What I'm trying to say is that it was never easy for us to be together because of your parents. Maybe you like this *Davis* because you think it will be easier; you think your parents would approve and you won't have to fight it."

After he said it, even Ray knew he didn't really feel that way. He knew Ashley too well to distill the situation down to something so trivial.

"Ray, I haven't even thought about what my parents would think. It's only been a few months. I don't even think my dad knows he exists."

Ray just nodded. Ashley had not only disarmed him, she'd eaten up the bullets and shot them back through his chest. "So? What do we do now?" he said.

"I don't know."

"You guys doing okay?" asked the wandering server.

"That all depends," Ray answered.

"Sorry?"

"We're fine," Ashley answered. "Thank you."

Ray took a sip of his drink. "So tell me about him," he said.

"Ray, don't."

"No, I'm serious. We're both adults here. I want you to be happy. Tell me about him."

"What do you want to know?"

"What's he like? How old is he? Who would win in a fight?"

Ashley laughed. "He's thirty-five," she said. "And you would actually like him, Ray."

"You sure about that?"

"Yeah, I am. He's not what you're picturing. He's not a stuffy, square lawyer with a part in the side of his hair and a briefcase in his hand. He's a cool guy. He plays piano, he plays basketball; he's funny, like you."

"No one's funny like me."

"Well, that's true."

"And he treats you well?"

"He does."

"How tall is he?"

"Why?" Ashley laughed.

"I'm just curious."

"Oh right, I forgot, we're adults."

"So?"

"I don't know. Five-ten. Five-eleven. This is weird. Can we change the subject?"

"Sure, wanna go back to your place again?"

"Ray!"

"It was worth a try."

"I should go," Ashley said.

"Are you serious? You didn't even finish your drink."

"Why start a new tradition?"

"Are you going to meet him?"

"Ray."

"Okay, okay, never mind."

"Will you walk out with me?" Ashley asked with sincerity.

Ray accepted the invitation and departed the hotel bar with Ashley, but not before leaving money for the two drinks along with a very healthy tip for the server.

Outside the doors of the hotel, Ashley wrapped her arms around Ray. Ray hugged her back, though it felt like an unfamiliar embrace. Ray had never attempted to look on Ashley as anything other than *his* girl, let alone hold her in his arms as someone else's. Ashley pulled away and put her hands on Ray's face. She gave him a kiss on the lips. It was a short, friendly kiss. "Call me, okay?" she said.

Ray nodded and then watched as Ashley walked away. She didn't look back, though Ray kept waiting, and hoping, that she would.

"Where you been?" Duncan asked when Ray returned home.

Ray tossed a small plastic bag onto the kitchen table and kept on walking by. Duncan pulled out the contents of the bag.

"Nice," Duncan said. "You got new SIM cards."

"The guy said we just have to call in and they can do the swap over the phone. We're going to need new numbers."

"That's fine," Duncan said.

"Where's Ruby?"

"Upstairs ripping tags off new clothes."

"What're you spending so much time on the computer for?"

"Porn," Duncan said.

"No, really?" Ray asked, peering over Duncan shoulder.

Duncan was looking at commercial real estate listings.

Ray left Duncan alone and decided to go bother Ruby instead. At the top of the stairs he could see that the door to her room was mostly closed. Ray approached quietly and nudged the door open just enough to see inside. Ruby was modeling an outfit in the full sized mirror that hung behind the closet door. She saw Ray's head in the reflection.

"You can come in," she said.

Ray entered the room. He walked up to Ruby and stood behind her. "This is a little tight on you." he said. He grabbed her waist firmly from behind.

"Fits fine," Ruby said.

Ray moved his hands around to her flat stomach and left them there to linger. "Feels pretty good," he said.

Ruby held her position in the mirror for a few moments, placing her hands on top of Ray's. Unable to help herself, Ruby turned abruptly and planted her lips on Ray's. She threw one of her arms over his shoulder and held the back of his neck as they continued to kiss. Ray slid his hands down her back and clutched her rear. His hands throbbed on her backside. Ruby let out a sigh; her deep, warm breath feathered Ray's cheek. With his hands still on Ruby's backside, Ray pulled her in even tighter, pressing their midsections up against one another. Ruby returned to his lips and kissed him even harder.

"I want you to fuck me," Ruby whispered in his ear.

Ray lifted Ruby from her feet and tossed her aggressively onto the bed. He closed the door to the room and made certain to lock it before he got on top of Ruby and pinned her hands above her head. Ruby writhed in delight and let out a short, high-pitched moan. With one hand still holding her arms above her head, Ray began to rip the clothes from Ruby's body. When he needed both hands, he let go of Ruby's arms allowing the eager girl to tug at his clothes, yanking his shirt up over his head and then going straight for the button on his pants.

Ruby and Ray disrobed one another and pressed their naked bodies together. Once again, Ray threw Ruby's arms up over her head and held them there before attacking her breasts and stomach with his other hand and with his mouth. Ruby bit her lip so not to make noise. Her legs moved up and down on the bed under the weight of Ray's body, until almost naturally, they spread apart and Ray's body slid down between them. With her arms still pinned above her head and Ray's mouth now on her neck, Ruby could feel Ray put himself inside her. She let out a deep breath as her body shuddered. Ray moved his pelvis back and forth. Ruby's head tilted back, extending her neck as she tried her hardest to hold in a cry of pleasure.

Ray let go of Ruby's arms, allowing her to finally touch the warm skin on his back. She dug her nails into his shoulders and held them there as he moved back and forth on top of her. With a jolt of energy Ruby tugged her body out from under Ray and got on top. Ray was receptive and allowed the smaller girl to move him with ease. Ruby, now straddling Ray, sat up revealing her body to him. Her breasts were not overly large, but on her thin frame they protruded like perfect ovals from her chest. Ruby took her hands from Ray's stomach and ran them through her hair.

Ray held Ruby's hips and helped her to speed up the motion. Ruby took one of her hands out of her hair and placed it on top of one of Ray's. She yanked his hand from her hip and placed it heavily onto her chest. Ray used both hands to grab Ruby's breasts and squeezed with just enough pressure to make Ruby moan with delight. Ruby threw her head back and ran her hands down her own neck and onto Ray's hands that were still holding on tightly. Ruby took in a short, heavy breath and held it in her lungs as her body exploded with orgasm. Ray felt it in his groin. The tensing, wet muscles of Ruby's manicured region caused Ray to near completion. He grabbed onto her hips and gave one last, hard, deep thrust, as he reached his own climax.

Ruby's body, like a vanquished marathon runner, wilted down onto Ray's. She lay there catching her breath, her head resting beside his. Ray put his arms on Ruby's hot, moist back, and squeezed her one more time before loosening every muscle in his body and forfeiting all control of where his limbs might land.

Ruby sighed with pleasure. Ray turned his head just enough to catch his reflection in the mirror behind the closet door. Ray was relaxed, content, and feeling well. For some reason, he was strongly compelled to turn away from his own reflection, though he couldn't say why.

CHAPTER 23

THAT EVENING, DUNCAN and Ray ventured over to O'Keefe's for a social visit. It was, after all, the closest pub to where they now lived. Ruby opted to stay at home and test the new cable they had installed earlier in the day. It had been a while since she had a quiet night to watch TV alone and the idea excited her more so than bending elbows with the boys in a dank pub.

"So," Duncan said on their way to the bar.

"So what?"

"So how is she?"

"What?"

Ray was taken aback. First of all he thought he and Ruby had managed to hoodwink their roommate, if not keep it quiet enough for him not to hear what had really gone on. But more than that, it was unlike Duncan to pose a question of that nature. They were not still in college, after all.

"How is she?" Ray asked.

"Yeah, how is she?" Duncan said.

Ray looked over at his friend.

"Ray, I'm not an idiot. We've been in Boston what…four days. I know she's here. I know you've seen her."

"Seen her? Oh fuck," Ray clued in. "You mean Ashley."

"So?" Duncan said.

"She's okay, I guess. She's got some boyfriend."

"Ouch. What, you meet him?"

"No. Just heard about him. He's a lawyer. Works in her office."

"She live with him?"

"No. It's only been a few months. She says it's not serious."

"How was it seeing her again?"

"Fine at first. Then torture."

"I'm sure."

"Dude, I thought everything would be better 'cause it's been so long. I mean I was fine after a while when she left. I stopped thinking about her; I went out with other girls. Then I saw her and in an instant it all came undone."

"I'm sure," Duncan said. "You two have always been like that."

"Yeah."

"Probably shouldn't have gone to see her at all."

"Probably not," Ray agreed.

"Yeah," Duncan said. "Probably shouldn't have fucked Ruby either."

Ray's head snapped to his friend.

They had reached the bar. Duncan swung the door open with a smile and held it for Ray.

As predicted by Charlene when describing Frank's trek, it took less than five minutes for Ray and Duncan to reach O'Keefe's. Though it was a few blocks away, there was a grassy park to cut through that dissected the walking time by half.

"There's something I want to check out first," Duncan said, still holding the door.

"What?"

"Something down the street. You can come if you really want to."

"Sure, I don't care."

"Why don't you just go in and grab a few pints, I'll be back in a minute."

Duncan wasn't trying to ditch Ray, and where he was going wasn't meant to be a secret, but for the first time since they met, Duncan was contemplating a venture that didn't involve his good friend. He didn't want the subject to be broached prematurely, even though both were fairly sure the other knew the situation.

Ray entered O'Keefe's without Duncan. It was busier than he had ever seen it, only having dropped in during daylight hours. Terry and Vinny were at their usual seats at the bar, and the man Vinny called Mike was sitting with them. Charlene was again behind the bar but had a second hand to assist her. A young man, in his early twenties, fetched glasses and filled pints on the command of the matriarch. However, it was the peculiar man again sitting alone in the corner that piqued Ray's interest.

Pete, the quiet loner that seemed to be in the bar each time Ray had visited, was in the same exact spot, like a picture on the wall. He didn't move, or talk to anyone; in fact he didn't do much of anything at all.

Charlene was bustling about, as was her helper, so Ray took the opportunity to get a closer look at the curious man.

Upon circling the belly-high wooden bar, Ray noticed that although Pete's face was still well hidden under his black hat, he wasn't looking down for no reason. Pete was reading. There was a book open under his nose, and on the chair beside the stranger were three other books, all stickered with library markings and complete with that noisy, clear, protective covering libraries put on all hardcover books. Ray approached the bar, satisfied that he had solved the issue of the secret agent in O'Keefe's. As he leaned up against the wood, Ray quickly noticed two distinct and unrelated things about the man.

1: Among the books Pete had in his possession was *God is not Great*, the very same book that Ray bought for Ruby in Omaha.

2: Pete was trying to hide more than his eyes under his hat. Though not close enough to get a proper look, Ray spotted what he thought to be multiple scars on the left side of Pete's face and neck.

Pete made a minor adjustment in his chair and for a fraction of an instant his eyes aligned with Ray's. It was as if he could feel Ray's gaze on the top of his head.

"You okay?" Charlene asked, appearing as if out of nowhere.

"Two pints, please," Ray said.

"Oh, Ray," Charlene said. "It's you."

Charlene pulled at the tap and beer came pouring out into the glass like liquid gold. "Can you believe it about Franky?"

"Franky?" Ray feigned.

"You didn't hear? Cops found him dead in the bathroom. Was there for days."

"Wow," Ray said. "That's too bad."

"Really is," Charlene agreed.

Charlene put the beers down in front of Ray and leaned in close.

"You can talk to him you know," she whispered, looking over at Pete. "He doesn't bite." Charlene smiled and walked away.

Ray took a sip of his beer and turned so that his back was against the end of the bar. Pete looked up once again. He looked at Ray for a fleeting moment, and then went back to his book.

Charlene didn't mean her words as a challenge, but something inside Ray made them feel that way. "What you reading?" Ray asked.

Pete lifted the book and revealed the cover. He didn't say anything, but did look up enough for Ray to see that the entire left side of his face and neck were not only scarred, but were also badly burned in several places. Upon inspection, Ray could see that one particularly large scar ran from just under his ear, down his neck, and ended just above his collar near his Adam's apple.

"I don't suppose you want any company?" Ray asked.

Pete hesitated for a moment and then pushed the chair beside him out a few inches.

Ray approached and sat down at the table.

"I'm Ray."

"Pete."

He spoke with a raspy, gruff, forced-out voice.

Ray lifted the familiar book off the chair beside him. "I've read this one," he said.

Pete took a look at the book and nodded.

"I've seen you in here before," Ray said.

"Library's depressing," Pete said as he looked around with a sly smile on his face.

Ray laughed.

"There you are," a voice said. Duncan had returned. "I'm getting a pint," he said without a second glance at Pete. "You guys okay?"

"I got you one. Here."

Duncan joined the table. He introduced himself to Pete, who returned the gesture.

"You from around here?" Duncan asked.

"Born and raised," Pete said. "You?"

"All over really. Here for now, though."

"Sorry to hear it."

Pete looked to be in his late thirties. The damage to the side of his face aged him, as did the black cap and darkness around his eyes.

"Your scars," Duncan said, unashamed. "From an accident?"

"You could say that."

"I don't mean to pry."

"It's okay."

Pete closed his book and placed it atop the others. He lifted his head, presenting the full measure of the damage. Besides a small patch of hair noticeably missing from above his ear, most of the harm was already visible. "Either of you guys ever serve?" he asked.

"No," Ray said.

Pete took a sip of his drink and looked back down at the table. "It's from an IED. Afghanistan," he said, raising his eyes once more. "Shrapnel almost tore my head clean off." Pete traced the long scar from beneath his ear down his neck with a finger. "The burns are residual. The hit put me on the ground and the heat singed my skin. Doc said some might clear up with time. Haven't yet."

"How long ago did it happen?"

"Sixteen months."

Pete put both hands on the table. On the back of his left hand, the only part visible under his long-sleeve shirt, burn marks pulled and riddled his skin. "Spent three months in MTF. Home for about a year now."

"Well we just moved into the neighborhood," Duncan said.

"And you've already found the nicest bar."

Pete removed his hands from the table. Both Duncan and Ray noticed that his left arm and hand didn't move very well.

"Yeah, well, we have a nose for class," Ray said.

"So what do you guys do?"

"Right now we're between jobs," Duncan said. "Just moved, right?"

"I saw you in here the other day. You were asking about Bill."

"He's an old friend from Vegas."

"A business friend?"

"If you're asking if we're taking bets, we're not."

"Okay," Pete said. He did his best to squeeze out a grin. "I had to ask, right?"

"No worries."

"You did business with Bill?" Ray asked.

"From time to time," Pete said. "I'm on Uncle Sam's dime for now so it doesn't leave a lot of room for hobbies. I only did it for fun, anyway. Why the hell not, right? But I'm not getting involved with Bixby."

"Bixby?" Duncan asked.

"Took over with the regulars. You know, when Bill died."

"I don't know him."

"He was in here," Pete said, "You saw him. Tall guy, tattoo of a spider on his neck, walks around with the big guy, Marco."

"Yeah," Ray said, nodding. "He had a few words with Terry?"

"That's him. Got a mean streak. Don't want to deal with it. Seen enough shit already."

"Is he on his own?" Duncan asked.

"On his own as far as I know. Lives around here. Was inside for a while for stabbing a guy in a fight and came out with a new attitude. Smarter now, calmer. Don't know about the gorilla he walks around with."

"Marco?"

"He's not from around here."

Pete took his last sip of his beer and clanked the empty glass down on the table.

"I got the next round," Duncan said.

"Not for me," Pete said. "One beer a day. That's it."

"You sure?"

"One beer a day."

"Okay."

"I will do a shot of whisky though, but it's every man for himself."

"I'm in," Duncan said.

"Sure," Ray agreed.

"Tell Charlene you want three for me. She'll know what you mean."

Duncan popped up to fill the order and returned balancing two pints and three full shots. Ray and Pete had changed the topic of conversation in his absence.

"I've been trying," Pete said. "That's what all these books are for."

Duncan passed out the drinks. "Thanks," Pete said. "I just can't seem to feel it anymore."

"So it's a feeling?" Ray asked.

"Used to be. Didn't you ever have it?"

"Never."

"Cheers," Pete said, holding up his shot glass and then downing it. Ray and Duncan followed.

"I always thought God was something you believed in," Ray said.

"It's both," Pete said.

"Both?"

Pete took a moment. "You ever been in love with a women?" he asked.

Ray gave a nod.

"Did you believe it, or did you feel it?"

"I believed it because I felt it."

"There ya go. Same thing. When you're by yourself and you're facing a decision, a really hard decision, do you feel alone or do you feel…something? Something leading you one way or another?"

"I feel something," Duncan said.

"Yeah, your conscience," Ray said.

"Could be," Pete said. "But I felt something else."

"And you don't anymore?" Duncan asked.

Pete shook his head slowly. "I've seen some fucked up shit," he said. "I don't know when or where I lost it, but I don't feel anything like that anymore."

"I can understand that," Ray said.

"Really? 'Cause I sure can't," Pete said.

CHAPTER 24

RAY AND DUNCAN left O'Keefe's in the early hours of the morning much more drunk than when they arrived. Having the luxury of walking home, they didn't take it easy on their running tab.

"How was your little stroll before?" Ray asked as they entered the outskirts of the park.

"Fine," Duncan said.

"See anything you liked?"

"Looked okay," Duncan said.

"Let me know if you want any help with, you know, whatever."

"I will."

"I mean I'm not sure how much I can help, but the offer stands."

"I'm kind of making it up as I go. It's just an idea right now."

"I'm pretty sure I can figure out what you're thinking."

"You probably can."

"When did you come up with the idea?"

"I think I've had it for a while. Talking to Kennedy helped."

"Kennedy? In Omaha? Why?"

"Just some of the things she said to me. I don't know; it made sense. I mean, what are we trying to do here anyway?"

"I haven't figured that out yet."

"I'm starting to think here is as good a place as any, right?"

Arriving at home, Ruby was not on the couch where they had left her. Ray and Duncan attempted to maintain a considerate level of quietude.

Duncan retired into his room leaving Ray to have one last beer and time alone to watch some TV. Ray caught up on the day's sporting events and watched a few minutes of a bad movie before reaching the bottom of his bottle.

He crept up the stairs and stopped in front of Ruby's door. The door was mostly closed, so he nudged it just a bit to see inside. Ruby was fast asleep. Ray stood at the door and watched her.

After a few moments Ray pulled the door back into the position he found it, and for the first time since he met Ruby, Ray went into the other room and lay down in a bed without her.

The office felt cooler than the other rooms. The futon was closer to the floor than the other beds, and he could feel the chill of the hardwood around him. The evenings were getting cooler and that particular night had a refreshing breeze that swept through the partially opened window.

Ray didn't fall asleep easily. He had a lot on his mind. Eventually he forced his eyes closed and was enveloped by the darkness.

Duncan was gone by the time Ray woke up in the morning. Ruby was back on the couch still in her pajamas and eating a bowl of cereal.

"Morning," she said.

"Hey."

Ray sat on the adjacent loveseat. Ruby put the bowl down on the coffee table. She picked up the remote and started to flip the channels. It was obvious to her that Ray was a little bit out of sorts. His eyes were still not completely open and by the lines on his face she could see that he had just woken up. "How'd you sleep?" she asked.

"Fine."

"You sleep on the futon?"

"Yeah."

Ruby waited a moment for Ray to add more. He offered nothing.

"Any reason?" she asked.

"Any reason what?"

"Any reason you slept in there?"

"You were out when I got home. I didn't want to wake you up."

"Uh huh," Ruby said.

"Honestly," he said. "I was hammered, and tired, and thought I was doing you a favor."

Ray got up from his seat and cuddled up to Ruby on the couch. The young girl couldn't help but smile. "I looked into your room and I couldn't see straight. I went to the washroom and then just wandered to the nearest bed."

"After yesterday, I would have thought, you know."

"I know. If it makes you feel any better I slept like shit."

"That makes me feel a *little* better."

"A little?"

"Just a little."

"Good. For real, though. I didn't mean anything by it at all. I missed you more than you missed me."

Ruby snuggled in closer to Ray, who was happy to have her do it.

"Where's Dun?" Ray asked.

"He went to meet some real estate person. Do you know what he's up to?"

"I think he's looking to start a business."

"I have to look for a job, too," Ruby said.

"What do you want to do?"

"Not be a waitress."

"That doesn't narrow it down much."

"I'm not really qualified for anything."

"What do you mean? Of course you are."

"Oh yeah? Like what?"

"Well, you're good with numbers."

"Yeah, and?"

"And what? That's a skill. You should do something with that."

"Like what?"

Ruby lifted her head from Ray's shoulder and looked him in the eyes.

"That's what you have to figure out," Ray said.

"Easy to say."

"Well, what did you think you were going to do when you left home?"

Ruby didn't answer.

"You're right in the middle of one of the education capitals of the world. You could always go back to school."

"It's too late to go back to school," Ruby said. She laid her head back on Ray's shoulder.

"Why? You don't have to go full time. Find classes that teach you what you want and work part time. Listen, it's just an idea, but it could be something worth looking into."

Duncan walked in the house holding papers in one hand and a plastic bag in the other. "Yo," he said. "You guys gotta try these bagels."

Duncan flung the bag onto Ray's lap.

"How was your meeting?" Ray asked.

"Pretty good," Duncan said. "Here, have a look."

On the table, Duncan laid out pictures and floor plans to an empty retail space not far from O'Keefe's.

"Tell me what we're looking at," Ray said, getting up from the couch.

"Seventeen hundred square feet of retail. Bathroom facility, room for an office."

"What's going in there?" Ruby asked.

"I was thinking about a Gym?"

"What kind?"

"Mixed martial arts."

"So, fighting."

"No, not fighting, Ruby. Martial arts."

"What's the difference?"

"When someone attacks you in a parking lot and you defend yourself, are you fighting?"

"Yes."

"No. Fighting is combat. You learn martial arts so you don't have to fight. It's a way to get to know your abilities, limitations, and to have control of your body. Idiots fight to prove they're tough. If you study martial arts you don't feel the need to do that, but you can defend yourself if you run into someone who does."

"Can girls do it?"

"They can, and they should."

"Okay," Ray said. "I like the idea. Have you checked if there are any others in the area?"

"I've looked," Duncan said. He pulled out a paper map of Boston. There were various red, green, and blue dots and notes scribbled across it. "The red dots are places for kids. The green are for adults, and the blue are for everyone. The ones that are circled teach more than one fighting technique. There aren't that many. Now, I'd go here," he said, pointing to a single black dot. "Right in the middle of Tufts, Harvard, and MIT."

"College kids," Ray said.

"Make it more about fitness and self defense than 'fighting'."

"I would do it," Ruby said.

"I hope so," Duncan said. "If there are girls there, the guys will come."

"So I guess you've changed your mind about staying in Boston then," said Ray.

"It's as good a place as any," Duncan shrugged.

"You could have done this back in Phoenix you know."

"Come on, Ray." Duncan gave Ray a stern look. "You really think we could have just stopped what we were doing and changed so easily? The whole idea was to get a fresh start. That's what I'm trying to do. Who knows if it will work out?"

"Anything I can do to help?"

"Well if I do it, I'll need to think of a way to get people to come. If either of you guys think of anything, let me know."

"You have a name for it yet?" Ruby asked.

"I was thinking, Max Fitness MMA."

"*Max*," said Ray.

"I don't get it," said Ruby.

"Max was the name of Duncan's teacher."

"And friend," Duncan added.

"So what's next?"

"Before I sign anything I want to find a place to buy equipment, see if I can even pull it off."

"And?"

"And I've made a few calls and sent some emails. I've only been at it a few days."

"Can I help?" Ruby asked.

"I'll let you know," Duncan said. "Maybe soon."

"It's a great idea, Dun."

"It feels pretty good. I think Max would be proud."

"Where did you come up with it?"

"I think I always had something like it in the back of my mind, but a new friend helped me see the real value of having a little business of your own."

"It was me, wasn't it," Ruby said fluttering her eyes.

"Of course it was," Duncan said, putting his arm around the girl and giving her a squeeze.

"You taking investors?" Ray asked.

"I may have to. I'll let you know."

Duncan began to clean up the papers on the table.

"What's that noise?" Ruby asked.

"That's me," Ray said.

Ray tugged a vibrating phone from his pocket and answered the call. "Hello? Hey, what's – you okay?"

Ray listened.

"I'm coming over," he said before hanging up the phone.

"What's up?" Duncan asked.

"Keys."

Duncan threw Ray the car keys. "What is it?" he asked again.

"She's sick, Dun. You know? I'll be back later."

Ruby just watched him go. "Who's sick?" she asked once the door had closed behind him.

Soon thereafter, Ray let himself into Ashley's apartment. He found her curled up in a ball on her bed. "I didn't know who else to call," she whimpered.

"It's okay," Ray said. "Where's Davis?"

"He's at work. But I want you here. He doesn't know. He doesn't get it."

Ashley was clearly ill. The color of her face nearly matched that of her white bed sheets. Ray climbed up on the bed and put his hand on her head.

"102," Ashley said.

"Okay, get under the covers."

Ray helped Ashley into her bed. He went to get a cold washcloth and located a bottle of aspirin in her washroom. "Take these," Ray said, handing her the pills and a glass of water.

Ashley took the pills.

When Ashley was younger, she contracted a severe case of atypical pneumonia that left her lungs in dreadful shape. For the following number of years, a standard cold or flu would have severe effects on the young girl. She was hospitalized on more than one occasion and put on ventilators simply to breathe well enough to sleep through the night. Ray had experience in dealing with many of Ashley's seemingly minor illnesses later in her life. Though her lungs had fully recovered and were much stronger than they were during her earlier years, the childhood trauma of near suffocation and panicked hospital visits left her scarred and terrified of illnesses. Ashley wasn't a hypochondriac, and she didn't wash her hands ten times a day to prevent germs; she went about her life as normal. However, at the onset of a virus that might seem conventional to others, Ashley's adolescent horrors brought out a fear in her that rivaled other, better-known phobias. Over the years she had experienced several debilitating panic attacks and went into shock on more than one occasion. It didn't help that her panic attacks were usually accompanied by true illness, which made the events that much more complex.

Once a sickness took hold in her body and she was a few days in, Ashley would naturally calm. Her wounded psyche eventually allowed her to accept an unfortunate yet benign diagnosis. Her fears would subside and she could ride out the illness like any other person would. The first few days, though, were still a problem for her. Ashley became a terrified little girl all over again when she felt she was getting sick, and her usually rational mind was lost.

Ray knew better than to try to talk Ashley down. Attempting to diminish her experience had proved detrimental more than once in the past. He learned the trick to help her cope. He learned to just be there for her.

"Do you want an Ativan?" Ray asked.

Ashley shook her head. "I want to sleep," she said.

"I'll sit with you 'til you fall asleep. I'm here, okay?"

Ray did as he said and waited for Ashley to nod off. He watched as she shook in bed like an animal left outside in winter.

Once he thought her asleep, he got up slowly from the bed and made for the other room. He left the door open just enough so that he could see her when he peered in, but closed enough so that he wouldn't disturb her sleep.

Ray took a seat on the couch and sent Duncan a text message informing him of the situation. Duncan would surely understand. He too had experience with Ashley's uncharacteristic reactions.

Ray put his phone back in his pocket and got up off the couch. He walked over to the mantle where the TV hung and picked up a framed picture. It had to be him, he thought. It had to be Davis.

The photo was of Ashley and a man embracing outside of Fenway Park. Who else could it be? Ray searched his mind but was already convinced.

"Ray," Ashley nervously called from the other room.

"I'm here."

"Ativan."

Ray fetched two little white pills from the marked bottle in Ashley's cabinet. The girl, again shaking from fear if not from the illness, placed them under her tongue and laid her head back on the pillow.

Ray couldn't help but lean over and kiss her on the forehead.

He sat in the room with her until the pills took effect and the trembling girl truly fell asleep.

CHAPTER 25

RAY WAS ON Ashley's couch watching TV a few hours later when he heard what sounded like a key in the door. He got up and approached cautiously. The door opened.

"Hi?" Ray said.

"Oh, hi," the man said, looking twice at the number on the door. Ray took a second but then recognized the face that had recently been burned into his memory.

"Davis," Ray said, pointing his finger like a gun.

"And you are?"

"Ray."

"Ray?"

"Ashley's friend, from Phoenix," Ray said, a little annoyed.

"Oh, *Ray*," Davis said. "Sure, sure. Hey, nice to meet you, Ray." Davis approached with arm held out. "What are you doing here?"

"Ash said that you were busy today, so I just came by to see if she was okay."

"Yeah, I called her office to talk to her and they told me she was home. I called her phone, but the answering machine kept picking up."

"Probably off."

"So…" Davis said, looking over Ray's shoulder. "Where's–"

"Sleeping."

"How she doing?"

Davis let himself into the apartment. He put his bag down on the kitchen counter and made his way to Ashley's room.

He was average looking, at least in Ray's estimation. Standing about the same height as Ray, Davis's suit and expensive shoes made him look more sophisticated than he probably was. His hair was neatly manicured and styled, and his chic, thin glasses irritated Ray instantly.

Davis peered in through the door of Ashley's room. He didn't dare go in and wake her. He shut the door quietly and walked over to the couch and sat down where Ray had been sitting.

Ray considered leaving right then, but he just couldn't pass up the opportunity to size up Ashley's new boyfriend.

"So what's wrong with her?" Davis asked.

"Probably just a flu," Ray said, sitting down in a chair beside the couch. "But you know Ashley."

"Actually, this is the first time I've seen her sick. But, yes, she's mentioned her difficulties."

"So you know she gets really freaked out and all that?"

"Sure. Yeah," Davis said. "Haven't seen it though. So, how scary is it?"

"Scary?" Ray said. "It's not *scary*, it's just a little anxiety."

"Has she been sleeping long?"

"Few hours."

"Have you been here the whole time?"

"Yeah, she was awake when I got here."

"And you stayed?"

"Yeah, I stayed," Ray said. "It's important that she knows someone's around. It makes her feel better."

"Uh huh, okay. Interesting. Why is that? Just in case something happens?"

"Yeah, I guess. So she knows she's not alone."

"Okay, I get it, I get it," Davis nodded. "Hey, thanks for the help, man."

"Right."

"So, are you in Boston for long, or…?"

"I'll be here a while," Ray said.

"I'm originally from Buffalo," Davis said. "I don't know if Ashley told you."

"I was just in Buffalo," Ray said. As soon as he said it, he cringed a little inside. Was he really making small talk with this guy?

"Really?"

"Well, Niagara Falls."

"Okay. Sure," Davis said. "Just for fun?"

"We went to the Falls, to the casino."

"So you were on the Canadian side then."

"Yeah."

"Did you go to any of the clubs?"

"Not really," Ray said. "We were only there for one night."

Ray looked at the clock on his phone. He was looking for a way out.

"Too bad, man. There are some pretty good clubs there."

"Yeah, I know," Ray said. He couldn't help but let out a little smirk.

"What?" Davis said. "Sundowner, right?"

Ray couldn't help but smile.

"I knew it," Davis said. "Crazy, huh?"

"It was pretty good."

"I've been going there since I was nineteen, man. I've got some crazy stories about that place."

"We saw a scrap out front."

"Really? I've never seen a fight there. The stories usually involve the girls."

"We were only there for a few hours. I'm not much of a strip club guy."

"I don't think I've been there in, what...over five years now. Or any club for that matter. I guess you just grow out of it or something. Who knows?"

Ray was beginning to hate Davis, but mostly because he was beginning to like him. He was friendly and unpresuming. He didn't for a second try to intimidate Ray with his position of superiority in Ashley's life, and he didn't show any intimidation from Ray's past with her. That, at least, was a commendable quality according to Ray. The guy could hold his own and was just confident enough to do it without being conceited.

Ray and Davis talked for a short while longer. When Ray did leave, Ashley still had not woken up.

When Ray got home, Ruby and Duncan were gone. Assuming they couldn't have gotten far without a car, Ray took a stroll over to O'Keefe's in search of his roommates.

It was approaching the early evening and the pub was beginning to get louder than it usually was during the day. Ray noticed Terry and Vinny in their spots up at the bar, but couldn't locate Ruby or Duncan.

"Hey," Ray said, sideling up beside Terry.

"Hey," Terry said.

"What's up Terry? Vinny?"

"Just hiding from the wife," Vinny said.

"You guys seen Duncan in here?"

"Your friend?" Terry asked. "I haven't seen him."

"Wasn't here today," Charlene added from behind the bar.

"Hmm."

"Can I get you one?" Charlene asked.

Ray tilted his head to see if Pete was at his usual table. He wasn't. "Ummm, sure," Ray said. "Why not."

Ray hopped up onto the stool beside Terry and graciously received his pint from Charlene.

"So what's going on?" Ray asked.

"Waiting for the Sox game," Vinny said, pointing up at the TV above the bar. "I got a good feeling about this. Those fuckin' Yanks ain't got shit tonight."

"They're playing the Yankees?"

"First game of three. I'm gonna clean up."

"We better," Terry added.

"You in on this game?"

"We both are," Vinny said.

"With who?"

"That little punk and his friend."

"Bixby?"

"Yeah," Terry said. "Piece of work that guy. But whaddaya gonna do?"

"Not the same as Bill?"

"Are you kidding?" Vinny said. "Billy had class. These guys are mooks. Fucking guys come in and collect their markers pretty much every day. Says he won't let me run a tab 'cause he doesn't trust me, or some shit. But fuck me if I'm up, right?"

"He's the only game around right now," Terry added.

"Guess so," Ray said. "What kind of action you guys play?

"Line," Vinny said, looking up at the TV screen. "We'll do some props from time to time. I'm good for one, maybe two bills if I'm feeling lucky. Billy's high rollers stopped coming around here though. And those fuckin' Gucci-wearing meatballs paid out. They were putting down a few g's a night. Guys like that ain't dealing with a puke like Bixby though."

"They used to come by here?"

"Sure did," Vinny said.

"Billy knew what he was doing. He greased up Nick just enough to let him work right outta here."

"Who's Nick?"

"The guy that owns the place, come on."

"You know, Vin," Terry said. "You got a big mouth."

"What?" Vinny said.

"You don't have to worry about me," said Ray.

"Hey, no offence. But this guy doesn't have to go telling every little thing."

"What?" Vinny said again. "He's a friend of Billy, you think he don't know?"

Ray took a sip of his beer. He didn't respond. He liked that Vinny had a loose tongue.

"Speak of the devil," Vinny said.

"You talking about me again?" Bixby said as he approached the bar.

"Where's your pal?" Vinny asked.

"What? You not happy to see me? Hey, Terry."

"Hey, Bixby," Terry said.

"Hey, Charlene," Bixby chirped. "A quick one over here."

Charlene nodded, though she didn't smile.

"Who's this?" Bixby asked.

"Ray, Bixby. Bixby, Ray," Terry said unenthusiastically.

Ray turned on his stool and put out his hand. "Hey," he said. Bixby shook his hand.

"He's a friend of Billy's," Vinny said.

"Oh, yeah?"

"I knew him," Ray said.

"Too bad what happened to him."

"Sure was."

"You staying for the game?"

"Was thinking about it."

Charlene put a pint of beer down on the bar. Bixby took the beer and dropped a ten-dollar bill on the wet circle the glass left behind on the wood.

"It's not too late to make it interesting," Bixby said. "I'd take your action."

Bixby was testing Ray. Upon hearing that he was a friend of Bill's, the newly crowned bet-taker was just short of peeing on the bar to make sure Ray knew it was his.

"No thanks," Ray said. "I'm not much of a sports fan."

"Okay, okay." Bixby said. "Char," he yelled. Charlene looked over. "His next one's on me." He pointed down over Ray's head.

"Thanks," Ray said, "but I'm good."

"T. Vinny. We good?"

"We're good, Bixby," Terry said.

"Good," Vinny agreed.

"Alright boys. I'll be around."

Bixby took his leave and made his way around the bar. He seemed to know everyone in the place, and considering how busy it was getting, Ray was mildly impressed.

By the time the game started, Ray was on his third beer and Bixby had left. The pub was nearing standing-room only, and on that night, the dull hum that was Ray's only experience of O'Keefe's had turned into a hearty roar.

Ray and Duncan had spent plenty of evenings watching sports in bars, but witnessing a Red Sox vs. Yankees game in a Boston area pub was a sight unlike anything Ray had seen before. In fact, Ray hadn't seen many live ballparks that could rival the energy of the place. The one thing he noticed missing was Pete. His table was occupied by what looked like a gaggle of college students challenging each other to chug their beers.

"Pete not here today?"

Charlene leaned over the bar. "Game day," she said. "Too many people."

The Red Sox pulled out a two run win that night, coming from behind in the seventh to take the lead. The bar celebrated as if they had just won the pennant. Terry and Vinny joined in the festivities, having made a couple of pennies on the victory.

Ray left the bar along with a smattering of others once the game ended. He returned home to a less-than-warm welcome. Ruby was lying on the couch watching a movie. She barely acknowledged his arrival. Ray knew something was wrong and he was pretty sure he knew what it was. "Where's Dun?" he asked from behind the couch.

"Upstairs," Ruby said.

Ray galloped up the stairs and found Duncan sitting on his bed with the computer on his lap and papers strewn across the mattress.

"You told her?" Ray asked.

"She knows," Duncan said.

"You told her."

"Ray, you ran out of the place. What did you want me to do?"

"What'd you tell her?"

"I think you can figure that out. What would you have said? You think I didn't look out for you?"

Ray dropped his head and looked at his feet.

"You'll figure it out, Ray," Duncan said, returning to the computer screen.

"Yeah."

Duncan chuckled.

"Thanks a lot, man," Ray said.

"Good luck."

CHAPTER 26

RAY SAT DOWN on the couch beside Ruby. She moved her feet to make room. Ray grabbed her ankles and pulled her legs onto his lap, returning her to the position in which he found her.

"I owe you an explanation," he said.

Ruby hit the mute button and looked over at Ray.

"Her name is Ashley, she–"

"Just tell me this," Ruby said. "Did you come here for her?"

"No," Ray said adamantly. "We came here for the money. That's the absolute truth; you can ask Duncan. The fact that she was here was a complete coincidence. An unfortunate one, actually."

"Why unfortunate?"

Ray thought for a moment. He wanted to choose his words very carefully.

"Look," he said. "I'm not going to lie to you and say I don't still have feelings for her. I probably always will. I know that now. Don't you have anyone like that in your life?"

"Go on," Ruby said.

"I didn't come here for her. But I did go see her because...fuck, I don't even know. How could I not? I had to.

But she's got a boyfriend, a life without me, and I have a life without her. The reason I went over there today was because–"

"Duncan told me," Ruby said.

"Told you what?"

Ruby rolled her eyes. "He told me about her anxiety attacks and all that. I know why you went."

"So you know nothing happened?"

"Yeah, today maybe. But that wasn't the first time you saw her, was it?"

"No," Ray said. "But I told you, she has a boyfriend."

"Why couldn't you just tell me about her?"

"What would I say? What would *you* say? Put yourself in my position. I didn't mean for any of this to happen."

"I would have told you."

"But there's nothing to tell."

"That's such a guy thing to say. Ray, you have to be honest with me, not talk to me just because you feel guilty about something. If you just would have told me–"

"Told you what?"

"–from the start about her then we wouldn't have had this problem."

"What should I have said?"

"How about I have an ex-girlfriend in Boston that I'd like to go see? How about–"

"But why should I have to tell you when it's not a big deal?"

"Because it is a big deal. It's a big deal to me because–"

"Because why?"

"Because obviously I have feelings for you, Ray!" Ruby blurted out.

Ray wasn't expecting to hear that just then from Ruby. Ruby wasn't expecting to say it either. In the quickening pace of the conversation she let out a thought that, once out, she was glad to have off her chest. Ray obviously suspected it, and though he most likely shared in the feeling he didn't want it out in the open. Instead, ever since Ray knew that he would be seeing Ashley again, once he had heard from Rico about Boston, not much in the way of a romance with Ruby could penetrate the shield he had put up. He cared for Ruby, of that he was sure. He had feelings for her that went far beyond the relationship that she and Duncan shared. Fortunately, and unfortunately, Ray never had to put much more thought to it – until just then.

"Ruby," Ray said.

"Never mind," she injected. "Forget I said anything."

"Yeah, 'cause that makes sense. I'll just forget it."

Ruby put her hands over her face in frustration, and embarrassment. "I didn't mean it like that," she said.

"Ruby–"

"Ray, don't say anything right now, because no matter what it is it's not going to help. I don't want to hear that you have no feelings for me and all this was just some playful crap to you, and I don't want to hear that you do have feelings for me right now, because then this whole thing with your ex-girlfriend will confuse me even more. Just, don't, okay?"

"Ruby–"

"Ray, I've had a long day. Just don't."

"Okay," Ray conceded.

"Now, how is your friend? Is she okay?"

Ray smiled and shook his head.

"What's so funny?"

"After all that you still want to know how she is?"

"I'm not upset with *her*, Ray. She didn't do anything."

"I don't know how she is, actually. Her boyfriend came home while she was asleep, so I left."

"You didn't say goodbye?"

"She was sleeping."

"She's not going to like that," Ruby said assuredly.

"Why? What do you mean?"

"She called *you*, right?"

"But her boyfriend came over."

"Yeah, but she called *you*."

"I'm not following."

"How long have they been together?"

"A couple of months."

"And how long have you known her?"

"Ten years."

"Then you really don't know much about women, do you?"

"I guess not," Ray said. "'Cause I have no idea what you're talking about."

"You're cute," Ruby said.

"So does this mean you're not mad at me anymore?"

"Wow. You *really* don't know much about women."

"What?" Ray laughed. "That was a perfectly normal question."

"Oh my God. Ray!" Ruby said in mocking frustration. "I was never mad at you. We're not in a fight. Don't you get that?"

"You were never mad at me?"

"No."

"Okay, then I really don't understand women."

"That's what I said."

Ray lunged over and jumped on top of Ruby. She let out a childish squeal and then laughed as Ray's weight pushed the air from her lungs.

Perhaps ill-timed, Ray peppered Ruby's neck with a handful of playful kisses.

"I guess things are okay?" Duncan said, clomping down the stairs in his bare feet.

"I don't know women," Ray said, removing himself from atop the girl.

"Yeah, big news. You okay, Rube?"

"I'm okay," she said. "Thanks, Dun."

"What's all this about?" Ray said, pointing back and forth between Ruby and Duncan.

"What?" Duncan asked.

"Me and Duncan bonded today," Ruby said.

"Oh really?"

"We bonded," Duncan affirmed as he poked his head into the nearby fridge.

Duncan came and joined the other two in the living room. He sat on the single seat beside the couch and took a bite of an apple. "What're we watching?" he asked, mouth full of apple chunks.

"I *was* watching *When Harry Met Sally*," Ruby said.

"Oh yeah," Duncan said, taking another bite. "Is that a new one?"

"Clever," Ruby said. "What have you been doing upstairs?"

"Work."

"How's that going?" Ray asked.

"Good."

"Anything I can help with?"

"Not really. Not yet anyway. I have to figure some shit out still."

"Well, just let me know."

"Me too," Ruby added.

"So where did you guys go today, anyway?" Ray asked. "When I got home you weren't here."

"We ran some errands," Duncan said. "You go to O'Keefe's?"

"Yeah. Dude, you should see that place during a Sox game. It's a completely different bar."

"Busy?"

"Packed. And loud."

"Next time," Duncan said.

"Can I finish my movie now?" Ruby asked.

The boys left Ruby to her movie. Duncan went back to his room and Ray kept him company for a while and caught him up on what happened with Ashley, Davis, and more recently with Ruby. After a while, Ray retired to bed a little earlier than usual.

When Ruby came upstairs sometime later, she was happy to see Ray in her bed. Thinking he was asleep, she quietly got undressed and crawled in beside him.

"What's that?" Ray said, his face in the pillow.

"What's what?" Ruby asked.

Ray pointed to the small table on Ruby's side of the bed. Ruby sat up and grabbed the stack of booklets. She flipped through them one at a time.

"Boston College, Cambridge College, Fisher College, Tufts University," Ruby said.

"So that's what you did today."

"It was Duncan's idea."

"It was *my* idea," Ray said, raising his head from the pillow.

"Okay, it was your idea. But Duncan and I went together."

"And?"

"And I have to decide what I want if I plan to start in September."

"And?"

"And...I'm thinking about Boston College," Ruby said. "Maybe accounting classes or something."

Ray put his head back down on the pillow. Ruby placed the pamphlets back on the table and got comfortable under the covers. Ruby shut her eyes and thawed into the silence of the room.

"My idea," Ray said into the stillness. He rolled over and put his arm over Ruby's body.

CHAPTER 27

"I FOUND IT," Duncan said.

He was plodding down the stairs at a regular pace and Ray wasn't certain he heard him correctly. He and Ruby had just woken up and were down in the kitchen looking for something to eat.

"You did what?" Ruby asked.

"I found it," Duncan said. "I think I found it."

"What?"

"A place for all the equipment I need."

"Oh," Ray said. "So that's good, right?"

"I noticed a bunch of local ads all over the place that kept leading me to the same guy. I finally e-mailed him and it turns out this guy is liquidating a bunch of shit from a gym that never opened. I don't know, something about some company trying to start one of those mega gyms and their funding fell through or whatever. Anyway, the details aren't worked out but the gear is brand new and they have way more than I need."

"So this is happening?" Ray said.

"Looks like it," Duncan said. "I'm meeting with the guy later today. If things go well, I'll be able to float the whole deal and have plenty of cash left over. It may not be as expensive as I thought."

"That's awesome," Ruby said. "Good for you, Dun."

"Hey, you read through those books?" Duncan asked.

"I did, and I think you were right."

"Are you going to do it?"

"I don't know," Ruby said. "It makes me really nervous."

"Wait," Ray said. "Slow down. What was he right about?"

"Boston College."

"You can just apply and get in?"

"It's a Professional Studies Certificate. It's not a degree or anything so I don't really need to *apply*, I just have to sign up…if there's still room."

"When do you have to decide?" Duncan asked.

"Soon," Ruby said. "I have until the end of the month to register. I think I want to go in and talk with someone about it though."

"You should," Ray said.

"So good news all around." Duncan clapped his hands together and smiled. "We should celebrate."

"Okay," Ruby said. "When?"

"Tonight? I have shit to do this afternoon. Ruby, see if you can make an appointment to talk to someone today 'cause I'm going that way and we can ride together."

"I'll call right now."

Ruby jogged up the stairs and disappeared.

"You good?"

"Fine," Ray said.

"Want to come with me?"

"If you want."

"I'm gonna go call that real estate agent."

Duncan jogged up the stairs and disappeared.

Ray was left alone in the kitchen. He stared out the back window. In plain sight, a squirrel was nibbling away at his breakfast. Ray watched intently. The tiny animal finished the meal and instantly bolted from sight. Ray wondered where the little guy was off to.

Duncan and Ruby came down the stairs together dressed and ready to go. Ray was on the couch flipping channels on the TV. "You coming?" Duncan asked him.

"When you leaving?"

"Now."

"Um, I'm okay."

"You sure? We'll wait for you."

"Nah. You guys go. I'm gonna stay here."

"Okay, your call. We'll be back later."

Ruby was a little disappointed that Ray didn't want to join them. She didn't say anything, but Ray's lack of enthusiasm took a little something away from hers. Before leaving, she leaned over the back of the couch and kissed Ray on the cheek. "See you soon," she said.

Duncan and Ruby left with the car.

The first stop for Duncan and Ruby was the retail space Duncan had already once inspected. It was less than a mile down on the same strip as O'Keefe's, but sat nestled between some nicer shops. There was a music store on one side and Starbucks on the other. The previous tenant of the space was a lady's wear shop that had recently been relocated. Duncan and Ruby sat in the car out front of the for-lease location and waited for the agent to arrive.

When Edita Maroni pulled up behind the Fifth Avenue, all parties exited their cars.

"Hi, again," Edita said, shaking Duncan's hand.

"Edita, this is my friend, Ruby."

Edita shook Ruby's hand.

"Do we want to go in again?" Edita asked.

Duncan and Ruby followed Edita into the store.

"The interesting thing is," she said, "it looks a lot smaller when it's empty. Once you get things in here it feels like a larger space. The washroom facilities are downstairs, as you remember, and the office can stay or you can easily take down the wall and you have even more room."

"I'd keep the office."

"That will save you some money in renovations."

"And it's ready for lease immediately?"

"That's right," Edita said, opening up her leather binder. "The lease would start on the first of the month. So that would be September first."

"What do you think, Ruby?" Duncan asked.

"Well, I like it," Ruby said. "But what do I know?"

"About as much as me."

"Obviously you'll change the floor?"

"Yeah, the carpet won't do. But I like the mirrored wall, I'd keep that."

"Yeah, I agree."

"How long has the place been available?" Duncan asked.

Edita consulted her binder once again. "The last tenant vacated...the end of last month," she said. "So less than four weeks."

Duncan looked around again, from ceiling to floor.

"It's a great location," Edita said. "You'll get a lot of foot traffic with a Starbucks next door."

"That's true."

"Do you want to think about it a while longer?"

"Ummmm..." Duncan pondered. "No. I don't think so. I think I'll take it."

"Okay," Edita said, closing her leather folder. "That's great."

"So now what?"

"Now, you can follow me to my office and we can start the paper work."

"Okay. Lead the way."

Edita led Duncan and Ruby out of the empty shop and locked the door behind them. Duncan let Edita pull out first and followed her as she made a U-turn on the street and headed towards her office.

Back home, Ray had fallen asleep on the couch. Duncan and Ruby had been gone for just over an hour, but for the first time since he left Phoenix, Ray was completely bored. He shut his eyes for lack of something better to do and soon fell prey to the late morning nap. The loop of Sports Centers had given way to a PGA golf tournament. The calming, dull sounds of lethargic commentators coupled with the soft-clapping crowd served as a potent lullaby.

Duncan and Ruby completed all the necessary paper work with Edita, and short of an unforeseen and unfortunate turn of luck, Duncan was the proud new owner of retail space in Sommerville.

Stop number two for the roving duo was the campus of Boston College, where Ruby had a meeting with an admissions counselor. They were early for their meeting but the counselor was gracious enough to take Ruby in right away, having left a gap for herself after her lunch break. Duncan planned on sitting out in the waiting area but both Ruby and the counselor, Ms. Coffer, invited him in.

"Some of our cert grads go on into bookkeeping positions, sure," Ms. Coffer said in response to one of Ruby's questions. She spoke softly and slowly and moved about in a similar manner.

"Small businesses, medium sized businesses, you name it," she said. "Or, some students continue on and use their course credits towards a degree, which you can also do."

"What sort of degree?" Ruby asked.

"You can use the credits towards an undergraduate Bachelors degree, or even as first steps towards becoming a CPA. The courses are all accredited and will remain on your transcript. But you certainly don't need to decide that now, honey."

"And I can do those degrees here?"

"The Cert Program is at Woods College, if you wanted to go on to complete your undergrad degree you could remain here, but at a different school at BC."

"Okay," Ruby said. "I think I get it. So this certificate program would be a good place to start?"

"There are many benefits to the program. It has a very flexible schedule so people with jobs can work around it. Or, you can take many classes at once and accelerate the program to finish early. It's a terrific gateway for things like job promotion, or change of career because it offers practical, hands-on knowledge. From our discussion on the phone earlier, and from what you've told me here, if you were looking to join a company or to start your own business you would have all the tools to be an effective bookkeeper, financial administrator, things like that."

"And how does this program compare to some of the other colleges in the city?" Duncan asked.

"I can't speak for the other schools," Ms. Coffer said. "But I can tell you that only a few offer a certificate program, and even fewer allow you to go on and use your credits towards a degree. And, as I'm sure you know, Boston College has a wonderful reputation, which is very important. When you go out and look for a job it's nice to have a good college on your resume. What I can do is put you in touch with someone that has taken this program in the past, you can speak with them and ask them all about it if you like. How does that sound?"

"That would be great," Ruby said.

"Okay then."

Ms. Coffer began typing away on her desktop computer. "Let me see where my student contacts are," she said to herself.

"And it's not too late to register for September?" Ruby asked.

"Well, you'll have to apply for each course separately. I can't say which, if any, would be full, but they are offered at various times so even if one class is full you may still be able to find the same course at a different time. Ah, okay, here we are."

Ms. Coffer pulled out a small sheet of paper from her desk and began to write down information from her screen. "Here is the name of two people that have taken the Accounting Cert Program," she said even slower than usual.

She completed scribbling and handed the paper to Ruby. "I'm not familiar with that gentleman there, but Amanda is a lovely girl who just finished the program last year."

"Amanda, huh?" Duncan said.

Ruby smiled.

"Do you know her?" Ms. Coffer asked.

"No," Ruby answered. "It's nothing."

"Oh. Well then do you have any other questions, hun?"

"I don't think so. Not right now at least."

"Okay, well you have my card, and I hope you'll call or e-mail if you think of anything else you'd like to talk about."

Duncan and Ruby thanked Ms. Coffer and left her office. On the way out, both couldn't help but comment on her soothing demeanor and gentle tone of voice.

The parking ticket they found on the windshield of the Fifth Avenue wasn't nearly enough to douse even one ember in the flame of their spirited mood.

Ray awoke on the couch, hungry and smelling foul. The golf tournament was still going strong, but it was of no interest to him at all. He located the remote under his butt and flicked off the TV. He got up off the couch, took a handful of cereal, and munched on it as he made his way slowly up the stairs.

Ruby and Duncan arrived at a warehouse on the outskirts of town. It was a massive one-story building that looked more like a factory than a place of business. They let themselves in through one of the open dock garage doors and were quickly greeted by a man pushing a cart.

"I'm supposed to ask for Tom Putero," Duncan said.

"Other end of the building, bro," the man answered. "You're going to want to head around to the front. There's a parking lot there, you'll see it."

Duncan took the direction and parked among a small cluster of cars in a place he would have called the back of the building, not the front.

Glass doors opened up to an office-like area complete with a receptionist. The walls of the office were of a normal height, but didn't come close to reaching the ceiling.

"I'm here to see Tom Putero," Duncan said to the young lady at the front desk.

"And your name?" she asked.

"Duncan Miller."

The receptionist picked up the phone and dialed a few numbers. "A Duncan Miller here to see you," she said. "He's up at the front."

Tom arrived in the reception area and introduced himself to Duncan and Ruby. "I thought you weren't coming until later," he said.

"We're ahead of schedule today."

"Must be nice. Follow me, guys, I think I know what you're looking for."

Duncan and Ruby followed Tom through the office area and came upon two brown double doors. Tom pulled one open and unveiled the inner workings of the building.

"So the guys that originally bought the stuff cancelled shipment," Tom said as he led them through immense wall-high metal shelving units packed with boxes and merchandise. "It's been taking up space in my warehouse for months."

At the end of a long aisle, Tom stopped and presented a cache of brand new gym equipment. "I've been selling it off piece by piece. Have a look and let me know if you can use anything. I can give you a good deal."

Duncan looked over the stash. There was too much to take in. "I need mitts, shields, targets," he said. "Ummm, a few hanging bags, a few standing bags, sparring gloves, headgear, foot guards, shin guards, and maybe a dummy or two if you have them."

"My friend, you've come to the right place," Tom said. "I got everything but the dummies."

Duncan picked up a still-bagged headgear and glove combo pack. "Is it all Warrior stuff?" he asked.

"The sparring gear is," Tom said. "I also got some Everlast stuff. The heavy bags, hanging kick bags, shields, stuff like that."

"You have hanging kicks and standing?"

"Oh yeah. You need the hardware? I got metal scaffolding so you can put them up anywhere: against a wall, from the ceiling, whatever. I got it all."

"Do you have any pictures of all this stuff set up?"

"I have all the pictures you need. Let's go to my office. I got the numbers there, too."

Duncan and Ruby followed Tom back to his office and sat down in the two chairs set up in front of his desk. Tom took out brochures and highlighted all the equipment he had in stock. He gave Duncan a printed sheet that broke down the original order by numbers (minus the bits and pieces he was able to unload prior to their meeting). After brief discussion, Tom and Duncan arranged a unit price for each individual SKU on Duncan's want-list. Tom was offering Duncan his wholesale price plus a small markup to help cover the storage and delivery costs. Duncan was extremely pleased with the offer. He tried his best not to show it.

"Let me do some measurements," Duncan said. "These numbers good for a while?"

"Could you ballpark what you're looking for?" Tom said. "I have other people interested."

"Ten to twelve heavies, ten to twelve hanging kicks, five or so standing, and…I'll probably take all your gloves, shields, heads, and shins."

"Well, okay. Then the numbers are good for a while. Just get back to me as soon as you can."

Duncan stood up and shook Tom's hand.

"I look forward to hearing from you," Tom said. "Young lady, it was nice to meet you, too."

Duncan and Ruby showed themselves out of the office and back to the car.

"Are those prices good?" Ruby asked.

Duncan handed her all the paperwork to hold while he drove. "Almost half off any other price I've gotten so far," he said.

"So that's awesome. But why do you need so many gloves and helmet things? There were, like, tons in there."

"'Cause when they're that cheap I can sell them myself," Duncan said. "People will want their own."

"Ah," Ruby said. "Smart."

Duncan pulled out of the parking lot and began the forty-minute drive back home.

Ray came out of an extra long shower and sat lazily down on the bed. He picked up his phone to check the time and noticed he had a missed call. He hit the callback button and waited for the ring.

"Hello?" a voice answered.

"Ash?" Ray said, surprised. "Who's number is this?"

"It's my home number," she said.

"Oh. How you feeling?"

"Can't you tell?" Ashley said, nose stuffed and voice labored.

"Yeah, but how are you *feeling*?"

"Much better. Thanks for coming over."

"No problem."

"You were gone when I woke up."

"Yeah, well, you know."

"You met Davis."

"I did."

"He said you were really cool."

"Yeah, well. I am, right?"

"Ray," Ashley said.

"What do you want me to say, Ash. I only spoke to him for a while. Yeah, he seems like a nice guy. But what do I know?"

"That's not what I was going to say."

"Oh. What were you going to say?"

"I was going to say…that I wanted it to be you. When I woke up. I wanted you here."

Ray said nothing.

"You there?"

"I'm here. I don't know what to say to that."

"You don't have to say anything. I just wanted you to know. When I woke up I wanted to see you, and you were gone. You didn't even say goodbye."

"I wasn't going to wake you."

"Why not? You could have said goodbye."

"Your boyfriend was there, Ash."

"He's not – yeah, okay, I know."

"It wasn't easy for me to just leave."

"I know."

"I wanted to be there for you."

"I know."

"I still love you, Ashley," Ray said.

There was a pause.

"I love you too," she replied.

CHAPTER 28

DUNCAN AND RUBY got home and found Ray back on the couch. If not for his damp hair and clean clothes they might have assumed he hadn't moved an inch since they left.

"How'd it go?" Ray asked.

"Went good," Duncan said.

Ruby jumped over the back of the couch and landed on Ray's head.

"And you, missy?" Ray asked.

"Good," Ruby said, entwined with him.

"Who's hungry?" Duncan asked.

"Starving," Ray said.

"Me too," Ruby shrieked.

"What's wrong with you? You drunk?"

"Nope."

"Let's do something touristy tonight," Duncan suggested.

"Like what?"

"Scalper tickets?"

"I'd do it," Ray said.

"Ruby?" Duncan asked.

"Can we eat first?"

"You're going to Fenway for the first time ever and all you can think about is food?"

"I'm also thirsty."

"What did you do to her?" Ray asked. "I've never seen her like this."

Ruby rolled off Ray and got up from the couch. "I'm going to get ready," she said. "You too." Ruby smacked Duncan across the shoulder as she ran past him and up the stairs.

"She's lost it."

"She's just happy," Duncan said. "And she's a girl so she's already a bit nuts. I'm going to get changed. Twenty minutes?"

"What time's the game?" Ray yelled as Duncan sprinted up the stairs.

"Seven, seven-ten? Check," his voice rang down.

"We won't have enough time for dinner."

Outside the stadium, Duncan tried to pay for the tickets himself but Ray made certain he covered at least half the cost by stuffing money into his pocket as he made the exchange. The scalper was asking far above average, but none of them cared. Ruby offered to pay too but was relegated to purchasing the first round of Fenway Franks. The first inning was just getting under way when they took their seats along the third base line. The atmosphere was electric on a perfect August night.

They enjoyed another round of Franks, a couple of warmish beers, and an entertaining seventh inning stretch that saw a fan rush the field.

The Yankees took the lead early and never let it go, which took some of the gusto out of the stadium, but seeing the green monster in person was worth the trip indeed.

After the game, Duncan led the others to the *Legal Seafood* restaurant, where a drunken patron was holding menus asking people if they preferred "smoking or non" as they walked into the establishment. Duncan didn't fall for the rouse but commended the youngish prankster on his ingenuity and guts. A male server soon de-railed the hoax and helped the man – who was wearing a Green Bay Packers outfit of all things – back to his table. His friends greeted him with a round of applause.

Duncan, Ray, and Ruby were shown to a table and each promptly ordered lobster dinners from a bubbly female server. It was to be another first for Ruby. Her first time at Fenway Park was followed by her first time having a full lobster set down before her. She'd tried lobster cakes, and one time had lobster bisque, but this was the first occasion where she was bibbed and handed a walnut cracker to properly attend to her dinner. Duncan and Ray gave her a few pointers along the way; how to properly extract the claw, which parts were most edible and which were best to leave alone, and finally, how to fold the remaining exoskeleton properly so that the server knows to remove it. The last tip was one initiated by Ray but quickly caught on to by Duncan, who was happy to play along. They never let Ruby in on the joke.

It was Ruby's idea to stop in at O'Keefe's on the way home. It was Duncan's idea to drop the car off at home first and make the short walk there instead.

The crowd at the bar was dispersing by the time they arrived. The Red Sox loss contributed heavily to the waning numbers inside. Neither Terry nor Vinny were there, nor was Pete.

Duncan claimed an empty table. Ray went to the bar. Ruby went to visit the little girl's room. They all met back at the table and clinked their pint glasses together to toast a good day.

A woman came over and sat down at the single empty seat beside Duncan. Though the thought was shared, no one came out and asked Charlene why she would hang out at work on her night off. Ray introduced her to Ruby and the two exchanged pleasant smiles and hellos.

"Where is everyone tonight?" Ray asked.

"Like who?" Charlene answered.

"Vinny, Terry, Mike…"

"Well, Vinny and Terry were here but Bixby came by and scared them off. Mike wasn't in at all today."

"Who's Bixby?" Duncan asked.

"The new Willy," Ray said. "What did he do to scare them off?"

"He just has this way of…I don't know; he makes the guys uneasy. I don't think they're scared of him or anything, but when he comes around to collect they don't want to be here."

"He was just here yesterday," Ray said.

"He's all over those guys."

"Does he get violent?" Duncan asked.

"No. Not really," Charlene said. "At least, he hasn't yet."

"That guy doesn't have a clue what he's doing," Ray said.

"Doesn't seem like it," Duncan agreed. "He comes to collect in person?"

"He does," Charlene said. "Why?"

"No reason. None of my business."

"Who is this guy?" Ruby asked.

"Just a kid from the neighborhood that eventually grew up," Charlene said.

"So, Charlene," Duncan said. "What about you?"

"Me?"

"Yeah, sure. You already know everything about everyone else in here. What's your story?"

"My story?"

"You married? Single? Have any big dreams? Wanna be a singer? Painter? Serial killer?"

"I've thought about the serial killer thing, but who hasn't, right? No, I'm just kidding. Let's see," Charlene looked up to the sky. "I'm single now, I used to be married–"

"Divorced?"

"Yup. Knocked me up when I was eighteen."

"So you have a kid."

"A daughter, Layla."

"How old is she?" Ray asked.

"Nice try," Charlene smiled, "but I'm not telling you how old I am. She's a teenager, that's all I'm saying."

"What's it like having a teenage daughter?" Duncan asked.

"Hell, but only sometimes. Most of the time she's my best friend in the world, so it's not so bad. And as for dreams, well, I used to be a pretty good dancer, but not so much anymore."

"Why not?"

"No time," Charlene said. "I live with a daughter that needs new clothes and with my mother who's getting up there. I have to work whenever I can. Plus, if Layla ever decides to go to college, well, I'll worry about that when it happens."

"So what," Ray said. "She's sixteen? Seventeen?"

"Funny. But no, to answer your question, I don't have time for dreams."

"Everyone has time for dreams," Ruby said.

"Not when they have bills like me they don't. Seems God has very small plans for me."

"I don't think God has anything to do with it," Ray said.

"He doesn't believe in God," Ruby offered.

"What, at all?" Charlene asked.

"At all."

"Neither should you," Ray said to Charlene.

"Why not?"

"Well you just said it yourself. He gives you a hard time. So what good is he anyway?"

"Just 'cause I have a hard time doesn't mean God doesn't exist."

"I guess you're right," Ray said. "The all-powerful, all-knowing, benevolent being chooses to make your life difficult."

Duncan just sat there and listened. He enjoyed not being the one on the receiving end of Ray's blaspheming for a change.

"God does things for his own reasons."

"Oh, Charlene," Ray said. "There are so many things wrong with that statement."

"It doesn't matter anyway. I believe there's a God, but I don't have to have all the answers. And if you don't think he exists then that's fine. But you're going to be the one fighting your whole life 'cause most people do believe."

"Now that's true," Ray said. "I am definitely in the minority. But there are more people like me than you think."

"It's harder to not believe I think," Ruby said. "It leaves you with so many questions."

"Maybe. But the answers you get from believing are all fake answers."

"Maybe fake to you," Charlene said.

"You're not going to get anywhere with him," Duncan said, sitting back in his chair. "The best thing to do is just nod and tell him he makes sense."

"You make sense," Charlene said.

"I know," Ray agreed.

"You should talk to Pete. He's always reading about that stuff."

"I have."

Charlene turned to look at Pete's usual spot. "Where'd he go?" she said.

"Game day. I thought he doesn't come in."

"Yeah, but he came in once the game was over. The crowd was gone but…that's so weird. I didn't see him leave. Anyway, anyone need another drink?"

"I'll come with you," Duncan said.

Duncan and Charlene went up to the bar together to refill everyone's drinks.

"You think he likes her?" Ruby asked.

"Duncan? I don't know. Maybe? He does like older women."

"I think he likes her."

"What makes you say that?"

"Just a feeling."

"Yeah, well, Duncan's hard to read. I'm surprised you get any sort of vibe at all."

"Hard to read?" Ruby said. "He was practically drooling over Kennedy in Omaha."

"He was?"

"Are you kidding? I don't get you sometimes. Are you oblivious to signals?"

"I don't know. Give me a signal and I'll tell you."

Ruby thought about it for a second and then reached her arm under the table and placed it on Ray's knee. Instead of leaving it there, she slowly progressed it up his leg until it reached his crotch. She grabbed a hold of the bulge between Ray's legs.

Duncan and Charlene returned to the table with fresh drinks; to Ray's surprise, Ruby left her hand where it was.

"What?" Duncan said, sitting back down.

"Nothing," Ray said.

Ruby gave the sensitive area a sturdy squeeze before removing her hand and taking her drink from Charlene. "Thanks," she said.

"Thank Duncan," Charlene said.

The foursome continued talking as their second round of drinks dwindled from their glasses. Though Charlene was ready for another, Ruby and Duncan – beginning to showing signs of wear – graciously declined. Ray wanted to stay but was coaxed otherwise by a simple look from Ruby.

"Okay," Ray said. "I'm gonna hit the washroom and then we'll go."

With all urinals occupied, Ray entered the lone stall. While inside, he heard the two other men mention something about a guy sitting on the floor by the bar. Ray mostly ignored it. On his way back to the table, Ray noticed that a few people were congregating at the other end of the bar. His curiosity was piqued and he couldn't help but head over in that direction. Ray turned the small corner at the end of the wood and saw that there was in fact someone on the floor behind Pete's usual table. At first, it simply looked like an old drunk wallowing on the ground, but as Ray took a second look, he could see that the old drunk was wearing a black cap. He couldn't see the man's face but there were many other telltale signs that it was indeed Pete. He cleared the growing throng. "Pete. You okay, man?" Ray asked, kneeling down to the ground.

"Sure," Pete said quietly.

Pete was sitting with his left side firmly up against the wall. In his left hand, Ray could vaguely make out what looked like the top of a bottle, and then it began to make sense. "You drunk?" Ray asked.

"No, are you?"

Charlene must have seen Ray's head disappear from sight as he bent down because she soon joined Ray on the floor with Pete. "Is that a bottle?" she asked.

"Maybe," Pete said. "Want some?"

Pete lifted and revealed a mostly empty bottle of Glenlivet. Charlene propped her head up and looked over to her right. "You took that from the bar?" she said.

"Nope," Pete said.

"Okay," Ray insisted. "Let's get you home."

Ray put his arm around Pete and tried to lift him from the ground. "No." Pete shouted, swatting Ray's arm away. "I can do it."

Duncan and Ruby arrived on the scene.

Pete began to rise to his feet, making certain that he still didn't show his left side. "He lives close," Charlene said.

"I can take him," Ray offered.

Pete got to his feet. His head still hanging low.

Pete lifted his chin just for a moment and his eyes met Ruby's. He quickly turned away in shame.

Pete leaned over to Charlene. "I'm sorry," he whispered.

"Don't worry about it for a second, Pete," Charlene said. "Ray's going to take you home."

"We'll come too," Duncan said. "Make sure you get home okay."

"Not the girl," Pete said ashamed.

"I don't have to go," Ruby said.

"You go with Ruby," Ray said to Duncan. "I can walk with him."

Followed closely by Ray, Duncan, Ruby, and Charlene, Pete exited the pub under his own diminished power. He was a fair sized man and though he hadn't been known to drink a lot at once, it seemed as though he could handle himself when drunk. Pete stood outside in the darkness with his right hand covering his left, which hung down beside his body like a wet rag. His head hung low and when he spoke, his harsh voice was even quieter than normal. "I'm okay to walk," he said, angling his face away from Ruby. "I'll leave you guys alone."

Pete turned and began to walk away. Ray took a few quick steps and caught up to him on the sidewalk.

Duncan and Ruby watched the pair as they dwindled into the distance under the streetlights. Charlene gave Duncan and Ruby a hug and went back into the pub for a few more cocktails. Duncan and Ruby turned in the opposite direction and began their own walk home.

When they arrived at Pete's house, Ray followed Pete up to his second floor apartment. Pete lived in a room he rented above someone's detached garage. Pete opened the unlocked door and walked in. He plunked down on his bed; it doubled as a couch during the day.

The grey room was fair sized for a bachelor apartment, but still fairly small for any adult to call home. About the size of a two-car garage with a small kitchen carved out of one corner. There were no signs of personality in the place at all. It was safe to say that Pete had forgone the use of an interior decorator. The lack of pictures on the wall, or even a proper paint job, gave the impression that Pete wasn't expecting to host many visitors. Either that or he simply didn't care.

"You gonna be okay?" Ray asked.

"I'm going to sleep, I think," Pete said.

Ray stood by the door.

Perhaps it was that Pete had become familiar with Ray, or that his current state robbed him of concern, but Pete began to disrobe. He struggled to pull his long sleeve shirt over the left side of his body, but managed to do it using only his right hand. Shirtless, Ray could see the extent of the burns to Pete's left side. Starting at his waist, Pete's torso and chest were wrinkled and charred. His left shoulder looked to bear the worst of the injury; his arm and elbow much the same. Pete turned to reposition his body and revealed only his unharmed right side. In the darkness of the room, he looked to Ray like two different people.

"You don't have to stay," Pete said, lying back on his bed.

"Okay," Ray said. "I'll catch you later then."

Ray turned to leave.

With his hand on the handle, Ray paused. Something made him turn back to Pete. "Why the sudden change?" he asked.

"Whah?"

"What happened to just one beer?"

"I guess things change, Ray."

Ray took a few steps into the dark room. He closed the door. A weak stream of light from the moon shone through the window and splattered on the wall just above Pete's head. Ray lifted a few items of clothing off a folding chair and took a seat. "Something happen?" he asked.

"Yeah," Pete said. "I got blown up."

Ray wondered if in that night Pete was celebrating – or mourning – the anniversary of his incident. Ray got up to leave, feeling he might be putting his nose where it didn't belong.

"They're cutting me off," Pete said, hearing Ray's footsteps on the hard wooden floor.

"What?"

"They're cutting me off," he repeated. "My time is up."

Ray turned back around.

"I'm now capable of *gainful employment*."

"Your disability–"

"I've been reduced. Not even enough to buy food for the month."

"What do they want you to do?"

"What's the difference?" Pete said.

"Get a job?"

Pete said nothing. He raised his hand and touched the left side of his face with the tips of his fingers. "You should go," he said.

"Is there anything I can do?"

"Yeah, sure. Find me a job I can do in the corner of a bar."

Ray watched the still man wallowing in the shadows. Pete didn't make another movement or say another word. Ray sat back down in the chair.

He watched Pete sleep for a short while before taking his leave.

Ray passed the bar again on the way home. He didn't consider stopping but could hear action still going on inside. He was heavy in thought.

When he got home the door was unlocked. He expected to see Duncan and/or Ruby sitting on the couch awaiting his return. Neither was there.

The house was silent.

Ray sat down at the kitchen table and lingered.

An hour passed. He stared out the window. When he finally got up, he moved about the house slowly and quietly. He walked up the stairs like a burglar.

There was a candle burning in Ruby's room and the sleeping girl was adorned in nothing but slinky white underwear. She had waited too long for Ray's arrival. Not wanting to wake her, Ray carefully leaned over Ruby and blew out the candle with a single breath. He covered the peaceful girl with the blanket. He watched her sleep.

After a few moments, Ray exited the room once more. He pulled out his phone and dialed a number as he strode down the stairs.

"Hey, Rico," Ray said. "I got a question for you."

CHAPTER 29

DUNCAN LEFT EARLY the next morning. He had managed to get Edita to let him into the store to take some measurements even though the deal had not yet officially closed. Ruby let Ray sleep and snuck downstairs to make a phone call. It had been a few days since Ruby spoke to her mother and she was eager to share the news with her. She was glad to hear a familiar voice, and even more excited that her return to school pleased her mother greatly. Upon hearing the news, Ruby's mom offered to help pay for the ambitious endeavor, a proposal Ruby quickly denied knowing too well of her mother's imperfect financial situation.

Ray awoke to the sound of an incoming text message on his phone. It was from Ashley; she cordially requested his attendance at her apartment at his earliest convenience, though her exact words were, "Alone. Come over when up."

Ray didn't get out of bed right away. He lay on his back and stared up at the ceiling. He let his thoughts run freely. Ruby was doing her best to remain quiet on the floor below, but the repetitive clanking of spoon to bowl was clear indication that she wasn't waiting for him to eat breakfast.

Ray finally rose, washed and dressed, and appeared down the stairs to a pajama-clad Ruby. She had the TV on but wasn't paying much attention. Instead she had forms and booklets open on the coffee table in front of her. She was filling out registration paperwork and organizing class schedules. "You going out?" she asked when she saw Ray.

"Yeah."

"Oh."

Ruby foolishly assumed that Ray would simply offer up his destination.

"Did Dun take the car?"

"Think so."

Ray put on his shoes at the front door. Ruby turned back to her paperwork.

"I'm going to see Ashley," Ray said. "See if she's okay."

"Okay," Ruby said, her eyes still down on her work.

"Just okay?"

"What else should I say?"

"Nothing. I guess." Ray pulled out his phone and dialed for a cab. Knowing he would have to wait at least five to ten minutes, he sat down on the couch beside Ruby. "Can I help?" he asked.

"Not really. Thanks, though."

"Is this your schedule?"

Ray lifted a stack of papers off the table.

"That's the calendar," Ruby said.

"Which ones do you have to take?"

"Ray," Ruby said, looking up. "I appreciate your interest but I have everything organized and I just need to get this done, so…"

"Okay, okay," Ray said. He put the papers back where he found them and left the couch. "I'll wait outside."

Ruby didn't stop him. When Ray shut the door behind him, Ruby sat back on the couch, clearly flustered. There was nothing she could have said or done differently to avoid the feeling. It was something she felt it in her gut as soon as Ray told her where he was going.

Ray arrived at Ashley's building by cab. He followed a building resident through the front door that would otherwise require someone to buzz him past. Ray walked up the stairs to Ashley's second floor apartment and knocked on the door. Ashley answered looking healthier than the last time he saw her. "Feeling better?" Ray asked.

"Much."

She got out of the way and Ray walked in. "Still not at work though." he said.

"It's been a rough few days."

Ray sat down on the couch. Ashley followed closely behind and sat down beside him.

"So?" Ray said.

"So?" Ashley repeated.

"What's up?"

"Not much. What's up with you?"

"Ash."

"What?"

Ray dropped his head and gave Ashley a familiar glare. She knew immediately that he knew she had something to say. "Sooooo…" she chirped, "I had a really long talk with Davis yesterday. Well, actually it started out as a bit of a fight."

Ray liked where this was going.

"And?" Ray coaxed.

"And…we decided it would be the best idea to take a little break."

"You did?" Ray smiled.

"That doesn't mean we're not together anymore. It just means we spend some time on our own…for now."

"Okay."

"Everything has happened so fast with him. It's been a crazy three months."

"I thought it was two months?"

"Did I say two? Well, technically it's been longer since our first date. I don't know."

Ashley knew. She was trying her best to soften the blow.

"Ah."

"Anyway, we see each other every day. We usually do something every night, so–"

"So you want some space. That's understandable."

Ray was secretly thinking, and hoping, that this had everything to do with him.

"That doesn't mean we can…you know," Ashley said.

"We can…what?"

"You know, Ray," Ashley smiled. "That one time was my fault and it was a mistake."

"A mistake?"

"You know what I mean. It wasn't a *mistake*, but I shouldn't have done it."

"Why not?"

"Ray!"

"What?"

"I don't want to get into this right now."

"Okay," Ray said. "So is that what you wanted to tell me?"

"I guess," Ashley said. "And I wanted to see you."

"I wanted to see you too."

CHAPTER 30

WHEN DUNCAN GOT home, Ruby was still working away at the coffee table. She had tried her best to focus on her task and not on her frustration with Ray. After all, he hadn't done anything dishonest or cruel.

Duncan put his notebook down on the kitchen table along with the tape measure he had borrowed from the basement.

"How'd it go?" Ruby asked.

"Good," Duncan said. He opened the fridge and pulled out the orange juice. "How are you doing? Can I help?"

"I'm almost done, actually," Ruby said. "But you could help me finish this one thing."

Duncan joined Ruby on the couch with the jug of orange juice in his hand.

"I have one more class to fit in," Ruby said. "I could add it to this day here, but that makes one really long day, or I could put it here and have another two-hour class."

"I would get it all over with on that day. Once you're there, you're there. Why would you want to go on Friday if you don't have to? This way, yeah, you have a super long Wednesday, but you have Fridays off."

"I was thinking that too. But that's a crazy Wednesday."

"It's not forever. A few months of hard work and you're done. Do it like a Band-Aid. Jump in with both feet."

"Any other clichés?"

"Kill two birds with one stone. Don't look a gift horse in the mouth."

"You–"

"Don't count your chickens before they're hatched. Two in the bush means…six…in…the basket? I don't know that one."

Ruby laughed.

Ray and Ashley spent a good portion of the early afternoon watching TV on the couch. They had found an ideal position intertwined with each other and didn't dare move for fear that they would lose it. It was as if no one on the planet had ever been as comfortable sitting with someone else. The way their heads were perfectly propped, their arms perfectly free, their legs perfectly positioned for ultimate support of the other. They were in a warm morning bed, a cool soothing bath, and a sensually arousing embrace all at the same time.

"Ray," Ashley said.

"Yeah?"

"I have to go to the washroom."

"No," Ray pleaded. "You can't."

"I know but I have to. I've been holding it in for an hour."

"We'll never get it back."

"Yes, we will."

Ashley broke the balance and leaped to her feet.

"Nooooooooo." Ray yelled.

Ashley ran to the washroom.

Upon her return, the pair tried in vain to regain the flawless pose, but they simply couldn't recapture the magic of the pretzel-like position. Finally settling on the classic big-spoon little-spoon model, Ashley, in front, picked up the remote to find something better to watch. As she did, Ray's hand gravitated away from her hip and landed on her partially exposed belly. He began to rub Ashley's skin as she flipped channels on the TV.

"You can't," Ashley said almost reluctantly, elbowing Ray's arm away.

"Can't what?"

"You know what."

"Okay, fine," Ray said. "But that's no fun."

"I know, but we can't."

"Okay," Ray said again.

Ray began kissing the side of Ashley's neck. Ashley lifted her shoulder making her neck much smaller and harder to reach. Ray simply pulled her hair back and started at the lobe of her ear. Ashley let out a quiet moan of pleasure with little frustration mixed in. "You can't do this," she said.

"I know," Ray whispered.

Ashley let Ray continue for a few more seconds before turning her body to face his. Ray moved from Ashley's ear to her mouth and they began to kiss. It was a quick and effortless transition, and it felt completely natural when Ray and Ashley began to make love on the couch.

Ruby had finished with all her paper work and schedule making. She turned her attention to helping Duncan translate his measurements and initial budget into an order of equipment from Tom. It wasn't a hard thing to do considering Duncan's plan was as well thought out as the drawing he had made that morning with Edita. Using the forms and prices that Tom had given him, he input each item one by one. Once worked out, Duncan's initial purchase total came to just under ten thousand dollars, a large sum, yes, but one significantly lower than what he had originally imagined.

Excited, Duncan called Tom on the phone and read him the order. Tom followed along and did his own calculations on the other end. When their totals matched, a large smile took hold on Duncan's face.

"Did you want more time to think about it?" Tom asked.

"Nope," Duncan said. "You can put through the order whenever you're ready."

"I don't need to put it through," Tom said. "I have everything you need here already. You let me know where and when you want it delivered and I'll have it there for you."

"Cash okay?"

"Better than okay."

"I'm taking possession on the first of the month. Assuming everything goes to plan, can we arrange delivery for the second?"

"The second, that's a Tuesday?"

"Yeah."

"Tell you what, you bring me the cash anytime in the next week and you've got a deal. I'll write you up a receipt and book your delivery with one of my guys while you're here."

"How's today?" Duncan said.

Tom laughed.

"If you can get here before 5:30, I'll be here."

"I'm on my way right now."

Duncan hung up the phone and smacked his hands together. "Want to go for a ride?"

"Are you going by BC?" Ruby asked.

"Sure. Let's do it."

Ruby organized all her papers into one neat pile before dashing up the stairs to get properly dressed. To Duncan's surprise, she came down in less than five minutes and the pair headed out the door with a jump in their step.

CHAPTER 31

CELEBRATING AT O'KEEFE's was becoming a familiar event for Ruby, Duncan, and Ray. After driving from bank, to school, to warehouse, and back, Ruby and Duncan grabbed a bite to eat at a local burger joint and were enjoying a pint at the bar before the sun had completely vanished from the August sky. Ray joined them at the table within an hour. He would have been there sooner but had trouble leaving Ashley's.

It was an unfortunate thing, Ruby thought to herself, that her mood was negatively impacted by Ray's arrival. She didn't want to feel that way. She tried her best to think positively and focused instead on the day's successes. Ray didn't bring up the topic of their earlier encounter, though he felt an unfamiliar distance growing between himself and Ruby.

"How's she feeling?" Duncan asked.

"Not great," Ray said. "We just watched a movie and hung out. She's still a little sick. What did you guys do?"

"Well, barring any unforeseen issues, you're looking at the newest Boston College student."

Ray put his hand on Ruby's leg and gave it a squeeze. Ruby barely acknowledged.

"And I am the proud new owner of 15 heavy bags, among other things, of course."

"Then it's congratulations to everyone," Ray said. He lifted his glass and took a sip of his beer.

"I just want to really thank you guys," Ruby said. "I don't know where I'd be without you."

"You don't have to thank us," Duncan said.

"No, really," she continued. "You've been so amazing."

Ruby might have been addressing both, but she was looking only at Duncan as she spoke.

"You're part of the crew," Ray added.

"I am?" Ruby said, finally looking at Ray. "I'm part of the *crew*?"

"You're not?"

Ray looked at Duncan. Duncan was wincing.

"You tell me," Ruby said. "Is that what I am? Part of the crew?"

"You don't want to be part of the crew." Ray said, hesitantly.

"Why wouldn't I, Ray? Who doesn't want to be part of a crew?"

"I'm gonna go get another drink now," Duncan said. He got up from the table with a full pint glass and sat down at the bar beside Terry, Mike, and Vinny.

"Did I say something wrong?" Ray asked.

"No, Ray, you did nothing wrong. It's my fault."

"What is?"

"See, I assumed you weren't like every other guy on the planet. But it turns out you're just as shitty at dealing with women as all the guys that came before you."

Ray knew exactly what she was talking about. He could have given her a whole catalog of lines, or delivered a laundry list of half truths and platitudes, but Ray knew she wouldn't buy any of it. What's worse, Ray was struck hard by the realization that Ruby was completely right about it all.

"Ruby," he said. "What can I say?"

"Nothing, *buddy*," Ruby mocked.

"Ruby, come on. You think this is easy for me?"

"I don't know Ray, I'm playing a guessing game over here."

"What do you want to know? I'll tell you anything."

"Are you being serious right now? You think I want to play twenty questions?"

"What do you want me to say, that I still love her? Okay, fine. I still love her. I probably always will. Do you want me to say that I hate that she has a boyfriend? Okay, I hate it. I want to take his head and rip it off his stupid neck. But that doesn't mean that I don't have feelings for you too, you know. I know that I'm fucking up. I know I am. But I'm doing the best I can. Is it fair? No, of course not. It's not fair to anyone. It's not fair to you, it's not fair to me, and it's not fair to that douche bag she's dating that actually seems like a pretty nice guy. But, you know, I've never been in a situation like this before. This isn't fucking Melrose Place or something. This is real life, and this shit isn't easy."

"I'll say."

"I wish it *were* easy, Ruby. I really do. I wish I could not think about her and be with you. Believe me, that would make my life so much easier. But right now I'm a little fucked in the head, and the last thing I want to do is feel like I hurt you, because that just makes it a million times worse."

"Oh, I'm sorry. Am I making you feel bad?"

"That's not what I meant."

"Of course not."

"Okay. Whatever. I'm an asshole. It's all me, I'm a piece of shit. Is that what you want to hear?"

"You think that's what I want to hear? You think any of that makes me feel better? That you're an asshole and don't know what to do?"

"What can I say to make you feel better? Tell me what you want to hear."

"The truth, Ray. That's all I wanted, ever. Just tell me the truth. I don't want to find out what's happening from Duncan, or have to put pieces together in my head. I just want you to be honest with me."

"I'm trying to be."

"You just don't get it."

"Then explain it to me."

"I can't, Ray! If you don't get it, then you don't get it."

Ruby got up from the table. Ray grabbed onto her wrist. "Don't go," he said.

Ruby paused but sat back down. She was noticeably ill-at-ease.

"I don't know what's going to happen," Ray said calmly. "But you have to know that I care about you. I don't want to lose you. I just can't say what's going to happen 'cause I really don't know."

Ruby got up from the table once again. This time Ray didn't try to stop her. "You still don't get it, Ray," she said. "I'm not a consolation prize."

Ruby walked away.

"I never said you were," Ray said to Ruby's back. But it was of no use. Ruby kept on walking and joined Duncan at the bar. Duncan could see that she was clearly upset and offered her his seat. He also offered a few words of condolence before returning to the table, and to Ray.

"So I'm going to need your help," Duncan said.

"With what?" Ray said, despondently.

"Next week I take possession of the gym. I'm getting equipment shipped and hopefully the floor pads, if I can get them delivered in time. Can you be there?"

"'Course," Ray said.

"Good," Duncan said. "And cheer up. She's a tough chick. She'll get by."

"Yeah, and what about me?"

"You're a tough chick, too."

"Fuck you," Ray said with a smile.

"You want my advice?"

"Sure."

"Just be her friend, Ray," Duncan said. "It's that simple."

"That simple?"

"If the only thing you're trying to accomplish is being her friend, then yeah, that's it."

"But what if I want more?"

"And one more thing—"

"What?"

"Remember that friends always have each other's backs."

"Yeah, I know"

"Always, Ray."

Ray looked over at the girl sitting at the bar amongst the middle-aged bar hounds. She was putting forth her best effort to be involved in their conversation.

Ray got up and walked over to her. He leaned up against the bar beside Ruby. "So, I think I should apologize," he said.

Ruby turned her head.

"No," Ray continued. "I should definitely apologize."

"I'm listening."

"I should have told you about Ashley from the start. That wasn't fair. Obviously."

"And?"

"And you're nobody's consolation prize. I know that. *Of course* I know that. Sometimes I'm just not very good at saying what I mean."

"So what do you mean?"

Ruby turned on her stool to face Ray.

"What I *meant* to say – in a charming way – is that there's definitely something between us. I'm not for a second trying to pretend there isn't. And even though we haven't known each other all that long, I care about you way too much to lose you. I have a past that I've collided with, and I can't say what's going to happen, but I promise, Ruby, *I promise* to be honest with you. I just need to work through a few things, so you're going to have to be patient with me, 'cause this is all new to me."

Ruby looked down at her feet.

"Can you do that?" Ray asked. "Can you give me some time and not give up on me as a friend?"

"I wouldn't give up on you as a friend, Ray," Ruby said, looking up and meeting his eyes.

"Okay. Good."

"But I'm also not waiting around for you to make some sort of decision."

"I know. I'm not asking you to."

"No more pulling me in with one hand and pushing me away with the other."

"No more."

"'Cause it makes me feel like shit."

"I'm shit."

Ruby couldn't help but laugh. "I'm serious, Ray."

"I know you are," Ray said. He took Ruby's hand. "I'm serious too. You only deserve good things and I promise to treat you that way."

Ruby held her gaze. "I believe you," she said. "So don't fuck it up."

"I won't."

"You better not."

"Can I buy you a drink?"

"Sure."

Ray kissed the back of Ruby's hand and returned it to its original resting place.

CHAPTER 32

THE FIRST OF the month arrived late the following week. Duncan got the keys from Edita and headed straight over to the store where Ray was already waiting. If everything went to plan, the guys installing the padded floor would arrive roughly four hours before the equipment from Tom, giving them plenty of time to complete the job of laying it down. Ruby was home, sick. Even though her and Ray had ceased their impromptu intimate encounters, Ray still somehow managed to pass along his flu. He had spent most of the past weekend in bed, suffering greatly – as men do – from a mild fever and an overabundance of mucus. Though the subject remained unbroached, it was lost on no one that Ray had no doubt been the conduit by which Ashley's illness had reached Ruby.

A new dynamic had begun to emerge between Ray and Ruby in the days since their heated encounter at the bar. Though only a handful in number, those days proved far more pleasant for Duncan. The flirting didn't completely desist, though it did return to a manner more innocuous, much like it had been before the sexual encounters began. Ruby still made certain to brush her chest against Ray as she slithered by him in tight spaces. Ray, too, would do things like put his hand on

Ruby's leg as he got up from the couch, or brush her hair back behind her ear. Duncan witnessed stolen glances and smiles, but didn't dare get involved. He had done his part to keep the peace; he now had other things on his mind.

Ray hadn't seen Ashley since their rendezvous on the couch. They had spoken a few times on the phone, but Ray's flu mixed with Ashley's recovery and subsequent days of catching up on work didn't allow for much opportunity to meet. Plus, along with Ashley's return to work, came more frequent encounters with Davis. Though she didn't dare mention that to Ray, his imagination played the villain.

Returning to life as normal had thrust Ashley into a more somber, tentative mood, and it was palpable even over the phone. Ray hesitated to use the word confusion, but in his own way, he knew what Ashley was going through. In fact, he knew it far too well. It was while lying in bed alone that Ray realized that, in fact, he and Ashley were experiencing almost identical predicaments. The one difference might have been Ashley's apprehension to commit fully in one direction, whereas Ray thought he knew he could. In the face of new and fledgling relationships, both Ray and Ashley were forced to take pause and reevaluate the once unshakable relationship they had with one another. Lying in bed, staring at a wad of crumpled up tissues, Ray realized that although his feelings for Ruby were true, Ashley's will was the only thing keeping him from returning to her bed. It was all in Ashley's hands.

The delivery of Duncan's floor mats was an hour late, and Tom's equipment truck thirty minutes early. Like bees around a hive, workers scurried and bumped into one another. Duncan did his best to reign in the collision of bodies and egos and relied heavily on Ray to manage one of the jobs when he was attending to the other. By the time the gym's twenty-foot-long overhead sign arrived, Duncan and Ray had everything mostly under control and flowing in an assembly line of foam, leather, and men in boots.

"It never occurred to you to spread this out over a few days?" one of the men installing the floor asked Duncan.

"Of course it did," Duncan said before simply turning away and continuing his duties.

First to finish were the sign guys who simply had to mount the white, black, and red behemoth above the front windows and door. Next to go were Tom's guys, who had unloaded all the equipment and helped Duncan set up the metal framework for his hanging bags. It was well into the evening when the entire floor had been installed, a job the Duncan thought would be the easiest to do. A few mis-measurements and an injured worker's back slowed the pace considerably. But alas, at a quarter after nine on the second of August, all the workers had gone and Duncan was left alone with his best friend in a nearly complete martial arts studio. If not for an unfurnished office, some equipment still bagged, and a few brown boxes in the corner, Duncan's month-long project would have come to fruition in one hectic day's work.

"Floor turned out good," Duncan said, bouncing up and down on the soft blue rubbery foam under his feet.

"I like it," Ray said.

"Thanks for the help, man." Duncan slapped Ray's hand and pulled him in close for a man-style half-hug.

"Anytime, buddy. Hey, I got something for you."

Ray went into the empty back office and came back with a brown paper bag.

"Are you serious?" Duncan said.

"This is from me and Ruby."

Ray tugged a 40 of malt liquor out of the paper bag and wiggled it in the air.

"Ha! I thought it was champagne."

"Hell no," Ray said. "That's gay. And not in the hip homosexual way, in the straight-dude-with-a-fanny-pack kind of way. One for the homies," Ray said as he opened the bottle and spilled the first bit on the floor.

"Hey!" Duncan yelled. "That's not even an hour old!"

"Oh suck it up, Suzie. It's fucking rubber."

Duncan paused for a second, waiting for Ray to make a move.

He didn't.

"Wipe it up," Duncan said calmly.

Ray finally did as he was told.

After a quick dinner, Duncan and Ray sauntered into O'Keefe's. It was an off day for the Red Sox so the bar was more airy than it had been in the recent past. At one table sat Bixby and Marco having a conversation with Terry. Ray tried to listen in as he walked by but couldn't catch anything of substance.

With a couple of pints, Ray and Duncan sat down at what was becoming their usual table.

"So, now you have to get people to show up," Ray said.

"Yeah," Duncan agreed. "The easy part is over."

"Have you figured out how you're going to do that?"

"I have a few ideas."

"If you need any help, just let me know."

"Mind if we take a seat?" Bixby said from over Duncan's shoulder.

Duncan offered him a chair.

Bixby and Marco sat down at the four-person table. Bixby didn't just sit down though; he turned the chair around and sat down with his arms resting on the back.

"Ray," Bixby said, pointing his finger. "And, Duncan?"

"That's right," Duncan said.

"This is Marco."

293

"Hey," Marco said.

Ray and Duncan both gave a nod.

"So, what's up?" Ray asked.

"Nothing's up," Bixby said. "Can't we just be friendly and say hello?"

"Sure."

"Okay, well that's what we're doing."

"Really, Bixby?" Ray said. "You wanna be friends?"

"Why wouldn't I?"

Both Duncan and Ray knew that Bixby had made his visit to size them up. Terry and Vinny looked on from the bar.

"Okay," Ray said. "Forget I said it. So, Bixby, is that your first name?"

"No."

"What is your name then?"

"Ryan."

"And what do you do, you know, for a living?"

"I have a few professions."

"Oh yeah? Like what?"

"I think you know what, Ray."

"I know you make some of the people in here feel uncomfortable. I know *that*."

"What do you mean, Ray?"

"Look, Bixby," Ray said, leaning forward. "I don't want to tell you how to manage your 'business', but if you're going to be running your numbers here, don't be showing up and intimidating your clients."

"Clients?"

"Yeah, see, that's your problem. You're not a businessman, you're a punk."

"I take offense."

"You should," Ray said. "I was insulting you."

Bixby didn't respond.

"Look," Ray said quietly. "Terry, Vinny, Mike, they're good guys. Not that you know how anyway, but they're not the kind of guys you make money from. You come into their bar and push them around and soon enough you're going to clear the place out."

"Hey, they came to me," Bixby said.

"Maybe. That may be. But it's never going to last. You don't know what the hell you're doing."

"And you do?" Marco chimed.

"Yeah, maybe I do."

"Okay, Ray," Bixby said. "So tell me what you know. Tell me what I'm doing wrong."

"Ray," Duncan said.

"First of all, you're never going to make a dime if you don't let the juice run. You come in here and collect the next day on these guys? That's amateur. You show up during the games? Amateur. You shouldn't ever show your face unless these guys are your friends, and I can tell you – no matter what you may think – these guys aren't your friends. What you need to do is become a ghost."

"Bill was here every day," Marco said.

"Like I said, if you're their friend."

"So I can't be friends with them?" Bixby said.

"Nope."

"And why is that?"

"I already told you," Ray said. "'Cause you're a punk. And maybe you think you're trying to be their friend, but you're not."

"Why don't you do things your way, and I'll do things my way. How about that?"

"That would be great, Bixby, except you're in here every day and you're getting in the way of me doing my things."

"So this is your bar now?"

"I didn't say that. But it is Terry's, and Vinny's, and Mike's, and Charlene's, and everyone else who cringes when you walk in."

"You don't know anything about me."

"I know what I see."

"I came over here to be friendly."

"Yeah, maybe you did, Bixby, maybe you did. But like everything else, you did it all wrong. You came over here and interrupted our conversation, you tried to be a tough guy by pretending you weren't sure who we were, when you know perfectly well who we are."

"Okay, *Ray*. I can see we've caught you at a bad time." Bixby got up, turned the chair back around, and pushed it up against the table. Marco got up too. "Next time I'll send a messenger and make sure we're not interrupting you. Duncan, you know your friend's a real cool guy."

"I don't care what you think of me," Ray said. "And I don't care if you come around here, you can do what you want. Just leave everyone else alone."

"Or what, Ray? What are you gonna do?"

"Just leave them alone, Bixby."

"Yeah, I thought so. Lot's of words and no balls."

Marco put his hand on Bixby's chest and pushed him back a bit.

"Yeah, hold him back. At least one of you has a brain," Ray said.

Marco turned abruptly and came back toward the table. Duncan's chair skidded across the floor as he got up and intercepted the larger man.

"Let it go," Duncan said, standing face-to-chin with Marco.

"And why should I listen to you?" Marco asked, peering down his nose.

"You don't have to," Duncan said. "But if you lay your hands on Ray, I'm going to have to get involved, and then you'll know."

"What are you going to do, little man?"

"Let's not find out tonight, Marco."

Duncan turned to his friend, still sitting at the table. "Ray."

"What?"

"Ray."

Ray got up from his chair and walked over to Bixby. Most eyes in the bar were watching the foursome.

"Look," Ray said to Bixby. "Just think about what I said, okay? There's a better way to do things, that's all."

Bixby didn't say anything. He just looked at Ray with a scowl.

"How do you think all that started?" Terry whispered to Vinny up at the bar.

"I have no idea," Vinny said. "But I wanted to see what Duncan was going to do."

"Really?" Charlene said. "'Cause I think what he just did was pretty impressive."

CHAPTER 33

RAY'S AGGRESSION AT the bar aroused some concern in Duncan. Usually mild of manner and not one to engage in confrontation, Duncan had always known Ray to be the peacekeeper. The only other time Duncan could recall Ray instigating an altercation was when Ashley's honor was involved. There was a certain look in Ray's eyes, and a singularity in his mind on that occasion; the same look that Duncan thought he saw again at O'Keefe's.

"She needs some time," Ray said to Duncan later that night on their way home from the bar. "She said she needs to think about things without distraction."

"What does that mean?" Duncan asked. "What distraction?"

"I don't know, me?"

"But she's still seeing the other guy?"

"What's your point?

"I didn't mean it like that, Ray. I'm asking if that's the case."

"She works with him, so yeah, she still sees him."

"No, I mean, is she still *seeing him,* seeing him?"

"Yeah, I guess," Ray snapped. "I don't know."

"Wow, okay. Ray, take it easy."

The following morning Duncan invited Ray to come with him on a few errands in an attempt to gauge his friend's mood, and in an effort to turn his mind onto other things. Ray declined the invitation but said he was feeling fine. He wanted instead to stay at home with Ruby. She was still sick and might have needed something. Ray wanted to be there to help her.

Duncan ventured out alone, stopping first at a local Kinko's to print up some flyers he had been working on.

Not a wizard with graphic design, the flyers looked rather pedestrian. However, with the aid of a friendly Kinko's employee – a longhaired teenager that smelled of marijuana and Axe Body Spray – the flyers took on a bit more character.

Duncan's plan was to litter the local college campuses with the yellow flyers that invited any and all females to attend free introductory classes. For two weeks, Max Fitness MMA was offering free membership.

His first stop was Tufts University. Duncan sought out and posted flyers on bulletin boards, lampposts, bus shelters, and anywhere else he could think of, or find. On his drive off campus, he got excited when he saw a single student waiting at a bus shelter having a glance at one of his postings.

Not sure what he expected, Duncan was surprised to find that the Harvard campus he visited next looked pretty much like any other. The students didn't look any smarter, the buildings were not any grander, and the streets had just as many cracks and potholes. One thing that did cause shock was the amount of money Duncan had to pay to park in one of the campus lots. A few more times visiting and he could have just as well enrolled as a student.

Duncan wandered the Harvard campus, taking in the culture and posting his yellow 8.5 x 11's.

Following Massachusetts Avenue, Duncan found himself entering the famous Harvard Yard. It was famous, of course, because Duncan had heard of it. The fall semester had not yet begun, but students already littered the flat, grassy square of the old school. Duncan passed by the John Harvard statue; he looked in on Massachusetts Hall. But it was outside Lamont Library that Duncan really got a taste of Harvard.

"Excuse me," a voice said. "You can't do that here."

Duncan was posting a flyer on a lamppost just outside the library when the young woman approached. She had broken off from a cluster of other student-looking folk leaving the library along with her.

"Oh," Duncan said, feigning vulnerability. "I can't?"

As the girl got closer, Duncan could see that though she still might have been younger than him, her teenage years were just as much a memory.

"No, you can't," the girl said. "But I didn't mean to startle you."

"That's okay. It's just that I've been posting a few around the yard and no one's said anything."

"So there's more?"

"There might be."

"Oh. Well, can I get you to take them down?" the girl winced.

"Sure," Duncan said. "I didn't know it wasn't kosher."

The girl looked him over. "You're not a student here, are you?" she said.

"No."

"I didn't think so."

"What gave it away? My sophisticated good looks?"

The girl laughed. "What's your name?" she asked.

"Duncan."

"I'm Kaya."

She reached out her arm.

"Hi, Kaya," Duncan said as they shook hands.

"Listen, Duncan. I'm walking towards the Old Yard, so I can help you with the others, if you want."

"Now, how could I pass up that offer?"

Duncan and Kaya began to traverse the path Duncan had taken through the yard. Duncan took the opportunity to get a better glimpse at the girl.

Kaya had an exotic look about her. Duncan didn't dare ask, but if he had to guess, he would say that she had a pedigree of both Caucasian and African American in her lineage. She had light blue eyes, which stood out against her cocoa skin. Her dark brown hair was long, and thick, and just a little bit curly, and it bounced off her neck and back like tiny little springs as she walked. Duncan stood just barely six feet and Kaya's eyes almost equaled his. Her figure was slight but fit, much like that of a runner, or volleyball player.

"Do you mind?" Kaya said. Duncan instantly thought he had been caught checking her out. Kaya was instead referring to the stack of flyers he was carrying.

"Oh," Duncan said, realizing his folly. He placed one of the flyers in Kaya's hand.

Kaya looked over the yellow paper as Duncan tore one of its brethren from a post along the way.

"So, I'm assuming you go here?" Duncan said, as they walked along and Kaya perused his ad.

"I do," she said. "I've been here for a while actually."

"What are you studying?"

"Mostly sciences. Is this your gym?"

"It is."

"So that's why you're posting these things."

"That's why. So how much longer do you have until you graduate?"

"Technically, I've graduated."

"So, what are you still doing here?"

"This week I'm showing around new students, which is why I was in the undergrad library. But I also do lab work on the campus."

"So, you're doing a post-grad or you're a graduate student?"

"Something like that."

"I'll tell you what, Kaya," Duncan offered. "If you tell me something about you, I'll tell you something really interesting about me."

Kaya laughed. "I don't mean to dodge your questions."

"What is it you do?"

"I do medical research. I just finished my PHD. What kind of gym is this?"

"None yet, really. It just opened and I haven't had a class. But the idea is to teach a mixture of fitness and martial arts."

"Like, Tae Bo."

"No," Duncan laughed. "Nothing like Tae Bo. Think of a class that makes you sweat out five pounds and teaches you how to defend yourself."

"So real martial arts then?"

"That's the idea. There are plenty of martial arts classes, and plenty of fitness classes, but I'm hoping to combine the two."

"So it's mostly for men?"

"You didn't read that did you," Duncan tugged at the flyer in Kaya's hand.

"Oh. Women free for two weeks."

"There ya go."

"You could teach someone how to, what, ward off a dangerous attacker?"

"Sure."

"Even someone like me?"

"Especially someone like you."

Duncan and Kaya came to a stop outside one of the buildings. "And the fact that I'm smaller than most men doesn't matter?"

"Nope," Duncan said. "Size doesn't matter."

"At all?"

Duncan thought for a second. He looked around his immediate radius.

"S'cuse me sir," Duncan said to a male student walking by.

"Me?"

"Could you help us out for just a second?"

"Sure?"

The young man walked over to Duncan and Kaya. He had a bag across his shoulder and was carrying a few books. "What's your name?"

"Manny."

"I'm Duncan, this is Doctor Kaya."

Kaya smiled.

"You're going to help us with a small experiment here. Is that okay?"

"Sure, I guess," Manny said. "What do I have to do?"

Manny was about the same size as Duncan, which gave him a reasonable strength advantage over Kaya. Being of a younger age, he hadn't yet fully developed, but by looks alone, he easily outweighed the girl by fifty pounds or more.

"This is going to be quick and painless," Duncan said.

"Okay."

"Well...quick."

Duncan took the books from Manny's hand.

"Okay Doc. If Manny were to attack you, say, try to steal your purse, what would you do?"

Kaya just looked at Manny.

"We'll do this slowly so no one gets hurt. Manny, go ahead and just grab hold of her shoulder or her arm or whatever."

303

Manny reached out and grabbed hold of Kaya's left arm just above her elbow. They both looked at Duncan. "Go ahead," Duncan said. "Get him off."

"Okay," Kaya said. "I guess I would do something like this."

Kaya raised her knee toward Manny's crotch, stopping short of actually making contact with his most sensitive parts. Even as deliberately as she made the motion Manny countered with one of his own. His leg instinctively came up and turned and his knee formed a shield in front his crotch.

"When you go with instinct and not education, size does matter," Duncan said. "You wouldn't have hurt Manny here with a kick to the nuts. He's bigger, more aggressive, and probably ready for something like that. You can see his leg would have easily deflected that kind of reaction."

"Okay," Kaya said. "So what should I have done instead?"

"Manny," Duncan said, taking a step toward the pair. "You can resist, okay?"

"Okay," Manny agreed, still holding on to Kaya's arm.

"Try this."

Duncan took Kaya's right hand and placed it with a light grip between Manny's thumb and index finger. "Now you're going to take a small step to your left, and as you do, pull his thumb back this way and then twist his wrist away from you and lift it.

"Twist and lift?"

"Yeah." Duncan gave Kaya a quick demonstration on her free hand. "Like this," he said.

"Got it. Now?"

"Sure. Just do it naturally, you don't need to do it fast or hard. Strength is not the most important thing. Manny, you can try to stop her."

"K, ready?" Kaya said.

Kaya followed Duncan's simple directions. She took a small step away from her pseudo-attacker with her right foot and pulled back to her left on his thumb and wrist as she pulled it up. Manny's grip was not only broken, but the stunned student fell to one knee under the seemingly light pressure of Kaya's progress. His wrist was turned backwards, and though she didn't put much pressure on it, it felt as though Kaya might tear his thumb right off. He couldn't help but laugh nervously at the result. "Ow," Manny said, still on the ground and under the influence of Kaya's will.

"Lesson one," Duncan said. "Size doesn't matter."

"Okay," Kaya said, relieving the grip and allowing Manny's wrist to return to normal. "So you show women how to beat up guys?"

"That's called Aikido. The purpose of techniques like that is not to start fights, it's to avoid them."

"Pretty cool," Manny said, rising to his feet and rubbing his wrist.

Duncan handed the victim back his books.

"Thanks you for your help, buddy," Duncan said.

"Can I have one of those?" Manny asked. Duncan handed Manny one of his flyers. "Thanks," he said as he continued on his way.

"Now it's your turn," Duncan said as he and Kaya began to walk again.

"My turn for what?"

"What kind of lab work do you do?"

"Right now I'm studying instances of peripheral neuropathy and incremental effects of organic, botanical treatment techniques."

"I see," Duncan said. "Want me to show you the wrist thing again?"

Kaya laughed. "It sounds like a mouthful, I know."

"No, no. I think one of the guys from my old softball team did the exact same thing."

"Really?"

"No, not really. And you like it?"

"I do."

"Well, that's the most important thing I guess."

"This is me," Kaya said, coming to a stop outside a building.

"Well, it was nice assaulting a student with you."

"And you."

"Off to work?"

"I have a few things to do."

"You wouldn't want to get a coffee or something instead, would you?"

"Um, now's not the best time."

"Okay. No problem. Thought I'd ask."

"You'll take down all the rest of the flyers, yeah? I wouldn't want you to get in any trouble."

"I promise."

"I'll hang on to this," Kaya said, flashing the flyer she still held in her hand.

She skipped up the first few steps of the building. "Nice meeting you, Duncan," she said with a graceful turn.

"You too."

Duncan did as he promised and removed the rest of the posted flyers. Returning to his car, he contemplated going back to the building into which Kaya had disappeared, if only to wait outside per chance to see her again. He thought for a few moments, but in the end decided against it. He returned to the car and headed for home.

CHAPTER 34

"I NEED TO see you."

"Okay, when?"

Ruby was feeling a little better and was occupying the couch beside Ray. When Ray got the phone call from Ashley, he excused himself upstairs for some privacy.

"Tonight?" Ashley said.

"Your place?"

"Sure. How's eight?"

"I'll see you then. Can I bring you anything?"

"No," Ashley said. "Just you."

Duncan walked into the house just in time to meet Ray at the bottom of the stairs.

"What're you smiling about?" Ray asked him.

"Me? Nothing. I'm not smiling."

"You're smiling. He's smiling."

"You're smiling," Ruby agreed, peering over the top of the couch.

"How you feeling?" Duncan asked.

"Better," Ruby said.

"Is that *Dumb and Dumber*?"

"If that's Seabass over there."

Duncan sat down on the chair beside the couch and put his feet up on the table. "Ray. *Dumb and Dumber*," he said.

"No kidding?" Ray said. "The sick one stole the remote from me."

"You gave it to me!" Ruby exclaimed.

"Now that you're back, I'm going out to get some food. Anyone want to come with me?"

"Bring me some soup," Ruby said.

"Grab me a sandwich or something," Duncan added, throwing Ray the keys without looking.

Ray shook his head and smiled at the friendly abuse. The truth was, he was glad to go alone.

Ray left the house without another word.

On his way out, he noticed a car in Frank's driveway. He immediately poked his head back into the house. "Hey Dun," he said. "You see the car at Frank's?"

Duncan got up and joined Ray at the front door. "I didn't even notice."

"Who do you think it is?"

Ruby sat up and craned her neck to peer out the window.

"No idea," Duncan said.

The front door of Frank's house opened and two women walked out. One of the women pointed over at Ray almost immediately. The second woman waved. Ray, confused, waved back. Duncan removed himself from the open door just to be on the safe side. Whoever those people were, they seemed to know that Ray had some sort of connection with the deceased homeowner. "Should I go over there?" Ray asked.

"Just leave it alone," Duncan said.

"Too late. They're coming here."

Ray walked out to intercept the incoming ladies on the driveway.

"Hi," Ray said.

"Hello," one of the women said.

"Are you Raymond?" the second asked.

"I am."

"Hi Raymond, I'm Elizabeth. I'm Mr. Rice's lawyer. This is Frank's niece Brenda."

"Brenda Tunney," the woman said, reaching out her hand.

"Oh, okay. Hi."

"Thank you for all your help."

"Don't mention it. I'm sorry for your loss."

"It was your girlfriend that found him?"

"It was. She's in the house. I'd introduce you, but she's sick right now."

"Oh, that's quite all right. Please tell her 'thank you' for me. It must have been an ordeal."

"So, are you the new owner of the house, or...?"

"I suppose I am," Brenda said, looking hesitantly to Elizabeth. "But I'm just in from New Hampshire for the day to take care of some of Uncle Frank's business. Unfortunately, I didn't know him very well."

"Oh," Ray said. "Well, he was a very good neighbor, I can tell you that."

"Thank you."

"We should get back to my office now, Brenda," Elizabeth said.

"Can I offer you a keepsake from Uncle Frank's house?" Brenda asked Ray. "I don't know how close you were but if you'd like, I'm just going to have to sell everything anyhow."

"That's nice of you," Ray said. "But I wouldn't feel right taking anything."

"Okay," Brenda said. She turned to Elizabeth. "I guess we should go then."

"Take care," Ray said. "It was nice meeting you."

"And you."

The two ladies crossed back over to the other side of the street. Ray went back into the house to inform his compatriots of the conversation.

"We heard," Duncan said. "We opened the window."

"What do you make of it?"

"Everything is fine. Let's just go on as usual."

"Okay. She said she barely knew him, and she'll make a killing on the house. Ruby, you okay with everything?"

"Not much we can do now," Ruby said. "I'm trying not to think about it."

"Okay," Ray said. "Business as usual."

"Business as usual," Duncan repeated.

"Soup and sandwich," Ray said. "See you in a bit."

Ray took an extraordinarily long time getting food, which brought up concern from Duncan and Ruby that something else was afoot. Upon his return, nearly two hours later, Duncan questioned him on his whereabouts.

"I didn't know you were in a hurry," Ray said.

"I wasn't in a hurry, but you said you were just running out to get some food."

"I did."

"So, what took so long?"

Ray unpacked the bags on the table by the kitchen. "I made a few other stops," he said.

"Where?" Duncan asked.

"What's the difference?"

Ray stopped unpacking the bags and sat down at the table.

"It's just that you've been acting weird lately."

"Weird?"

"You've been a little secretive, yeah."

"Secretive?"

"Ray…"

"If you have to know, I stopped by Pete's place to say hi."

Ruby sat back and allowed the boys to hash out the issue. "And since when do we keep tabs on each other, Dun?" Ray continued.

"It's not tabs, Ray."

"Then what is it?"

"Nothing, never mind."

"No, tell me. You say I'm acting weird, I want to know what that means."

"Never mind, just let it go."

"Let it go?"

"Yeah, let it go. We don't need to talk about it."

"What's going on here?" Ray asked.

"What, can't I be concerned about you?" Duncan said.

"Concerned about me? What're you, my mother?"

Duncan smiled coyly. Ray smiled back.

After a moment, Duncan lunged across the room at his friend, who expected his advance and received the brunt.

"Is this how boys argue?" Ruby asked as Duncan pinned Ray to the ground.

To his credit, Ray was putting up a good fight. To *his* credit, Duncan was going easy on his under-matched friend. After a few playful slaps to the face, Duncan relieved Ray of any further abuse. He left his friend on the floor and snatched up the bags from the kitchen table.

Duncan, Ruby, and Ray ate their late lunches as Ruby flipped the channels on the TV.

"When do your classes start?" Ray asked.

"Monday," Ruby said.

"You ready?"

"Not at all."

"You excited?"

"A little scared."

"Why scared?"

"I don't know. It's so new and unknown. I have to change my whole lifestyle and become a student again. I don't think I even remember how. I guess change makes me nervous."

"Uh oh," Ray said.

"What?"

"You hear that, Dun? Change."

"I heard," Duncan said.

"So what's wrong with that?" Ruby asked. "Most people don't like change."

"Dun, you wanna take this?"

"Take what?" Ruby asked.

"When we were first thinking about leaving Phoenix the whole 'change' discussion came up a lot."

"People aren't afraid of change," Duncan said. "They're afraid of failure."

"What do you mean?" Ruby asked.

"Change isn't the problem. It's losing what they think they have that makes people nervous."

"I don't have anything to lose."

"Not true, you said it yourself. You have a certain lifestyle, things you're used to, a way of thinking." Duncan could see that Ruby wasn't following. "Look," he said. "What if I were to say that I was taking away your house? That would be pretty scary, right? But what if I said I'm taking away your house and replacing it with a furnished mansion that's all paid for? I bet that change wouldn't scare you, would it? And that's a pretty big *change*. People don't like change in their jobs, right? But what if I were to offer you a new job that was way more fun and paid you a million dollars? That wouldn't make you nervous, would it? You'd probably be pretty excited."

"I guess."

"It's not change that's frightening, it's loss, and failure. When people are faced with a new situation they're afraid they

312

won't succeed, not that it's unknown or different. Good things are unknown and different, too, but we're not afraid of those, we get excited about them. The new house, the better job – not scary at all."

"So, what you're saying is, I'm really afraid that I might fail at this whole school thing?"

"Why else would you feel nervous about something you clearly want?"

"Because I could be making a huge mistake."

"You also could be making the best decision of your life. Look, you're going to succeed, and it's going to lead to better things. But that's not the point. What I'm saying is change is just a word people give to the fear of failure."

"You're saying it's about perspective," Ruby said.

"See, Ray, she hasn't even started school yet and she's already smarter than you."

"And cuter," Ray said.

Ruby leaned over on the couch and laid her head on Ray's shoulder. Ray put his arm around her.

It would be so easy with Ruby, Ray thought to himself. To really *be* with her would take such little effort. She was smart and sensitive and knew how to manage him. She was far more attractive than he thought he deserved and though she often professed trepidation, Ruby's fearlessness for life made her even more attractive.

It was as if Ray had an anchor around his waist, though, something hard and heavy holding him down.

Ray put his hand on Ruby's hair and kissed the top of her head. Ruby looked up and she and Ray locked eyes. For a moment, Ray felt a stirring in his stomach. It was just a simple look from Ruby, but it moved him in a way it hadn't done before.

With delicate wording, Ray informed Ruby and Duncan of his evening's plans. He told them that because Ashley was feeling much better, she wanted to see him to thank him for his help. It was a friendly get-together between friends. Ruby pretended not to care but her overcompensated ambivalence was obvious.

It was with a little bit of guilt and a little bit of excitement that Ray excused himself from the house that evening.

CHAPTER 35

"COME IN," ASHLEY said as she opened the door.

Ray had stopped on the way to pick up a bottle of wine. "I brought this for you," he said, handing her the bottle. Ashley took it from Ray and put it on the counter. Ray took a seat on the couch and waited for Ashley to join him.

Ashley looked great. She had fully recovered from her illness, but that wasn't it. She was wearing a pair of old jeans and a small light blue T-shirt. She looked just like Ray remembered her when they were younger.

"Should I open this?" Ashley asked.

"Up to you."

Ashley opened the bottle and poured some wine into two small glass cups. Ever since her visit to France, Ashley ceased to use the North American standard wine glasses. She brought the wine over to the couch and handed one to Ray.

"How's Duncan?" she asked.

"Good. He opened the gym."

"That's good. Good for him."

"Yeah. He's pretty excited about it."

"Did you tell him I said hi?"

"Of course I did."

Ray put his hand on Ashley's leg. Ashley quickly got up and went back to the counter to retrieve the bottle of wine. "For later," she said, returning to the couch. "So what's up with you? Are you working, or…"

"Umm, I'm still figuring things out."

"Do you have any idea what you want to do?"

"I know what I *don't* want to do, does that count?"

"I guess," Ashley said, taking a sip of her drink. "You should probably decide soon though."

"What's the rush?"

"How long are you going to go on figuring out what you don't want to do?"

"I don't know, until I figure out what I *do* want to do?"

"You've been doing that for years."

"Yeah. And if I have to I'll do it for more. I don't want to do something just for the sake of doing it. There has to be more to life than that. Why wouldn't I wait until I figure out what it is I really want with my life?"

"You can do that," Ashley said. "But why not do something else in the meantime?"

"If you're asking about money, I have plenty. I don't rely on anyone."

"It's not about money, it's about having a life."

"I have a life."

"What did you do today?"

"What did *you* do today?"

"I went to work."

"Okay, and did you enjoy it?"

"Not really."

"So then what are you talking about? You go to a job you hate, and I don't?"

"Don't you want to be…I don't know, organized?"

"I'm not organized?"

"You think you are?"

"I don't think I'm *dis*organized, if that's what you mean. I might not get up at 6 a.m. every morning to go to an office, but that's not what everyone wants. That doesn't make your life complete."

"I never said it did. But you should have something to do. You know, some sort of work, or passion for something to fill your time."

"I fill my time just fine."

"It can be something as simple as volunteering somewhere, if you don't need the money."

Ray paused to digest Ashley's questioning.

"Why are you on me about this now?"

"'Cause I care about you."

"But what's this all about? Why the sudden inquisition?"

"It's hardly an inquisition."

"If you could, wouldn't you leave your job tomorrow? If you won the lottery, would you go into the office?"

"I would," Ashley said without hesitation.

"Liar."

"I would. I've spent a lot of time getting good at what I do and I care about my job. I may not love it every day, but that doesn't mean I only do it for the paycheck. I care about the people I help and the work I do."

"Okay, so you're a bad example. Most people would quit their jobs."

"Did you win the lottery or something?"

"No."

"Then what are you talking about?"

"Ashley!" Ray snapped. He put the glass down on the table. "What's going on?"

"Nothing, I'm just trying to—"

"To what? Do you have something you want to say to me? 'Cause if there's something you're trying to say then just say it because–"

"I'm moving in with Davis," Ashley spouted.

Silence.

Ray wasn't expecting her to say anything like that. His mind raced to find alternate meanings to her words, but there were none. There could only be one meaning for the sequence of syllables Ashley had just uttered, there was no way around them. Like the poor passerby crushed on the sidewalk by a falling piano, Ray's entire body felt lifeless. The only sensation he could recognize was the pain in his chest.

"Say something," Ashley said.

"What do you want me to say?"

"I hate when people say that. Just say what's on your mind. Say what you're thinking."

"You don't want me to say what I'm thinking."

"Yes I do, Ray," Ashley said.

"No, you really don't."

"So you're upset."

"Upset?" Ray snapped. He got up from the couch and stood over Ashley. "Are you fucking kidding me? You just told me you're moving in with a guy you've known for two months."

"I've known him a lot longer than that."

"We had sex on this couch less than a week ago, you said you love me."

"I do love you."

"Okay," Ray said, throwing his hands in the air. "This is insane. You can't say you love me and then tell me you're moving in with some other guy."

"I do love you, Ray, but I'm not *in* love with you."

"Oh really? What movie did you steal that from?"

"It's true."

"What does that even mean?"

"It means–"

"I know what you think it means, Ashley. But you don't tell someone you love them and then add some sort of explanation why it's actually *not* the case. Either you love someone or you don't."

"It's not that simple."

"Maybe not for you."

"That's not fair," Ashley said. "This isn't easy for me, you know."

"Easy for you? This isn't easy for you? You have two guys that want to be with you and you don't seem to give a shit about either of them. I don't know what's going on with Davis but you obviously haven't been honest with him. Did you tell him we've been having sex? You sleep with me one day, and push me away the next. You've been unbelievably selfish, which shouldn't surprise me, you always only think of yourself–"

"I do not!"

"You can't fuck with people like that, Ashley. You can't just pull someone in with one hand and push–"

Ray stopped suddenly. Something had clicked. He dropped his hands and stood up straight.

"What?" Ashley said, recognizing Ray's instant hesitation.

"Fuck me," Ray whispered.

"What happened?"

"I get it."

Ray sat back down on the couch. He took a moment to compose himself before turning to Ashley. "I think you're crazy and stupid for moving in with this guy," he said. "But I may be the last person that should be yelling at you about it."

"Okaaaaay."

"So, I think, yeah, I think I'm gonna go now."

"What's going on? You're scaring me."

Ray had already gotten up and begun walking toward the door.

"You're acting kinda funny, Ray. You sure you're okay?"

"Believe me, there are a million things going on inside my head right now," Ray said, standing at the door. "I'm sure once it all registers, I'll have plenty to say to you. But right now, I think I just want to be alone. So, yeah, that's it. Goodbye, Ashley."

Ray walked out of Ashley's apartment and didn't look back. He wasn't ready to go home and face Ruby, so he stopped at O'Keefe's to kill time, and to untangle the knots in his head.

"Ray," Vinny yelled as soon as he walked through the door.

"Hey guys," Ray said. "I need a drink."

Charlene overheard Vinny's cry of welcome and had already begun pouring a pint for Ray. She dropped the pint in front of him at the bar and, upon request, added a shot of whisky to the order. Ray lifted his elbow and stretched his neck and dropped the shot into his gullet like he was trying to put out a fire down there. "One more, Char," Ray said. "Please."

"You okay, buddy?" Vinny asked from the next stool.

"I will be."

"Leave him alone," Terry said. "Sometimes you just need to get drunk, right Ray?"

Charlene refilled the little shot glass and Ray sucked it down without hesitation. "Thanks," he said. "That'll do for now."

Ray turned the shot glass over and slid it down the bar. "Wooo," he bellowed. "I needed that."

"Girl trouble?" Vinny asked.

"Vinny," Ray said. "They're all trouble."

"Hey!" Charlene said with a smile.

"Not you, of course," Ray said.

Ray managed to shake off some of the earlier shock, at least for the time being.

"Hey, Ray," Charlene said, "Could you help me with something over here?"

"Uh, sure," Ray said.

Ray walked over to the corner of the bar where the servers would pick up their drinks, if there were any servers. "What's up?" Ray asked.

"How's Pete?" Charlene asked quietly.

"He's okay," Ray said. "I saw him today, actually. He's doing better."

"Okay, good. I haven't seen him in here since, you know."

"Just a bad night, that's all. But I have a feeling he'll be around soon."

"Yeah?"

"Yeah. Soon. Trust me."

"Okay." Charlene said with a pause. "Am I missing something?"

"No," Ray said, tapping the back of Charlene's hand. "Everything will be just fine. Pete's fine."

"Okay, now I know I'm missing something."

"I'll let him know you asked about him."

Ray returned to his stool and did his best to get involved with a conversation between Terry and Vinny concerning the off-season signings of the Boston Bruins, and the chances they had of making it all the way in the coming season.

Ray didn't dare mention to them, or to anyone, that he had always been a New York Rangers fan. He didn't mention, either, the secret he and Pete had been keeping. They would all find out soon enough.

PART III

CHAPTER 36

AT 9 A.M. ON a Monday morning, Ruby officially became a student again. That same day Duncan had completed all the necessary adjustments and formally opened the gym for business. For both, day one was slow. Ruby's was spent surrounded by unfamiliar faces; regrettably, Duncan's was not. The only person to stop by the gym that day was Ray, who came in around lunchtime to bring his friend some food and help rearrange bits of furniture in the office. It was later in the afternoon that Ruby stopped by, too. And she brought a friend.

About mid-way through the day, Ruby noticed that there was a girl that seemed to be tracing her every step. By the time Ruby entered her third class and saw the same girl, she decided to sit down beside her.

"I think we have a few classes together," Ruby said.

"I think we do," the girl agreed. "We sat across from each other this morning."

"I'm Ruby."

"Lacy."

Lacy looked older than Ruby, and even though she was curious, Ruby didn't feel right about asking her. "What do you think so far?" Ruby asked.

"Too soon to tell. The first teacher seemed pretty cool, but what's with that woman teaching Managerial?"

Ruby laughed. "I was thinking the same thing. It's one thing to be old fashioned, but she's taking it a little too far."

"Right? I mean who dresses like that?"

Ruby and Lacy continued chatting, but the level of their voices lowered as the rest of the seats began to fill.

After class, Lacy and Ruby sat together outside and compared schedules. They had all the same classes, naturally, and only two of them were at different times during the week. In an attempt to keep her evenings free, Lacy had scheduled a morning class on Friday; Ruby had not.

The girls had one last class to attend before their first day as returning students came to a close. Their last instructor let the class go after only an hour, having little more planned than a brief personal introduction and handing out a syllabus. Lacy was kind enough to offer Ruby a ride home.

On the trip from the campus back to Somerville, Ruby told Lacy about Duncan and Ray, and about Max Fitness's first day in operation. It was Lacy's idea to stop by and say hello.

"Duncan, Ray," Ruby said. "This is Lacy. Lacy, Duncan and Ray."

Lacy introduced herself to the boys. It was evident to all that she took an interest in Duncan right away. The foursome seemed to branch off into two couples during Duncan's attempt at a tour. Ray and Ruby began messing around with one of the heavy bags while Lacy tried on a pair of gloves and questioned Duncan on his hopes for the gym.

"I'd like to make it more like a club," Duncan said. "You know, a place where everyone knows each other and feels like they belong to something. There are so many gyms out there. I think I have to do something a little different if I want it to work."

"How has the reception been so far?" Lacy asked.

"You tell me," Duncan said, presenting the empty gym.

"I'm sure things will pick up."

"Hope so."

"I'd take classes," Lacy said. "How much does it cost?"

"For the first few weeks it's free."

"Really?"

"Yeah. Which really means I have two more weeks to figure out how to charge people."

Lacy laughed.

"I'm messing around with the idea of charging a membership fee," Duncan said. "It would be a monthly cost and you could come as much as you want."

"Like a country club or something like that."

"I haven't figured out how it would work yet."

"Well," Lacy said, sliding her hands into a pair of blue gloves. "Let's say you have 100 members…"

"Okay."

"And let's say you charged $100 a month. So that's $10,000 a month, and $120,000 a year."

"If only."

"Plus you could do additional things, like personal sessions or special classes, you could charge for those too."

"True."

Lacy put one of the blue foam helmets on her head. Duncan helped her with the chinstrap.

"So what do I do?" Lacy said, bouncing on her toes with her hands now in fists. "Show me what to do."

"I wanna fight, too," Ruby said from across the room.

She ran across the floor and grabbed a pair of gloves and a helmet from the wall.

The two girls playfully sparred.

"So what's going on with you and Ruby?" Duncan asked quietly.

"Nothing," Ray said innocently.

"Yeah, nothing," Duncan said. "All those looks and touches. Seems like nothing."

"What looks?"

"Dude."

Ray looked at Ruby with a smile on his face.

Ruby and Lacy had wrestled each other to the ground. Ruby straddled Lucy and was fake punching her in the chest.

"You win," Lacy shrieked. "You win."

Ruby threw her arms up in the air before dismounting her new friend and helping her to her feet.

"You guys want to grab a drink?" Ray asked. "On me."

"Sure," Ruby said. "Lacy?"

"Around here?" Lacy asked.

"There's a place just down the street."

Taking off her gloves, Lacy looked up to the clock on the wall. "Sure," she said. "I'm not much of a drinker though."

"Dun?" Ray said.

"I'm going to hang out here a bit longer."

"Did you put that ad in the paper?" Ruby asked.

"Yeah. It runs tomorrow."

"So then what are the odds that someone will come by today?" Ray asked. "Come on, call it a day."

"Yeah," Lacy said. "You should come."

"Give me an hour," Duncan said. "If no one comes by I'll close up until tomorrow."

"Okay," Ray said. "Ladies…"

The two girls took off their gear and placed it all back where they found it.

Lacy drove Ray and Ruby over to the bar, leaving the Chrysler for Duncan to join them later.

There was an early Red Sox game that day so O'Keefe's was busy. There were still enough empty tables that the trio had their choice.

"Can I get you guys something?" a young man asked.

"Sure," Ray said a little surprised. "I've seen you here before, right?"

"I help out from time to time," the fair-faced man said.

"What's your name again?"

"Sash."

"Okay, Sash. Just tell Charlene that Ray and Ruby will have the usual and...Lacy?"

"I'll have whatever you guys are having, I guess."

"Three please."

"Do you have a tab, er...?"

"Just for the day," Ray said. "We pay before we go."

Sash went off to fill the order.

Ray looked around the bar. It was a rare sight, but Terry was not in his seat. Vinny and Mike both caught Ray's eyes and the three exchanged a distant hello with a nod. Ray caught a glimpse of Pete's table. The table was occupied. The occupant got a special nod from Ray when he looked up. After his longest hiatus since returning to Boston, Pete was back at O'Keefe's.

"So cute," Ruby said.

"Totally," Lacy agreed.

"Who?" Ray inquired, returning his attention to the girls.

"You," Ruby mocked. "Sash, that's who."

"Really?" Ray said, trying to catch another glimpse of the young waiter. "Why is he cute?"

"Oh, I don't know," Ruby said. "Cute blond hair, cute face, tight, hot body."

"He's a child," Ray said.

"A hot child," Lacy added.

The girls giggled to each other.

"Want me to hook you up with him?" Ray asked Ruby.

"Could you?"

"Sash," Ray yelled across the bar. The young man looked over.

"Ray!" Ruby nudged.

Sash approached the table without the drinks.

"How old are you?" Ray asked.

"Eighteen."

"You can serve alcohol at eighteen?"

"Just can't drink it. Pretty stupid, huh?"

"You from around here?"

"Sash," Charlene called from behind the bar.

"Be right back," Sash said, taking his leave from the table. He returned moments later with three pints. "Charlene says hi," he said, placing the glasses on the table.

"You got a girlfriend?" Ray asked.

"Who's asking?"

"Oh! A bit of an attitude, I like it."

Sash smiled.

"What do you think of my friends here?" Ray continued.

"Pretty hot."

"Ray!" Ruby said. "Ignore him. He's an idiot."

"Sash," Charlene called once again.

"What're your names again?" Sash asked.

"Ray, Ruby, Lacy," Ray said, pointing to each.

"Ray, Ruby, Lacy," the boy repeated. "Ray, Ruby, Lacy."

"So hot," Lacy said again once the server disappeared from earshot.

"Stop drooling."

Ray found himself fighting back pangs of jealousy. It wasn't that the girls found Sash attractive that bothered him – even he could admit that the boy had good looks – what bothered Ray was that Ruby flirted so openly in front of him. In all the time he had known her, Ruby never showed interest in any other guys. She had certainly never displayed sexual desire for anyone other than Ray. It was the first time Ray acknowledged to himself that Ruby was available to anyone she wanted. He didn't like it. He didn't like it at all.

Duncan arrived at the bar long before the hour was up. No one had come by the gym and with nothing left to set up or organize, Duncan gave in to temptation, and to defeat.

"Where's Ray?" Duncan asked, sitting down beside Lacy.

Ruby pointed to the other end of the bar.

"Pete's back," Duncan said.

Ray was sitting at Pete's table with his back to Duncan.

"No one came?" Lacy asked.

Duncan shook his head. "Maybe tomorrow."

"It's gonna take time. My dad opened his own store years ago. It takes a while for things to pick up. Now he has three stores around the city and plans to open more."

"What kind of stores?" Ruby asked.

"Pool and hot tub stuff."

"And they're successful?" Duncan asked.

"Very," Lacy said. "And I should know. I do his books."

"Ooohhh," Ruby said. "Now I get it."

"Get what?" Duncan asked.

"Accounting program." Lacy said.

"Right, sorry. That makes sense. So you've been doing the bookkeeping without any training?"

"It's not hard," Lacy said. "I mean there are things I don't know how to do, which is why I'm in school now. But to run one or two stores isn't that difficult. It just takes time. Accounts payable, receivable, payroll, invoicing. It's all pretty straightforward on a small scale."

"I did that kind of stuff at the bar," Ruby said. "Well, not all of it, but I helped the manager. He wasn't that good with numbers."

"What you're saying is you could do all that stuff now?" Duncan asked Ruby.

"Sure she could," Lacy said. "Anything she doesn't know how to do she could figure out easily. I did."

"I see," Duncan said. He looked over at Ruby. "You want a job?" he asked her.

"Me?" Ruby said.

"Lacy already has one."

"You mean work for you?"

"Yes."

"As your bookkeeper?"

"Yes."

"Are you serious?"

"Yes."

"Okay!"

"Good. It's settled," Duncan said.

"What's settled?" Ray asked, sitting down at the table.

"I thought Pete wasn't coming in anymore?"

"Things change."

"And when there's a Sox game on."

"Well, there he is."

Duncan got up from the table and took a few steps toward the bar. "Anyone need anything?" he asked. Everyone at the table waved him off. Ruby and Ray had been refilled just prior to his arrival and Lacy was still nursing her first. Duncan rested up against the wood and said hello to the regulars, and to Charlene.

"He's hot too," Ruby said.

"I know," Lacy said. "*So* hot."

"Very funny," Ray said.

"I was being serious," Lacy said. "Is he single?"

"He is," Ruby said. "You guys should go out or something."

"I don't know, maybe another time."

"Another time?"

"I'm kind of seeing someone off and on. It's complicated."

"It always is," Ray said.

Duncan got a drink and instead of returning to the table, he meandered over and sat down with Pete. Ray watched him do it. "Uh oh," he said.

"What?" Ruby asked.

"Never mind. It's nothing. So Lacy, how old you are?" Ray asked.

"Twenty-five, and you?"

"Twenty-one."

"Funny," Ruby said. "He's twenty-eight. I'm twenty-three."

"You're only twenty three?" Lacy gasped.

"Yeah why?"

"No, nothing," she laughed. "I thought you were older than me. But that's a compliment. I swear."

"Older than you? Really?"

"Yeah, I don't know. Are you mad?"

"No, not at all."

"So how old is Duncan?"

"Thirty."

Lacy followed Ray's gaze and they both fixated on the table where Pete and Duncan sat. Duncan looked over his shoulder and caught Ray's eye. Ray looked away. After a few more minutes Duncan returned to the table; he didn't sit down.

"Can I talk to you?" Duncan said to Ray.

"Now?"

"Yes."

"Sure."

"Outside."

"Is everything okay?" Ruby asked.

"It's fine," Ray said as he followed Duncan's path to the door.

"What was that about?" Lacy asked, once the boys were out of sight.

"I have no idea. But I really wanna know."

CHAPTER 37

"HAVE YOU THOUGHT this through?" Duncan asked, coming to a halt by the curb.

"Thought what through?" Ray answered.

"Ray."

"Was it that obvious?"

"Pete's not going to lie. And I saw the book. I knew right away. It's your style."

"What do you want me to say?"

"Why, Ray?"

"Why?"

"Yeah, why?"

Ray looked at Duncan with a mixture of guilt and frustration. "Why not?" he said, though he knew that answer would not suffice.

"That's the best you can do? Why not? And why drag Pete into it?"

"Pete was more than willing."

"But it was your idea."

"Of course it was my idea."

"How long has it been going on?"

"I called Rico last week."

"Rico's involved?" Duncan asked, surprised.

"Yeah, why?"

"I thought we left all that behind, Ray. I thought that was the whole point of coming here."

"Yeah, well, it was. But what do you want me to do? I can't open a gym or go back to school. I had to do something. The opportunity just came up."

"Came up?"

"Yeah, Pete needed help and I needed something to do."

"So how does this work?" Duncan asked, feigning calm.

"What do you mean, how does it work? You showed me how it works."

"I didn't mean it like that. I mean…you know what I mean, Ray."

"Same deal as Phoenix. Pete takes the calls, Rico gets his vig, and we split the points."

"And you?"

"I make sure everything runs smoothly."

"Are you taking bets from Terry and the guys in there?"

"No," Ray said.

"Good."

"Pete is."

"Are you serious?"

"Yeah, why?"

"What do you need that for? You know we don't shit where we eat, Ray."

"It's not us anymore, Dun. It's me and Pete. And that douche Bixby was pissing me off."

"Is that what this is about?"

"What?"

"Is this about Bixby?"

"No."

"Then explain it to me, Ray, 'cause I don't get it."

Ray motioned Duncan away from the street. Their voices were getting louder and attracting attention from passersby. Ray slunk into the small alleyway beside the bar. Duncan followed.

"What do you want, man?" Ray pleaded. "I tried to leave it behind, but what else can I do? You've got your thing going on. Ruby has hers and–"

"And Ashley has hers." Duncan interrupted.

"Why do you think Ashley has anything to do with it?"

"Tell me she doesn't. Tell me all this doesn't have anything to do with her."

Ray paused. Perhaps he didn't fully accept the role that Ashley played in his decision. Staring down at his feet in the alley beside O'Keefe's, Ray began to realize that Ashley's words might in fact have been a powerful stimulus.

"This is all on you," Duncan said. "I'm not getting involved."

"I know."

"At all, Ray. I'm not helping you out with this one."

"I know."

"And don't you think about getting Ruby involved either."

"I won't."

Duncan noticed his hand on his hip and quickly removed it. "I'm assuming Bixby knows what's going on?"

"I don't know," Ray said. "I'm sure he does, but I haven't run into him yet. We've been taking most bets from Willy's guys over the phone. Rico has his old book and he called them all. You should've seen it the first few days. The phone was ringing like mad."

"Really?"

"These guys were dying to give us their money."

Duncan couldn't help but smile.

"Look," Ray said. "Everything will be fine. Pete needed a hand and I needed something, too. It's probably just temporary."

"I still don't think it's a good idea."

"You got a better one?"

"That's something you have to figure out yourself, Ray."

"Yeah, well the only thing I can come up with is a list of things I *don't* want to do."

Duncan put up his hand, Ray grabbed hold of it and they hugged. "Let me know when shit comes down from Bixby," Duncan said. "And it *will* come down."

"I can handle it," Ray said, patting his friend on the back.

Though most of him was disappointed, a small part of Duncan was happy for Ray. He knew that Ray was having a hard time in Boston, and maybe a little organization would be a positive thing. He didn't want to tell Ray what to do, but Duncan had it in his mind from the start that he would do everything he could to ensure that the situation was temporary. And though he said otherwise, Duncan would always make sure that he had Ray's back.

"Have you thought about what you're going to tell the girl?" Duncan asked just before reentering the bar.

"I don't think she needs to know right now," Ray said.

"Your funeral," Duncan said, grabbing the wooden door and opening for Ray.

"What was that about?" Ruby asked as the pair sat back down.

"Just guy stuff," Ray said. "Nothing important."

"Oh, I see. Sports, facial hair, big tits…stuff like that?"

"Pretty much."

"Fine, don't tell me. Let's go to the bar." Ruby got up, took Lacy by the hand, and led her to the empty stools beside Terry.

"That went well," Duncan said.

"Women."

"You have a box?"

Duncan was referring to a drop box where he and his clients could exchange monies owed.

"I have a box," Ray said.

"And you trust Pete?"

"Wouldn't you?"

"I don't know, Ray. I don't know him that well."

"I trust Pete. You saw the book, he's using our system. He can't hide anything."

"Yeah, I saw the book. I knew it right away."

"The system is good."

"I know the system is good," Duncan said. "It's my system."

"Uh, *our* system."

"Everything was pretty much done long before you came along."

"Yeah, right. Who came up with the grids?"

"Okay, the grids were yours," Duncan admitted.

"Damn right the grids were mine. You were using those stupid icons."

"They weren't icons."

"Whatever they were. Dumb."

"You finished?"

Ray mouthed the word "dumb" and then took a sip of his beer.

CHAPTER 38

IT WAS WEDNESDAY when the first real customers walked through the doors of Duncan's gym. Two zaftig ladies in their early thirties arrived just before 6 p.m., each holding a newspaper coupon for a free class. Duncan was far too preoccupied to check if the coupons were legitimate, he simply ushered in the would-be students with a smile. Duncan found himself a little nervous, something he never imagined he would be. He had prepared in his mind how he thought initial classes would go, but faced with the reality of it, his mind went mostly blank. At five after six, when it was clear that no one else would arrive for the session, Duncan began his instruction.

He started with simple stretching and heart rate exercises. He incorporated some defense techniques in the movements. The two ladies mirrored his punches, kicks, and lunges. He could see that his two students, Carol and Lana, were unaccustomed to strenuous activity and brought down the intensity accordingly.

The goal of Duncan's first class was to get his new and only students used to specific movements that would be incorporated into more complex actions and reactions that were soon to follow, should they continue their training.

Duncan had the women performing lunges and twists they felt were strange. At first they found the motions a tad comical, but giggles quickly vanished once they attempted the more complicated moves. Nearing the end of the hour, Duncan could see the ladies were still a little confused to the purpose of the unorthodox class. To assuage their concerns, Duncan had them use a few of the moves in an impromptu, choreographed Capoeira-style sparing exercise. The women were overjoyed when they realized how the movements they had been practicing actually had a practical use. Duncan, too, could hardly contain his smile. The women began to understand it was all meant to build up into something bigger. By the way their bodies ached, they also knew that Duncan was getting them to work muscles they didn't know they had. They liked that, too.

Duncan allowed the ladies to stay long after the hour ended. He showed Carol and Lana around the gym and introduced them to some of the equipment. Holding a heavy bag for Lana to punch, he heard a voice come from the front door.

"Hello?" the voice said.

Duncan turned to see who it was.

"Hi," Duncan said, releasing the bag just before Lana gave it one last punch. The bag swung just enough to graze Duncan's balls, which caused him to flinch awkwardly.

"Oops," Lana exclaimed. "Sorry!"

"It's okay. My fault."

Carol let out the laugh she had tried in vain to hold in.

"Okay, ladies," Duncan said. "It was really nice meeting you. I hope to see you again. There is a schedule at the front and one online. And your first two weeks are on me."

Carol and Lana looked at one another with brows raised.

"Nice meeting you," Carol said, holding out her hand. "Thanks for the class."

Duncan made sure that both women took a slew of info cards before walking them to the front door. With his first customers gone, and his first class finished, Duncan could turn his attention to the recent visitor.

"Hi, Kaya," Duncan said.

"I guess I missed the class."

"First customers."

"Don't they have to pay to be customers?"

"Okay, first students." Duncan relented. "Are you here to—"

"Not today," Kaya said. "I'm not really dressed for it."

"Oh."

"I was just driving by and wanted to see how it was going."

"Slow so far. Come in, I'll show you around."

Kaya followed Duncan into the open space of the studio. He gave her what he considered a lack luster tour; there wasn't really much to see, save for a few hanging bags and some small equipment neatly organized by the front.

"Manny came to find me," Kaya said as the walkabout came to an end.

"Manny?"

"The student whose arm I nearly tore off in the yard."

"He's okay, right?"

"Oh yeah, he's fine," Kaya assured. "Actually, he wanted to know where he could find you. He wanted to know if this was yours." Kaya pulled a yellow flyer out of her bag and handed it to Duncan. "He found it outside the library."

"Ah," Duncan said. "I guess I didn't get them all."

"I guess not," Kaya smiled.

"So...oops?"

"I guess he hasn't come in yet, then."

"Not yet."

"He seemed pretty interested, so you might be seeing him."

"I'll keep my eyes open."

"Okay. Well, thanks for the tour–"

"Is that it?"

"What do you mean?"

"Is that why you came by?"

"Well, yeah," Kaya said.

"Is that the only reason?"

Duncan marveled at her smooth, flawless skin. The way the lights bathed her face made her appear like a living doll. Duncan could only imagine how his own red, sweaty face must have looked.

"Well, like I said," Kaya continued. "I was driving by so I thought I would stop in–"

"Have dinner with me?" Duncan interrupted.

Kaya was caught off guard.

"What? Now?"

"I know I'm a little sweaty, but I could wash up."

"No, it's not that...I don't care if...I mean you look..." Kaya stopped herself. The self-assured PhD had begun to babble. She shook her head with a smile and looked up into Duncan's eyes. "Sure," she said. "Okay."

Duncan used the newly refurbished washroom to clean himself up and change his clothes. Kaya offered to drive but Duncan suggested they walked instead. On a previous stroll from the gym to O'Keefe's, Duncan had come upon a few restaurants he thought to try. He informed Kaya that he hadn't yet sampled any of them, so her suggestion of where to stop was as good as his own. Together, they decided on a small Italian place with interesting specials chalked on a board out front.

Further down the road, Ray was just sitting down with Pete at O'Keefe's. There was yet another Red Sox game on that night and the bar was filling up as the early innings had come and gone.

"Bixby was here today," Pete said quietly.

"And?"

"He was asking about you."

"Did he say anything else?"

"Not really. He just asked where you were."

"Okay."

"Just okay?"

"Yeah. I was expecting that."

"He didn't look happy."

"Does he ever?"

"What're we going to do about it?"

"Nothing. There's nothing to do. He doesn't have any claim on the bar, or the area. In fact, I would argue that we do. We're taking over for Willy, who was here long before Bixby arrived."

"You think he'll buy that?"

"Probably not," Ray said.

"If you hang around long enough you'll find out. He said he'd be back tonight."

Though he pretended not to be phased, the prospect of coming face-to-face with Bixby made Ray nervous. Bixby was not the type of guy Ray was used to dealing with. He was a street thug, probably more prone to violence than the college kids and upper crust clientele to whom Ray was accustomed. And, even when the tiniest prospect of violence had arisen in the past, Ray could always count on his partner for security, if not simply peace of mind. But Pete was not Duncan, and Duncan was nowhere to be seen.

In a completely related matter, Ray fired a quick text to Duncan inviting him to O'Keefe's for a beer. Duncan's response was blunt: *at dinner. Maybe after* it read.

"Mind if I join?" Terry asked from over Ray's shoulder.

"Have a seat," Ray said.

Terry sat down and gave Pete a smack on the shoulder – the good one. "What's the good news, Pete?" Terry said.

"Same story."

"You have me in there?"

Terry tilted his head to see the scribbles in the book that lay open in front of Pete.

"I do."

"So you have me for tonight?"

"I do. You and Vin and Mike."

"I'm up," Terry said to Ray.

"Good," Ray said. "I don't want you to lose."

"Yeah, right," Terry said with a chortle.

Ray put his hand in the middle of the open black book, pulled it close to himself and swung it around. Taking a peek down, Ray flipped a few pages backward. "See this?" Ray said, covering the top of the page with his hand and displaying the bottom half to Terry.

"What about it?" Terry asked, looking down at the book.

"That's thousands."

Terry took a moment to interpret what he was looking at. "What are all those icons?" he asked.

"Don't worry about that. Look at the numbers."

"So you've got some big bettors. What of it?"

Ray pulled the book back, closed it, and returned it to Pete. "You guys aren't going to make us rich, and you're not gonna make us poor. We'll take your action all day long, and we love it, but believe me, we want you to win. I'd be happy to pay you out."

"Okay, so how about letting me off when I'm down?"

"Let me put it this way," Ray said with a smile. "You've got a high ceiling. I won't come asking unless your number starts to look like the ones I just showed you. If you're a few hundred in the hole, your tab is good with me."

"That's a lot better than Bixby," Terry said.

"How did Bill do it?"

"End of the month," Pete said.

"Yeah, well, let's try it my way for now."

"Sounds good to me," Terry agreed. "Vinny can get up there so watch out for him."

"I'll keep my eyes open."

Terry stayed at the table with Pete and Ray until he could see the bottom of his glass. He then returned to his seat at the bar to take in the rest of the game, and the rest of another pint.

Ray was three beers and four more innings when Pete's prophecy came to fruition. Bixby and Marco walked into O'Keefe's just after nine o'clock.

CHAPTER 39

IT WAS BOTH good and bad that Bixby kept his distance from Ray for the first little while. It was good because Ray didn't have to face the issue at hand and could wait it out a while longer. It was bad because Ray didn't have to face the issue at hand and had to wait it out a while longer. With a confrontation no doubt pending, Ray decided to check on his missing friend once again. This time, Ray added the side note that he may, indeed, need some assistance.

Bixby sat at a table on the other end of the bar. He didn't even look over to Ray, not once. He just sat there and sipped his beer. It was obvious that Terry and the guys were also trying to keep their distance. Though they all saw Bixby come in, none dared to make eye contact.

The baseball game ended not long after. The Sox had lost which led to the bar emptying out faster than if they had won. Ray was ready to leave; he had plans to meet Ruby at home. The two had been getting along well and Ray was looking forward to his rendezvous with her. He wasn't about to let Bixby hold him hostage at O'Keefe's.

Pete offered to walk out with him – perhaps in an effort to ensure backup for himself – which Ray quickly accepted.

He got up and Pete soon followed. Neither made eye contact with Bixby or Marco as they said goodbye to Charlene and the guys at the bar. They walked out the front door and onto the sidewalk.

"Okay," Ray said. "I guess–"

"Hey guys," Bixby said, swinging the door open with a little extra verve. Marco caught the door as it swung back at his face; he held it in place for a second and then followed his comrade out.

"Never mind," Ray said to Pete.

"I think we should just–" Pete began.

"You two have been busy," Bixby said. "I didn't know you were involved too, Pete. I had to find out from Vinny. I hope you weren't expecting that guy to keep your secret."

"I–"

"I thought we cleared everything up, Ray. I thought we were cool."

"I know you think it does," Ray said. "But this has nothing to do with you. This is Bill's book. He was here long before you were."

"So you're just taking over for Bill, huh?"

"Bixby." Ray took a step closer to the taller man. "I don't think you want to take this any further." Bixby took his own step forward. The two were nearly face-to-face. "You don't know what you're getting yourself into," Ray continued. "This goes a long way past you and me. There are more people involved than you know."

"Oh yeah?"

"Yeah. And these aren't the kind of people you want to fuck with. They take what they do very seriously."

"You trying to make me believe you're a gangster, Ray? You think I'm stupid?"

"I never said I was a gangster. But let me ask you something. Why do you think Bill – a middle aged, overweight puppy dog – was able to carry on the way he did for so long? You think he was on his own? You think he didn't have someone looking out for him? You're not the first person to come along and step on our feet."

"I was around before you got here."

"We were always here, Bixby," Ray said, looking straight into the man's eyes. "We knew what you were up to long before we got to town. You think because Bill is gone you can just show up and no one will care? You think we would let you do that?"

Bixby said nothing.

"Let it go, Ryan. You're in over your head."

"Okay," Bixby nodded. He lowered his eyes and contemplated the words. "But let me ask you something, Ray." He looked back into Ray's eyes. "You think I'm on my own? You think it's just me and Marco and no one is behind us?"

"Actually," Ray said. "Yeah, I do."

Bixby scowled. "Then maybe we should just settle this right now." He took up the last bit of space between him and Ray.

"What's going on?" Duncan said, as he and Kaya approached on the sidewalk.

Bixby stepped down from Ray's face.

"Hey, Dun," Ray said calmly, though he was overjoyed to see his friend.

"Everything okay?"

"We were just talkin'," Bixby said, visibly effected by Duncan's arrival. Marco stepped forward and took up position beside his cohort. "This is our business," the goliath said. "And you're looking for trouble, Ray."

"Come on," Bixby said to Marco. "We'll see him again when his bodyguard isn't here."

"I don't give a shit about him," Marco said.

"Go home, Marco," Duncan said.

"You going to make me?"

Duncan gently pulled Kaya behind his body as Marco drew closer.

"Don't," Duncan said. "Don't do it. Right now we have no problem, Marco. Don't make it a problem."

"You're not a problem for me."

"Not yet."

"Bixby," Ray said. "This is between us. Don't get Duncan involved."

"Hey, waddaya gonna do?"

"Marco!" Ray said. "Don't do it."

"Hey!" a voice rang out. It was Charlene. She had come outside to see what was happening. "What the fuck? Bixby, I warned you about this."

"Don't look at me," Bixby said.

Charlene walked right over and stood in front of Marco. "None of this shit here, okay?"

Marco stared at the much smaller women.

Duncan lifted his chin, signaling to Ray to head back inside. Ray obliged and he and Pete started back for the door. Duncan took Kaya's hand and went to join his friend.

"See you soon, Ray," Bixby said.

"Not here," Charlene said. "You guys aren't welcome anymore."

"Oh no?" Bixby said mockingly.

Marco turned and brushed past Charlene. He made sure to bump her shoulder just a little.

Duncan saw him do it.

With a sudden jolt and swift heel to the back of the leg, Duncan dropped Marco to one knee and wrapped his arm around his neck. Ray stepped in front of Charlene and backed her up to where Kaya was standing. Pete shielded the two women as Ray turned to Bixby.

"Alright!" Bixby yelled. "Duncan, alright."

"Alright," Marco squeezed out as he held onto the arm that was cutting off the air to his lungs. Duncan took a moment and then let Marco loose with a forward shove that put the big man on all fours.

"Charlene–" Bixby started.

"Just go," Charlene said. "And don't come back." She turned and stomped back inside. Pete, Ray and the girls followed behind. Duncan held the door open. "Let it go, guys," he said. "Let it go."

All eyes were on the group as they came back into the bar. "Everything's fine, okay?" Charlene said, annoyed.

The buzz resumed as people went back to their drinks and conversation. "Sorry about that," Charlene said.

"None of this is your fault," Ray said quietly. But Charlene wasn't interested. She walked back behind the bar.

Duncan, hoping to leave the incident behind, found an empty table and sat down with Kaya. Pete followed Charlene back to the bar where Terry and Vinny quickly asked what had happened outside.

"Thanks, Dun," Ray said sitting down at the table.

Duncan didn't respond. Even though he knew to expect it, he was still perturbed at the whole ordeal.

"I'm Ray."

"Kaya."

The two shook hands.

"Nice to meet you."

Ray could see that Duncan was unhappy. It wasn't the first time he had helped Ray out of trouble, and it wasn't going to be the last, but this time something was different. Perhaps it was that Duncan warned Ray that it would happen. Perhaps it was that it happened in front of Kaya.

"I'll leave you two alone," Ray said. He got up from his seat. "Drinks are on me." Ray threw his bankcard down on the table. "You know the code."

Ray took a spot at the bar. He lingered there for only a few minutes before taking his leave for the night.

CHAPTER 40

RUBY WAS CURLED up under a small blanket reading a book on the couch. Ray could see her through the window as he approached the house; he stopped to watch the unsuspecting girl. He was mesmerized by how perfect she looked as the dim light hit the angles of her face just right. Her calm and pleasant expression made her look like a painting, and the way all her hair fell over to one side of her neck made Ray feel a rush of adrenaline.

His feelings for Ruby had begun to change. He had always been attracted to the girl, but that was not much of an accomplishment to say the least. He had always liked her; from the moment he met her to the morning after he woke up beside her. But as time wore on, and Ashley started to wear off, Ray began to feel Ruby in his gut. When he looked at her, he wanted to touch her. When he touched her, he could feel it in his bones. He looked forward more and more to the time he got to spend with Ruby, and marveled at how quickly time disappeared when he did.

As if by some twinge of extra-sensory perception, Ruby looked up and out the window at Ray. Standing on the lawn, Ray simply raised his hand and smiled. Ruby smiled too.

He hopped the steps and walked into the house.

"You're late," Ruby said.

"Don't ask," Ray said.

"Why, what happened?"

"It's a long story."

"I want to hear it," Ruby said, concerned.

Ray knew that he would eventually have to tell Ruby all about Pete, and Rico, and Bixby, and what he had been up to the past few weeks, but that didn't mean he wouldn't try to put it off as long as he possibly could. "Did you know that Duncan was on a date tonight?" Ray asked.

"No. Why? Is that weird?"

"It's not weird. He just usually tells…never mind."

"What happened tonight?" Ruby asked again, sitting up on the couch.

Ray remained silent.

"You don't want to tell me?"

"It's not that."

Ray wanted badly to forget the whole thing. Not sure why, he felt guilty and a little ashamed. He was worried that Ruby might think less of him, but he remembered his promise to the girl.

"Wanna take a walk, or something?" he asked.

"Sure," Ruby agreed.

They began a leisurely stroll down the street. Neither said anything for the first while. Ray was searching for the right way to tell Ruby about how he had reverted to his once and only lifestyle; the same he had just recently and happily left behind in Phoenix.

The only thing audible was the hypnotizing sound of their feet on the pavement.

Duncan was doing far better back at O'Keefe's. He had no trouble explaining to Kaya about leaving Phoenix, what he did there, and why he wanted it to end. Kaya, a lifelong academic, was more than understanding and even forgiving about Duncan's less than reputable choices as a younger man. Kaya, too, got into her past, including the not-so-nice boyfriend who's aggression forced her to call the police more than once. Kaya was not proud of the story, but was forthcoming when Duncan brought up the topic of past relationships. He had wondered aloud why Kaya was still single.

"I'm taking bets again," Ray said, keeping his eyes on the path ahead.

"What do you mean?" Ruby asked, knowing full well what he was talking about.

"I called my contact is Vegas and I've taken over for Bill."

Ruby searched for the right thing to say. "Okay, and you're telling me this because…"

"Because I don't want to keep secrets from you."

"I kinda knew already."

"You did?"

"I'm not stupid, Ray. I can hear you and Duncan talking. I live there too."

"You're not mad?"

"Why would I be mad?"

"Disappointed?"

"Why would I be disappointed?"

Ray and Ruby had reached the park. Their pace decreased as they ambled lazily through the grass. Ray took Ruby by the hand. She locked fingers with him and they continued to stroll. "I was just worried you'd be disappointed," Ray said.

"It's your life, Ray. You know? I mean, I can't tell you what to do. It might not be the best thing in the world, but it's your choice. If it makes you happy, then it makes you happy."

"It's just for now," Ray said, placating Ruby and perhaps himself. "Pete does most of the work anyway. It's more like I'm helping him. It's just until I find something else."

Ruby stopped walking. Ray – still holding on to her hand – followed suit. "Ray," she said. Ray turned to face her. A nearby lamppost cut through the shadows and lit up her face just enough so that Ray could see the color in her eyes. "I'm not mad, or upset, or disappointed." Ruby took half a step closer to Ray. He clenched her hand tightly, and though there was hardly enough room to pass an apple between their bodies, Ray inched closer and put his free arm around Ruby's waist. Ruby took in a heavy breath.

"I just want you to be happy," she said.

"You make me happy," Ray said.

"I do?"

Ray nodded. Ruby could feel her chest thumping. She wondered to herself if Ray could hear it through the silence of the empty field.

"I think I'm in love with you, Ruby," Ray said, inching even closer.

"You are?"

"I think I've been in love with you for a while."

Ruby's chest raised and lowered as blood coursed heavy through her veins. "I think I love you, too," she said.

Ray's head tilted and their noses rubbed past each others. Ruby's eye's closed; she could feel Ray's breath on her cheek. Ruby made the last move to bridge the tiny gap that remained between their lips.

They had kissed before, but never like this. They kissed like they invented it.

Ruby had always felt something for Ray, and if not for his muddled state of mind, Ray would have realized that he had always felt it for her, too. Finding clarity in the darkness of the park, Ray had put all else behind him and understood that he could never be "just friends" with Ruby, and that he didn't want to.

They kissed in the darkness, and in the silence.

"How nice," a voice rung out, followed by the sound of car doors slamming. A car had pulled up to the curb only fifty yards away. Bixby leaned back against the passenger side door; Marco leaned over the top from the driver's side.

"Text Duncan," Ray said quietly as he released his grip on Ruby. Ruby hid herself behind Ray's body and followed his direction.

At first Ray thought about simply walking the other way, towards O'Keefe's, and ignoring Bixby completely. Something inside made him do the opposite. Ray began to walk casually towards Bixby and the dimly lit street. Ruby followed closely behind, her hand holding on to Ray's.

"Bixby," Ray said as he got closer. "How's this going to end?"

"You tell me," Bixby said, his arms folded. He pushed off the car using only his back and came to meet Ray on the sidewalk. "You started this, Ray."

"Let's just go home," Ruby said.

"What're you doing here?" Ray asked.

"Why don't you get in the car," Bixby said. "Let's go for a ride."

"You're kidding, right?"

"No."

"That's not going to happen, Bixby. I'm not getting in your car."

Bixby took a step closer to Ray.

Ray took Ruby's hand once again and turned to walk back home. With a jump in his step, Marco circled around the car and impeded their path. "Are you serious?" Ray said. He looked over his shoulder into the darkness of the park. He made it seem arbitrary, but his purpose was sure; he was looking for Duncan.

"You can go home," Bixby said to Ruby. "We just want to talk to Ray."

"I'm not going anywhere," Ruby said.

Marco reached his arm out to grab Ruby but she recoiled. "Hey!" Ray yelped. "Don't touch her."

"Or what?" Marco said.

"You're in over your head."

A car approached and then whizzed by. It wasn't a Fifth Avenue. The foursome stood on the elbow of a tight turn in the road; if Duncan was to arrive by car, he would appear as if from nowhere.

Ray knew that if he couldn't end the confrontation, he had to delay it as long as possible. Even though Duncan wasn't happy with him, he would never leave him out to hang. Ever.

"We can take care of ourselves," Bixby said, boxing Ray and Ruby in on the sidewalk between he and Marco.

"Okay," Ray said. He gripped Ruby's hand as if holding on to her would keep her safe. "Say what you want to say right here."

"Nah," Bixby said. "Get in the car."

"You watch too many movies, Bixby. You think people fall for that shit?"

"We could always *put* you in the car."

"You're not going to touch anyone, and you know it." Ray said.

"Marco, help Ray into the car."

Marco made a move for Ray, who finally let go of Ruby's hand. As he released her, he did so with a motion that pushed her back a step, though she instinctively got out of the way. Ray looked one last time to his left; Duncan was nowhere to be found. Not willing to wait for Marco to take hold of him, Ray turned around quickly and lunged for Bixby's waist. The tackle propelled both men off the sidewalk and onto the trunk of the parked car.

"Ray!" Ruby yelled. She wasn't trying to stop him. She was trying to warn him. As Ray gained the upper hand on Bixby, Marco wrapped his arm around Ray's neck and began to peel him off. He pulled Ray back onto the curb when Ray bent over as far as he could and introduced his elbow to Marco's most private of parts. In obvious pain, Marco let go his grip. Ray stepped away quickly, his foot landing half on the curb, and half off, causing him to stumble backwards into Bixby. Bixby tried to grab onto Ray, if only by instinct. Ray's momentum caused both men to roll off the back of the car and propelled them out into the street. The timing was wretchedly perfect. If it happened ten thousand more times, it probably couldn't have happened like that again. The incoming car tried to break when it saw the two men explode into its path, but it was going too quickly, and it was already too close. The skidding car made contact with the two men and sent Bixby rolling up onto its hood. The windshield cracked as Bixby's body collided with it and then rolled across the hood and back onto the road.

The car came to a screeching stop; it's headlights illuminating the waft of smoke the tires had swept up into the air.

Bixby lay bloodied on the asphalt, but he was still conscious. From his vantage, lying on the warm road, he could hear only faint noises and echoes. The streetlights above looked like halos, and beyond them the sky was black and empty. Bixby's eyes struggled to focus. When they did, they focused out onto the road. There lay Ray.

Ray was lying motionless, on his back, only a few yards from Bixby. His elbow lay on the road and his forearm was up in the air, as if it were being held there by a string.

Ruby immediately ran over and knelt down beside Ray.

"Ray," she said softly, her hand upon his chest, her eyes filled with fear. "Ray," she said again, only louder.

It was then that Ruby saw the pool of blood beginning to spread from under Ray's head.

The headlights of the car glistened in the purplish-red liquid. "No," Ruby whispered. She touched her hand to Ray's head and then quickly pulled it away. Bixby's chest rose up and down as he searched for breath and watched as Ruby tended to the other man. Down on one knee, Marco looked on in shock from the curb.

"Ray?" a voice rang out.

"Duncan?" Ruby yelled. She turned to look but was blinded by the headlights of the car. Ruby began to feel sick. She hoped with everything inside of her that anyone but him would emerge.

"Call an ambulance," the voice said. "Now!"

Out from behind the lights of the car Duncan came running. He quickly got down beside Ray to survey the damage. His hands were up in the air as if he didn't know where he could or could not touch.

"Don't move him," Kaya said, arriving and kneeling down beside Duncan. "We need an ambulance, now."

"We have to do something," Duncan said.

"They fell," Ruby said, choked with tears. "They were fighting and they fell into the street."

Duncan looked over at Marco who still hadn't moved from the curb. He shifted his glance back to Bixby.

A faint siren could be heard in the distance.

The ambulance arrived in minutes, along with a barrage of other sirens and flashing lights. Firefighters tended to Bixby, who was now speaking and responding to their questions. Three EMTs rushed to Ray's side, shooing the others away. A second ambulance arrived and emergency workers hurried Bixby into its belly on a backboard. Ray needed to be treated much more lightly.

Ray, still unconscious, was outfitted in a neck brace and gauze was placed behind his head to quell the pooling blood. In what all seemed like a haze of rotating red lights and frantic, scurrying bodies, he was finally lifted and put into an ambulance. The ambulance hurried off from the scene.

"Ma'am," a police officer said.

Ruby was still watching the taillights of the ambulance dart away.

"Ma'am," the man said again.

"Ruby," Duncan interjected.

"Can I talk with you, ma'am?" the officer said.

Ruby followed the police officer onto the sidewalk where Marco and an unfamiliar stranger were already talking with other cops.

"Who's he?" Ruby asked.

"Did you see what happened?" the officer asked.

"Yeah," Ruby said. "I was here. Who's that guy?"

"Could you explain the events to me, please?"

"They were arguing."

"Who was arguing?"

Ruby paused and looked to Duncan who had followed her to the roadside.

"Tell him, Ruby," Duncan said. "It's okay."

"They started arguing about something," Ruby said. "Bixby wanted Ray to, uh, get into the car but Ray didn't want to. Marco went at Ray to try to...push him into the car and then

Ray and Bixby started fighting. They tripped over the...curb and fell into the street. Then the car, just, came."

"Did you witness the car strike the men?" the officer asked. Ruby nodded.

"How would you describe the speed of the car?"

"I don't know," Ruby said. "I just heard the skid and then saw it."

"Were you involved in any way in the altercation between the two men?"

"No."

Duncan put his arm around Ruby, whose tears had dried and left dark lines down her cheeks. The officer asking the questions was called over to the other men.

"We should go to the hospital," Ruby said.

"We will," Duncan said. "Ky went to get the car."

"Who?"

"Kaya, the girl I was with."

"I don't understand," Ruby said.

"What?"

"Who's that guy?" Ruby asked yet again.

"Which guy?"

"Him." She pointed to the man, still surrounded by blue uniforms.

"That's the driver," Duncan said.

Ruby perked up her sagging body. "It wasn't you?"

"Me?" Duncan said. "What, driving the car? No. It wasn't me. Did you think it was me?"

Ruby took a closer look at the car that had caused the damage. It was the same color as the Fifth Avenue, it was even similar in build, but it was not the Fifth Avenue. It was a light blue Chrysler Imperial.

Ruby turned and threw her arms around Duncan.

"You thought it was me," he said, clutching the girl.

She nodded her head as it pressed into his shoulder.

Kaya had retrieved the car and pulled up just down the street from the accident scene.

Duncan took Ruby by the hand and briskly walked her to the awaiting car. The police officer saw, and did nothing to stop them.

Already in the driver's seat, and knowing the area better than Duncan, Kaya drove the trio to the nearby hospital.

CHAPTER 41

WAITING TO HEAR the news on Ray's condition was a dreadfully painful task. As if she hadn't already done enough, Kaya sat and waited with Ruby and Duncan the entire time. She was holding Duncan's hand in her lap. Duncan's knee bounced incessantly up and down.

A doctor finally came through the double doors to share the diagnosis more than two hours after they had arrived. Duncan and Ruby rushed over to meet her.

"We've stabilized him for now," the doctor said after a terse introduction. "I would still classify his condition as critical, however. He sustained several injuries to his sternum but we've managed to stop all the bleeding in the area. He has a collapsed lung and multiple broken ribs."

Duncan shook his head in disgust.

"What concerns me the most, though, is the trauma to his head," the doctor continued. "He fractured his skull and has a very serious concussion. Unfortunately, the damage is such that we don't yet know the full extent."

"Will he recover?" Duncan asked. "I mean his brain…"

"A concussion is essentially a contusion, okay, like a bad bruise. In other words right now Raymond has a badly bruised brain. We're going to be monitoring him very closely and I can update you as soon as we know more. We need the swelling to go down a bit though. Once it does, we'll be able to have a closer look."

"When does the swelling go down...usually?" Ruby asked.

"It's hard to say. Each injury is different."

"Okay..."

"Look," the doctor said, taking off her surgical cap. "I feel a little silly saying this, but your friend is really lucky to be alive right now. Our concern is the next twenty-four hours."

"Can we see him?" Duncan asked.

"I can take two of you in."

"Go," Kaya offered. Duncan kissed her on the cheek and he and Ruby followed the doctor through the doors. She led them into Ray's room and then left. The whole of Ray's upper head was wrapped in white hospital gauze. He looked peaceful, lying on his back with his arms by his side. Neither Duncan nor Ruby wanted to say it, but to them, Ray looked as if he could have been dead. His chest rose and lowered shallowly as he sucked tiny breaths of air into his injured chest. A beige tube protruded from his right side, just beneath his underarm, and led into what looked like a briefcase.

"That's helping his lung return to form," a nurse said as she brushed in past the silent pair.

"Is that blood?" Ruby was referring to the contents of the briefcase.

"Yes," said the nurse. "It's a typical procedure. He responded well to it, actually. His lung inflated almost immediately after the surgery, which is good."

The nurse injected a solution into Ray's IV line and checked various readings on the machines. Ruby took a chair from against the wall and pulled it up to the bed. She sat down, leaned over, and put her hand into Ray's.

The nurse finished her duties and left the room to tend to other patients.

"I'm going to take Kaya home," Duncan said, standing at the foot of the bed.

"Already?"

"She doesn't need to be here."

"Okay," Ruby said. She found it a little strange that Duncan was so eager to leave, but didn't make mention of it out loud. "I'm going to stay," she said.

"I'll come back and get you."

Back in the waiting area, Kaya was sitting beside a face familiar to Duncan.

"Duncan," Ashley said with tears in her eyes.

"Hey, Ash."

Duncan embraced the girl.

Davis had accompanied Ashley to the hospital, and the group of four was formally introduced to one another. Duncan explained to Ashley all he knew of Ray's condition. "Can I see him?" she asked.

"I don't think so," Duncan said. "I snuck in."

Duncan said goodbye to Ashley and didn't waste any more time before leaving the hospital with Kaya. He took her by the hand and led her back to the parking lot.

"Don't you want to stay with him?" Kaya asked as they zigzagged through the rows of parked cars.

"Ruby's there," Duncan said. "It's pretty late. You shouldn't have to deal with this."

"I'm okay, Duncan," Kaya said as they reached the Fifth Avenue. Duncan opened the passenger door for her. She didn't get in. "Duncan," she said. "What is it?"

Duncan didn't answer.

He looked down to his feet.

"It's okay," Kaya said, taking his hand. "What is it?"

Duncan shook his head. "I don't know," he said. "I'm so...I'm so fucking angry."

"You're allowed to be angry."

"I should've been there," Duncan said. "I should have done something sooner. Fuck!"

"You're angry at yourself?" Kaya asked, bewildered.

"He's always had my back, Ky. Always. And I wasn't there for him when he needed me to have his. I was too caught up in my own shit. I knew he needed help. I fucking knew this was going to happen. I told myself I wasn't going to get involved, like I was proving a point or something."

In a move that caught Duncan by complete surprise, Kaya reached up her hands, placed them on Duncan's face, and calmly kissed him on his lips.

"What was that for?" Duncan asked.

Kaya just smiled.

"Do it again," Duncan said.

Kaya once again raised her hands up to Duncan's face. Duncan was ready for it this time and met her lips halfway.

CHAPTER 42

RUBY AND DUNCAN quickly became favorite visitors on the hospital floor. By day three, all the staff knew them by name and welcomed them with status updates on their friend's condition.

Ray hadn't yet opened his eyes, as was to be expected, but his other injuries were mending at an encouraging pace. The tube leading into his chest was to be pulled out that afternoon, which is why Duncan and Ruby made a special trip to the hospital together. Duncan, whose classes had recently seen a boon from two attendees to three, closed the gym early to be in attendance. Ruby took the day off school, and waited for Duncan to drive rather than taking the bus alone as she had the two days prior.

Arriving in Ray's room, Duncan and Ruby were met by an unexpected guest. Sitting in a wheelchair near Ray's bed in a full-leg cast and a cumbersome body brace was Ryan Bixby.

"Has he woken up yet?" Bixby asked, keeping his eyes on Ray.

"No," Duncan said, brushing past the injured man's chair.

"What happened to you?" Ruby asked, disgusted.

"Broken hip, broken pelvis, broken femur."

"Is that all?" Duncan said.

"I'm being held together with fucking pins."

Duncan had always regarded Bixby as nothing more than a stupid kid trying to act tougher than he was. He wasn't interested in making peace, but at least for the time being, he thought Bixby might have had enough abuse. He just wanted him gone, and gone for good.

"Duncan Miller," a voice said from the doorway.

A pretty, blonde girl entered the room with coffee cup in hand.

"You were supposed to call me when you got here," Duncan said, embracing the girl.

"Ruby, this is Nikki. Nikki, Ruby."

"Ray's sister?" Ruby asked.

"Hi," Nikki said, shaking Ruby's hand. "Cute."

Ruby smiled shyly.

"And who's this?" Nikki asked of Bixby.

"He was just leaving," Duncan said.

Bixby turned his chair and began wheeling out of the room. He stopped at the door and turned his head as if he were about to say something. Instead, Bixby wheeled out into the hall and disappeared.

"What was that about?" Nikki asked.

"Don't ask," Duncan said. "How long have you been here?"

"I got in this morning."

Nikki looked much different than Duncan remembered. She had come to stay with them in Phoenix a few years prior and was, at the time, still sporting a few dreadlocks in her long messy hair. She had since cut her tresses to a shoulder's length and had apparently discovered a quality shampoo. She dressed like someone her own age and even seemed to walk with less of a lazy gait.

Nikki sat down in a chair by Ray's bedside.

"Has the doctor been in yet?" Duncan asked.

"Not yet."

He couldn't help but hold his inquisitive gaze on Nikki. She looked like a completely different person.

"So, what's new with you?" Duncan asked. "What are you doing now?"

"You wouldn't believe me if I told you," Nikki said.

"Don't tell me you got a real job?"

"Nope."

"Didn't think so."

"I started my own business."

"You? You started your own business? The girl that slept on our couch for forty-eight hours straight?"

"I was sick," Nikki said to Ruby.

Ruby smiled.

"You weren't sick," Duncan said.

"I was too."

"You were drunk."

"I had alcohol poisoning."

"So tell me about this business."

"What can I tell you? I met this girl in a class I was taking. We started hanging out and one day I was at her place and she was showing me all her artwork, and this stuff was – Duncan, I'm telling you – this stuff was incredible. I asked her why she doesn't try to sell any of it. Long story short, I started taking her paintings around to galleries and now I represent her...and four other artists."

"You're an *art dealer*?"

"More like a manager."

"Never would have guessed."

"Ray never told you this?"

"When was the last time you spoke to him?"

Nikki looked at her motionless brother. "Months," she said forlornly. "And what about you, Duncan?" she continued. "Are you still–"

"No. Not anymore. Not since we left Phoenix." Duncan said. "I'm actually working on something new for myself."

"And you, Miss Ruby?"

"Back at school," Ruby said.

"I never could figure out how to do well in school."

"You just said you were taking a class," Duncan said.

"It was an acting class, Duncan."

"Well look at this fuckin' mess," a voice said from the doorway.

Duncan turned to see the most recent visitor. "You gotta be kidding me," he said.

It was Rico. To Duncan's surprise, he had made an unannounced trip to Boston. He brought along Kentucky Joe. "How did you hear?" Duncan asked.

"Pete," Rico said, walking into the room with the big man behind him. "Hey, Dun," Kentucky Joe said.

Duncan welcomed his old Las Vegas cohorts and introduced them to the women.

"He looks good," Rico said with a simper. "How's he doing?"

"He hasn't woken up yet," Nikki said.

"Three days?" Rico asked, already knowing the answer.

Duncan nodded.

"And what's this thing?"

"That's for his lung," Ruby said. "But they're supposed to come take it out…ten minutes ago."

"Uh huh," Rico said, surveying the situation. "Is there anything I can do to help? Duncan?"

"The fact that you came is enough, Rico."

371

Kentucky Joe sat down in a chair beside Nikki. He didn't know Ray nearly as well as Rico, or anyone in the room for that matter, but he looked sincerely upset by the situation.

"What about something to eat?" Rico asked. "How about some food? Ladies?"

The doctor arrived with Ray's nurse in tow.

"I see someone has a lot of friends," the doctor said.

"Hi, Doc," Nikki said.

"There are way too many of you in here," the nurse insisted in the friendliest way possible. "Two at a time is the most."

"We were just leaving," Rico said.

Kentucky Joe got up and gave Ray a pat on the shoulder.

"We'll just be in the hall," Rico said.

"I don't want to see this," Nikki said. She followed the two men out of the room.

Ruby and Duncan remained as the male doctor tended to Ray.

The doctor put on surgical gloves and pulled back the sheets that covered Ray's body. The nurse aided by lifting Ray's gown and exposing his side. The area under Ray's armpit was covered in tape, no doubt to hold the tube in place. The nurse began to peel away the white layers. The cut looked to be about two inches long and perfectly straight; the work of a steady hand and scalpel. Protruding from the opening was the tube that disappeared into Ray's sternum. Ruby didn't look directly at the wound.

"Now usually I have to brace the patient for this because it's one of the more painful parts," the doctor said, placing his hand on Ray's chest. He then took hold of the tube. "But considering the circumstances…"

Without further warning, the doctor yanked the tube from Ray's chest as if he were trying to start a lawn mower. Ray's body wobbled back and forth from the reverse pressure of the doctor's hand still holding his side. The nurse ducked in to get a closer look at the now re-opened incision and began to re-bandage the region.

"It doesn't need stitches?" Duncan asked.

"No," the doctor said. "It's mostly muscle in that area. It will close up nicely on its own."

"And that's it?"

"That's it."

"Doctor," the nurse said.

No one had seen it but the nurse, but she insisted Ray had moved on his own.

"It could be a reaction to the pain of pulling out the tube," the doctor said, getting up close to Ray. "You know how they say that getting stabbed isn't nearly as bad as pulling the knife out…"

Ray moved again. This time everyone saw. His arm moved outward, away from his body.

"Okay," the doctor said. He immediately took out his penlight and went to look in Ray's eyes. As he lifted the lid of Ray's left eye, both of the patient's eyes slowly opened. "Raymond," the doctor said.

Ruby came closer and squeezed Duncan's arm.

"Hello there," the doctor said.

Ray tried to reach over to grab his side where the nurse was still working. "Try to stay still," the doctor said, intercepting Ray's arm.

"He's awake," Ruby whispered as she propped up on her toes to get a better look over the doctor's shoulder.

"Raymond," the doctor said. "You're in the hospital. My name is Dr. Green. Your friends are here with me. Okay?"

Ray said nothing.

"Raymond, what's my name?"

Ray, again, said nothing.

"Raymond, do you know who these people are?" The doctor got out of the way so that Ray could clearly see Duncan and Ruby.

Ray nodded slowly.

Ruby smiled.

"Good. Do you know their names?"

Ray thought for a moment. He shook his head with a look of confusion on his face.

"Okay," the doctor said. "When was the last time he had imaging done?" he asked the nurse.

The nurse put Ray's chart in front of the doctor. Nikki, having heard bits and pieces of the conversation, came into the room.

"He's awake," Ruby said.

The nurse scurried around the bed performing all sorts of checks and calculations. The doctor wrote vigorously on the chart.

"My head…" Ray squeezed out.

"You were in an accident, Raymond. Just relax. We'll give you something for the pain."

Rico and Kentucky Joe were not in the hall when the doctor pulled out Nikki, Duncan, and Ruby. He left the nurse to perform her tasks while he updated the group on Ray's situation. "Right away, I would say he definitely has a degree of post-traumatic amnesia," he said. "I don't know the level of severity. I told him my name and he wasn't able to recall it moments later. He recognizes your faces, which is good, but he can't bring up your names. Symptoms like this are not uncommon for someone in his condition."

"But he'll eventually be able to remember, right?" Duncan asked.

"Traumatic amnesia usually wears off. But until we know the degree, and pinpoint exactly what we're dealing with, I don't want to make any assumptions. We're going to get him tested again and see what we can find out. We'll give him a good scan, and see if we can't find out more."

"Thank you, Doctor," Nikki said.

"Can we go talk to him?" Ruby asked.

Another nurse brushed past the group and went into Ray's room.

"I want to get a few more tests done right now."

"Okay," Duncan said. "Why don't we go for a walk or something?"

"I'd like to stay if that's okay," Nikki said. "I know he doesn't remember my name but – I'd like to stay. It might be good if he sees a familiar face."

"That would be fine," the doctor said.

Nikki followed the doctor back into the room, leaving Duncan and Ruby in the hall.

Duncan could see that Ruby was overwhelmed. He wrapped his arms around his friend and gave her a tight hug. The girl returned the gesture. Hospital traffic washed back and forth down the hall as Duncan and Ruby remained in their embrace.

CHAPTER 43

AS IF FROM nowhere, Rico and Kentucky Joe appeared out front of the hospital and injected themselves into the walking path of Duncan and Ruby.

"Where'd you go?" Duncan asked.

"We had something to take care of," Rico said.

Duncan didn't have to ask any more. He knew quite well what Rico meant, and where he had been. It wasn't by accident that it was the hulking Kentucky Joe that accompanied Rico on his trip. Rico wanted to introduce himself, and Joe, to young Bixby who was in the same hospital as Ray. Duncan didn't need to know the specific details of Rico's meeting to forecast the result. No matter what happened from then on, interference from Bixby would no longer be a concern.

It was doubtful that Rico used any sort of physical coercion because that just wasn't his style. He had instead a talent for getting a stalwart message across simply with words, an enviable skill and one that often came in handy in his line of work.

"He opened his eyes," Duncan said.

"That's great," Rico said. "Is he talking? Should we say hello?"

"Nah," Duncan said. "They pretty much kicked us out. They're doing some tests. He probably wouldn't remember you anyhow. He has some kind of amnesia."

"No shit?"

"He didn't remember us."

"At all?"

"He knew our faces. He knew that he knew us, but didn't know our names."

"I've seen that before," Kentucky Joe said. "It'll all come back."

"Doctor said it should."

"It will," Joe said. "Bad concussion I bet."

Duncan nodded. "So how long you guys here for?" he asked.

"Just tonight," Rico said. "We fly out in the morning."

"You have plans, or–"

"We have a few things to do. First was to see Ray."

"Well, we're going to hang around here for a while but do you want to meet later on for a drink or something?"

"Sure," Rico said.

"Sounds good," Joe agreed.

"There's a place called O'Keefe's not far from here. If you take Highland–"

"Already know where it is, Dun," Rico interrupted, putting his hand on his old friend's shoulder. "We'll see you there later on. We'll wait for you."

"Right," Duncan said, cluing in. "See you in a few hours then."

"It was nice to meet you, Ruby," Rico said.

"You too," Ruby agreed.

During a walk around the area, which included a stop at a coffee shop, Ruby told Duncan of her and Ray's mutual confession the night of the accident. It came as no surprise to

Duncan that the two had finally admitted their feelings for one another.

The pair returned to hospital and to Ray's room. Nikki was still there, sitting beside Ray's bed, reading a book. Ray was asleep.

"The doctor said he would be sleeping a lot," Nikki whispered. "He's still really out of it."

"What did the doctor say?" Duncan asked.

"Not much. They mostly just talked to Ray. They would tell him something and then a few minutes later ask him to repeat it. One of the nurses kept saying her name, he would repeat it, and then a few minutes later he couldn't remember it. He did seem to remember that I was his sister, though."

"That's good," Ruby said.

"That was the one thing he got right."

"But they didn't say anything else to you?" Duncan asked.

"They said that just waking up and talking is a really good thing. His whole right side is banged up so it pretty much hurts him to move his body. They pumped him full of pain killers and said he should be out for the rest of the night."

"He looks better," Ruby said, standing over the bed.

The scrapes and scratches on the side of Ray's face had begun to heal. A little color had reappeared in his cheeks, and the bandages around his head remained a stark white. He didn't look nearly as dire as he did only forty-eight hours prior, though that was just Ruby's visual assessment mixed with hopeful thoughts.

"Can I take you ladies out for dinner?" Duncan asked. "You need a break, Nik. Bring your stuff back to our place and let's go get something to eat."

"I should go grab a hotel room," Nikki said.

"Come stay with us," Ruby encouraged. "We have plenty of room."

"It's no trouble, really," Nikki said. "Don't put yourselves out."

"Who are you?" Duncan said. "You're staying with us. That's the end of it."

The trio stayed with Ray a little while longer before Duncan drove the girls home and got Nikki set up in Ray's room. Ray had recently replaced the futon with a proper bed, so Duncan didn't feel bad about putting Nikki in her brother's office-turned-bedroom. Ray had decided not long after his conversation with Duncan in the bar that if he were ever to sleep in Ruby's bed again, he would have to be invited to do so. With little fanfare, he purchased a mattress set and basic metal frame later that week.

Duncan took the women to a nearby Greek restaurant. He called Kaya along the way to see if she would join, but she was bogged down with work and regretfully declined. Though the conversation at dinner sometimes wandered from the topic, much of the time was spent talking about Ray. Nikki wanted to know what had happened to lead up to the accident. Duncan filled her in. It was the first time hearing some of the grittier details for Ruby, too. She knew what Ray was up to, but Rico's affiliation and appearance in Boston finally made sense to her by the time the main course arrived.

Midway through dinner Nikki excused herself from the conversation to take a phone call. She got up and walked away from the table. She stood in the alcove of the restaurant and spoke on her Blackberry.

"She's really nice," Ruby said in her absence.

"If you would have seen her a few years ago…I don't even recognize her."

"Really? It's so hard to imagine."

Nikki returned to the table and put her phone back in her bag. "Sorry," she said.

"What's all that about?" Duncan asked.

"What?"

"That grin on your face. Who were you talking to?"

"What grin?"

"I know who she was talking to," Ruby said.

"Who?" Duncan asked.

"What are you guys talking about?"

"Nikki has a boyfriend," Ruby said.

"How do you know?" Duncan asked.

"I can tell."

"Ruby," Nikki said, blushing.

"Oh, wow," Duncan said. "Was Nikki just talking to her boyfriend?"

"What is this, middle school?"

"What's his name?"

"I'm not talking about this."

Nikki picked up her fork and tried her best to ignore the pair.

"Is he tall?"

Nikki took a bite of food.

"Is he rich?"

"What's his name?" Ruby asked.

Nikki put down her fork. "If I tell you his name will you let it go?"

"I knew it," Ruby said.

"Sure," Duncan agreed. "Just his name."

"Fine. Jacob. His name is Jacob. Happy?"

"What does he do?" Duncan asked.

"You said…he's an art dealer."

"Okay. And…"

"And I met him at a show. We hit it off. No big deal."

"How long have you been dating?" Ruby asked.

"Nine months."

"Do you love him?" Duncan asked.

"Duncan!"

"What? That's a perfectly good question."

"She loves him," Ruby said with a smile.

Nikki looked at Ruby with a friendly scowl. "Where'd you find her?"

"Utah," Duncan said.

"You're from Utah?"

"I'm from Kansas," Ruby said.

"Now I'm confused."

"That's a story for another time," Duncan said. "I want to hear more about Jacob."

Nikki obliged and magnanimously answered all of their queries, and for a short time they were able to put their minds to something other than Ray. When the bill came, both Nikki and Ruby reached for their wallets, though Duncan wouldn't have any of it. He graciously paid the bill and escorted the ladies back to the car.

"Is there anywhere to get a quick drink around here?" Nikki asked on the drive. "I could really use one."

"I think we can find a place," Duncan said.

O'Keefe's was busy. It was Terry's birthday so all the regulars were there, and they were in a fine mood. Terry was in particularly good spirits, having imbibed more than his usual share. Through the crowd, Duncan could see Rico and Joe sitting with Pete at his usual table. Duncan led the women in that direction. In a serendipitous turn, the patrons at the table directly beside Pete's vacated their seats just as Duncan and the ladies arrived. They wasted no time occupying the coveted chairs and setting up camp beside Pete and their out-of-town friends.

Instead of waiting for Sash to make his way to the table, Duncan excused himself almost immediately to obtain libations and to say hello to Terry, Charlene, and the rest of the folks at the bar.

"It's so great that you came to see Ray," Ruby said.

"He's my brother," Nikki said.

"I know, but still. I know you guys aren't that close."

"Is that what Ray said? That we're not that close?"

"Well, no, not really."

"What did he say? Did he tell you what happened? I can't believe he still hasn't gotten over it."

"Gotten over what?"

"It's a family thing. Never mind. It's just like him to hold it against me forever."

"Did you do something?"

"It's complicated. I mean, I'm not saying I'm innocent, but it's been years. Things change."

"I'm sure he's happy you're here."

Duncan returned to the table with a jug of beer and three glasses. After serving the ladies, he poured himself a share. He surprised himself with how uninterested he was in the conversation going on at the table adjacent. He felt removed from the business of Rico and Pete, and took satisfaction in the sudden emancipation.

At the behest of Rico, the two tables were eventually pushed together and the two parties became one. There was no talk of business for the rest of the night, only friendly banter and a plenty of anecdotes involving a certain absent friend.

CHAPTER 44

NIKKI EXTENDED HER stay and remained with Duncan and Ruby in her brother's room. Duncan was pleased to see Ruby flourish in the presence of another female; she and Nikki had become instant friends.

Both Ruby and Duncan did their best to get back to their normal routines, but still made time to visit Ray each day. School was ramping up for Ruby and she made every attempt to juggle her work, care for Ray, and help Duncan at the gym. She had begun her employ for Duncan, taking over all of the gym's financial concerns – with a little help and advice from Lacy along the way.

Still in the hospital, Ray was progressing well. The surgical wound on his side was healing and he was even beginning to get out of bed and walk around on his own. His memory was returning more each day, and with the help of the nurses, Ray's cognition was almost back to full capacity. The day of the accident, however, was permanently erased from Ray's mind. He couldn't recall any of the events that led up to his encounter with Bixby and Marco, and according to the doctors, he most likely never would. When Ruby heard that, she wondered to herself if he would ever recall what he said to her in the park, right before the trouble started.

A few more days passed by and the doctors were nearly ready to let Ray go home, if not for the ruthless headaches he was still experiencing. They wanted to keep him just a little while longer to make certain they covered every base.

"Have you seen this?" Ruby said, walking into Duncan's gym one afternoon after class.

"That all depends," Duncan said. "If you mean a newspaper, then yes; if you mean *that* newspaper, then no."

"Look," Ruby said, holding the paper in front of Duncan's face.

Duncan took the paper from Ruby's hand and began to peruse the article to which she was referring.

"Wow," Duncan said. "This is...not good."

"Well," Ruby said, "I mean, yeah, of course it's bad. But–"

"I know. You never want anyone to get hurt."

While waiting for Lacy after class, Ruby picked up a paper and inadvertently came upon an article outlining a story that was becoming news across the city. There had been a recent string of sexual assaults being reported on the campus of Harvard University. With the school year in full swing the grounds were littered with new and returning students, and the dorms were overflowing with co-eds. The perpetrator – or perpetrators – was targeting students, and college campuses around the city were being advised to take extra precautions.

"This is today's paper," Duncan said. "That could explain why I've been getting more calls than usual."

"What kind of calls?"

"People asking all kinds of things. What kind of classes, how much, where we are. Things like that."

"You think it has something to do with this?"

"If it's in this paper it could be in all the college papers."

"And you hung all your flyers on the campuses."

Kaya walked into the gym, also with a newspaper in hand.

"Good timing," Duncan said.

Kaya gave Duncan a kiss. "Hey, Ruby," she said, giving her a hug. "I called you but I got your machine so I thought I'd come by," Kaya said.

"You saw the article," Duncan said. "You know anything about it?"

"No, I just found out today, but everyone on campus is talking about it. I wanted to let you know."

"Tough situation," Duncan said. "On one hand… No. Never mind. I'm not going to say it."

"Well, the girls that reported it are okay, right?" Ruby said.

"Says so," Kaya agreed.

"Let's not talk about it. I don't want to feel like an asshole," Duncan said.

"Let's just hope they find the guy," Kaya said.

"Yes," Duncan said.

Duncan tried hard to contain his enthusiasm. It wasn't something to be celebrated, after all. It couldn't be helped, though, that if by some twist of fate, Duncan were to benefit because of someone else's malicious actions. It wasn't his doing. He shouldn't feel guilty about it; it was the universe at work.

Ruby usually went straight to the hospital after class but had made an exception that day to show Duncan the newspaper article. After the short visit, Kaya offered to drive her back that way so she could resume her routine and leave the car for Duncan. Ruby accepted. Duncan saw the two girls out and watched as they drove off together down the road.

It was not long after that Carol and Lana – Duncan's two original customers – arrived at their usual time. They had been coming twice a week since their first lesson with Duncan and were due for another session. A pair of women joined them for a class the week prior, but the two bubbly youngsters had not since returned. Duncan wasted no time launching the ladies into their workout.

Nikki was at the hospital when Ruby arrived in Ray's room. Ray, however, was not there.

"Another CT?" Ruby asked.

"Last one, apparently," Nikki said. "They said he might be able to go home tomorrow."

"Really?"

"He'll have to come back for check-ups though."

"That's okay. At least we can get him home."

"Hey, that guy Ryan came back," Nikki said.

"He did? What did he say?"

"Not much. Ray wasn't all that happy to see him."

"He's an asshole."

"And someone named Pete came by, too. He has…" Nikki motioned to the side of her face.

"Yeah. He's a friend of Ray's"

Just then, Ray limped into the room followed closely behind by a nurse with an empty wheelchair. "See," Ray said. "I made it."

"Hi, Nikki," the nurse said.

"Is he being an ass?" Nikki asked.

Ray climbed into bed.

"No, he's fine."

"Thanks for your help, Tanya," Ray said.

"Goodbye, Ray. Bye girls."

"I'm starving," Nikki said. "You guys want something? I'm going out."

"I'm okay," Ray said.

"No thanks," Ruby agreed. "Want me to come with you?"

"No. You just got here. Keep him company. I'll be back in a bit."

Ruby took a seat on Ray's bed.

It was the first time they had been alone since the night of the accident. Ruby lay back and carefully cuddled up to Ray's healthier left side. He tried to move to receive her but was inflicted with a jolt of pain.

"Don't move," Ruby said. She propped herself up on her elbow and surveyed the situation. She carefully reached over and wrapped her arm around Ray's neck and pressed her ear onto the left side of his chest.

"Ray," Ruby said, lying carefully on his body. "Do you remember anything from that night?"

"Nothing," Ray said. "It's like when you wake up from a dream, you know? I mean, when I try really hard, I can see really vague pictures, but they don't feel real."

"Do you see me and you in the park?"

"No," Ray said. "Nothing."

"Right before Bixby showed up?"

Ray shook his head. "Why?" he asked.

"I was just curious."

"Did something happen in the park?"

"Ray."

"Yeah?"

"You stink."

Ray let out a little chuckle.

"You need a shower," Ruby said.

Ruby walked into the washroom and turned on the water in the shower. Ray limped over and eventually arrived. Ruby helped him out of his gown and made sure the dressing on his cut was covered with a special plastic bandage so it wouldn't get wet. With Ruby's help, Ray stepped into the shower and stood under the warm spray. Ruby handed him the soap and watched as he struggled to wash himself using only one arm. He winced as he tested the various ways in which he could and could not move his body.

Ruby watched for a few painful moments, then got up from her perch on the counter, left the washroom and closed the door of Ray's room. She returned to the washroom and closed that door, too. There was no lock on the door but Ruby didn't care. She pulled her top up over her head. She removed her pants. She unclasped and removed her bra and then dropped her underwear to the ground.

She stepped into the shower with Ray.

The water poured over her hair and ran down her back. Ruby stood up on her toes and kissed Ray on the cheek as she carefully took the bar of soap from his hand. Ruby positioned Ray under the running water. Ray closed his eyes as she rubbed the soap between her palms and then pressed the lather against his chest. Slowly, and with delicate care, Ruby began to wash Ray's body.

When she was done with the soap, Ruby moved out of the way and helped Ray rinse off. She watched as the sudsy water fell down into the drain. She looked onto Ray's stubbly cheeks and chin. As Ray let the last of the soap rinse away, Ruby reached onto the counter and grabbed the shaving cream from the toiletry kit Nikki brought from the house. She shook the can and pressed a healthy blob into her palm. Careful still, she applied the cream to Ray's face and neck. She then picked up the razor and surveyed his whitened face. She paused.

"Up or down?" she asked, before pressing the blade to Ray's cheek.

"Down." Ray smiled.

Ruby took the first stroke.

"A little harder," Ray said, his eyes fixed on Ruby's face; hers still fixated on his cheek.

"Sorry," Ruby said, meeting his eyes. "I'm used to doing legs."

Ruby took another try and was more successful.

She didn't rush the job. She was enjoying the task as much as it seemed he was. Once complete, she used her hands to remove the remainder of the cream from Ray's face, taking extra care to swipe the last bit from his lips.

Ray hesitated for only a second before tilting his head and pressed his lips against Ruby's. He wrapped his good arm around the small of her back and pulled her close to his body. Ruby was sure not to put any pressure on Ray's right side.

By the time Nikki returned, Ray was back in his hospital gown and lying in bed with his eyes closed. Ruby was in a chair beside the bed catching up on all the latest celebrity gossip from the random magazines that had accumulated in the room.

"He shaved," Nikki whispered, looking at the face of her brother.

"He took a shower," Ruby said. "But he got dizzy afterwards. It must have been the hot water."

"Well, it's good that he got cleaned up. He looks better."

Nikki sat down beside Ruby and picked up one of the magazines from the ledge.

"Where'd you go?" Ruby asked.

"I just went for a walk. I had a coffee and a sandwich. Shit, I should have brought you something."

"It's okay. I'm not much of a coffee drinker."

"Okay, good. Then I don't feel so bad."

"You shouldn't."

"Ruby," Nikki said, looking across her shoulder to the girl sitting next to her, then to her brother, then back at Ruby again. "Why is your hair wet?"

CHAPTER 45

RAY WAS OFFICIALLY released from the hospital the next morning. Ruby regretted not being there to help him get settled at the house, but she knew that Nikki could take care of it, so she went instead to class.

Nikki and Duncan made certain that Ray was comfortable at home. He was still very tired, and by the time he got into his bed, he was experiencing a fairly severe headache. Nikki gave her brother a couple of pills and shut the blinds in the room so that the sun wouldn't peer through. Duncan was eager to get to the gym but he didn't want to leave until Ray had fallen asleep. He sat on the couch downstairs with Nikki until the early afternoon.

When Duncan got to the gym, he was pleased to find a number of phone messages waiting for him. He was even more pleased when his four o'clock class had seven new participants – all female, all students. The group had come from a Tufts University dorm, one of the girls holding Duncan's yellow flyer. The five o'clock class had only three students, but that was still an improvement from the day before.

It was at five minutes to six o'clock that Duncan couldn't help but phone Kaya, and Ruby, who was now at home with

Ray, to tell them that his next class was going to have at least sixteen participants. Ruby was elated for her friend and wanted to see the spectacle for herself. After hanging up the phone, she began the short walk over to the gym.

Kaya, on the other hand, was less than excited when Duncan told her the news. Duncan was disappointed. It turned out, however, that it wasn't a lack of enthusiasm that stayed her excitement, but instead a simple lack of surprise. Through a little investigative questioning, Duncan quickly uncovered that Kaya had not only visited each of the dorms at Harvard with flyers from Duncan's gym, but she had also spoken with each of the resident advisors so that they too could spread the word. More than a dozen of the students waiting for Duncan's next class came from those dorms. Of the group, three of them were guys, and one of the guys was Manny.

By the time the class started, there was a total of twenty-two students, by far the most Duncan had ever taught. When she arrived, Ruby could barely sneak by the cluster of sweaty bodies. She didn't want to disturb the class so instead snaked her way through to the office in the back and watched from the door.

The most successful day of Max Fitness drew to a close just after eight o'clock. Duncan and Ruby went straight home where both Nikki and Kaya were waiting. Ray had been up for most of the day but was feeling weak and tired so he remained in bed.

Duncan took a fast shower and rejoined the group of ladies who had already reached the bottom of a bottle of wine. Nikki was on the phone, altering her travel arrangements yet again, when Kaya opened a second bottle of red. Duncan was used to a male dominated house, but he welcomed the shift in hormonal balance.

Nearing ten o'clock, and the completion of the second bottle of wine, a rap came at the front door. Duncan got off the couch to see who it was.

"Hey, Mark," Duncan said.

"Hi, Duncan. Am I interrupting something?"

"No, not at all, come on in."

"Actually," Mark said, poking his head into the house. "Would it be okay if we spoke outside?"

"Sure," Duncan said.

Duncan followed Mark out and closed the door behind him. Mark cut right to the chase.

"My brother is coming back," he said.

"From New York?"

"It's a long and boring story, but they'll be back sometime next month. I'm really sorry to do this to you, but–"

"But we have to leave."

"You have to leave," Mark repeated. "I mean, not today or anything."

"Listen," Duncan said, "It is what it is, right?"

"I'll be giving you guys your last month's deposit back anyway. You've already paid for this month so, as far as I'm concerned, we're square. They're not coming back for at least four weeks so you can stay until then. There's no rush."

"It's not a problem."

"Hey," Mark said. "Thanks for understanding. I'm really sorry. If there's anything I can do to help you guys…"

"I may just take you up on that."

"Let me know," Mark said. "Again, really sorry."

Duncan shook Mark's hand and went back inside after watching him drive off. He didn't want to break the news to Ruby right away so he said that Mark just had a small concern to run by him. Duncan made sure to say that he would fill

Ruby in on it later, so as not to make it seem he was hiding anything from her. For Ruby, that was good enough.

As the night was winding down, Duncan invited Kaya to spend the night. Nikki brought up the topic of sleeping arrangements. With Ray back in his bed, Nikki was roomless, or so it would seem.

"You can take my room," Ruby offered. "I'll stay with Ray."

"I couldn't do that," Nikki said.

"Me and Duncan could go back to my place," Kaya said.

"No, really, Nik," Ruby said. "I'd be happy to do it. You take my room and I'll sleep with Ray."

Nikki caught Duncan's silent endorsement of the proposal from across the room.

"Are you sure?" Nikki asked.

"Positive."

"Then I'm going to go up to my *new* room," Nikki said. She stood up from the chair, gave Ruby a hug, and wished everyone a goodnight.

There was enough wine left to fill up Kaya's and Ruby's glass one more time. Duncan was happy to sit the last round out.

"So I have some news," Duncan said.

"You do?" Ruby responded.

"It's not good news, though, so don't get excited."

"Uh oh."

"Well it's not *bad* news either."

"Out with it."

"We have to move out," Duncan said.

"I knew it," Ruby said without hesitation. "I said there was a problem. Didn't I say there was a problem? When you went outside with Mark. I knew it"

"She did," Kaya agreed.

"Why is it a problem? We just have to find a new place to stay," Duncan said. "Mark's brother is moving back. Not a big deal."

"'Cause I like it here," Ruby said. "I just got used to it."

"You can get used to a new place."

"When do we have to leave?"

"We have three, four weeks."

If she were less inebriated, Ruby might have been more contentious. But things being as they were, she didn't let the news bother her for very long.

"I'm about ready for bed," Kaya said. "I'll meet you upstairs."

Kaya gave Ruby a hug and kissed Duncan on the cheek as she passed him by.

"I'll be up in a minute," Duncan said.

Ruby and Duncan remained in the living room.

"Ruby," Duncan said once Kaya was out of earshot. "I know you've only had a second to think about it, but—"

"But what?"

"I'm going to look for a place on my own."

"You mean to live alone?"

"Yeah. I'm thirty years old and I've never lived on my own. I've been thinking about it a lot actually, even before Mark said we have to leave."

"Okay."

"Okay?"

"Yeah, okay. What else can I say? I get it."

"Well that was easy."

"I'm not the issue, Duncan. You haven't told Ray yet."

"The first concern is to get Ray better," Duncan said. "I'll worry about telling him once he's back to being himself again."

"So we shouldn't tell him we have to leave?"

"Oh, no. We should definitely tell him that. I just don't want to add any additional stress, you know? We've lived together for a decade."

"No problem."

"Well then, my dear," Duncan said, rising to his feet. "I'm off to bed."

"Night, Duncan."

Ruby took her last swig of wine and then sprung to her feet as well. She collected the empty bottles and purple stained glasses and placed them all in the kitchen sink. She locked the front door and shut off all the lights before making her way upstairs.

After using the washroom for all her nightly duties, Ruby slowly opened the door to Ray's room. The light from a bedside lamp lit up most of Ray's face. He was sitting up in bed, reading a book.

"You're awake," she said softly.

"I'm awake," Ray said with a smile.

Ruby crept into the room and shut the door behind her.

"Want some company?"

"If it's you, I do."

"Your sister is taking my room so you're stuck with me."

Ray reached over with his left arm and threw the covers down, exposing the empty side for Ruby. She stripped down to her underwear, removed her bra from under her T-shirt, and slid into bed beside Ray. Ray threw his book onto the table beside him. Ruby cuddled up close.

"I could hear you guys talking," Ray said.

"You could? Did you hear what we were saying?"

"No. But you know when you were a kid and your parents had friends over but made you go to bed early. It was like that. I felt ten years old. I could hear the rumblings of a party going on but not much more."

"I really like your sister," Ruby said.

"She's okay."

"She's better than okay, Ray. Why are you so mean to her?"

"I'm not mean to her."

"She came in as soon as she heard you were hurt and she hasn't left since. She sat in the hospital with you for days."

"I know."

"Then what is it? What's the story with you two?"

"I don't want to get into it."

"Why not?"

"Because it will sound stupid."

"Try me."

"Let's just say that she wasn't there when someone else really needed her. Yeah, she's here now and that's great, but I think she's doing it 'cause she feels bad."

"Feels bad for you?"

"Feels bad that she abandoned my mother when she was dying."

"Oh."

"I don't want to talk about it."

"Then I have some other news," Ruby said.

"What?" Ray asked, pulling Ruby in closer. Ruby rested her head on the left side of Ray's chest.

"We have to leave."

"Leave?"

"The house. We have to leave the house. That guy Mark came by tonight. His brother is coming back or something so we can't stay."

"Do we have to leave now?"

"Three or four weeks."

"Oh," Ray said. "That's okay."

"I guess so."

"We can get an apartment or something."

Ruby smiled.

"So you still want to live with me?" she asked.

"'Course I do."

"What about Duncan?"

"Duncan can come if he wants, but what if it were just us?"

"Just me and you?"

"Yeah."

"Are you asking me to move in with you…some more?"

"Ruby," Ray said. "Would you continue to move in with me?"

Ruby reached up and kissed Ray's lips.

Not wanting to linger too long with her weight upon him, Ruby returned to her original position after reaching over and turning off the lamp. She closed her eyes.

"We were in the park," Ray said.

Ruby's eyes opened.

"That night. We were standing in the park, just you and me. It almost doesn't seem real, but I can…I can see it."

Ruby propped herself up and looked at Ray through the darkness. "Do you remember anything else?" she asked.

"I think so," Ray said.

"I think I remember saying something."

Ruby nodded.

"I think I told you…" Ray looked down and met her eyes. "I think I said 'I love you'."

Ruby's heart jumped. She wanted to climb on top of Ray and hug him until he couldn't breathe. But she knew she couldn't. "Do you remember what I said?" she asked.

"Remind me," Ray said.

"I said– 'I love you too'."

"Did you?"

Ruby nodded coyly.

She pulled her body up the bed and they began to kiss. Ray's hand clasped the hair behind Ruby's head, and if not for his physical limitations, he would have grabbed her entire body.

Ruby lay back down on Ray's chest and gently caressed his right side. "Does it still hurt?" she asked.

"Only if I move. But for the first time my head feels okay. The stitches are a little itchy but, I mean, that's nothing."

"Shhh," Ruby said.

"What?"

"You hear that?"

Ray and Ruby looked into the air and listened intently into the silence. In the lowest region where sometimes only hopeful sounds lived, they each thought they heard the faint noises of what could only be Duncan and Kaya making love.

CHAPTER 46

NIKKI WAS THE first to rise the next morning. Being in yet another strange room, in another strange bed, didn't lend to an ideal night's sleep. The sun had long since risen and she was content to start her day and call it a partial victory. She made her way downstairs quietly and put on a pot of coffee. She was pouring her first cup when Kaya snuck into the kitchen to join her. Nikki poured a mug for Kaya and the two sat down at the table and whispered.

Duncan came along not long after and joined the ladies. He wasn't a drinker of the java so instead he enjoyed the company.

Voices downstairs eventually rose from a whisper, and Ruby's eyes opened to the sounds. She looked over to Ray who was still fast asleep on his back, a position not foreign to him in his current condition. She didn't want to wake him and instead slid from the bed, clothed herself, and crept from the room. On her way downstairs she met Kaya who was now on her way up.

"Morning," Kaya greeted at the top of the stairs. "Did we wake you?"

"No," Ruby lied. "I was up."

"I made coffee. Duncan and Nikki are downstairs."

Ruby smiled.

Ruby never had a large family, and certainly never knew a well functioning one. She took great pleasure in the full household, even if it was made up of people unrelated.

Ruby gave Kaya a hug.

"What was that for?" Kaya asked.

"I don't know."

"You're adorable," Kaya said with a smile.

Ruby fumbled around in the fridge a bit before joining Duncan and Nikki at the table. Their conversation, it seemed, had picked up from where it left off the night before.

"Most places start leases at the beginning of the month, so that doesn't give us much time," Duncan said.

"I told Ray," Ruby said.

"How is he?" Nikki asked.

"He's good, actually. His head was better."

"What did he say when you told him?" Duncan asked.

"He asked if I would move in with him."

"Really?" Nikki said.

Nikki and Duncan shared a glance. "It looks like I have to find my own place then," Duncan said.

"We can look together," Ruby offered. "I've never done it on my own."

"Okay."

"Where do we start?"

"I'll get the computer."

Duncan disappeared up the stairs. When footsteps came from that direction, Ruby and Nikki were expecting to see Duncan, computer in hand. To their surprise, it was Ray. He carefully pulled up a chair at the table as the girls watched.

"Hey," he said, as if nothing were amiss.

Ruby got up from her chair and wrapped her arms around his neck from behind.

"How you feeling?" Nikki asked.

"Better," Ray said. "Still tired though."

"Me and Duncan are going to go look for places today," Ruby said, letting him go. "I told him that we are moving in together."

"I want to come," Ray said.

"No chance," Nikki injected.

"Ruby," Duncan's voice rang from upstairs.

"I'm gonna go get ready," Ruby said. She kissed Ray on the cheek and ran towards Duncan's voice.

"You want some coffee?" Nikki asked her brother.

"No," Ray said. "I'll have some water though."

Nikki got up to fill the request.

"Hey, Nik," Ray said as his sister turned on the tap and held her finger under the running water.

"Yeah?" Nikki said.

"Have I said thank you yet?"

Nikki filled a glass with cold water.

"No. But you don't have to."

Ray got up out of his chair awkwardly. He approached his sister at the sink and put his good arm around her shoulders for a hug.

"Thank you, Nicole," he said.

Nikki used the arm not holding the glass to return the hug from her injured brother. "You're welcome," she said.

"You're a good sister."

Nikki's eyes welled, though she dared not shed the tears. Her big brother rarely showed her affection, and she didn't want to sully the occasion by making it seem like such a big deal.

Ray made his way back to the table and sat down. Nikki put the glass of water in front of him and turned away. "I have to go back soon," she said, pretending to rearrange the glasses in the sink.

"How soon?"

Nikki collected herself and sat back down at the table. She told him all about her job, about Jacob, and about all the other things he had missed over the past year. As Ray listened to Nikki he realized he was beginning to see her differently. She was still his little sister, sure, but she was also a person. She had her own life and troubles and she was doing the best she could. Whatever grudge once remained, warranted or not, washed away with the glass of water he drank.

Ruby, Duncan, and Kaya all appeared back in the kitchen and buzzed around Ray and Nikki like flies. Kaya was readying to return to campus for some work while Duncan and Ruby grabbed a quick bite before they were off to start hunting for homes. And just as quickly as they came, the three were out the door, leaving the siblings alone at the table once again.

"What do you want to do today?" Nikki asked.

"I don't know. I'd like to get out of the house though. I haven't been outside in forever."

"Are you okay to go out?"

"I'd like to try. Wanna…go for a walk or something? You can tell me more about Jacob."

"Yeah," Nikki said. "I'd like that."

CHAPTER 47

IT WAS LATE afternoon when Ruby returned home, alone. Excited, she called for Nikki and Ray before she even got in all the way.

No one answered her call.

"Hello?" she said into the silent house.

Still, there was no answer.

Ruby ran up the stairs and opened the door of Ray's room. It was empty. Ruby became worried. She ran back downstairs and looked out to the backyard. Nikki was there, walking on the grass and talking on her phone.

Ruby opened the back door.

"Where's Ray?" she whispered, so not to disturb the call.

Nikki pointed to the sky and mouthed the word "upstairs."

Confused, Ruby shut the door and walked back up the stairs to look for Ray again. He wasn't in the washroom. He wasn't in his bed.

Ruby then found Ray, asleep in her bedroom.

Ruby shut the door quietly and walked back down the stairs. Nikki came in through the back door, her phone call completed.

"How's he feeling?" Ruby asked.

"Okay. We went for a walk and he got a little dizzy. He went to lie down about an hour ago."

"Was that Jacob? On the phone?"

"No, that was for work."

"Oh."

"I spoke to Jacob right before that."

"Do you have a picture?" Ruby asked, joining Nikki at the sink to help her clean the glasses and coffee mugs.

Nikki wiped her hands on a towel and pulled out her phone. She pulled up her photo album and displayed a picture of her boyfriend. Ruby took the phone from her hand. "Cute!" she said.

"I know, right?"

"Very cute."

"He's a bit older, but the age difference doesn't matter."

"How old is he?"

"Thirty seven."

"Oh! That's nothing. Yeah, he looks about that age. So what he's—"

"Eleven years older than me."

"That's nothing," Ruby assured. She handed the phone back to Nikki.

"Hey," Nikki said. "How did the search go?"

"Pretty good. We only got to see three places 'cause Duncan had to go into work. Two of them were dumps, but one was really nice."

"That's good."

The girls finished cleaning and retired to the sofa. Nikki curled her heels in underneath her and took up the corner. Ruby sat in the other corner in a similar position.

"I should tell you," Nikki said. "I'm leaving tomorrow morning."

"Really? Why? Do you have to?"

"I do. I've missed so much and I have an opening on Monday I *have* to be at."

"Does Ray know?"

"He knows."

Ruby reached across the couch and embraced Nikki. "I'm going to miss you," she said.

"I'll be calling a lot to check on him, and on you. So you won't miss me that much."

Ruby returned to her side of the couch.

"And visit. You have to come visit."

"I will."

"And bring Jacob next time."

"Okay," Nikki laughed.

Nikki and Ruby went upstairs to see if Ray was still asleep. He had been up there a long time. They peered through the door like doting parents. Ray was still out.

"So what now?" Ruby whispered.

"Let's go do something," Nikki said, closing the door quietly. "He'll be fine."

Word had spread around the campuses of Boston about Max Fitness and Duncan's first class of the day was jammed. In another first, Duncan actually had to suggest people come back for a later session because there simply wasn't enough room. By the time Nikki and Ruby arrived, they had to maneuver past a crowd standing by the door.

The police had tracked down and captured the perpetrators of the campus assaults. Two nineteen year-old boys were arrested, detained, and charged on three counts of unlawful entry and sexual assault. Nevertheless, Max Fitness was becoming a hot spot for students, both male and female.

"I need to hire another instructor," Duncan said to the girls in the office between classes. "I can't handle this myself."

Ruby couldn't contain her smile.

"See those four girls over there? They were here yesterday. And today they brought their friends."

"Amazing," Nikki said.

"Do you need me to stay?" Ruby asked.

"We need to make a job posting."

"I just helped Jacob hire an assistant," Nikki said. "I can help."

"Not now," Duncan said.

"Why not? I'm leaving tomorrow."

"You're leaving?"

"I have to go back," Nikki said. "But Ray and I had the talk."

"You did?"

"What talk?" Ruby asked.

"Fill her in," Duncan said, "I have to get back out there. If you guys want to work on a job posting I'll buy both of you dinner and give Ruby a raise."

"I don't make any money yet," Ruby said.

"Yeah, well, neither do I."

Duncan escaped into the throng of Lycra-clad students and left Ruby and Nikki in the office.

"What talk?" Ruby asked.

"I think it has something to do with you," Nikki said.

Ray woke up and skulked out of the room like a zombie. He walked downstairs expecting to find a full house, but instead found no one at all. He went to the fridge, pulled out some ingredients, and began the ordeal of making a sandwich with only one good arm.

By the time the next class let out, Nikki and Ruby had already produced a fair draft of the job posting in the back office. Duncan was impressed by the effort and suggested only a few tweaks needed to be made.

"Get out of here, you two" Duncan said. "Leave it open on the computer and I'll look at it again before I leave."

With that, Duncan threw himself back out to the gym floor.

Ray sat down on the couch and turned on the TV. He had finished his sandwich and wanted to do anything but go back to bed. He settled on an afternoon Sox game, put the remote down, and began easy arm exercises the therapist at the hospital instructed him to start on his own.

As they were leaving the gym, Ruby and Nikki ran into Kaya, literally. She was trying to make her way in while they were walking out. The mass of people standing in the alcove forced the threesome to nearly knock one another over.

"Hey!" Ruby said, realizing it was Kaya.

"Oh my God," Kaya said. "Look at this place."

Kaya caught Duncan's eyes and smiled. Duncan broke his stern demeanor and smiled back warmly.

"Come on," Ruby said. "Let's all do something."

Ruby locked arms with Kaya and led her back out through the door. The three girls disappeared from Duncan's sight, though he had little time to concern himself with the matter.

CHAPTER 48

THE LADIES MET Duncan back at the gym later that evening. The last class for the day was ending and he was showing signs of fatigue. They waited in the office for the last of the students to leave. Duncan locked the door around 9:15 and fell down onto the matted floor.

"Long day?" Kaya said, as the girls emerged from the back. Duncan got up and gave Kaya a weary hug.

"I'm starving," he said.

"Us too," Ruby agreed.

Duncan thought for a moment, but it was Nikki that spoke first. "I have an idea," she said.

Ray had fallen asleep on the couch. The game was long since over and the local news show was recapping the result when he awoke. He tilted upwards and looked around. He cringed as he made a sudden movement, forgetting for a split second he was in a delicate state.

He didn't know it yet, but Ray had been awoken by the sound of car doors slamming. Nikki, Kaya, Ruby, and Duncan had arrived home and walked into the house, each carrying a paper bag.

"We brought dinner," Nikki said, tapping her brother lightly on the head as she walked behind the couch.

"Hi," Ruby said, kissing his cheek from a similar position.

"I need a shower," Duncan said, dropping a bag on the kitchen table.

"Go," Kaya said. "We'll set everything up and wait for you."

Ray tried to take in all the commotion. After yet another long and lazy day he was momentarily overwhelmed.

Kaya and Nikki unpacked the bags and laid all the food out on the table. Ruby began pulling out plates and cutlery and setting it all to the side.

"What's going on?" Ray asked.

"Family dinner," Ruby said. "It's Nikki's last night. We weren't going to leave you out."

"How you feeling?" Nikki asked.

"Fine." Ray got up from the couch slowly and waddled over to the table.

"Sit down," Nikki said. "We'll take care of it." Ray did as he was told. With his elbows on the table, Ray put his hands to his eyes as if he were playing a game of peek-a-boo with an infant. He was feeling groggy indeed. As the food was laid out around him, Ray removed his hands and perused the various dishes. Though he had little appetite, he looked forward to trying to eat.

Duncan came downstairs refreshed and took a seat at the table with the rest of the group. Together they dined on roasted chicken, potato salad, coleslaw, and green beans.

Midway through the meal, Ray had given up trying to force-feed himself. The painkillers turned his stomach into what felt like the tumble cycle of a clothes dryer, so he could only eat a little before beginning to feel full and almost nauseated.

"So Kaya was telling us all about her work today," Nikki said.

"Then maybe you could explain it to me," Duncan said. "'Cause I still don't really understand it."

"Which part?" Kaya asked.

"All of it. But mostly the part about what it is you actually do every day."

"Research. That's probably the easiest way to put it."

"On animals?" Ruby asked.

"No, no, we use a cell-based model."

"Which means?"

"Which means a lot of time in the lab looking through microscopes at Petri dishes and not injecting living creatures."

Duncan heard his phone ring from upstairs but decided that whoever it was could wait.

"Do you like what you do?" Nikki asked.

"I do," Kaya said. "But it's really hard to get funding so I'm always applying for grants and filling out paper work."

"Doesn't the school pay for it?"

"Yes and no. They pay for parts, like lab time and equipment, but I need funding to survive."

"You heard they caught those guys that were breaking into the dorms, right?"

"Yeah. They weren't students."

"Just assholes," Nikki said.

"Do you live on campus?" Ruby asked.

"Near campus, not on it," Kaya said. "I rent an upstairs apartment from a professor. He lives downstairs with his wife. He could probably get a lot more for the place than I'm paying, but I don't think he needs the money."

"That's good," Ruby said.

"Want a roommate?" Duncan asked in jest.

"That depends," Kaya said. "Who's asking?"

"I was only kidding."

"I do have room."

"Are you being serious?"

Kaya nodded. "Wanna move in with me?" she asked.

Ruby, Nikki, and Ray all exchanged glances. Duncan put down his fork.

"Uh, I'd move in with you, if you're being serious," Duncan said.

"Okay," Kaya said flippantly.

"That's a pretty big move, you two," Nikki said.

"Why?" Kaya asked.

"Well, you know, you've only known each other for–"

"How better to get to know someone?"

"True."

"Yeah," Duncan said.

"So there," Ray said, adding the final jab to his sister.

"So you're accepting my offer?" Kaya asked.

"How could I refuse?" Duncan said.

There was a knock at the door. Duncan was the first to get up. He walked over to the window and peered to the side to see who it was. "It's Mark," he said.

Instead of inviting Mark in, Duncan opened the door and simply went outside to meet him.

"Everything okay?" Duncan asked.

"Hey, Duncan," Mark said. "This time I know I'm disturbing something."

"No, really. It's okay."

"I called but no one answered so I just stopped by on my way home."

"My phone was upstairs."

"Oh. Well, I just wanted to tell you something. I don't know why I didn't think of it sooner but I may know of a place for you guys, if you're interested."

"Oh yeah?"

"My uncle has an apartment he rents out. It's not far from here, and the price is really reasonable."

"How many bedrooms?"

"That's the thing," Mark said. "There's only two and one is pretty small. It's not as big as this place."

"That may be okay," Duncan said. "Would it be available soon?"

"It's empty. There's even some furniture in there you guys could use if you wanted."

"Can we take a look?"

"I'm sure I can get the key whenever you want. Just let me know."

"Okay, that's great. Hey, thanks Mark."

"No problem. You know where to find me."

Duncan watched Mark drive away before going back inside.

"What was that about?" Ruby asked.

"Mark says his uncle may have an apartment to rent."

"An apartment?"

"Where is it?" Ray asked.

"I don't know exactly," Duncan said, sitting back down in his chair. "He said it wasn't far from here, though."

"You should go see it," Nikki said.

"When can we see it?" Ray asked.

"Whenever you want," Duncan said.

"Can we see it tonight?" Ruby asked.

Duncan laughed. "I'll call Mark after dinner and see when we can go."

"How about that," Nikki said. "Looks like everyone is finding a new place to live tonight."

"Not me," Kaya said.

"But you're getting a roommate. That's pretty good, too."

Dinner ended sometime later and Duncan went to call Mark as soon as they were through cleaning up. Ray accompanied him upstairs into his room. The call was brief and to the point. Mark informed Duncan that the earliest he could get the key and take them over was the coming Monday morning. Ray knew the news would disappoint Ruby, so he recruited Duncan to inform her.

"I have class Monday morning," Ruby said. "And I can't miss it. Unless I can get Lacy to – no, I can't miss it."

"I can go," Ray said.

"But I want to be there."

"Are you sure you're okay to go?" Nikki asked.

"I'll be fine," Ray said. "It's still a few days away and it's just a ride in a car."

"Dammit," Ruby said.

"You can see it another time, Ruby. And who knows, it could be a dump."

"I guess."

The group had moved onto the couches and chairs near the front of the house. The days were getting noticeably shorter, and cooler. The sun had completely vanished from the sky and outside it was as dark as it was ever going to get.

"I have to start packing," Nikki said. "Not that I have much."

"What time is your flight?" Duncan asked.

"Nine. So I have to leave here pretty early."

"Do you want me to drive you?"

"No," Nikki said. "I appreciate it though. I'd rather take a cab and not wake everyone up."

"Are you sure?"

"Positive, really."

Nikki got up from her seat on the couch and began to make her way upstairs to start packing her bag. "Need any help?" Ruby asked.

"No," Nikki said. "I'm okay."

Ruby didn't accept the answer and followed Nikki up. "I'll keep you company at least," she said.

"What are you guys doing tonight?" Ray asked.

"Are we still going?" Duncan asked Kaya.

"We don't have to," she said.

"Where?" Ray asked.

"I still want to. I wanna meet them."

"Okay, so we'll go," Kaya said. "My friends Chris and Emily are having people over tonight."

"What time again?" Duncan asked.

"Any time."

Duncan looked at the clock. "I'll go get dressed."

"What you're wearing is fine."

"I have to make a decent first impression with your friends, Ky."

"Then don't go," Ray said.

Duncan made his way upstairs.

"I'm coming," Kaya said.

"Me too," Ray added. "I wanna lie down."

Ruby and Nikki were in Ray's room packing her things. Duncan and Kaya were in Duncan's room trying on various shirts. Ray was in Ruby's room, carefully positioning himself in her bed.

Ray had reached the point where he could move his right arm with considerably less pain. He still had plenty of scrapes along his back, and his shoulder still showed signs of bruising, but his range of motion had greatly increased. Besides his head, only Ray's ribs and hip caused him discomfort when he moved around, though he had perfected a limited range and adapted his movements accordingly.

As he lay on his back he could hear stirring in both of the adjoining rooms. If not so tired, he might have joined. But instead, Ray shut his eyes and rubbed his temples with his hand.

Duncan and Kaya said their heartfelt goodbyes to Nikki before departing the house for the night. Leaving Ray to rest, Nikki and Ruby occupied the lower floor of the house and chatted away most of the night. They even tapped into Duncan's stash of beer hiding in the fridge.

Before retiring for the night, Nikki looked in on Ray. She wanted to say goodbye to her brother, but he was already asleep. She closed the door slowly and continued to his room where she was to spend the night.

Ruby thought to wait up for Duncan when she realized that he most likely wasn't going to be returning home at all that night. She instead basked in the quiet and flipped channels on the TV alone in the dark.

It was close to 3 a.m. when Ruby awoke on the couch. She had fallen asleep to an infomercial for a miniature blender that did the exact same thing as a regular sized one. She peeled herself from the couch, slunk up the stairs and crawled into bed beside Ray. The cool of the mattress and unused pillow against her warm body brought her instant joy. She was asleep again before the smile faded from her face.

It was only a few hours later that Nikki sat on the couch, waiting. It was still dark outside and through the window she could see the headlights of the cab as it pulled up the driveway. She took hold of her bags and quietly made her way to the front door.

"Hey," a voice whispered from the stairs.

Ray was inching his way down, eyes partially closed, his hair going every which way. "I thought I heard you," he said.

"You're up."

"I wake up every few hours."

Ray made it to the bottom of the stairs and stood with his sister. "So, you're leaving," he said.

"I'm leaving."

Ray rubbed his hand through his messy hair. "You know," he paused.

"I know, Ray," Nikki said. She leaned forward and put her arms around her big brother. Ray awkwardly did the same.

"Thanks, Nik," he said.

"You're welcome."

"I'll call you soon, okay?"

Nikki smiled.

Ray held the door open and watched his sister climb into the back of the cab. He held his arm in the air as the yellow car pulled out of the driveway and made its way down the dim street.

"Everything okay?" Ruby asked as Ray got back into bed.

"Yeah. Nikki just left. Go back to sleep."

"Nikki," Ruby mumbled as she drifted off again.

CHAPTER 49

DUNCAN DIDN'T RETURN home until late Sunday night. In what was becoming the norm, he had spent a long and busy afternoon at the gym. Full classes and his first one-on-one personal training session meant by the time he arrived at home he wanted nothing more than to rest.

Ray and Ruby had spent a lazy day at home. Ray was able to move about on his own more and more which gave Ruby time to herself to catch up on some school work and update the books for Max Fitness. The only money coming in to date was from the one-on-one sessions that had only recently commenced. Both Duncan and Ruby were looking forward to the end of the first month, which was quickly approaching. They were mostly interested to see how many of the multitudes would stick around and pay.

Lacy was right when she told Ruby she would be able to handle the bookkeeping. So far, Ruby had little trouble applying the few skills she had already learned and had in place an efficient system of all expenditures.

That night, now just a trio once more, Ruby, Duncan, and Ray prepared pasta and rented a movie on TV. It was a quiet Sunday night, but they welcomed it.

Getting into bed that night, Ray attempted to alter his sleeping position and found that he could lie on his left side with minimal discomfort. For the first time, he didn't need any pills to subdue the pain or to help him sleep. The only reason he had trouble dozing off was because he was looking forward to the next morning. With Duncan's help, Ray had begun hatching a bit of a plan for himself and Ruby. He was greatly looking forward to seeing it through.

Ruby left for class early Monday morning but was sure to remind both Duncan and Ray to call her with any updates on the apartment they were to see that day. They promised they would.

Throughout her morning classes, Ruby checked her phone incessantly for missed calls or text messages. Around lunchtime she still had not heard from either of the guys. She finally placed a call to Duncan's cell phone, only to be met with the voicemail greeting. Duncan eventually replied with a text in the early afternoon and told her that the place was just fine, and that they were still in negotiations with Mark's uncle.

Returning home after a restless and unproductive day, Ruby was surprised – if not a little suspicious – that the guys were still not home. She placed another call to Duncan.

"I'm at the gym," Duncan said.

"Where's Ray?"

"Kaya came to meet us. I had to get to work and we still weren't done. She's with him now."

"What's taking so long? Is the place nice or what?"

"Ruby, you know I'd love to talk to you but I can't right now. I have a class starting. I'm sure Ray will want to tell you everything himself anyway."

"Ahhh!" Ruby shrieked in mock anger. "When's he going to be home?"

"Shouldn't be long."

"Duncan…"

"Gotta go, Rube. Speak soon."

Duncan hung up the phone.

When Ray finally did arrive at home, Ruby was even more annoyed by the lack of communication. "Well?" she said as Ray waddled in with Kaya behind him. She got up from the couch and met them at the door.

"We got the place," Ray said with a smile.

Ruby threw her arms around Ray a little too enthusiastically which sent a sharp pain through his chest.

"Sorry, sorry," she said, releasing him from her grasp. "So what does it look like?"

"It's not big," Ray said.

"Did you see it?" Ruby asked Kaya.

"No," Kaya said. "I met them at Ed's house."

"Who's Ed?"

"Mark's uncle."

"It's only eight hundred square feet," Ray interjected.

"So?" Ruby said. "What's wrong with that?"

"Nothing. I'm just saying."

"I want to go see it."

"Ruby," Ray said. "I'm exhausted. Tomorrow, I promise. There's something I want to show you, anyway, and it's too late now."

"I can't stay guys," Kaya said. "I have to get going."

"Can't you stay for a bit?" Ruby asked.

"Thanks so much, Ky. I owe you one," Ray said while making his way to the couch.

"I can't, Rube. I have a class."

"Skip it."

"I can't, it's my first class…and I'm dating the teacher."

"Ohhhhh. Does Duncan know you're coming?"

"Not yet," Kaya smiled. "See you guys soon. Get some rest, Ray."

"Bye, Ky," Ray said. "You're the best."

Ruby joined Ray on the couch. He did look tired and as curious as Ruby was, she didn't want to pester him.

"How you feeling?" Ruby asked, stroking the back of his head.

"Head hurts," he said with a wince.

"Really? You haven't had a headache for a while."

"I know, it's weird. It hurts right here." Ray rubbed his hand just over his ear.

"Want some pills?" Ruby asked.

"Not yet," Ray said. "Maybe it'll go away."

"Well you have to go back to the hospital on Wednesday for a checkup. So just hang on 'til then."

"I'll try," Ray said with a smile.

Ruby got up from the couch and picked up her school bag from the front door. She began setting up her books on the kitchen table. Before she sat down to get to work she went over to Ray, took his face in her hands, and kissed his lips. Ray's eyes were closed, but he smiled and caressed her leg lovingly.

Ruby worked away while Ray nodded off on the couch. Both Ray's nap and Ruby's work didn't last very long. Ruby was done her work in just over twenty minutes and though she tried to stay quiet so Ray could sleep, Ray's eyes popped open as soon as she got up from her chair. "I need to wake up," he said. "I'm feeling so groggy."

"Take a cold shower."

"I could. I'd rather take a warm one though."

"That will make you more groggy."

"Who says?"

"A cold shower will wake you up. A hot one will tire you out."

"What about a medium shower with some company. I still can't reach a few spots you know."

Ruby smiled. "I might be able to help you out with that," she said.

Ray was sitting up on the couch. Ruby sauntered over and straddled Ray's legs so that they were face-to-face. She leaned down and kissed him again. Ray wrapped his arms around her waist.

"Both arms," Ruby said, impressed.

"I'm pretty talented."

"Does your shoulder still hurt?" Ruby asked as she gently kissed his collarbone.

"It's starting to feel a little better."

"What about here?"

Ruby lifted Ray's shirt and peppered his chest with kisses.

"Not bad."

"And here?" Ruby moved her way up to Ray's neck and continued her treatment.

"I think we need to move this upstairs," Ray said.

Ruby got up off the couch and tugged Ray along with her. Moving with more spring than he had in a long time, Ray followed Ruby up the stairs.

They didn't reach the shower for a good thirty minutes, thanks to long overdue sexual activity that unfortunately exposed Ray's still-tender areas. Once in the shower, however, Ruby did as she promised and gave Ray a full rubdown with a bar of soap. Ray had forgotten to place the protective covering over his bandage, though he cared little for the small issue with Ruby's magical hands navigating his body. "You'll have to remind me to return the favor one day," Ray said.

"Soon enough," Ruby said. "There will be plenty of time for that."

"There's only one shower in the apartment."

"Then we'll have to do this more often."

"It really does help conserve water."

"Of course."

"Anything for the environment."

Ruby's rubdown was nearing completion. Ray pressed his soapy skin up against her slim figure. He placed his hand on the back of her neck and brought her lips in close. They remained in the shower long after they were both duly clean.

Duncan arrived home later that night, at what had become his usual time. Ray was lying on the couch with his legs up on Ruby's lap when his friend simply swooped through the door and ran up the stairs.

"Hi Duncan," Ruby yelled.

"Hey guys," Duncan yelled back, already halfway up the stairs.

After only three minutes in his room Duncan shot back down carrying a freshly packed bag. He changed his shoes at the front door and slung the bag back over his shoulder.

"Bye, Duncan," Ruby said as the door opened.

"Bye guys, good show." Duncan said as the door closed behind him.

"Who was that?" Ray asked.

That night, Ray had introduced Ruby to *Bored to Death*, a little known HBO show that Ray and Duncan claimed as their own little best kept secret.

"What are we doing about furniture?" Ruby asked between episodes.

"There's some already there," Ray said. "And whatever we don't have we can collect as we go."

"Oh shit, I forgot to call my mom back."

Ruby leaped from the couch. Ray paused the progress of the show and waited patiently for her return.

As they were nearing the end of the first season, and the clock was nearing 1 a.m., Ruby decided she could save the last few episodes for another night. Ruby and Ray ambled up the stairs and together climbed into bed. Ray, now able to lie on his left side, assumed a position so that he and Ruby were facing one another on their pillows.

"And what about pots and pans and stuff like that?" Ruby asked.

"That's nothing."

"Cutlery, plates, cups?"

"Easy to get."

Ray rubbed his head just over his ear where he had earlier complained of pain.

"Still hurting?" Ruby asked.

"No," Ray said. "It's fine."

"So you gonna miss Duncan?"

"I've lived with the guy for almost ten years."

"It's like I'm breaking up a couple."

"You're my couple now," Ray said, his eyes closing in the darkness. Ruby ran her fingertips over Ray's face. "I'm falling asleep," he said.

"Okay."

"Hey, Ruby," Ray said softly.

"Yeah?"

"I love you."

"I love you too," she whispered.

CHAPTER 50

DUNCAN CAME HOME fairly early the next morning. Kaya had a class and he was eager to see if there were any responses to the job posting he had placed in the paper and online. He had given out an e-mail address in the ad rather than a phone number. He figured that if he were teaching his classes he wouldn't be able to answer the phone as easily.

Ruby's eyes opened when she heard Duncan rumbling in the next room. To her happy surprise, Ruby noticed Ray's right arm resting across her body, just as it had so many nights before. Ray had taken to sleeping on his left side but this was the first occasion since the accident that he fell into his old routine of holding her as they slept. Not wanting to wake him, Ruby carefully slid out from underneath his grasp.

Ruby put on a pair of sweatpants and went to see Duncan in his room.

"Hey," she said, leaning against his doorframe.

"Look," Duncan said, flipping an open newspaper page to the end of the bed on which he sat. Ruby came into the room and took a seat at the foot of the bed beside where the paper had landed. She read the job posting that she had helped to write. "Any responses yet?" she asked.

"Just one so far, but the guy is hugely under-qualified."

Duncan clicked away at the computer.

"It's still early."

"I know. I'm not worried. How's Ray?"

"Still sleeping. He seemed better last night. He had a bit of a headache but nothing bad."

"Did you guys talk about the apartment?"

"Not really. He said he wanted to show me something. I don't know. I made him promise to take me there today."

"I'm sure he will. Why don't you wake him up?"

"Nah," Ruby said with a wave of her hand. "Let him sleep."

"What time's class today?" Duncan asked, closing the lid of the computer.

"I'm skipping class. Today is exam review, but I've got it all down already."

"Pretty confident."

"What time do you have to be at work?"

"I'll go in around noon. I'm starting personal training with a new client."

"Hey, did someone surprise you yesterday?"

"What? Oh, you mean Kaya," Duncan chuckled. "Yeah, I think she had fun."

Duncan got up from the bed and changed his shirt. In his haste, he had forgotten to pack a new one the night before.

"Wanna go grab some breakfast?" Duncan asked.

Ruby went back into her room. Ray was still fast asleep. She quietly changed her clothes and snuck out to the washroom to clean up. Duncan was already downstairs waiting by the time she was done. "It's just us," she said, reaching the bottom of the stairs. Duncan opened the door as Ruby approached.

It was a chilly morning. Instead of walking, Duncan and Ruby drove to a nearby diner for breakfast. They chatted about work, and about their upcoming moves. Duncan was apprehensive whenever the topic of the new apartment came up. He told Ruby that he wanted Ray to be the one to tell her all about it, and that she would have to wait to see it herself.

Upon returning home, Ruby went upstairs to see how Ray was fairing, and to give him the strawberry Danish she had brought. She opened the door to see that Ray was still asleep. He looked so peaceful. Ruby almost felt bad about waking him.

Ruby flicked the light switch on and off a few times in an attempt to rouse him. It didn't work. Leaving the light on, Ruby walked into the room. "Raaayyy," she sang.

She noticed that Ray hadn't strayed even an inch from the position in which she had left him hours earlier. A tiny spark of concern ignited in her belly. As she got closer, that tiny flame grew to a wildfire of fear when she realized that Ray's face was uncharacteristically pale, and that his body looked slumped over. "DUNCAN!" she screamed out.

"Ray?" she said, finally shaking him on the shoulder.

Ray didn't move.

Ruby yelled for Duncan again.

Duncan arrived at the door. Ruby stepped away from the bed. "Something's wrong," she said.

Duncan approached the bed. He was the first to notice the blood on the pillow beneath Ray's head. "Call an ambulance, Ruby. Hurry."

Ruby ran for the phone.

"Ray," Duncan said, shaking his friend's body. "Ray!"

Duncan turned Ray so that he was lying on his back. He pressed two fingers to Ray's neck. He rested his ear to his chest. "Ruby!" he yelled.

Ruby came back into the room with phone in hand. "They're coming," she said. Ruby stood and surveyed the situation. She could feel her heart pounding through her chest.

"The blood," she said. Duncan ducked his head down to get a closer look. There was more blood on Ray's right ear.

"What do we do?" Ruby asked. "I'm feeling a little…"

Ruby's face was as white as the sheets on the bed. "Sit down, Ruby," Duncan instructed, fearing she was about to faint. "Just breathe."

Ruby sat down on the dressing chair and put her hands on her knees. "I'm feeling…light headed," Ruby said.

"Put your head between your knees."

Ruby did as instructed as Duncan got up on the bed.

"His ribs," Ruby said, looking up and seeing Duncan pressing heavily up and down on Ray's chest.

"He's not breathing, Ruby. I'm not worried about his ribs!"

The sound of a siren began to split the air. "They're coming," Ruby said, removing her head from between her knees and heading to the front door.

"Breathe, Ray," Duncan whispered, blowing air into his friend's mouth.

Once again, a unit of firefighters arrived first. One of the men leaped from the back of the truck carrying a bright yellow bag.

"He's not breathing," Ruby said.

"How old is he?" the fireman asked, bounding up the steps in front of the house.

"Twenty-eight."

An ambulance arrived.

EMT workers jogged into the house behind Ruby and the firefighters.

"What do we have?" a woman in a blue jumpsuit asked as she burst through the door of Ruby's bedroom.

"Male, late twenties. He's not responding."

"He had a head injury," Duncan offered.

"What kind of injury, sir?" the EMT asked as she knelt beside Ray's body.

"He was hit by a car a few weeks ago. He had a concussion, broken ribs–" Duncan said.

"Okay, clear out," the EMT said. "I need everyone out." One of her colleagues was rubbing two heart paddles together.

Duncan took Ruby by the arm and walked her down the stairs and out the front door. He wanted to get her far away from that room. He sat Ruby down on the front steps of the house, took position beside her, and wrapped his arm around her shoulder. Ruby placed her head back between her knees and breathed deeply.

Duncan rubbed her back and took notice of the few neighbors that had come out of their houses to see what all the commotion was about.

Ruby looked up.

She stared straight out into the street. She did not say a word.

From where she was sitting, everything seemed calm. It was quiet. She could hear the wind rustling through the drying trees. She could hear birds chirping, and watched as a few brown leaves fell lightly from their branches. The lights from atop the street-lined vehicles pulsed through the air and fell on her face. Ruby touched her fingertips to the palms of her hands; they felt cold and rough.

Ruby and Duncan sat. They waited.

They didn't know what else they could do.

CHAPTER 51

RAY DIED EARLY Tuesday morning. Doctors at the hospital told them later that day that he had suffered a ruptured brain aneurysm and passed away in his sleep. He had been gone long before Ruby had called for help; long before the medics had arrived. There was nothing the doctors could do. They told the grieving pair that in all likelihood Ray had felt no pain at all, though it offered little consolation at the time.

Duncan drove Ruby home and they sat down on the couch together in silence.

"We have to call Nikki," Duncan said.

"Okay," Ruby agreed, stoically.

"I'll do it," Duncan said, rising from his seat.

Duncan walked upstairs to call Ray's sister. Ruby could only hear mumbles from where she sat. The conversation did not last long.

Duncan returned to the sofa and sat back down beside his friend. "She's going to try to come in tonight," Duncan said, more concerned about the girl in his immediate presence.

Ruby reached for the remote and turned on the TV. She flipped the channels. "Ruby," Duncan said.

"Yeah?"

Duncan searched for the right words.

"Nothing," he said.

Duncan slid over so that he was sitting right beside her. Ruby put her head on his shoulder as she continued to press the buttons on the remote.

The TV hummed.

The channels flipped.

Ruby sighed.

"There's nothing on," she said.

CHAPTER 52

RUBY AND DUNCAN didn't talk about what happened. For the rest of the day and all that night they avoided bringing up Ray's name at all. The word simply didn't exist. Ruby lay on the couch in front of the TV and didn't move. Duncan walked around the house doing various useless chores, every once in a while stopping to check his e-mail. "This guy's no good," he mumbled.

Kaya called yet again in the late afternoon. She asked if there were anything she could do. Kaya was eager to come over, but Duncan thought it would be better if he kept Ruby company alone, if only for the time being. He told Kaya that Ruby hadn't spoken a word of what had happened and it didn't seem like she was going to any time soon. "She's probably still in shock," Kaya suggested.

"Could be," Duncan agreed. "Whatever it is, I wanna stay with her."

"And what about you? How are you doing?"

"I'm…just…I don't even know. I mean I thought he was dead when I saw him lying on the street that night. I was more freaked out then. I don't know. Maybe it hasn't even sunk in yet."

"I really want to see you," Kaya said.

"I really want to see you, too. I'm just worried about Ruby. I don't know how she would react if people were around."

"I understand. I can't even imagine what she must be feeling."

"Can you come by tomorrow?" Duncan asked. "Kaya, I don't want you to feel like I'm pushing you away."

"I don't feel like that. Really, don't worry. Call me tomorrow and I'll come over whenever you want."

"Thanks for understanding, Ky."

"I'll speak to you soon, okay?"

"For sure," Duncan said.

It was approaching midnight when Duncan rejoined Ruby on the couch. For a few moments he watched Ruby as she watched TV. Duncan wanted to talk to Ruby about everything. Instead, he just turned his head and watched TV along with her.

Ruby fell asleep on the couch and stayed there through the night. Duncan also fell asleep, but woke up around 2 a.m. and went upstairs to bed. On the way to his room, Duncan stopped in front of the old office and peered through the door. All of Ray's stuff was still strewn about. Duncan closed the door.

In the morning Duncan came downstairs to see Ruby still on the couch in front of the flickering TV. She was barely awake, but when he looked over he could see that her eyes were opening every few minutes or so. Duncan didn't say anything.

A cab pulled up on the driveway nearing ten a.m.. Duncan looked out the front window. "Ruby," he said. Ruby slowly perched up on the couch so that she could see out the window. She got up off the couch. She walked over to the front door and yanked it open.

Duncan had always known Ruby to be strong willed. The first night he met her, alone on the road, underneath the fist of a stranger, the girl didn't shed a tear. But when Ruby and Nikki laid eyes on one another, all the strength and self-control she had always displayed simply washed away. The girls walked toward one another and embraced each other heavily. The tears held themselves back no longer. It was the first time Ruby had showed emotion over Ray's death. For all Duncan knew, it could have been the same for Nikki. Something had happened when the women saw one another that made everything real. They stood in front of the house holding each other, neither wanting to be the first to let the other go. They cried in each other's arms.

Duncan came outside, took care of the cab fare, and sent the taxi on its way.

The girls, eventually collecting themselves as best they could, started for the house, though they remained entwined. Duncan followed behind carrying Nikki's bags.

Perhaps it was the mere presence of another woman, or perhaps it was just time, but Ruby had opened the floodgate and began to grieve.

At Duncan's request, Kaya came by later that day. The four friends, reunited, tried to find whatever solace and comfort they could from one another.

Nikki's boyfriend, Jacob, arrived early the following day and secured a hotel for them. Nikki wanted to stay at the house with Duncan and Ruby, but at the same time, was happy not to have to sleep in Ray's empty room. Jacob, too, insisted they not impose; Duncan and Ruby understood completely and took no offence to Nikki's arrangements.

The next few days were ones of sorrow. Duncan had never before prepared a funeral, and he found no consolation or sense of closure in doing so. He didn't involve Ruby in the project, but instead found incredible help and support from Kaya. Kaya was a pillar, holding up the house during those few days. Without her, it seemed, things might have began to crumble.

Ray's funeral was held on a Saturday. Ruby stood at the front, as did Duncan. Jacob held Nikki's hand and tried his best to comfort her. Pete came and so did Charlene. She brought with her condolences from Ray's friends at the bar. Terry, Vinny, Mike, and the others got together and sent flowers. Rico sent his best wishes along with his sincerest regrets that he couldn't make it out. Duncan would later find out that his Las Vegas friend and former associate covertly covered the majority of the funeral costs. Quinton and Courtney came in from Omaha; Ray's childhood friends Adam and Tim made the journey to Boston, too. Lacy stood by Ruby and at one point took her friend's hand. Ashley was there, accompanied by Davis. The pair stood discreetly near the rear.

During the burial, Duncan eyes wandered. In the shadows, among the trees in the distance, his eyes came upon a figure leaning on crutches. When the man saw that Duncan took notice, he slunk away, never to return.

Duncan was still standing with Ruby, Kaya, Nikki, and Jacob as the funeral ended. As the crowd dispersed, Ashley approached to offer a word.

"Can I talk to you?" Duncan asked, before Ashley could speak.

"Sure," Ashley agreed.

Duncan led her away onto the cemetery grounds. Davis, ever the gentleman, introduced himself and offered his sincere condolences to the group that remained.

The rest of the mourners said their goodbyes to one another and floated away like leaves in the wind. Duncan returned a few minutes later. He wrapped his arm around Ruby's and began to lead her away from the pile of dirt that stood beside the open grave.

As they walked, Ruby was the only one to look back at the workers shoveling earth over Ray's lowered casket.

Nikki returned to her hotel room with Jacob. They wanted to change their clothes and make arrangements for their trip back home before meeting back up with Duncan, Ruby, and Kaya. Duncan and Ruby dropped Kaya off at her house where she too needed to attend to some things before returning to the group.

Duncan and Ruby arrived at home to half-filled moving boxes and feelings of emptiness. Neither needed to voice what was on their minds; it was a shared sensation. The house was not theirs any longer, and it certainly felt that way. There was something missing now, and it was something that could never be restored. It was time for them to leave.

It was easy for Duncan to arrange to move in with Kaya a week or so sooner, but he had to pull some strings to get Ruby into the new apartment earlier than planned. She didn't want to stay at the house alone, and Duncan wouldn't think of letting her. He had spoken to Ed and worked out all the details at the same time he was planning for Ray's funeral. As soon as she was ready, Ruby could move in, even though the apartment wouldn't really be hers until the beginning of the month.

At first, Ruby was disillusioned about going through with the move. It was supposed to be her and Ray's apartment, after all. But after a sincere and candid conversation with Kaya and Nikki, Ruby quickly agreed that it was still the best thing for her to do. Ray would have wanted it no other way.

As planned, Duncan, Ruby, Kaya, Nikki, and Jacob met up later that night at a restaurant to celebrate Ray's life. Quinton and Courtney joined the gathering at Duncan's request.

They ate, they drank, they talked, and there was even some laughter. It was only fitting that after the meal they all retired for a drink at O'Keefe's.

When they walked into the bar, they were welcomed warmly and sat among those that knew Ray. It wasn't about the money, but instead the gesture, that Duncan allowed the bar patrons to pick up the tab for the group at the end of the night. It was their way of showing their respect, and perhaps their way of saying the things for which they didn't have the words. What does one say, after all, to someone who's lost a brother, a lover, or a friend so close that would make the hurt lessen in any way?

CHAPTER 53

DUNCAN AND RUBY were leaving the house for good. Duncan had packed up the last of Ray's things and he spent an extra moment alone in Ray's empty room. "You ready?" Ruby asked from the doorway.

"In a minute," Duncan said. He was sitting on Ray's bed. Ruby put down her bag and came into the room. She sat down on the side of the bed beside Duncan. The pair didn't say a word.

They just sat.

"Hello?" a voice from downstairs called.

Duncan and Ruby's moment was broken. They gathered themselves, and their things, and went downstairs.

"Hey, Mark," Duncan said.

"Looks like you guys are all packed up."

"Yeah, we didn't have much."

Mark helped Duncan and Ruby pack up the car and Duncan returned the keys to his brother's house.

"Hey," Mark said as they were preparing to leave. "I'm really sorry about Ray."

"Thanks," Duncan said, shaking the man's hand. "Thanks for everything."

Duncan and Ruby sat in the car on the driveway and took one last look at the house.

Duncan turned on the car and backed out slowly, nodding to Mark as they rolled by.

And like that, Duncan and Ruby were off.

CHAPTER 54

THE FIRST STOP for the pair was Kaya's house. There wasn't much for Duncan to carry in; he only had his clothes and one box of papers for the gym. Both Ruby and Duncan remained at Kaya's until the late afternoon when Ruby's curiosity got the better of her. "Can we go see the place already?" she said.

"You coming?" Duncan asked Kaya.

"No," Kaya said. "You guys go. I'll be here when you get back."

Kaya gave Ruby a hug. Duncan gave Kaya a kiss. "I'll be home soon," he smiled.

Duncan parked the car in a visitor's parking spot in the front of a building. Getting out of the car, Ruby's eyes peered up to the top of the structure.

Duncan grabbed Ruby's bags from the trunk and led her to the side entrance where he used a plastic fob on a key ring to open the locked door.

"Where you going?" Ruby asked as Duncan bypassed the elevators completely.

"Nice lobby, huh?" Duncan said.

Ruby followed Duncan up to the small desk at the front of the building where behind it sat a man in a blue jacket.

"Hello," the man said.

"Hi," said Duncan. "This is Ruby, she's moving in today."

"Okay," the man said, running his hand down a ledger. "Do you have an elevator booked?"

"No," Duncan said. "This is all we have."

"Oh. Can I give you a hand?"

"I think we're okay."

"Okay. Well, my name is Darryl. If you need anything, here's the number to call."

Darryl handed Ruby a card. "Thank you," she said.

"I think you have something for me," Duncan said.

"What's the name?" Darryl asked.

"Duncan Miller."

Darryl rummaged through a drawer of letters and small packages. "Yup," he said, pulling out a long manila envelope. He handed it to Duncan. "Could I get you to sign for that here?"

Duncan signed for his package. "Thanks," Darryl said. "Have a good one."

"What is that?" Ruby asked as they made their way back to the elevators.

"It's for you. I'll show you upstairs."

The elevator door opened and the pair got in. "Well?" Ruby said, waiting for Duncan to push a button.

"Twenty-six," Duncan smiled. Ruby pressed the button and watched the door close on the lobby.

"To the right," Duncan said as they exited the elevator. "All the way to the end."

Duncan followed Ruby down the hall to apartment 2601.

"Oh, hi," a young man said, exiting the apartment directly across the hall. "Are you moving in?"

"I am," Ruby said.

"Just her," Duncan added.

"Then I'm your new neighbor."

The man moved his small bag of trash from his right hand to his left and extended his palm. "Trevor," he said.

"Ruby. This is my friend Duncan."

"Hi Ruby. Duncan. Well I'll let you get all set up. If you need anything I'll be home."

"Thanks."

"No problem."

Trevor began his walk down the hall. "Welcome to the building," he turned to say.

Duncan held out the keys for Ruby. Ruby put down her bag and happily snatched the key ring. She unlocked the door and opened it slowly. Duncan followed her in. They both put down their bags in the small foyer and walked to the middle of the main room.

Duncan gave Ruby a second to take it all in.

There was a couch, a coffee table, and a TV at one end of the apartment. The bedroom door was open and Ruby could see that there was an undressed bed and a small dresser inside. She walked around and poked her head into the bathroom.

"Well?" Duncan finally asked.

"It's so...cute," Ruby said, grinning.

She went into the kitchen and opened the cupboards. They were empty. She opened the fridge to find only a box of baking soda and a few bottles of water. She then walked over to three large windows that made up almost the entire far wall of the apartment. She looked out across the city.

"West," Duncan said.

Ruby turned to face him. "It faces west," Duncan said again. "The balcony faces north, but because you're on the corner you're looking out west if you're over there."

Ruby turned and looked out the window again.

Duncan went back to the front door and picked up the envelope he had received from Darryl. He pulled out the contents and laid it out on the kitchen counter. "Ruby," he beckoned.

Ruby turned from the window and walked over to Duncan.

"What is it?" Ruby asked, leaning up against the opposite side of the counter and tilting her head to see the papers.

"You need to sign these."

"The lease," Ruby inferred.

"Not exactly."

"It looks like legal stuff."

"Ruby," Duncan said. "There's something I need to tell you, and I want you to just listen, okay?"

"Okay," Ruby said. "Should I be nervous?"

"No."

"Okay…"

"Ruby," Duncan said again, "Ray never actually rented this place."

Ruby looked at Duncan and waited for more. "I don't get it," she said.

"When we came to meet Ed here a few weeks ago he and Ray got to talking. Ed was telling Ray that the place had been empty for months. He said that renting it out had become more of a hassle than it was worth and that he wanted Ray to sign for a minimum of a year, at least. Me and Ray had a bit of a talk, and well…"

"Yeah?"

"Ray didn't sign the lease, Ruby. Ray bought the place."

"I don't understand," Ruby said, a look of apprehension on her face.

"Ray didn't rent it. He bought it. These aren't lease papers. They're ownership papers."

Ruby looked down to the legal sized bundles of paper on the counter.

"But how…what does that…"

"When you sign these papers, you'll own the place," Duncan said.

Ruby looked up and met Duncan's eyes. "Are you being serious?" she asked.

"We had to pull some strings and do a little fancy paperwork to get it done, but we managed to do it. This is your condo now, Ruby."

"But how…how did you do that? Wasn't everything–"

"Ashley's a pretty good lawyer after all. And Ed was happy to re-sign the papers with your name on it."

Duncan flipped the papers open and showed Ruby that the seller had already autographed in all the necessary places. "See," he said. "All you have to do is sign your name."

"I can't believe this," Ruby said. "I can't. I can't do it."

"You can, Ruby."

"You should be the one–"

"Ray bought this place for you; for both of you. I was never supposed to live here."

Ruby looked down at the papers and saw her name typed below the empty "Buyer" lines upon which she was meant to sign. "But…I don't have a pen," she said.

Duncan fumbled through the drawers in the kitchen and came up short.

"Wait here," he said.

Duncan left the apartment. Ruby took the papers in her hand and looked over the legalese.

Duncan knocked on apartment 2602. Trevor came to the door. "Hey," he said. "Duncan, right?"

"Trevor," Duncan pointed. "How you doing?"

"Good, man. What can I do you for ya?"

"Could we just borrow a pen?"

"Course!" Trevor said. "Come on in."

Trevor went in to fetch a pen. Duncan stood just inside by the door.

"So how is it helping your girlfriend move?" Trevor asked.

"We're just friends," Duncan said.

"Oh, really? Sorry 'bout that."

"No problem."

Trevor returned to the door holding a few pens. "I'm not sure if they work, so take a couple," he said.

"Thanks."

"Hey," Trevor said, halting Duncan's exit. "I don't want to be too forward, but does that mean she's single?"

"Well, something like that. She just lost her boyfriend."

"New breakup, huh?"

"No," Duncan said. "She *lost* him."

"Oh." Trevor said, his demeanor changing from smile to unease. "Oh, wow."

"So for now she probably doesn't need–"

"Say no more," Trevor said. "I'm good at being a friend, too."

"Thanks for the pens."

"Yeah, sure. Tell her to just keep'em."

Trevor showed Duncan out the door.

Duncan went back into the apartment where he watched as Ruby signed the papers in triplicate. Duncan signed as witness where it was required.

"I can't believe this," Ruby said, completing the last of the forms.

"Congratulations. You're the proud new owner of about 800 square feet in the sky."

"I still can't believe it," Ruby said again. "I just wish…"

"I know," Duncan said. "So do I."

Ruby turned and wrapped her arms around Duncan. "Do you need me to help you with anything?" he asked.

"No," Ruby said with tears in her eyes. "You've done more than enough already."

"Then I'm going to get going," Duncan said. "I want to stop by the gym on my way home. There are some things I need to take care of. I start interviewing people tomorrow."

"Call me later, okay?"

"For sure. And get some rest tonight," Duncan said, standing at the door. "It's going to be a really busy week coming up. I need you at work."

Ruby smiled.

Duncan took his leave along with the signed papers, which he planned on returning to Ashley himself.

Ruby stood in the middle of her new apartment. She couldn't contain the feelings she was experiencing. She was elated and saddened. She was excited and fearful. But most of all, Ruby simply couldn't believe what had happened to her in the few months that had passed since she first left home. Everything had come rushing in at once and Ruby let out a scream of joy that belied the tears that were falling from her eyes.

CHAPTER 55

DUNCAN PULLED UP in front of Ashley's apartment and buzzed her number. The door clicked and he pulled it open.

"Hey," Ashley said, opening her front door for him. Duncan held out the envelope. "Thank you, Ashley," he said.

"Did it go okay?" she asked.

"It went fine."

"Good."

"You did good, Ash," Duncan said.

Ashley nodded and took the papers from Duncan. "Do you want to come in for a second?"

"No. I can't. But thanks."

Duncan turned and walked down the hall.

"Hey, Duncan," Ashley said from a distance.

Duncan turned.

"Gimme a call or something," she said.

Duncan raised his arm in a wave and continued to walk away.

Duncan went straight from Ashley's apartment over to the gym. He pulled the car up in front into what was becoming his usual spot. Walking up to the door Duncan fiddled with his keys, looking for the one that would open the door. It only took a second for him to realize that he had mistakenly given the key to the gym to Ruby when he handed her the ones to her new apartment.

Standing in front of the impenetrable door, Duncan just turned and took a seat on the small ledge in front of the window to think of his best solution. After a moment, Duncan's thoughts shifted. It was one of the first times Duncan had been alone since Ray had died. Memories of their time together came rushing in. All the years in Phoenix working and living together swept through his memory. And of course, the recent trip they took driving to Boston lay freshest in his mind. Duncan thought about all the times he had bailed Ray out of trouble, and how he wouldn't have wanted it any other way. But mostly Duncan thought about how much he missed his best friend. A lump began to form in Duncan's throat. It was an unfamiliar feeling, but he welcomed it.

And that's when it happened.

Duncan looked down to his feet. As if it had come from nowhere, a small, gray cat had sidled up beside him and perched beside his leg. The cat looked up and met Duncan's eyes. Duncan looked down and he and the animal stared at one another. And then, just as simply as it had arrived, the small cat weaved its way through Duncan's feet and began to walk away down the sidewalk. Duncan watched it as it went.

Before the cat turned the corner and vanished completely from Duncan's sight, it stopped. It looked back to Duncan once again and let out a soft, satisfied purr. Duncan smiled and began to cry.

With tears in his eyes, he looked up to the sky. It was painted with bright oranges and purples as white clouds wiped across the darkening blue of the horizon. Duncan started to laugh. A tear let go its grasp and rolled down his cheek, but

Duncan continued laughing. He shook his head and looked back down to the sidewalk below.

Pulling out his cell phone, Duncan dialed a number.

"Kaya," he said, clearing his throat and composing himself the best he could. "I'm coming home."

CHAPTER 56

BACK AT THE apartment, Ruby had finished unpacking what little she had brought with her. She was standing at one of the large windows, looking out at the very same colors in the sky. From her vantage, she could see the remainder of the sun as it danced atop the horizon.

She put her hand on the glass and leaned in closer.

She stood in silence and watched with a grin as the sun began to disappear behind the end of the earth.

Tears rolled down her face and tickled her cheeks.

She pressed her palm against the glass and watched as the sun continued to fall away. Ruby thought about her mother. She thought about her grandmother. She thought about Ray.

With pain, sadness, and utter jubilation in her heart, Ruby's watery face was hijacked by a smile.

The sun had gone away.

All that remained in view were a few shards of light that pierced upward in the distance like yellow ribbons into the sky. From her own apartment, Ruby had watched the sun go down. The only thing missing was that particular someone with whom she longed to share it. But for reasons she felt though couldn't describe, Ruby knew that share it with him she did.

BOUNDLESS

www.BradCotton.com
Twitter: @bradcott0n
Facebook: facebook.com/bradcotton

Prinia Press